RESURRECTION!

The last of the five girls didn't look peeled, she looked burnt. She bore only a rough resemblance to a human being. She might have been shaped out of mud by a dim-witted child who gave her no fingers or toes or breasts, and poked fingers into the mud to make her eyes. Her crust made papery, crackling sounds as she shuffled past the fire, and pieces flaked off.

A motley crew, thought the girl cuffed to the limb.

She wondered if any of them would have enough sense to find the key and unlock the handcuffs.

She doubted it.

In fact, they didn't seem to be aware of her presence at all.

Whatever else they might be, they were the victims of the Reaper.

—From "Mess Hall" by Richard Laymon

BOOK OF THE DEAD

Edited by
John Skipp and Craig Spector

BANTAM BOOKS
NEW YORK · TORONTO · LONDON · SYDNEY · AUCKLAND

BOOK OF THE DEAD
A Bantam Spectra Book / July 1989

PRINTING HISTORY

FOREWORD copyright © 1989 by George Romero
INTRODUCTION: ON GOING TOO FAR copyright © 1989 by John Skipp
and Craig Spector
BLOSSOM copyright © 1989 by Chan McConnell
MESS HALL copyright © 1989 by Richard Laymon
IT HELPS IF YOU SING copyright © 1989 by Ramsey Campbell
HOME DELIVERY copyright © 1989 by Stephen King
WET WORK copyright © 1989 by Philip Nutman
A SAD LAST LOVE AT THE DINER OF THE DAMNED copyright © 1989
by Edward Bryant
BODIES AND HEADS copyright © 1989 by Steve Rasnic Tem
CHOICES copyright © 1989 by Glen Vasey
THE GOOD PARTS copyright © 1989 by Les Daniels
LESS THAN ZOMBIE copyright © 1989 by Douglas E. Winter
LIKE PAVLOV'S DOGS copyright © 1989 by Steven R. Boyett
SAXOPHONE copyright © 1989 by Nicholas Royle
ON THE FAR SIDE OF THE CADILLAC DESERT WITH DEAD FOLKS
copyright © 1989 by Joe R. Lansdale
DEAD GIVEAWAY copyright © 1989 by Brian Hodge
JERRY'S KIDS MEET WORMBOY copyright © 1989 by David J. Schow
EAT ME copyright © 1989 by Robert R. McCammon

SPECTRA and the portrayal of a boxed "s" are trademarks of
Bantam Books, a division of Bantam Doubleday Dell Publishing
Group, Inc.

ISBN 0-553-27998-X

Published simultaneously in the United States and Canada

Bantam Books are published by Bantam Books, a division of Bantam Doubleday
Dell Publishing Group, Inc. Its trademark, consisting of the words "Bantam
Books" and the portrayal of a rooster, is Registered in U.S. Patent and Trademark
Office and in other countries. Marca Registrada. Bantam Books, 666 Fifth Avenue,
New York, New York 10103.

PRINTED IN THE UNITED STATES OF AMERICA

RAD   12 11 10 9 8 7 6 5

DEDICATION

For
Tom Allen
[1938–1988]

God bless you, man.
Wherever you are . . .

Acknowledgments

You know that an idea's time has come when the green lights extend clear to infinity. This book, which was conceived one fine summer afternoon by a miracle of serendipity on a back porch in Pennsylvania, and which by all rights should have been one hell of a difficult sell, breezed straight through to fruition with scarcely a hitch.

It's been a long time coming, and there are a lot of people we'd like to thank; for their patience and support, for their enthusiasm and professionalism, and, most of all, for their friendship.

Special thanks must certainly go to Lou Aronica, Pat LoBrutto, Janna Silverstein, Robert Simpson, Susan Sherman, Katherine Schupf, and all the fine folks at Bantam; Adele Leone and Richard Monaco, Mark Zeising, George and Chris Romero, Tom Savini, Everett Burrell and Greg Nicotero, Dave Schow, Marcus Nickerson, Jesse Horsting and *Midnight Graffiti*, Richard Rubenstein, Salah Hassanein, TK & BAM, the *Fango* gang, our long-suffering families, and Lise Rogers, perhaps the most benign copy editor in all of human history.

We'd like to extend extra special *uberthanks* to the writers who contributed to this book. They kick big moby butt, and they keep us honest.

Last, but hardly least, we'd like to thank all of those (too numerous to list) who participated in the creation of the *Dead* trilogy; and to the millions who have taken those zombies into their hearts without ever once becoming them.

Thanks, guys. We owe you one.

Now buy this book.

FOREWORD

BY GEORGE ROMERO

It was 1967 when I saw my first walking corpse. I was a struggling filmmaker living, among other struggling filmmakers, in Pittsburgh, Pennsylvania. I remember someone asking, "If you want to make movies, how come you stay in Pittsburgh? I mean. . . . this ain't exactly Hollywood." "No," I replied, "It sure ain't. That's sort of why I like it here. Besides, Hollywood isn't the only place where the dead can walk. No, sir. On those rare and mystical occasions when the dead do decide to rise up and walk, they walk any damn place they feel like walkin'."

I'd seen walking corpses in E.C. comics and in the movies, but I'd never seen one in the, er. . . . flesh. Not until that summer of '67. I saw a lot of them that summer up around Evans City, Pa., a few miles from Mars. My friends, the other filmmakers I mentioned, and I took moving pictures of them. In the Spring of '68 those pictures were released to the public. You may have seen them. Quite a few people have. My friends and I were (and still are) thankful for how well those pictures were received.

I saw the dead walk again in 1978. Saw them walk yet another time in 1984. I took moving pictures of them each of those times and those pictures, like the first ones, were released to the public. The public. . . . or at least a certain portion of it. . . . seems to have an interest in the walking dead.

Not long ago I was talking with two friends of mine, John Skipp and Craig Spector, who suggested that while the dead were walking in Pittsburgh, they were probably walking in other places as well. After all, whoever. . . . or whatever. . . . causes the dead to walk, isn't going to go to all that trouble just to terrorize Pittsburghers. These things tend to be more than just localized phenomena. "Maybe we can find some first-hand stories from other parts of the world," they said. "If we can collect enough stories we might be able to publish a book. A. . . . Book of the Dead."

I remembered that conversation back in 1968. "They walk any damn place they feel like walkin'." Was that me that spoke those words so boldly? God. I was so young, then, so naïve. Willing to admit that I knew about the dead. Willing to ignore the recriminations, the denunciations of society. I even found pride in what I was doing, in what I was saying. Times were different then. Ah, the sixties.

But these are the eighties. The self-centered, get-rich-and-look-good-at-all-costs eighties. Sure, I thought to myself. There are stories out there, alright. There have to be. But trying to find them. . . . that's gonna be next to impossible. I said to my friends, "Go ahead. If you can find somebody who knows about the walking dead. . . . somebody who's willing to admit it, that is. . . . I'll eat my hat."

I didn't think John and Craig would come up with anything. I figured there were few out there who knew the movements of the dead and that those few, fearing ridicule, would probably clam up when approached. I'm amazed at the list of necrophiles who were willing to appear in this volume. I regret the derision these brave souls have subjected themselves to by admitting their knowledge of matters beyond the grave. I know, from experience, that there are those out there who will judge them to be either mad or in league with the Devil. I offer my thanks to all the contributors here. They have renewed my faith and made me feel. . . . much less alone.

I've selected a knit stocking cap, black and gold, with a Steeler emblem on the side. Is it okay if I put some spaghetti sauce on it?

INTRODUCTION

ON GOING TOO FAR
OR
FLESH-EATING FICTION:
NEW HOPE FOR THE FUTURE

"What's going to come out of those people who think that
Night of the Living Dead *isn't enough?"*

Robert Bloch

There is always, as they say, the next frontier.

The function of the pioneer is to penetrate the unknown: to delve into those culturally uncharted places and report back on what they've found. All progress is based on the willingness of a few to venture into uncharted territory, check it out, come to terms with it, and make it a place where we all can dwell.

It's not the most enviable position in the world. There's an old adage, culled from our own nation's vainglorious past: *the pioneer is the guy with the arrows in his back.* It's a dangerous job, scoping out the frontier; most people are more than happy to follow in the pioneer's footsteps. Once the road is paved, and it's safe to come in, you're one heartbeat away from the chain stores and the franchises, all frantically hawking the hitherto unheard-of, rendering the frontier a frontier no longer.

Making it accessible.

Making it safe.

And when the last pioneer stops dead in his tracks, pitches camp, and settles in for the rest of his days, you can bet your coonskin cap that somebody else will soon be there to push it just a little bit farther. Despite the public outcry that it's time to stop, we've gone far enough, thank you—or perhaps, ironically, *because* of it—another hand-

5

ful of intrepid souls will feel the itch to probe a little deeper.

To expand the horizon.

To go too far.

> *"Horror is that which we have not yet come to terms with."*
>
> Ramsey Campbell

This is a book of zombie stories. Not only that, it's the god-damndest book of zombie stories you've ever seen. We would even go so far as to venture that this may be the most *overt* anthology of original horror fiction ever assembled.

Does this sound like we're pleased?

Sorry. We just can't help ourselves, for several very good reasons. First, because of the uniformly inspired and intimately visionary quality of the work herein. Second, because of the seemingly endless stream of mind-blowing spike points that the authors have graced us with: flaming frozen moments of dread and wonder that you will never in a million years forget.

Third, because it allowed all involved to pay homage to the films of George A. Romero, a wild frontiersman in the grandest tradition. By running the heart of his brazen cosmology through their distinctive filters, they have breathed *even more fire* into his already vibrant archetypal landscape. No tiny task, that.

And fourth, because we The Editors had a hand in goosing this glorious sucker into existence, thereby doing our part to stretch the boundaries of modern horror fiction just a little bit further.

Because, have ye no doubt, until fairly recently it seemed as though the body of traditional horror fiction had reached the coast and settled there. It was more than happy to homestead the territories, tilling the fertile soil opened up by Lovecraft, Machen, Poe and James, not to mention Bloch and Matheson and Serling and Blatty and yes, even Stephen King.

This is not, in itself, a bad thing. The world could do worse than to suffer a surfeit of such vision. But still, the call which came to all of them keeps right on calling. Extending the invitation.

This book is but one response: a vicious backhand serve into the beyond, a missile unleashed and beyond calling back, a fleet of cerebral ships in the time-honored tradition of all challengers of the flat earth and the legend "here there be dragons".

This is a book that goes too far, and invites you along for the ride.

> *"Zombies are the liberal nightmare. Here you have the masses, whom you would love to love, appearing at your front door with their faces falling off; and you're trying to be as humane as you possibly can, but they are, after all, eating the cat. And the fear of mass activity, of mindlessness on a national scale, underlies my fear of zombies."*
>
> *Clive Barker*

In 1968, *Night of the Living Dead* first appeared on America's silver screens. Shot in jarringly mundane, schizo-*verite* black and white, this stunning tale of The Day That Hell Met Earth was a virtual Pandora's Box of cinematic firsts. While Sam Peckinpah was doing his part to usher in the age of explicitness by blasting Ernest Borgnine into teensy little bits in *The Wild Bunch,* Romero dared to give us a pair of darling young lovers and send them heroically off into danger, only to blow them to flaming smithereens, then let the camera hang around while a gaggle of rotting guys and gals next door devoured their crispy innards.

Night was daring in other ways, as well: it featured a strong black male as its pivotal character. *And* did an end run around the tidy horror convention of *good vs. evil,* subbing the far more morally ambiguous and provocative equation of *living vs. dead.*

But perhaps most significantly, *Night* was the first horror film to give shape to the dawning fear that the American Dream, such as we knew it, was dead.

Now, of course, *Night* is a legend in its own right, with a permanent seat in New York's Museum of Modern Art and a warm spot all its own in the hearts of those who trip the dark fantastic. Not satisfied with that, Romero went on to create 1979's *Dawn of the Dead,* the film that successfully encoded his worldview forevermore on the cultural nervous system. From that moment on, his vision of a world overrun by the living dead was more than just a nifty plot device: it was a legitimate modern *mythos* every bit the equal to Lovecraft's own, if not that of the eternally-squabbling Greeks.

Dawn was also the first major film to defy the dreaded MPAA (Motion Picture Association of America) by refusing to dilute into an R-rated version while simultaneously refusing to accept an X, the skull-and-crossbones which would have placed it on the marquee right next to *Deep Throat* and *Debbie Does Dallas.* It went out, instead, unrated, in flat-out refusal to play the censorship game.

This unwillingness to compromise would have doomed a lesser film. But there had never been anything like the nonstop cavalcade of technicolor sploosh that Romero unleashed with *Dawn.* When audiences the world over went nuts for the thing, the age of splatter had truly arrived.

And with it, the battle over how much is *too* much pitched into predictable overdrive.

George Romero, God bless him, had gone too far.

> *"Overexposure to violent images is desensitizing us to violence. Because it now takes more and more violence to make us feel shock and revulsion, media violence has to become more and more graphic to be profitable. We are addicted—and we're about to overdose."*
>
> Tipper Gore

> *"My position is simple: I detest the Vomit Bag School of Horror, whether on screen or on the printed page— books and stories and films featuring gore for gore's sake, designed strictly for the purpose of grossing out an audience. Swill in a bucket. Sewer slime as 'entertainment'."*
>
> William F. Nolan

"You know you're successful when you've pissed off your parents."

David J. Schow

There was no question that *Dawn of the Dead* was desensitizing. After two hours and however many minutes (depending on which cut you saw) of exploding heads and rippling viscera, it got awfully hard to give a damn about the no-longer-humans and their violent *au revoirs*. In certain respects, it is the ultimate dehumanization flick, because you can no longer afford to think of these blueish-green people as *people*. They're not people anymore: they are shambling dead things that want to eat you. To regard them as more is potentially fatal. The sense of dehumanization is pointedly not by accident.

But there are also moments of intense, perverse and profoundly disturbing *rehumanization*. One vivid example of this can be found in Romero's third (and last, to date) foray into zombieland: 1985's *Day of the Dead*. Specifically, the sequence where the scientist, Sarah, is forced to amputate her lover's zombie-bitten arm, in a desperate attempt to stop the infection before it claims his life.

At this point, the levels of horror are many; you can take your pick as to which hurts the worst. Is it the moment when the machete cleaves into Miguel's arm, then takes several meticulously unbearable seconds to saw through the bone? Is it the moment when the limb finally severs, then flops in gruelingly authentic deadpan to the floor? Or perhaps the moment comes seconds later, when she brings the torch up to his dripping stump, setting off a bio-frenzy of sizzling, blackening cauterization?

All of that takes place on the first level, the ground floor of being. It's fear as a matter of simple biology: the flesh, surrendering to the laws of physics. By itself, it's most certainly horrifying, and it plays from the understanding that you can flinch if you want to . . . the camera simply won't do your flinching for you.

But, as critics of the overt mode are quick to point out, simple carnography is easy. Just train your gaze on the icky thing in motion, and you need go no further. Lord knows that the cinescape is redolent with empty goo and spew, loveless as your average quickee porn loop and meaningless as popping a zit.

But this brings us to the second level, which takes place on the stripped-naked faces of the people to whom this horror is occurring. There is Miguel's terrible shriek of realization, of a pain and loss far beyond the physicality of the moment; there is the near-lethal voltage of tension in the Mexican standoff between Rhodes' men, who want to destroy him, and Sarah, who are fighting to save his life. And then there is the unspeakable anguish on Sarah's face in the aftermath, as her rigorously maintained composure unravels.

Again: by itself, this would be more than bad enough; and, as the critics of the overt mode are quick to point out, that is precisely where we *should* stop. To go any further is to pander, to lower oneself into the slag-pit of cheap sensationalism.

But the advocates of the *less is more* school of horror are specialists in the art of averting their eyes, and their *modus operandi* tends toward a far more irrational brand of fear. It's the insistence that the unknown *remain* unknown, the oblique and introspective terror of an ostrich with its head in the sand. It takes the axiom *what I don't know can't hurt me* to its logical conclusion: *I never even knew what hit me.* It is, with all due respect, an evasion of the most fundamental sort.

Which brings us to the third level: the level of gestalt, of fusion and reintegration. At this point, you can no longer detach; the unknown has become tangible and all too real, beyond cheapening on the one hand or denial on the other. You can see the wet hole and the charred stump, yes; but beyond that—and in vital, visceral conjunction— you can know how it feels to be a part of it.

That is the essence of horror's frontier: meat meeting mind, with the soul as screaming omniscient witness. It is the point at which true illumination becomes possible: neither one nor the other but both, and more. There is no sacrifice of one for the other. Such sacrifice is worse than pointless.

To go too far is to come that much closer to having it

all; and in dangerous times like these, we *need* it all if we are to survive.

> *"You must choose:*
> *Do you wish to see (perceive) nothing, or do you want to see things as they really are?*
> *It is not hard to see things as they really are, it is simply a matter of tearing down walls, ridding oneself of defenses and presumption, rendering oneself vulnerable, an idiot, a fool.*
> *But it is not easy to see things as they really are, because it is painful, it is real, it requires response, it's an incredible commitment.*
> *To go nine-tenths of the way is to suffer at every moment utter madness.*
> *To go all the way is to become sane.*
>
> *Most people prefer blindness.*
> *But most people are a dying race."*
>
> Paul Williams

We are a culture suffused with violence. Pick up the newspaper. Turn on the TV. Look out your window. Death and mindless brutality have permeated every aspect of our lives to such a degree that there is no escape, no place safe to hide. And while violence *per se* is certainly nothing new, it might be safe to assert that during the twentieth century some dark, twisted component of the human spirit has come of age. And in doing so, given rise to a radical twist in the nature of Absolute Values in relation to *life as it is.*

When the first poison gas blew through the trenches of Belgium and France, something fundamentally twisted. When the first ovens fired at Auschwitz and the first mushroom clouds bloomed over Hiroshima and Nagasaki, something twisted. When we watched the First Lady scrambling onto the back of the Presidential limo to scrabble at the skittering pieces of her husband's skull, something twisted. When we were force-fed napalm and body bags for breakfast, lunch and dinner, courtesy of network news and the public's need to know, something twisted.

When oppressed peoples rioted in the streets or were led off to slaughter, when it became all too clear that our fearless leaders were more often than not bald-faced businessmen who sold us out in the name of profit, when killer cultists who listened to The Beatles carved up Sharon Tate and her unborn baby, ushering in an era of serial killers and Khmer Rouge, drive-by shooters and day-care rapists, hijackings and knee-cappings, death squads and body dumps . . .

Something twisted. And it keeps on twisting, in the winds of change.

Viewed in this light, Tipper Gore's statement takes on a provocatively comic bent. She states that we're about to o.d. on violence, as if violence were something new, or as if the overdosing process were of itself a negative thing. As if, were we simply to stop looking at it—to just say *no*— the carnage would simply *go away,* or at least recede to a more "reasonable" level.

It's a reasonable enough assumption, with one minor flaw. It doesn't work. It never has. And it never will.

Perhaps because as a culture we've seen too much, and don't know what to do with it, we have become disoriented. The old maps grow frayed at the edges; whole new vistas open up where before there was the fog and the fading to black. The currents shift before we've adjusted to the last wave that struck us, and we don't know where we stand anymore.

It's understandable, in such times, to wish to dig in: to hold still, to not venture into even more uncertain realms. Or better yet, to return to the last place we felt comfortable. The last place we felt we knew.

Your Humble Editors would offer that it is better to press on: to squint past the old horizon and look beyond, to see what comes next. If there's anything that will help us come to grips with how far over the edge we've gone, that thing is to do what pioneers have always done.

To go too far.

Until we've gone all the way.

"I don't know how you *perceive my mission as a writer, but for me it is not a responsibility to reaffirm*

> *your concretized myths and provincial prejudices. It is
> not my job to lull you with a false sense of the rightness
> of the universe. This wonderful and terrible occupation
> of recreating the world in a different way, each time
> fresh and strange, is an act of revolutionary guerrilla
> warfare. I stir the soup. I inconvenience you. I make
> your nose run and your eyeballs water."*
>
> *Harlan Ellison*

Which brings us back to the book at hand.

You hold in your hands a world of hurt: a psychic neutron bomb disguised as a bunch of zombie stories, able to vaporize the conventions of a genre while leaving the glory and terror intact. You hold in your hands a universe of grisly possibility, replete with all of the hope and humanity supportable by such a place.

Not bad for a book of zombie stories.

The contributors responded to our invitation with an enthusiasm that both stunned and delighted us. We asked for their most intense vision. But we never expected the level of intensity that came pouring in, story after story. It just *came:* so strong, so personal, that we knew a genuine nerve had been struck.

Everybody knows something about the world of the walking dead.

This is our way of probing the boundaries, penetrating the unknown, making sense of the nonsensical and the abhorrent. It has been brought to you by a handful of the wildest frontiersmen that this world has to offer, guys who have gone to the edge and have the arrows in their backs to prove it. We won't catagorize or count off their accomplishments to date; by the time you read this, they will already have blazed new trails to follow.

Read these people. Read every goddam thing they write. They are not writing for no reason. Each in their own way, they are pushing us toward *understanding:* the noblest cause that a human being can undertake.

If we are to rise above this nightmare, we must first make peace with the monster inside ourselves: that shambling dead thing that would tear us apart and eat us alive, never questioning why. We, the inhabitants of the latter half of the twentieth century, ride a razor's edge. A new dark age beckons on the one side. A renaissance, on the other.

If there is any hope for the future, it surely must rest upon the ability to stare unflinchingly into the heart of darkness.

Then set our sights on a better place.

And prepare ourselves.

To go too far.

—Skipp & Spector
York, Pa., 1989

Blossom

BY CHAN MCCONNELL

"Each of us has a moment," Quinn told her. "The moment when we shine; that instant when we are at our absolute best. Just as each of us has an aberration, a hidden secret. Some might call it a perversion, though that's rather a rough word. Crude. Nonspecific. Is it a perversion to do that thing you're best at, to enjoy your individual moment?"

Amelia nodded vaguely, watching the older man through her glass of Sauvignon Blanc. He was going to answer his own obtuse question, and the answer he had already decided upon was no. It was the puffery that preceded the crunch—was she going to fuck him tonight, or not? She was positive he had already answered that one in his head as well. Dinner had run to ninety-five bucks, not counting the wine or the tip. Dessert had been high-priced, higher-caloric, chocolate, elegant. Cabs had been taken and token gifts dispensed.

She had worked in loan approvals at Columbia Savings for nine months, riding the receptionist's desk. Older men frequently asked her out. When Quinn invited her to dinner, a weekend date, she had pulled his file, consulted his figures, and said yes. All the girls in the office did it. He drove a Jaguar XJS and was into condo development.

The dinner part had been completed two hours ago. Now it was *his place*. When your income hit the high six figures there was no such animal as date rape. Amelia had herpes. It was inactive tonight. Best to stay mum; it was like compensation. To her certain knowledge she had never bedded bisexuals or intravenous drug users, and in truth she feared contracting AIDS in the same unfocused way she feared getting flattened in a crosswalk by a bus. It

15

could happen. But probably not. There was no way in the world either of them could fit a condom over their mouths, so it was academic. Right?

Quinn's watery gray eyes glinted as he rattled on about aberrations and special moments. Probably the wine. It had gotten to Amelia half an hour ago, a fuzzy vino cloud that put her afloat and permitted her to tune out Quinn's voice while staring past him, to nod and generate tiny noises of acknowledgment on a schedule that allowed him to believe she was actually listening. She had disconnected, and felt just fine. She took a deep, languorous breath, keeping him on the far side of her wine glass, and stifled the giggle that welled within her. Oh my yes, she felt nice, adrift on a cumulus pillow of gasified brain cells. She would look past him, through him, in just this way when he was on top of her, grunting and sweating and believing he had seduced her . . . just as he now believed she was paying attention.

She rewound back to the last utterance she cared to remember and acted upon it. "I have an aberration," she said. She added a glowing smile and toyed with a long curl of her copper hair. Just adorable.

His interest came full blast, too eager. "Yes? Yes?" He replaced his wineglass on the clear acrylic tabletop and leaned forward to entreat her elucidation.

She played him like a catfish on a hook. "No. It's silly, really." *Look at my legs,* she commanded.

Through the tabletop he watched her legs recross. The whisper of her stockings flushed his face with blood. His brain was giddy, already jumping forward in time, to the clinch. "Please," he said. His voice was so cultured, his tone so paternal. He was losing control and she could smell it.

She kept a childlike killer smile precisely targeted. "Well. Okay." She rose, a slim and gracile woman of thirty-four, one who fought hard to keep what she had and had nothing to show for her effort except a stupid airhead bimbo job at Columbia Savings. So much bitterness, there beneath the manner and cosmetics.

There was a tall vase of irises on an antique end table near the fireplace. Firelight mellowed all the glass and

Scandinavian chrome in the room, and danced in the floor-to-ceiling wraparound windows of Quinn's eighth-floor eyrie. He kept his gaze on her. The fire was in his eyes as well.

Every inch the coquette, Amelia bit off the delicate chiffon of the iris. Chewed. Swallowed. And smiled.

Quinn's face grew robust with pleasure. His old man's eyes cleared.

"Ever since I was a little girl," she said. "Perhaps because I saw my cat, Sterling, eating grass. I like the flavor. I don't know. I used to think the flower's life added to mine."

"And this is *your* . . ." Quinn had to clear his throat. "Aberration. Ah." He left his chair to close up the distance between them. It became evident that his erection was making him blunder.

Amelia's eyes dipped to notice, bemused, and she ate another flower. She had made a point of telling Quinn she liked lots of flowers, and he and his Gold Card had come through in rainbow colors. All over the penthouse were long-stemmed roses, carnation bouquets, spring bunches, mums, more.

Quinn found the sight of Amelia chewing the flowers throat-closingly erotic. His voice grew husky and repeated her name. It was time for him to lunge. "Let me show you my specialty. Dear Amelia. My aberration."

She had been tied up before. So far, no big deal. Quinn used silk scarves to secure her wrists and ankles to the mahogany poles of the four-poster bed. With a long, curved, ebony-handled knife he halved the front of her dress. Into the vanilla highlands of her breasts he mumbled promises of more expensive replacement garments. His hands lost their sophistication and became thick-fingered, in a big masculine hurry, shredding her hose to the knees and groping to see if she was as moist as his fantasies. Then he was thrusting. Amelia rocked and pretended to orgasm. This would be done in a hurry. No big deal.

He withdrew, still hard, saying, "Don't be afraid." She had been falling asleep.

She expected him to go for the knife again, to stroke her nipples with its razor edge or tease her nerve endings with mock danger. Instead, he reached into a headboard compartment and brought out a rubber mask festooned with sewn leather and buckles and shiny gold zippers. It almost made her laugh. She protested. The contraption engulfed her head like a thick, too-tight glove. She thought of getting stuck in a pullover sweater, only this material was definitely nonporous. Her lungs felt brief panic until the thing was fully seated and she could gulp air through the nose and mouth slits.

Then Quinn resumed pushing himself into her, his prodding more urgent now. He broke rhythm only to zip the holes in the mask shut.

Fear blossomed loud in her chest, becoming a fireball. She pulled in a final huge draught of air before he zipped the nose shut, and wasted breath making incomprehensible muling noises against the already-sealed mouth hole. She could not tell him now of her congenital lung problems, that respiration was sometimes a chore. When the weather was wrong, she had to resort to prescription medication just to breathe. It had never come up, all through dinner. They had been too busy with aberrations and prime moments and eating flowers. . . .

All she could feel now was a slow explosion in her chest and the steady pounding down below, in and out. She began to buck and heave, thrashing. Quinn loved every second of it, battering her lustily despite her abrupt lack of lubrication. The friction vanished when he came inside her.

Panting, he lumbered immediately to the bathroom. When he returned, Amelia had not changed position, and he finally noticed she was no longer breathing.

Sometimes it went down this way, he thought. The price of true passion, however aberrant. But she was still moist and poised at the ready, so he opted to have one more go.

He huffed with surprise when she began to squirm beneath him again. He went *aahhh* and started stroking rigid and slippery in a fast tempo. That was it—she had fainted. Sometimes it went down that way as well—orgasm put them in the Zone for a while. She would awaken on highburn and come her teeny secretary brains right out.

Her jaw wrenched around at a ridiculous angle and bit into the leather muzzle of the mask from within, shredding a hole. A drop of Quinn's sweat flew to mix with the blood staining her teeth and the vomit clogging her throat, and before Quinn could make sense out of what he thought he saw, Amelia bit his nose off.

In the brief second before the pain hit, Quinn thought of that crazy shit on the news. Cannibal attacks on the eastern seaboard. Some whackpot scientist had claimed that dead people were reviving and eating live people. It was all Big Apple ratshit. Yet it flashed through Quinn's mind right now because Amelia had bitten his nose off *and was chewing it up and swallowing the pieces.*

His throat flooded with the foaming pink backwash of inhaled blood. He made a liquid gargling noise as he tried to recoil, to back out of her, to get the hell away from this fucking lunatic, but she had a deathgrip on him belowdecks, as well.

Then Quinn was able to yell, and he did because he could feel the ring of vaginal muscle increasing pressure, locking up beyond the circumference of his cock. The more he tried to pull out, the harder he got. He'd heard of men getting stuck in wine bottles the same way. You can't compress a liquid. Blood was a liquid. His panic erection was vised with no options. He shoved wildly against the bed, blood pumping from the cavern in his face. He began hitting her with both fists, but she was beyond feeling a thing.

When he felt the muscle sever his penis like a wire cutter, he began to scream hoarsely. None of his neighbors would pay any mind. Weird games, aberrations, were the standard menu at Quinn's. Suddenly freed, he sprawled backward. Blood gushed, ruining the carpet and sputtering from his crotch. He watched the stump of his still-stiff manhood vanish into the slick red chasm between Amelia's legs, overwhelmed by the sight of it being swallowed whole by the orifice that had bitten it off.

Quinn hit the floor and kept screaming until catatonia blanketed him.

It took Amelia about half an hour to gnaw through her bonds. She spent another hour and a half eating Quinn.

During her meal the life left his body, and the queer radiations mentioned on the news did their alien work. By then there was not enough left of his corpse to rise, or walk, or eat anyone else. The pieces lolled around on the floor, feeling the first pangs of a new hunger, unearthly and unsatisfiable.

Her savaged dress dropped away. Swaying side-to-side she found her way into the room where they had dined when they were alive. Sparks of remembered behavior capered through her dead brain matter, evaporating for the last time. She began eating the flowers in their vases, in no hurry to begin her nightwalk. The flowers were alive, but dying every moment. Their life might become hers. When she stopped, all the bouquets had been stripped.

Eventually Amelia found her way to a door, and moved into the world to seek others of her newborn kind. Never again would she be as beautiful. It was her moment, just as Quinn had said. She blended with the shadows, a striking, cream-skinned nude with flower petals drifting down from her mouth, ochre, mauve, bright red.

Mess Hall

BY RICHARD LAYMON

Jean didn't hear footsteps. She heard only the rush of the nearby stream, her own moaning, Paul's harsh gasps as he thrust into her. The first she heard of the man was his voice.

"Looks to me like fornication in a public park area."

Her heart slammed.

Oh God, no.

With her left eye, she glimpsed the man's vague shape crouching beside her in the moonlight, less than a yard away. She looked up at Paul. His eyes were wide with alarm.

This can't be happening, Jean told herself.

She felt totally helpless and exposed. Not that the guy could see anything. Just Paul's bare butt. He couldn't see that Jean's blouse was open, her bra bunched around her neck, her skirt rucked up past her waist.

"Do you know it's against the law?" the man asked.

Paul took his tongue out of Jean's mouth. He turned his head toward the man.

Jean could feel his heart drumming, his penis shrinking inside her.

"Not to mention poor taste," the man added.

"We didn't mean any harm," Paul said.

And started to get up.

Jean jammed her shoes against his buttocks, tightened her arms around his back.

"What if some *children* had wandered by?" the man asked

"We're sorry," Jean told him, keeping her head straight up, not daring to look at the man again, instead staring at Paul. "We'll leave."

"Kiss goodbye, now."

Seemed like a weird request.

But Paul obeyed. He pressed his mouth gently against Jean's lips, and she wondered how she could manage to cover herself because it was quite obvious that, as soon as the kiss was over, Paul would have to climb off her. And there she'd be.

Later, she knew it was a shotgun.

She hadn't seen a shotgun, but she'd only given the man that single, quick glance.

Paul was giving her the goodbye kiss and she was wondering about the best way to keep the man from seeing her when suddenly it didn't matter because the world blew up. Paul's eyes exploded out of their sockets and dropped onto *her* eyes. She jerked her head sideways to get away from them. Jerked it the wrong way. Saw the clotted wetness on the moonlit trunk of a nearby tree, saw his ear cling to the bark for a moment, then fall.

Paul's head dropped heavily onto the side of her face. A torrent of blood blinded her.

She started to scream.

Paul's weight tumbled off. The man stomped her belly. He scooped her up, swung her over his shoulder, and started to run. She wheezed, trying to breathe. His foot had smashed her air out and now his shoulder kept ramming into her. She felt as if she were drowning. Only a dim corner of her mind seemed to work, and she wished it would blink out.

Better total darkness, better no awareness at all.

The man stopped running. He bent over, and Jean flopped backward. She slammed something. Beside her was a windshield plated with moonlight. She'd been dumped across the hood of a car. Her legs dangled over the car's front.

She tried to lift her head. Couldn't. So she lay there, struggling to suck in air.

The man came back.

He'd been away?

Jean felt as if she had missed a chance to save herself.

He leaned over, clutched both sides of her open blouse, and yanked her into a sitting position. He snapped a handcuff around her right wrist, passed the other bracelet beneath her knee, and cuffed her left hand. Then he lifted her off the hood. He swung her into the car's passenger seat and slammed the door.

Through the windshield, Jean saw him rush past the front of the car. She drove her knee up. It bumped her chin, but she managed to slip the handcuff chain down her calf and under the sole of her running shoe. She grabbed the door handle. She levered it up and threw her shoulder against the door and started to tumble out, but her head jerked back with searing pain as if the hair were being torn from her scalp. Her head twisted. Her cheekbone struck the steering wheel. A hand clasped the top of her head. Another clutched her chin. And he rammed the side of her face again and again on the wheel.

When she opened her eyes, her head was on the man's lap. She felt his hand kneading her breast. The car was moving fast. From the engine noise and the hiss of the tires on the pavement, she guessed they were on the Interstate. The highway lights cast a faint, silvery glow on the man's face. He looked down at her and smiled.

The police artist sketch didn't have him quite right. It had the crewcut right, and the weird crazy eyes, but his nose was a little larger, his lips a lot thicker.

Jean started to lift her head.

"Lie still," he warned. "Move a muscle, I'll pound your brains out." He laughed. "How about your boyfriend's brains? Did you see how they hit that tree?"

Jean didn't answer.

He pinched her.

She gritted her teeth.

"I asked you a question."

"I saw," she said.

"Cool, huh?"

"No."

"How about his eyes? I've never seen anything like that. Just goes to show what a twelve-gauge can do to a fellow. You know, I've never killed a *guy* before. Just sweet young things like you."

Like me.

It came as no surprise, no shock. She'd seen him murder Paul, and he planned to murder her too—the same as he'd murdered the others.

Maybe he doesn't kill them all, she thought. Only one body had been found. Everyone talked as if the Reaper had killed the other six, but really they were only *missing.*

Maybe he takes them someplace and keeps them.

But he just now said he kills sweet young thing*s*. Plural. He killed them all. But maybe not. Maybe he just wants to keep me and fool with me and not kill me and I'll figure a way out.

"Where are you taking me?" she asked.

"A nice, private place in the hills where nobody will hear you scream."

The words made a chill crawl over her.

"Oooh, goosebumps. I like that." His hand glided over her skin like a cold breeze. Jean was tempted to grab his hand and bite it.

If she did that, he would hurt her again.

There'll be a world of hurt later, she thought. He plans to make me scream.

But that was later. Maybe she could get away from him before it came to that. The best thing, for now, was to give him no trouble. Don't fight him. Act docile. Then maybe he'll let his guard down.

"Do you know who I am?" he asked.

"Yes."

"Tell me."

"The Reaper."

"Very good. And I know who you are, too."

He knows me? How could he? Maybe followed me around on campus, asked someone my name.

"You're Number Eight," he said. "Just think about that. You're going to be famous. You'll be in all the newspapers, they'll talk about you on television, you'll even end up being a chapter in a book someday. Have you read any books like that? They'll have a nice little biography of you, quotes from your parents and friends. The bittersweet story of your brief but passionate relationship with that guy. What was his name?"

"Paul," she murmured.

"Paul. He'll get a good write-up, himself, since he's the

first guy to die at the hands of the Reaper. Of course, they'll realize that he was incidental. You were the intended victim, Paul simply an unlucky jerk who got in the way. He got lucky, then he got unlucky. Good one, huh? Maybe I'll write the book myself. He got off and got offed. Or did he? Which came first? Did he go out with a bang?"

"Why don't you shut up?"

"Because I don't want to," he said, and raked a path up her belly with a single fingernail.

Jean cringed. Air hissed in through her teeth.

"You should be nice to me," he said. "After all, I'm the one making you famous. Of course, some of the notoriety may be a trifle embarrassing for you. That book I was telling you about, it'll have a whole lot about today. Your final hours. Who was the last person to see you alive. And of course, it won't neglect the fornication in the park. People read that, a lot of them are going to think you were asking for it. I suppose I'd have to agree with them. Didn't you know any better?"

She *had* known better. "What about the Reaper?" she'd asked when the movie let out and Paul suggested the park.

"He'll have to find his *own* gal."

"I mean it. I'm not sure it's such a great idea. Why don't we go to my place?"

"Right. So your demented roommate can listen through the wall and make noises."

"I told her not to do that anymore."

"Come on, let's go to the park. It's a neat night. We can find a place by the stream."

"I don't know." She squeezed his hand. "I'd like to, Paul, but . . ."

"Shit. Everybody's got Reaperitis. For godsake, he's in *Portland.*"

"That's only a half hour drive."

"Okay. Forget it. Shit."

They walked half a block, Paul silent and scowling, before Jean slipped a hand into the rear pocket of his pants and said, "Hey, pal, how's about a stroll in the park?"

"Didn't you know any better?"

His hand smacked her bare skin.

"Yes!"

"Don't you ignore me. I ask you a question, you answer. Got it?"

"Yes."

The car slowed. The Reaper's left hand eased the steering wheel over and Jean felt the car slip sideways. It tipped upward a bit, pressing her cheek against his belt buckle.

An off-ramp, she thought.

The car stopped, then made a sharp turn.

A cold tremor swept through Jean.

We're getting there, she thought. Wherever he's taking me, we're getting there. Oh, Jesus.

"You thought it couldn't happen to you," he said. "Am I right?"

"No."

"What, then? You were just too horny to care?"

"Paul would've kept on pouting." Her voice was high, shaky.

"One of those. I hate those sniveling, whiny pouters. Take me, for instance—I never pout. That's for the losers. I never lose, so I've got no reason to pout. I make *other* people lose."

He slowed the car, turned it again.

"I hate pouters, too," Jean said, trying to keep her voice steady. "They stink. They don't deserve to live."

He looked down at her. His face was a vague blur. There were no more streetlights, Jean realized. Nothing but moonlight, now.

"I bet you and I are a lot alike," she said.

"Think so, do you?"

"I've never told anyone this before, but . . . I guess it's safe to tell you. I killed a girl once."

"That so?"

He doesn't believe me!

"Yeah. It was just two years ago. I was going with this guy, Jim Smith, and . . . I really loved him. We got engaged. And then all of a sudden he started going with this bitch, Mary Jones."

"Smith and Jones, huh?" He chuckled.

"I can't help it if they had stupid names," she said, and wished she'd taken an extra second to think up names that sounded *real,* damn it. "Anyway, he spent less and less time with me, and I knew he was seeing Mary. So one night I snuck into her room in the sorority and smothered her with a pillow. Killed her. And I enjoyed it. I laughed when she died."

He patted Jean's belly. "I guess we are two of a kind. Maybe you'd like to throw in with me. I can see some advantages to an arrangement like that. You could lure the pretty young things into my car, help me subdue them. What do you think?"

She thought that she might start to cry. His offer was just what she had wanted to hear—and he knew it. He knew it, all right.

But she went along, just in case. "I think I'd like that."

"That makes it an even fifty percent," he said.

The front of the car tipped upward. Again, Jean's cheek pressed his belt buckle.

"You're the fourth to try that maneuver. Hey, forget about killing me, I'm just your type, let's be partners. Four out of eight. You're only the second to confess a prior murder, though. The other one said she pushed her kid sister out of the tree house. I sure do pick 'em. Two murderers. What are the chances of that?"

"Coincidence," Jean muttered.

"Nice try."

His right hand continued to fondle her. His left hand kept jogging the steering wheel from side to side as he maneuvered up the hill.

She could reach up and grab the wheel and maybe make them crash. But the car didn't seem to be moving very fast. At this speed, the crash might not hurt him at all.

"Let's hear the one about your rich father," he said.

"Go to hell."

He laughed. "Come on, don't ruin the score. You'll make it a hundred percent if you've got a rich father who'll pay me heaps of money to take you back to him unscathed."

She decided to try for the crash.

But the car stopped. He swung the steering wheel way over and started ahead slowly. The car bumped and rocked. Its tires crunched dirt. Leafy branches whispered and squeaked against its sides.

"We're almost there," he said.

She knew that.

"Almost time to go into your begging routine. Most of them start about now. Sometimes they hold off till we get out."

I won't beg, Jean thought. I'll run for it.

He stopped the car and turned off the engine. He didn't take the key from the ignition.

"Okay, honey. Sit up slowly and open the door. I'll be right behind you."

She sat up and turned toward the door. As she levered the handle, he clutched the collar of her blouse. He held onto it while she climbed out. Then he was standing, still gripping her collar, knuckles shoving at the back of her neck to guide her around the door. The door slammed shut. They passed the front of the car and moved toward a clearing in the forest.

The clearing was milky with moonlight. In the center, near a pale dead tree, was a ring of rocks that someone had stacked up to enclose a campfire. A pile of twigs and broken branches stood near the fire ring.

The Reaper steered Jean toward the dead tree.

She saw wood already piled inside the wall of rocks, ready for a match.

And she felt a quick glimmer of hope. *Someone* had laid the fire.

Right. *He* probably did it. He was up here earlier, preparing.

She saw a rectangular box at the foot of the tree.

A toolbox?

She began to whimper. She tried to stop walking, but he shoved her forward.

"Oh please, please, no! Spare me! I'll do anything!"

"Fuck you," Jean said.

He laughed.

"I like your guts," he said. "In a little while, we may take a good look at them."

He turned her around and backed her against the tree.

"I'll have to take off one of the cuffs, now," he explained. He took a key from the pocket of his pants and held it in front of her face. "You won't try to take advantage of the moment, will you?"

Jean shook her head.

"No, I didn't think so." He shot a knee up into her belly. His forearm caught her under the chin, forcing her back as she started to double. Her legs gave out. She slid down the trunk, the barkless wood snagging her blouse and scraping her skin. A knob of root pounded her rump. She started to tumble forward, but he was there in front of her upthrust knees, blocking her fall. She slumped back against the trunk, wheezing, feeling the cuff go away from her right wrist, knowing this was it, this was the big moment she'd been waiting for, her one and only chance to make her break.

But she couldn't move. She was hurting and dazed and breathless. And even if she hadn't been disabled by the blow, her position made struggle pointless. She was folded, back tight against the tree, legs mashing her breasts, arms stretched out over her knees, toes pinned to the ground by his boots.

She knew she had lost.

Strange, though. It didn't seem to matter much.

Jean felt as if she were outside herself, observing. It was someone else being grabbed under the armpits, someone else being lifted. She was watching a movie and the heroine was being prepared for torture. The girl's arms were being raised overhead. The loose cuff was being passed over the top of a limb. Then, it was snapped around the girl's right hand. The Reaper lifted her off her feet and carried her out away from the trunk. Then he let go. The limb was low enough so she didn't need to stand on tiptoes.

The man walked away from his captive. He crouched on the other side of the ring of rocks and struck a match. Flames climbed the tented sticks. They wrapped thick, broken branches. Pale smoke drifted up. He stood and returned to the girl.

"A little light on the subject," he said to her. His voice sounded as faint as the snapping of the fire behind him.

This is okay, she thought. It's not me. It's someone else
—a stranger.

It stopped being a stranger, very fast, when she saw the
knife in the Reaper's hand.

She stood rigid and stared at the dark blade. She tried to
hold her breath, but couldn't stop panting. Her heart felt
like a hammer trying to smash its way out of her chest.

"No," she gasped. "Please."

He smiled. "I knew you'd get around to begging."

"I never did anything to you."

"But you're about to do something *for* me."

The knife moved in. She felt its cool blade on her skin,
but it didn't hurt. It didn't cut. Not Jean. It cut her
clothes instead—the straps of her bra, the sleeves of her
blouse, the waistband of her skirt.

He took the clothes to the fire.

"No! Don't!"

He smiled and dropped them onto the flames. "You
won't need them. You'll be staying right here. Here in the
mess hall."

Somewhere in the distance, a coyote howled.

"That's my friend. We've got an arrangement. I leave a
meal for him and his forest friends, and they do the
cleanup for me. None of this 'shallow grave' nonsense. I
just leave you here, tomorrow you'll be gone. They'll come
like the good, hungry troops they are, and leave the area
neat and tidy for next time. No fuss, no bother. And you,
sweet thing, will be spared the embarrassment of returning
to campus bare-ass."

Squatting beside the fire, he opened the toolbox. He
took out pliers and a screwdriver. He set the pliers on the
flat top of a rock. He picked up the screwdriver. Its shank
was black even before he held it over the fire. Jean saw the
flames curl around it.

"No!" she cried out. "Please!"

"No! Please!" he mimicked. Smiling, he rolled the
screwdriver in his hand. "Think it's done yet?" He shook
his head. "Give it a few more minutes. No need to rush.
Are you savoring the anticipation?"

"You bastard!"

"Is that any way to talk?"

"HELP!" she shouted. "HELP! PLEASE, HELP ME!"

"Nobody's going to hear you but the coyotes."

"You can't do this!"

"Sure, I can. Done it plenty of times before."

"Please! I'll do anything!"

"I know just what you'll do. Scream, twitch, cry, kick, beg, drool . . . bleed. Not necessarily in that order, of course."

He stood up. Pliers in one hand, screwdriver in the other, he walked slowly toward Jean. Wisps of pale smoke rose off the shank of the screwdriver.

He stopped in front of her. "Now where oh where shall we begin? So many choice areas to choose from." He raised the screwdriver toward her left eye. Jean jerked her head aside. The tip moved closer. She shut her eye. Felt heat against its lid. But the heat faded. "No. I'll save that for later. After all, half the fun for *you* will be watching."

She shrieked and flinched rigid as something scared her belly.

The Reaper laughed.

She looked down. He had simply touched her with the nose of the pliers.

"Power of suggestion," he said. "Now, let's see how you like some *real* pain."

Slowly he moved the screwdriver toward her left breast. Jean tried to jerk away, but the handcuffs stopped her. She kicked out. He twisted away. As the edge of her shoe glanced off his hip, he stroked her thigh with the screwdriver. She squealed.

He grinned. "Don't do that again, honey, or I might get mean."

Sobbing, she watched him inch the screwdriver toward her breast again. "No. Don't. Pleeease."

A rock struck the side of the Reaper's head. It knocked his head sideways, bounced off, scraped Jean's armpit, and fell. He stood there for a moment, then dropped to his knees and slumped forward, face pressing against Jean's groin. She twisted away, and he flopped beside her.

She gazed down at him, hardly able to believe he was actually sprawled there. Maybe she'd passed out and this was no more than a wild fantasy. She was dreaming and pretty soon she would come to with a burst of pain and . . .

No, she thought. It can't be a dream. Please.

A dim corner of her mind whispered, *I knew I'd get out of this.*

She looked for the rock thrower.

And spotted a dim shape standing beside a tree on the far side of the clearing.

"You got him!" she shouted. "Thank God, you got him! Great throw!"

The shape didn't move, didn't call back to her.

It turned away.

"No!" Jean cried out. "Don't leave! He'll come to and kill me! Please! I'm cuffed here! He's got the key in his pocket. You've gotta unlock the cuffs for me. Please!"

The figure, as indistinct in the darkness as the bushes and trees near its sides, turned again and stepped forward. It limped toward the glow of the fire. From the shape, Jean guessed that her savior was a woman.

Others began to appear across the clearing.

One stepped out from behind a tree. Another rose behind a clump of bushes. Jean glimpsed movement over to the right, looked and saw a fourth woman. She heard a growl behind her, twisted around, and gasped at the sight of someone crawling toward her. Toward the Reaper, she hoped. The top of this one's head was black and hairless in the shimmering firelight. As if she'd been scalped? The flesh had been stripped from one side of her back, and Jean glimpsed pale curving ribs before she whirled away.

Now there were *five* in front of her, closing in and near enough to the fire so she could see them clearly.

She stared at them.

And disconnected again.

Came out of herself, became an observer.

The rock thrower had a black pit where her left eye should've been. The girl cuffed beneath the tree was amazed that a one-eyed girl had been able to throw a rock with such fine aim.

It was even more amazing, since she was obviously dead. Ropes of guts hung from her belly, swaying between her legs like an Indian's loincloth. Little but bone re-

mained of her right leg below the knee—the work of the
Reaper's woodland troops?

How can she walk?

That's a good one, the girl thought.

How can *any* of them walk?

One, who must've been up here *a very long time,* was
managing to shamble along just fine, though both her legs
were little more than bare bones. The troops had really
feasted on her. One arm was missing entirely. The other
arm was bone, and gone from the elbow down. Where she
still had flesh, it looked black and lumpy. Some of her
torso was intact, but mostly hollowed out. The right-hand
side of her rib cage had been broken open. The ribs on the
left were still there, and a shriveled lung was visible
through the bars. Her face had no eyes, no nose, no lips.
She looked as if she might be grinning.

The girl beneath the tree grinned back at her, but she
didn't seem to notice.

Of course not, dope. How can she see?

How can she walk?

One of the others still had eyes. They were wide open
and glazed. She had a very peculiar stare.

No eyelids, that's the trouble. The Reaper must've cut
them off. Her breasts, too. Round, pulpy black disks on
her chest where they should've been. Except for a huge
gap in her right flank, she didn't look as if she'd been
maimed by the troops. She still had most of her skin. But
it looked shiny and slick with a coating of white slime.

The girl beside her didn't seem to have any skin at all.
Had she been peeled? She was black all over except for the
whites of her eyes and teeth—and hundreds of white
things as if she had been showered with rice. But the rice
moved. The rice was alive. Maggots.

The last of the five girls approaching from the front was
also black. She didn't look peeled, she looked burnt. Her
body was a crust of char, cracked and leaking fluids that
shimmered in the firelight. She bore only a rough resemblance to a human being. She might have been shaped out
of mud by a dim-witted child who gave her no fingers or
toes or breasts, who couldn't manage a nose or ears, and
poked fingers into the mud to make her eyes. Her crust

made papery, crackling sounds as she shuffled past the fire, and pieces flaked off.

A motley crew, thought the girl cuffed to the limb.

She wondered if any of them would have enough sense to find the key and unlock the handcuffs.

She doubted it.

In fact, they didn't seem to be aware of her presence at all. They were limping and hobbling straight toward the Reaper.

Whose shriek now shattered whatever fragile force had allowed Jean to stay outside the cuffed stranger. She tried to keep her distance. Couldn't. Was sucked back inside the naked, suspended girl. Felt a sudden rush of horror and revulsion . . . and hope.

Whatever else they might be, they were the victims of the Reaper.

Payback time.

He was still shrieking, and Jean looked down at him. He was on his hands and knees. The scalped girl, also on her knees and facing him, had his head caught between her hands. She was biting the top of his head. Jean heard a wet ripping sound as the girl tore off a patch of hair and flesh.

He flopped and skidded backward, dragged by the rock thrower and the one with the slimy skin. Each had him by a foot. The scalped girl started to crawl after him, then grunted and stopped and tried to pick up the pliers. Her right hand had no fingers. She pawed at the pliers, whimpering with frustration, then sighed when she succeeded in picking up the tool using the thumb and two remaining fingers of her other hand. Quickly, she crawled along trying to catch up to her prize. She scurried past Jean. One of her buttocks was gone, eaten away to the bone.

She gained on the screaming Reaper, reached out and clamped the pliers to the ridge of his ear and ripped out a chunk.

Halfway between Jean and the fire, the girls released his feet.

All six went at him.

He bucked and twisted and writhed, but they turned him onto his back. While some held him down, others tore at his clothes. Others tore at *him*. The scalped one took the pliers to his right eyelid and tore it off. The burnt one snatched up a hand and opened her lipless black mouth and began to chew his fingers off. While this went on, the armless girl capered like a madcap skeleton, her trapped lung bouncing inside her ribcage.

Soon the Reaper's shirt was in shreds. His pants and boxer shorts were bunched around his cowboy boots. The scalped girl had ripped his other eyelid off, and now was stretching his upper lip as he squealed. The rock thrower, kneeling beside him, clawed at his belly as if trying to get to his guts. Slime-skin bit off one of his nipples, chewed it, and swallowed. The girl who must've been skinned alive knelt beside his head, scraping maggots off her belly and stuffing them by the handful into his mouth. No longer shrieking, he choked and wheezed.

The dancing skeleton dropped to her bare kneecaps, bent over him, and clamped her teeth on his penis. She pulled, stretching it, gnawing. He stopped choking and let out a shrill scream that felt like ice picks sliding into Jean's ears.

The scalped girl tore his lip off. She gave the pliers a snap, and watched the lip fly.

Jean watched it too. Then felt its soft plop against her thigh. It stuck to her skin like a leech. She gagged. She stomped her foot on the ground, trying to shake it off. It kept clinging.

It's just a lip, she thought.

And then she was throwing up. She leaned forward as far as she could, trying not to vomit on herself. A small part of her mind was amused. She'd been looking at hideous, mutilated corpses, such horrors as she had never seen before, not even in her nightmares. And she had watched the corpses do unspeakable things to the Reaper. With all that, she hadn't tossed her cookies.

A lip sticks to my leg, and I'm barfing my guts out.

At least she was missing herself. Most of it was hitting the ground in front of her shoes, though a little was splashing up and spraying her shins.

Finally the heaving subsided. She gasped for air and blinked tears out of her eyes.

And saw the scalped girl staring at her.

The others kept working on the Reaper. He wasn't screaming anymore, just gasping and whimpering.

The scalped girl stabbed the pliers down. They crashed through the Reaper's upper teeth. She rammed them deep into his mouth and partway down his throat, left them there, and started to crawl toward Jean.

"Get *him*," she whispered. *"He's* the one."

Then Jean thought, maybe she wants to help me.

"Would you get the key? For the handcuffs? It's in his pants pocket."

The girl didn't seem to hear. She stopped at the puddle of vomit and lowered her face into it. Jean heard lapping sounds, and gagged. The girl raised her head, stared up at Jean, licked her dripping lips, then crawled forward.

"No. Get back."

Opened her mouth wide.

Christ!

Jean smashed her knee up into the girl's forehead. The head snapped back. The girl tumbled away.

A chill spread through Jean. Her skin prickled with goosebumps. Her heart began to slam.

It won't stop with him.

I'm next!

The scalped girl, whose torso was an empty husk, rolled over and started to push herself up.

Jean leaped.

She caught the tree limb with both hands, kicked toward the trunk but couldn't come close to reaching it. Her body swept down and backward. As she started forward again, she pumped her legs high.

She swung.

She kicked and swung, making herself a pendulum that strained higher with each sweep.

Her legs hooked over the barkless, dead limb.

She drew herself up against its underside and hugged it.

Twisting her head sideways, she saw the scalped girl crawling toward her again.

Jean had never seen her stand.

If she can't stand up, I'm okay.

But the *others* could stand.

They were still busy with the Reaper. Digging into him. Biting. Ripping off flesh with their teeth. He choked around the pliers and made high squeaky noises. As Jean watched, the charred girl crouched over the fire and put both hands into the flames. When she straightened up, she had a blazing stick trapped between the fingerless flaps of her hands. She lumbered back to the group, crouched, and set the Reaper's pants on fire.

The pants, pulled down until they were stopped by his boot tops, wrapped him just below the knees.

In seconds they were ablaze.

The Reaper started screaming again. He squirmed and kicked. Jean was surprised he had that much life left in him.

The key, she thought.

I'll have to go through the ashes.

If I live that long.

Jean began to shinny out along the limb. It scraped her thighs and arms, but she kept moving, kept inching her way along. The limb sagged slightly. It groaned. She scooted farther, farther.

Heard a faint crackling sound.

Then was stopped by a bone white branch that blocked her left arm

"No!" she gasped.

She thrust herself forward and rammed her arm against the branch. The impact shook it just a bit. A few twigs near the far end of it clattered and fell.

The branch looked three inches thick where it joined the main limb. A little higher up, it seemed thin enough for her to break easily—but she couldn't reach that far, not with her wrists joined by the short chain of the handcuffs. The branch barred her way like the arm and hand of a skeleton pleased to keep her treed until its companions finished with the Reaper and came for her.

She clamped it between her teeth, bit down hard on the dry wood, gnashed on it. Her teeth barely seemed to dent it.

She lowered her head. Spat dirt and grit from her mouth. Turned her head.

The Reaper was no longer moving or making any

sounds. Pale smoke drifted up from the black area where his pants had been burning. The charred girl who had set them ablaze now held his severed arm over the campfire. The slimy, breastless girl was pulling a boot onto one of her feet. The skinned girl, kneeling by the Reaper's head, had removed the pliers from his mouth. At first Jean thought she was pinching herself with them. That wasn't it, though. One at a time, she was squashing the maggots that squirmed on her belly. The rock thrower's head was buried in the Reaper's open torso. She reared up, coils of intestine drooping from her mouth. The rotted and armless girl lay flat between the black remains of the Reaper's legs, tearing at the cavity where his genitals used to be.

Though he was apparently dead, his victims all still seemed contented.

For now.

Straining to look down past her shoulder, Jean saw the scalped girl directly below. On her knees. Reaching up, pawing the air with the remains of her hands.

She can't get me, Jean told herself.

But the others.

Once they're done with the Reaper, they'll see that bitch down there and then they'll see me.

If *she'd* just go away!

GET OUT OF HERE!

Jean wanted to shout it, didn't dare. Could just see the others turning their heads toward the sound of her voice.

If I could just kill her!

Good luck on that one.

Gotta do something!

Jean clamped the limb hard with her hands. She gritted her teeth.

Don't try it, she thought. You won't even hurt her. You'll be down where she can get at you.

But maybe a good kick in the head'll discourage her.

Fat chance.

Jean released the limb with her legs. She felt a breeze wash over her sweaty skin as she dropped. She thrashed her feet like a drowning woman hoping to kick to the surface.

A heel of her shoe struck something. She hoped it was the bitch's face.

Then she was swinging upward and saw her. Turning on her knees and reaching high, grinning.

Jean kicked hard as she swept down.

The toe of her shoe caught the bitch in the throat, lifted her off her knees and knocked her sprawling.

Got her!

Jean dangled by her hands, swaying slowly back and forth. She bucked and tried to fling her legs up to catch the limb. Missed. Lost her hold and cried out as the steel edges of the bracelets cut into her wrists. Her feet touched the ground.

The scalped girl rolled over and crawled toward her.

Jean leaped. She grabbed the limb. She pulled herself up to it and drove her knees high but not fast enough.

The girl's arms wrapped her ankles, clutched them. She pulled at Jean, stretching her, dragging her down, reaching higher, *climbing* her. Jean twisted and squirmed but couldn't shake the girl off. Her arms strained. Her grip on the limb started to slip. She squealed as teeth ripped into her thigh.

With a *krrrack!*, the limb burst apart midway between Jean and the trunk.

She dropped straight down.

Falling, she shoved the limb sideways. It hammered her shoulder as she landed, knees first, on the girl. The weight drove Jean forward, smashed her down. Though the girl no longer hugged her legs, she felt the head beneath her thigh shake from side to side. She writhed and bucked under the limb. The teeth kept their savage bite on her.

Then *had* their chunk of flesh and lost their grip.

Clutching the limb, Jean bore it down, her shoulder a fulcrum. She felt the wood rise off her back and rump. Its splintered end pressed into the ground four or five feet in front of her head. Bracing herself on the limb, she scurried forward, knees pounding at the girl beneath her. The girl growled. Hands gripped Jean's calves. But not tightly. Not with the missing fingers. Teeth snapped at her, scraping the skin above her right knee. Jean jerked her leg back and shot it forward. The girl's teeth crashed shut. Then Jean was off her, rising on the crutch of the broken limb.

She stood up straight, hugging the upright limb, lifting its broken end off the ground and staggering forward a few steps to get herself out of the girl's reach.

And saw the others coming. All but the rotted skeletal girl who had no arms and still lay sprawled between the Reaper's legs.

"No!" Jean shouted. "Leave me alone!"

They lurched toward her.

The charred one held the Reaper's severed arm like a club. The breastless girl with runny skin wore both his boots. Her arms were raised, already reaching for Jean though she was still a few yards away. The rock thrower had found a rock. The skinned girl aswarm with maggots picked at herself with the pliers as she shambled closer.

"NO!" Jean yelled again.

She ducked, grabbed the limb low, hugged it to her side and whirled as the branchy top of it swept down in front of her. It dropped from its height slashing sideways, its bony fingers of wood clattering and bursting into twigs as it crashed through the cadavers. Three of them were knocked off their feet. A fourth, the charred one, lurched backward to escape the blow, stepped into the Reaper's torso, and stumbled. Jean didn't see whether she went down, because the weight of the limb was hurling her around in a full circle. A branch struck the face of the scalped girl crawling toward her, popped, and flew off. Then the crawling girl was behind Jean again and the others were still down. All except the rock thrower. She'd been missed, first time around. Out of range. Now her arm was cocked back, ready to hurl a small block of stone.

Jean, spinning, released the limb.

Its barkless wood scraped her side and belly.

It flew from her like a mammoth, tined lance.

Free of its pull, Jean twirled. The rock flicked her ear. She fell to her knees. Facing the crawler. Who scurried toward her moaning as if she already knew she had lost.

Driving both fists against the ground, Jean pushed herself up. She took two quick steps toward the crawler and kicked her in the face. Then she staggered backward. Whirled around.

The rock thrower was down, arms batting through the maze of dead branches above her.

The others were starting to get up.

Jean ran through them, cuffed hands high, twisting and dodging as they scurried for her, lurched at her, grabbed.

Then they were behind her. All but the Reaper and the armless thing sprawled between his legs, chewing on him. *Gotta get the handcuff key,* she thought.

Charging toward them, she realized the cuffs didn't matter. They couldn't stop her from driving. The car key was in the ignition.

She leaped the Reaper.

And staggered to a stop on the other side of his body.

Gasping, she bent over and lifted a rock from the ring around the fire. Though its heat scorched her hands, she raised it overhead. She turned around.

The corpses were coming, crawling and limping closer. But they weren't that close.

"HERE'S ONE FOR NUMBER EIGHT!" she shouted, and smashed the rock down onto the remains of the Reaper's face. It struck with a wet, crunching sound. It didn't roll off. It stayed on his face as if it had made a nest for itself.

Jean stomped on it once, pounding it in farther.

Then she swung around. She leaped the fire and dashed through the clearing toward the waiting car.

It Helps
If You Sing

BY RAMSEY CAMPBELL

They could be on their summer holidays. If they were
better able to afford one than he was, Bright wished them
luck. Now that it was daylight, he could see into all the
lowest rooms of the high rise opposite, but there was no
sign of life on the first two floors. Perhaps all the tenants
were singing the hymns he could hear somewhere in the
suburb. He took his time about making himself present-
able, and then he went downstairs.

The lifts were out of order. Presumably it was a repair-
man who peered at him through the smeary window of
one scrawled metal door on the landing below his. The
blurred face startled him so much that he was glad to see
people on the third floor. Weren't they from the building
opposite, from one of the apartments that had stayed unlit
last night? The woman they had come to visit was losing a
smiling contest with them. She stepped back grudgingly,
and Bright heard the bolt and chain slide home as he
reached the stairs.

The public library was on the ground floor. First he
strolled to the job center among the locked and armored
shops. There was nothing for a printer on the cards, and
cards that offered training in a new career were meant for
people thirty years younger. They needed the work more
than he did, even if they had no families to provide for. He
ambled back to the library, whistling a wartime song.

The young job-hunters had finished with the newspapers. Bright started with the tabloids, saving the serious
papers for the afternoon, though even those suggested that

42

the world over the horizon was seething with disease and
crime and promiscuity and wars. Good news wasn't news,
he told himself, but the last girl he'd ever courted before
he'd grown too set in his ways was out there somewhere,
and the world must be better for her. Still, it was no wonder that most readers came to the library for fiction rather
than for the news. He supposed the smiling couple who
were filling cartons with books would take them to the
housebound, although some of the titles he glimpsed
seemed unsuitable for the easily offended. He watched the
couple stalk away with the cartons, until the smoke of a
distant bonfire obscured them.

The library closed at nine. Usually Bright would have
been home for hours and listening to his radio cassette
player, to Elgar or Vera Lynn or the dance bands his father used to play on the wind-up record player, but something about the day had made him reluctant to be alone.
He read about evolution until the librarian began to har-
rumph loudly and smite books on the shelves.

Perhaps Bright should have gone up sooner. When he
hurried round the outside of the building to the lobby, he
had never seen the suburb so lifeless. Identical gray ter-
races multiplied to the horizon under a charred sky; a pair
of trampled books lay amid the breathless litter on the
anonymous concrete walks. He thought he heard a cry,
but it might have been the start of the hymn that immediately was all he could hear, wherever it was.

The lifts still weren't working; both sets of doors that
gave onto the scribbled lobby were open, displaying thick
cables encrusted with darkness. By the time he reached
the second floor he was slowing, grasping any banisters
that hadn't been prised out of the concrete. The few lights
that were working had been spray-painted until they resembled dying coals. Gangs of shadows flattened themselves against the walls, waiting to mug him. As he
climbed, a muffled sound of hymns made him feel even
more isolated. They must be on television, he could hear
them in so many apartments.

One pair of lift doors on the fifth floor had jammed
open. Unless Bright's eyes were the worse for his climb,
the cable was shaking. He labored upstairs to his landing,

where the corresponding doors were open too. Once his head stopped swimming, he ventured to the edge of the unlit shaft. There was no movement, and nothing on the cable except the underside of the lift on the top floor. He turned toward his apartment. Two men were waiting for him.

Apparently they'd rung his bell. They were staring at his door and rubbing their hands stiffly. They wore black T-shirts and voluminous black overalls, and sandals on their otherwise bare feet. "What can I do for you?" Bright called.

They turned together, holding out their hands as if to show him how gray their palms looked under the stained lamp. Their narrow bland faces were already smiling. "Ask rather what we can do for you," one said.

Bright couldn't tell which of them had spoken, for neither smile gave an inch. They might be two men or even two women, despite their close-cropped hair. "You could let me at my front door," Bright said.

They gazed at him as if nothing he might say would stop them smiling, their eyes wide as old pennies stuck under the lids. When he pulled out his key and marched forward, they stepped aside, but only just. As he slipped the key into the lock, he sensed them close behind him, though he couldn't hear them. He pushed the door open, no wider than he needed to let himself in. They followed him.

"Whoa, whoa." He swung round in the stubby vestibule and made a grab at the door, too late. His visitors came plodding in, bumping the door against the wall. Their expressions seemed more generalized than ever. "What the devil do you think you're doing?" Bright cried.

That brought their smiles momentarily alive, as though it were a line they'd heard before. "We haven't anything to do with him," their high flat voices said, one louder than the other.

"And we hope you won't have," one added while his companion mouthed. They seemed no surer who should talk than who should close the door behind them. The one by the hinges elbowed it shut, almost trapping the other before he was in, until the other blundered through and squashed his companion behind the door. They might be fun, Bright supposed, and he could do with some of that. They seemed harmless enough, so long as they didn't stumble against anything breakable. "I can't give you much time," he warned them.

They tried to lumber into the main room together. One barged through the doorway and the other stumped after him, and they stared about the room. Presumably the blankness of their eyes meant they found it wanting, the sofa piled with Bright's clothes awaiting ironing, the snaps he'd taken on his walks in France and Germany and Greece, the portrait of herself his last girlfriend had given him, the framed copy of the article he'd printed for the newspaper shortly before he'd been made redundant, about how life should be a hundred years from now, advances in technology giving people more control over their own lives. He resented the disapproval, but he was more disconcerted by how his visitors looked in the light of his apartment: gray from heads to toes, as if they needed dusting. "Who are you?" he demanded. "Where are you from?"

"We don't matter."

"Atter," the other agreed, and they said almost in unison: "We're just vessels of the Word."

"Better give it to me, then," Bright said, staying on his feet so as to deter them from sitting: God only knew how long it would take them to stand up. "I've a lot to do before I can lie down."

They turned to him as if they had to move their whole bodies to look. Whichever responded, the voice through the fixed smile sounded more pinched than ever. "What do you call your life?"

They had no reason to feel superior to him. The gray ingrained in their flesh suggested disuse rather than hard work, and disused was how they smelled in the small room. "I've had a fair life, and it's only right I should make way for someone who can work the new machines. I've had enough of a life to help me cope with the dole."

His visitors stared as if they meant to dull him into accepting whatever they were offering. The sight of their faces stretched tight by their smiles was so disagreeably fascinating that he jumped, having lost his sense of time passing, when one spoke. "Your life is empty until you let him in."

"Isn't two of you enough? Who's that, now?"

The figure on his left reached in a pocket, and the overalls pulled flat at the crotch. The jerky hand produced a videocassette that bore a picture of a priest. "I can't play that," Bright said.

His visitors pivoted sluggishly to survey the room. Their smiles turned away from him, turned back unchanged. They must have seen that his radio could play cassettes, for now the righthand visitor was holding one. "Listen before it's too late," they urged in unison.

"As soon as I've time." Bright would have promised more just then to rid himself of their locked smiles and their stale sweetish odor. He held open the door to the vestibule and shrank back as one floundered in the doorway while the other fumbled at the outer door. He held his breath as the second set of footsteps plodded through the vestibule, and let out a gasp of relief as the outer door slammed.

Perhaps deodorants were contrary to their faith. He opened the window and leaned into the night to breathe. More of the building opposite was unlit, as if a flood of darkness were rising through the floors, and he would have expected to see more houses lit by now. He could hear more than one muffled hymn, or perhaps the same one at different stages of its development. He was wondering where he'd seen the face of the priest on the videocassette.

When the smoke of a bonfire began to scrape his throat, he closed the window. He set up the ironing board and switched on the electric iron. It took him half an hour to press his clothes, and he still couldn't remember what he'd read about the priest. Perhaps he could remind himself. He carried the radio to his chair by the window.

As he lifted the cassette out of its plastic box, he winced. A sharp corner of the cassette had pricked him. He sucked his thumb and gnawed it to dislodge the sliver of plastic that had penetrated his skin. He dropped the cassette into the player and snapped the aperture shut, then he switched on, trying to ignore the ache in his thumb. He heard a hiss, the click of a microphone, a voice. "I am Father Lazarus. I'm going to tell you the whole truth," it said.

It was light as a disc jockey's voice, and virtually sexless. Bright knew the name; perhaps he would be able to place it now that the ache was fading. "If you knew the truth," the voice said, "wouldn't you want to help your fellow man by telling him?"

"Depends," Bright growled, blaming the voice for the injury to his thumb.

"And if you've just said no, don't you see that proves you don't know the truth?"

"Ho ho, very clever," Bright scoffed. The absence of the pain was unexpectedly comforting: it felt like a calm in which he need do nothing except let the voice reach him. "Get on with it," he muttered.

"Christ was the truth. He was the word that couldn't deny itself although they made him suffer all the torments of the damned. Why would they have treated him like that if they hadn't been afraid of the truth? He was the truth made flesh, born without the preamble of lust and never indulging in it himself, and we have only to become vessels of the truth to welcome him back before it's too late."

Not too late to recall where he'd seen the priest's face, Bright thought, if he didn't nod off first, he felt so numbed. "Look around you," the voice was saying, "and see how late it is. Look and see the world ending in corruption and lust and man's indifference."

The suggestion seemed knowing. If you looked out at the suburb, you would see the littered walkways where nobody walked at night except addicts and muggers and drunks. There was better elsewhere, Bright told himself, and managed to turn his head on its stiff neck toward the portrait photograph. "Can you want the world to end this way?" the priest demanded. "Isn't it true that you wish you could change it but feel helpless? Believe me, you can. Christ says you can. He had to suffer agonies for the truth, but we offer you the end of pain and the beginning of eternal life. The resurrection of the body has begun."

Not this body, Bright thought feebly. His injured hand

alone felt as heavy as himself. Even when he realized that
he'd left the iron switched on, it seemed insufficient reason
for him to move. "Neither men nor women shall we be in
the world to come," the voice was intoning. "The flesh
shall be freed of the lusts that have blinded us to the
truth."

He blamed sex for everything, Bright mused, and instantly he remembered. EVANGELIST IS VOODOO WID-
OWER, the headline inside a tabloid had said, months ago.
The priest had gone to Haiti to save his wife's people, only
for her to return to her old faith and refuse to go home
with him. Hadn't he been quoted in the paper as vowing
to use his enemies' methods to defeat them? Certainly he'd
announced that he was renaming himself Lazarus. His
voice seemed to be growing louder, so loud that the
speaker ought to be vibrating. "The Word of God will fill
your emptiness. You will go forth to save your fellow man
and be rewarded on the day of judgment. Man was made
to praise God, and so he did until woman tempted him in
the garden. When the sound of our praise is so great that
it reaches heaven, our savior shall return."

Bright did feel emptied, hardly there at all. If giving in
to the voice gave him back his strength, wouldn't that
prove it was telling the truth? But he felt as if it wanted to
take the place of his entire life. He gazed at the photograph, remembering the good-byes at the bus station, the
last kiss and the pressure of her hands on his, the glow of
the bus turning the buds on a tree into green fairy lights as
the vehicle vanished over the crest of a hill, and then he
realized that the priest's voice had stopped.

He felt as if he'd outwitted the tape until a choir began
the hymn he had been hearing all day. The emptiness
within him was urging him to join in, but he wouldn't
while he had any strength. He managed to suck his bottom lip between his teeth and gnaw it, though he wasn't
sure if he could feel even a distant ache. Voodoo widower,
he chanted to himself to break up the oppressive repetition
of the hymn, voodoo widower. He was fending off the
hymn, though it seemed impossibly loud in his head, when
he heard another sound. The outer door was opening.

He couldn't move, he couldn't even call out. The numbness that had spread from his thumb through his body had sculpted him to the chair. He heard the outer door slam as bodies blundered voicelessly about the vestibule. The door to the room inched open, then jerked wide, and the two overalled figures struggled into the room.

He'd known who they were as soon as he'd heard the outer door. The hymn on the tape must have been a signal that he was finished—that he was like them. They'd tampered with the latch on their way out, he realized dully. He seemed incapable of feeling or reacting, even when the larger of the figures leaned down to gaze into his eyes, presumably to check that they were blank, and Bright saw how the gray, stretched lips were fraying at the corners. For a moment Bright thought the man's eyes were going to pop out of their seedy sockets at him, yet he felt no inclination to flinch. Perhaps he was recognizing himself as he would be—yet didn't that mean he wasn't finished after all?

The man stood back from scrutinizing him and turned up the volume of the hymn. Bright thought the words were meant to fill his head, but he could still choose what to think. He wasn't that empty, he'd done his bit of good for the world, he'd stood aside to give someone else a chance. Whatever the priest had brought back from Haiti might have deadened Bright's body, but it hadn't quite deadened his mind. He fixed his gaze on the photograph and thought of the day he'd walked on a mountain with her. He was beginning to fight back toward his feelings when the other man came out of the kitchen, bearing the sharpest knife in the place.

They weren't supposed to make Bright suffer, the tape had said so. He could see no injuries on them. Suppose there were mutilations that weren't visible? "Neither men nor women shall we be in the world to come." At last Bright understood why his visitors seemed sexless. He tried to shrink back as the man who had turned up the hymn took hold of the electric iron.

The man grasped it by the point before he found the handle. Bright saw the gray skin of his fingers curl up like charred paper, but the man didn't react at all. He closed his free hand around the handle and waited while his companion plodded toward Bright, the edge of the knife blade glinting like a razor. "It helps if you sing," said the man with the knife. Though Bright had never been particularly religious, nobody could have prayed harder than he started to pray then. He was praying that by the time the first of them reached him, he would feel as little as they did.

Home Delivery

BY STEPHEN KING

Considering that it was probably the end of the world, Maddie Pace thought she was doing a good job. *Hell* of a good job. She thought that she just might be coping with the End of Everything better than anyone else on earth. And she was *positive* she was coping better than any other *pregnant* woman on earth.

Coping.

Maddie Pace, of all people.

Maddie Pace, who sometimes couldn't sleep if, after a visit from Reverend Peebles, she spied a dust-bunny under the dining room table—just the thought that Reverend Peebles *might* have seen that dust-bunny could be enough to keep her awake until two in the morning.

Maddie Pace, who, as Maddie Sullivan, used to drive her fiancé Jack crazy when she froze over a menu, debating entrées sometimes for as long as half an hour.

"Maddie, why don't you just flip a coin?" he'd asked her once after she had managed to narrow it down to a choice between the braised veal and the lamb chops . . . and then could get no further. "I've had five bottles of this goddam German beer already, and if you don't make up y'mind pretty damn quick, there's gonna be a drunk lobsterman under the table before we ever get any food *on* it!"

So she had smiled nervously, ordered the braised veal . . . and then lay awake until well past midnight, wondering if the chops might not have been better.

She'd had no trouble coping with Jack's proposal, however; she accepted it and him quickly, and with tremendous relief. Following the death of her father, Maddie and her mother had lived an aimless, cloudy sort of life on Deer Isle, off the coast of Maine. "If I wasn't around to

51

tell them women where to squat and lean against the wheel," George Sullivan had been fond of saying while in his cups and among his friends at Buster's Tavern or in the back room of Daggett's Barber Shop, "I don't know what the hell they'd do."

When he died of a massive coronary, Maddie was nineteen and minding the town library weekday evenings at a salary of $41.50 a week. Her mother was minding the house—or had been, that was, when George reminded her (sometimes with a good, hard shot to the ear) that she had a house that needed minding.

He was right.

They didn't speak of it because it embarrassed them, but he was right and both of them knew it. Without George around to tell them where to squat and lean to the wheel, they didn't know what the hell to do. Money wasn't the problem; George had believed passionately in insurance, and when he dropped down dead during the tiebreaker frame of the League Bowl-Offs at Big Duke's Big Ten in Yarmouth, his wife had come into better than a hundred thousand dollars. And island life was cheap, if you owned your own home and kept your garden weeded and knew how to put up your own vegetables come fall. The *problem* was having nothing to focus on. The *problem* was how the center seemed to have dropped out of their lives when George went facedown in his Island Amoco bowling shirt just over the foul line of lane nineteen in Big Duke's (and goddam if he hadn't picked up the spare they needed to win, too). With George gone their lives had become an eerie sort of blur.

It's like being lost in a heavy fog, Maddie thought sometimes. Only instead of looking for the road, or a house, or the village, or just some landmark like that lightning-struck pine in the Altons' woodlot, I am looking for the wheel. If I can ever find the wheel, maybe I can tell *myself* to squat and lean my shoulder to it.

At last she found her wheel; it turned out to be Jack Pace. Women marry their fathers and men their mothers, some say, and while such a broad statement can hardly be true all of the time, it was true in Maddie's case. Her father had been looked upon by his peers with fear and admiration—"Don't fool with George Sullivan, chummy," they'd say. "He's one hefty son of a bitch and he'd just as soon knock the nose off your face as fart downwind."

It was true at home, too. He'd been domineering and sometimes physically abusive . . . but he'd also known things to want and work for, like the Ford pickup, the chain saw, or those two acres that bounded their place on the left. Pop Cook's land. George Sullivan had been known to refer to Pop Cook (out of his cups as well as in them) as one stinky old bastid, but there was some good hardwood left on those two acres. Pop didn't know it because he had gone to living on the mainland when his arthritis really got going and crippled him up bad, and George let it be known on the island that what that bastid Pop Cook didn't know wouldn't hurt him none, and furthermore, he would kill the man or woman that let light into the darkness of Pop's ignorance. No one did, and eventually the Sullivans got the land. And the wood, of course. The hardwood was logged off for the two wood stoves that heated the house in three years, but the land would remain. That was what George said and they believed him, believed *in* him, and they worked, all three of them. He said you got to put your shoulder to this wheel and *push* the bitch, you got to push ha'ad because she don't move easy. So that was what they did.

In those days Maddy's mother had kept a roadside stand, and there were always plenty of tourists who bought the vegetables she grew—the ones George *told* her to grow, of course, and even though they were never exactly what her mother called "the Gotrocks family," they made out. Even in years when lobstering was bad, they made out.

Jack Pace could be domineering when Maddie's indecision finally forced him to be, and she suspected that, loving as he was in their courtship, he might get around to the physical part—the twisted arm when supper was cold, the occasional slap or downright paddling—in time; when the bloom was off the rose, so as to speak. She saw the similarities . . . but she loved him. And needed him.

"I'm not going to be a lobsterman all my life, Maddie,"

he told her the week before they married, and she believed him. A year before, when he had asked her out for the first time (she'd had no trouble coping then, either—had said yes almost before all the words could get out of his mouth, and she had blushed to the roots of her hair at the sound of her own naked eagerness), he would have said, "I *ain't* going to be a lobsterman all my life." A small change . . . but all the difference in the world. He had been going to night school three evenings a week, taking the ferry over and back. He would be dog tired after a day of pulling pots, but he'd go just the same, pausing only long enough to shower off the powerful smells of lobster and brine and to gulp two No Doz with hot coffee. After a while, when she saw he really meant to stick to it, Maddie began putting up hot soup for him to drink on the ferry ride over. Otherwise, he would have had no supper at all.

She remembered agonizing over the canned soups in the store—there were so *many*! Would he want tomato? Some people didn't like tomato soup. In fact, some people *hated* tomato soup, even if you made it with milk instead of water. Vegetable soup? Turkey? Cream of chicken? Her helpless eyes roved the shelf display for nearly ten minutes before Charlene Nedeau asked if she could help her with something—only Charlene said it in a sarcastic way, and Maddie guessed she would tell all her friends at high school tomorrow and they would giggle about it—about *her*—in the Girls' Room, because Charlene knew what was wrong; the same thing that was always wrong. It was just Maddie Sullivan, unable to make up her mind over so simple a thing as a can of *soup*. How she had ever been able to decide to accept Jack Pace's proposal was a wonder and a marvel to all of them . . . but of course they didn't know how, once you found the wheel, you had to have someone to tell you when to stoop and where exactly to lean against it.

Maddie had left the store with no soup and a throbbing headache.

When she worked up nerve enough to ask Jack what his favorite soup was, he had said: "Chicken noodle. Kind that comes in the can."

Were there any others he specially liked?

The answer was no, just chicken noodle—the kind that came in the can. That was all the soup Jack Pace needed in his life, and all the answer (on that one particular subject, at least) that Maddie needed in hers. Light of step and cheerful of heart, Maddie climbed the warped wooden steps of the store the next day and bought the four cans of chicken noodle soup that were on the shelf. When she asked Bob Nedeau if he had any more, he said he had a whole damn *case* of the stuff out back.

She bought the entire case and left him so flabbergasted that he actually carried the carton out to the truck for her and forgot all about asking why she had wanted all that chicken soup—a lapse for which his wife Margaret and his daughter Charlene took him sharply to task that evening.

"You just better believe it," Jack had said that time not long before the wedding—she never forgot. "More than a lobsterman. My dad says I'm full of shit. He says if it was good enough for his old man, and his old man's old man, and all the way back to the friggin' Garden of Eden to hear *him* tell it, if it was good enough for all of *them,* it ought to be good enough for me. But it ain't—*isn't,* I mean—and I'm going to do better." His eye fell on her, and it was a loving eye, but it was a stern eye, too. "More than a lobsterman is what I mean to be, and more than a lobsterman's wife is what I intend for you to be. You're going to have a house on the mainland."

"Yes, Jack."

"And I'm not going to have any friggin' Chevrolet." He took a deep breath. "I'm going to have an *Oldsmobile.*" He looked at her, as if daring her to refute him. She did no such thing, of course; she said yes, Jack, for the third or fourth time that evening. She had said it to him thousands of times over the year they had spent courting, and she confidently expected to say it *millions* of times before death ended their marriage by taking one of them—or, hopefully, both of them together.

"More than a friggin' lobsterman, no matter what my old man says. I'm going to do it, and do you know who's going to help me?"

"Yes," Maddie had said. "Me."

"You," he responded with a grin, sweeping her into his arms, "are damned tooting."

So they were wed.

Jack knew what he wanted, and he would tell her how to help him get it and that was just the way she wanted things to be.

Then Jack died.

Then, not more than four months after, while she was still wearing weeds, dead folks started to come out of their graves and walk around. If you got too close, they bit you and you died for a little while and then *you* got up and started walking around, too.

Then, Russia and America came very, very close to blowing the whole world to smithereens, both of them accusing the other of causing the phenomenon of the walking dead. "How close?" Maddie heard one news correspondent from CNN ask about a month after dead people started to get up and walk around, first in Florida, then in Murmansk, then in Leningrad and Minsk, then in Elmira, Illinois; Rio de Janeiro; Biterad, Germany; New Delhi, India; and a small Australian hamlet on the edge of the outback.

(This hamlet went by the colorful name of Wet Noggin, and before the news got out of there, most of Wet Noggin's populace consisted of shambling dead folks and starving dogs. Maddie had watched most of these developments on the Pulsifers' TV. Jack had hated their satellite dish—maybe because they could not yet afford one themselves—but now, with Jack dead, none of that mattered.)

In answer to his own rhetorical question about how close the two countries had come to blowing the earth to smithereens, the commentator had said, "We'll never know, but that may be just as well. My guess is within a hair's breadth."

Then, at the last possible second, a British astronomer had discovered the satellite—the apparently *living* satellite —which became known as Star Wormwood.

Not one of ours, not one of theirs. Someone else's. Someone or something from the great big darkness Out There.

Well, they had swapped one nightmare for another,

Maddie supposed, because *then*—the last *then* before the TV (even all the channels the Pulsifers' satellite dish could pull in) stopped showing anything but snow—the walking dead folks stopped only biting people if they came too close.

The dead folks started *trying* to get close.

The dead folks, it seemed, had discovered they *liked* what they were biting.

Before all the weird things started happening, Maddie discovered she was what her mother had always called "preg," a curt word that was like the sound you made when you had a throatful of snot and had to rasp some of it up (or at least that was how Maddie had always thought it sounded). She and Jack had moved to Genneseault Island, a nearby island simply called Jenny Island by those who lived there.

She had had one of her agonizing interior debates when she had missed her time of the month twice, and after four sleepless nights she had made a decision . . . and an appointment with Dr. McElwain on the mainland. Looking back, she was glad. If she had waited to see if she was going to miss a third period, Jack would not even have had one month of joy . . . and she would have missed the concerns and little kindnesses he had showered upon her.

Looking back—now that she was *coping*—her indecision seemed ludicrous, but her deeper heart knew that going to have the test had taken tremendous courage. She had wanted to be sick in the mornings so she could be surer; she had longed for nausea. She made the appointment when Jack was out dragging pots, and she went while he was out, but there was no such thing as *sneaking* over to the mainland on the ferry. Too many people saw you. Someone would mention casually to Jack that he or she had seen his wife on *The Gull* t'other day, and then Jack would want to know who and why and where, and if she'd made a mistake, Jack would look at her like she was a goose.

But it had been true, she was with child (and never mind that word that sounded like someone with a bad

cold trying to rake snot off the sides of his throat), and
Jack Pace had had exactly twenty-seven days of joy
and looking forward before a bad swell had caught him
and knocked him over the side of *My Lady-Love,* the lobster boat he had inherited from his Uncle Mike. Jack
could swim, and he had popped to the surface like a cork,
Dave Eamons had told her miserably, but just as he did,
another heavy swell came, slewing the boat directly into
Jack, and although Dave would say no more, Maddie had
been born and brought up an island girl, and she knew:
could, in fact, *hear* the hollow thud as the boat with its
treacherous name smashed her husband's head, leaving
blood and hair and bone and brain for the next swell to
wash away from the boat's worn side.

Dressed in a heavy hooded parka and down-filled pants
and boots, Jack Pace had sunk like a stone. They had
buried an empty casket in the little cemetery at the north
end of Jenny Island, and the Reverend Peebles (on Jenny
you had your choice when it came to religion: you could
be a Methodist, or if that didn't suit you, you could be a
Methodist) had presided over this empty coffin, as he had
so many others, and at the age of twenty-two Maddie had
found herself a widow with an almost half-cooked bun in
her oven and no one to tell her where the wheel was, let
alone when to put her shoulder to it.

She thought she would go back to Deer Isle, back to her
mother, to wait for her time, but she knew her mother was
as lost—maybe even *more* lost—than she was herself, and
held off.

"Maddie," Jack told her again and again, "the only
thing you can ever decide on is not to decide."

Nor was her mother any better. They talked on the
phone and Maddie waited and hoped for her mother to
tell her to come home, but Mrs. Sullivan could tell no one
over the age of ten anything. "Maybe you ought to come
on back over here," she had said once in a tentative way,
and Maddie couldn't tell if that meant *please come home*
or *please don't take me up on an offer which was really just
made for form's sake,* and she spent sleepless nights trying
to decide and succeeding in doing only that thing of which
Jack had accused her: deciding not to decide.

Then the weirdness started, and that was a mercy, because there was only the one small graveyard on Jenny (and so many of the graves filled with those empty coffins —a thing which had once seemed pitiful to her now seemed another blessing, a grace) and there were two on Deer Isle, bigger ones, and it seemed so much safer to stay on Jenny and wait.

She would wait and see if the world lived or died.

If it lived, she would wait for the baby.

That seemed like enough.

And now she was, after a life of passive obedience and vague resolves that passed like dreams an hour or two after getting out of bed, finally *coping*. She knew that part of this was nothing more than the effect of being slammed with one massive shock after another, beginning with the death of her husband and ending with one of the last broadcasts the Pulsifers' TV had picked up—a horrified young boy who had been pressed into service as an INS reporter, saying that it seemed certain that the president of the United States, the first lady, the secretary of state, the honorable senator from Oregon (which honorable senator the gibbering boy reporter didn't say), and the emir of Kuwait had been eaten alive in the White House ballroom by zombies.

"I want to repeat," the young reporter said, the fire-spots of his acne standing out on his forehead and chin like stigmata. His mouth and cheeks had begun to twitch; the microphone in his hand shook spastically. "I want to repeat that a bunch of dead people have just lunched up on the president and his wife and a whole lot of other political hotshots who were at the White House to eat poached salmon and cherries jubilee. Go, Yale! Boola-boola! Boola-fuckin-boola!" And then the young reporter with the fiery pimples had lost control of his face entirely, and he was screaming, only his screams were disguised as laughter, and he went on yelling *Go, Yale! Boola-boola!* while Maddie and the Pulsifers sat in dismayed silence until the young man was suddenly swallowed by an ad for Boxcar Willy records, which were not available in any store, you could only get them if you dialed the 800 number on your screen, operators were standing by. One of little Cheyne Pulsifer's crayons was on the end table beside the place where Maddie was sitting, and she took down the number before Mr. Pulsifer got up and turned off the TV without a single word.

Maddie told them good night and thanked them for sharing their TV and their Jiffy Pop.

"Are you sure you're all right, Maddie dear?" Candi Pulsifer asked her for the fifth time that night, and Maddie said she was fine for the fifth time that night (and she was, she was *coping* for the first time in her life, and that really *was* fine, just as fine as paint), and Candi told her again that she could have that upstairs room that used to be Brian's anytime she wanted, and Maddie had declined her with the most graceful thanks she could find, and was at last allowed to escape. She had walked the windy half mile back to her own house and was in her own kitchen before she realized that she still had the scrap of paper on which she had jotted the 800 number in one hand. She dialed it, and there was nothing. No recorded voice telling her all circuits were currently busy or that number was out of service; no wailing siren sound that indicated a line interruption (had Jack told her that was what that sound meant? she tried to remember and couldn't, and really, it didn't matter a bit, did it?), no clicks and boops, no static. Just smooth silence.

That was when Maddie knew—knew for sure.

She hung up the telephone slowly and thoughtfully.

The end of the world had come. It was no longer in doubt. When you could no longer call the 800 number and order the Boxcar Willy records that were not available in any store, when there were for the first time in her living memory no Operators Standing By, the end of the world was a foregone conclusion.

She felt her rounding stomach as she stood there by the phone on the wall in the kitchen and said it out loud for the first time, unaware that she had spoken: "It will have to be a home delivery. But that's all right, as long as you remember, Maddie. There isn't any other way, not now. It will have to be a home delivery."

She waited for fear and none came.

"I can cope with this just fine," she said, and this time she heard herself and was comforted by the sureness of her own words.

A baby.

When the baby came, the end of the world would itself end.

"Eden," she said, and smiled. Her smile was sweet, the smile of a madonna. It didn't matter how many rotting dead people (maybe Boxcar Willy among them) were shambling around on the face of the world.

She would have a baby, she would have a home delivery, and the possibility of Eden would remain.

The first news had come out of a small Florida town on the Tamiami Trail. The name of this town was not as colorful as Wet Noggin, but it was still pretty good: Thumper. Thumper, Florida. It was reported in one of those lurid tabloids that fill the racks by the checkout aisles in supermarkets and discount drugstores. DEAD COME TO LIFE IN SMALL FLORIDA TOWN! the headline of *Inside View* read. And the subhead: *Horror Movie Comes to Life!* The subhead referred to a movie called *The Night of the Living Dead,* which Maddie had never seen. It also mentioned another movie she had never seen. The title of this piece of cinema was *Macumba Love.* The article was accompanied by three photos. One was a still from *Night of the Living Dead,* showing what appeared to be a bunch of escapees from a lunatic asylum standing outside an isolated farmhouse at night. One was a still from *Macumba Love,* showing a woman with a great lot of blond hair and a small bit of bikini-top holding in breasts the size of prize-winning gourds. The woman was holding up her hands and screaming at what appeared to be a black man in a mask. The third purported to be a picture taken in Thumper, Florida. It was a blurred, grainy shot of a human whose sex was impossible to define. It was walking up the middle of a business street in a small town. The figure was described as being "wrapped in the cerements of the grave," but it could have been someone in a dirty sheet.

No big deal. Bigfoot Rapes Girl Scouts last week, the

dead people coming back to life this week, the dwarf mass murderer next week.

No big deal until they started to come out everywhere. No big deal until the first news film ("You may want to ask your children to leave the room," Dan Rather introduced gravely) showed up on network TV, creatures with naked bone showing through their dried skin, traffic accident victims, the morticians' concealing makeup sloughed away either in the dark passivity of the earth or in the clawing climb to escape it so that the ripped faces and bashed-in skulls showed, women with their hair teased into dirt-clogged beehives in which worms and beetles still squirmed and crawled, their faces alternately vacuous and informed with a kind of calculating, idiotic intelligence; no big deal until the first horrible stills in an issue of *People* magazine that had been sealed in shrink-wrap like girly magazines, an issue with an orange sticker that read *Not For Sale To Minors!*

Then it was a big deal.

When you saw a decaying man still dressed in the mud-streaked remnants of the Brooks Brothers suit in which he had been buried tearing at the breast of a screaming woman in a T-shirt that read *Property of the Houston Oilers,* you suddenly realized it might be a very big deal indeed.

Then the accusations and the saber rattling had started, and for three weeks the entire world had been diverted from the creatures escaping their graves like grotesque moths escaping diseased cocoons by the spectacle of the two great nuclear powers on what appeared to be an undivertable collision course.

There were no zombies in the United States, Tass declared: This was a self-serving lie to camouflage an unforgivable act of chemical warfare against the Union of Soviet Socialist Republics. Reprisals would follow if the dead comrades coming out of their graves did not fall down decently dead within ten days. All U.S. diplomatic people were expelled from the mother country and most of her satellites.

The president (who would not long after become a Zombie Blue Plate Special himself) responded by becoming a pot (which he had come to resemble, having put on at least fifty pounds since his second-term election) calling a kettle black. The U.S. government, he told the American people, had incontrovertible evidence that the only walking dead people in the USSR had been set loose deliberately, and while the premier might stand there with his bare face hanging out and claim there were over eight thousand lively corpses striding around Russia in search of the ultimate collectivism, *we* had definite proof that there were less than forty. It was the *Russians* who had committed an act—a *heinous* act—of chemical warfare, bringing loyal Americans back to life with no urge to consume anything but other loyal Americans, and if these Americans—some of whom had been good Democrats— did not lie down decently dead within the next *five* days, the USSR was going to be one large slag pit.

The president expelled all Soviet diplomatic people . . . with one exception. This was a young fellow who was teaching him how to play chess (and who was not at all averse to the occasional grope under the table).

Norad was at Defcon-2 when the satellite was spotted. Or the spaceship. Or the creature. Or whatever in hell's name it was. An amateur astronomer from Hinchly-on-Strope in the west of England spotted it first, and this fellow, who had a deviated septum, fallen arches, and balls the size of acorns (he was also going bald, and his expanding pate showcased his really horrible case of psoriasis admirably), probably saved the world from nuclear holocaust.

The missile silos were open all over the world as telescopes in California and Siberia trained on Star Wormwood; they closed only following the horror of Salyut/ Eagle-I, which was launched with a crew of six Russians, three Americans, and one Briton only three days following the discovery of Star Wormwood by Humphrey Dagbolt, the amateur astronomer with the deviated septum, et al. He was, of course, the Briton.

And he paid.

They *all* paid.

* * *

The final sixty-one seconds of received transmission from the *Gorbachev/Truman* were considered too horrible for release by all three governments involved, and so no formal release was ever made. It didn't matter, of course; nearly twenty thousand ham operators had been monitoring the craft, and it seemed that at least nineteen thousand of them had been running tape decks when the craft had been—well, was there really any other word for it?—invaded.

Russian voice: Worms! It appears to be a massive ball of—

American voice: Christ! Look out! It's coming for us!

Dagbolt: Some sort of extrusion is occurring. The portside window is—

Russian voice: Breach! Breach! Suits!

(Indecipherable gabble.)

American voice: —and appears to be eating its way in—

Female Russian voice (Olga Katinya): Oh stop it stop the eyes—

(Sound of an explosion.)

Dagbolt: Explosive decompression has occurred. I see three—no, four—dead—and there are worms . . . everywhere there are worms—

American voice: Faceplate! Faceplate! *Faceplate!*

(Screaming.)

Russian voice: Where is my mamma? Where—

(Screams. Sounds like a toothless old man sucking up mashed potatoes.)

Dagbolt: The cabin is full of worms—what appears to be worms, at any rate—which is to say that they really *are* worms, one realizes—they have extruded themselves from the main satellite—what we took to be—which is to say one means—the cabin is full of floating body parts. These space-worms apparently excrete some sort of aci—

(Booster rockets fired at this point; duration of the burn is seven point two seconds. This may or may not have been attempt to escape or possibly to ram the central object. In either case, the maneuver did not work. It seems likely that the chambers themselves were clogged with worms and Captain Vassily Task—or whichever officer was then in charge—believed an explosion of the fuel tanks themselves to be imminent as a result of the clog. Hence the shutdown.)

American voice: Oh my Christ they're in my head, they're eating my fuckin br—

(Static.)

Dagbolt: I am retreating to the aft storage compartment. At the present moment, this seems the most prudent of my severely limited choices. I believe the others are all dead. Pity. Brave bunch. Even that fat Russian who kept rooting around in his nose. But in another sense I don't think—

(Static.)

Dagbolt: —dead at all because the Russian woman—or rather, the Russian woman's severed head, one means to say—just floated past me, and her eyes were open. She was looking at me from inside her—

(Static.)

Dagbolt: —keep you—

(Explosion. Static.)

Dagbolt: Is it possible for a severed penis to have an orgasm? I th—

(Static.)

Dagbolt: —around me. I repeat, all around me. Squirming things. They—I say, does anyone know if—

(Dagbolt, screaming and cursing, then just screaming. Sound of toothless old man again.)

Transmission ends.

The *Gorbachev/Truman* exploded three seconds later. The extrusion from the rough ball nicknamed Star Wormwood had been observed from better than three hundred telescopes earthside during the short and rather pitiful conflict. As the final sixty-one seconds of transmission began, the craft began to be obscured by something that certainly *looked* like worms. By the end of the final transmission, the craft itself could not be seen at all—only the squirming mass of things that had attached themselves to it. Moments after the final explosion, a weather satellite snapped a single picture of floating debris, some of which was almost certainly chunks of the worm-things. A severed human leg clad in a Russian space suit floating among them was a good deal easier to identify.

And in a way, none of it even mattered. The scientists and political leaders of both countries knew exactly where Star Wormwood was located: above the expanding hole in earth's ozone layer. It was sending something down from there, and it was not Flowers by Wire.

Missiles came next.

Star Wormwood jigged easily out of their way and then returned to its place over the hole.

More dead people got up and walked.

Now they were all biting.

The final effort to destroy the thing was made by the United States. At a cost of just under six hundred million dollars, four SDI "defensive weapons" satellites had been hoisted into orbit by the previous administration. The president of the current—and last—administration informed the Soviet premier of his intentions to use the SDI missiles, and got an enthusiastic approval (the Russian premier failed to note the fact that seven years before he had called these missiles "infernal engines of war and hate forged in the factories of hell").

It might even have worked . . . except not a single missile from a single SDI orbiter fired. Each satellite was equipped with six two-megaton warheads. Every goddamn one malfunctioned.

So much for modern technology.

Maddie supposed the horrible deaths of those brave men (and one woman) in space really hadn't been the last shock; there was the business of the one little graveyard right here on Jenny. But that didn't seem to count so much because, after all, she had not been there. With the end of the world now clearly at hand and the island cut off —*thankfully* cut off, in the opinion of the island's residents—from the rest of the world, old ways had reasserted themselves with a kind of unspoken but inarguable force. By then they all knew what was going to happen; it was only a question of when. That, and being ready when it did.

Women were excluded.

It was Bob Daggett, of course, who drew up the watch roster. That was only right, since Bob had been head selectman on Jenny since Hector was a pup. The day after the death of the president (the thought of him and the first lady wandering witlessly through the streets of Washington, D.C., gnawing on human arms and legs like people eating chicken legs at a picnic was not mentioned; it was a little too much to bear, even if the bastid and his big old blond wife *were* Democrats). Bob Daggett called the first men-only Town Meeting on Jenny since someplace before the Civil War. So Maddie wasn't there, but she heard. Dave Eamons told her all she needed to know.

"You men all know the situation," Bob said. He had always been a pretty hard fellow, but right then he looked as yellow as a man with jaundice, and people remembered his daughter, the one on the island, was only one of four. The other three were other places . . . which was to say, on the mainland.

But hell, if it came down to that, they *all* had folks on the mainland.

"We got one boneyard here on the island," Bob continued, "and nothin' ain't happened yet, but that don't mean nothin' *will*. Nothin' ain't happened yet lots of places . . . but it seems like once it starts, nothin' turns to somethin' pretty goddam quick."

There was a rumble of assent from the men gathered in the basement of the Methodist church. There were about seventy of them, ranging in age from Johnny Crane, who had just turned eighteen, to Bob's great-uncle Frank, who was eighty, had a glass eye, and chewed tobacco. There was no spittoon in the church basement and Frank Daggett knew it well enough, so he'd brought an empty mayonnaise jar to spit his juice into. He did so now.

"Git down to where the cheese binds, Bobby," he said. "You ain't got no office to run for, and time's a-wastin'."

There was another rumble of agreement, and Bob Daggett blushed. Somehow his great-uncle always managed to make him look like an ineffectual fool, and if there was anything in the world he hated worse than looking like an ineffectual fool, it was being called Bobby. He owned property, for Chrissake! He *supported* the old fart, for Chrissake!

But these were not things he could say. Frank's eyes were like pieces of flint.

"Okay," he said curtly. "Here it is. We want twelve men to a watch. I'm gonna set a roster in just a couple minutes. Four-hour shifts."

"I can stand watch a helluva lot longer'n four hours!" Matt Arsenault spoke up, and Davey told Maddie that Bob said after the meeting that no frog setting on a welfare lily pad like Matt Arsenault would have had the nerve enough to speak up like that if his great-uncle hadn't called him Bobby, like he was a kid instead of a man three months shy of his fiftieth birthday, in front of all the island men.

"Maybe so," Bob said, "but we got enough men to go around, and nobody's gonna fall asleep on sentry duty."

"I ain't gonna—"

"I didn't say *you,*" Bob said, but the way his eyes rested on Matt Arsenault suggested that he *might* have meant him. "This is no kid's game. Sit down and shut up."

Matt Arsenault opened his mouth to say something more, then looked around at the other men—including old Frank Daggett—and wisely sat down again.

"If you got a rifle, bring it when it's your trick," Bob continued. He felt a little better with Frere Jacques out of the way. "Unless it's a twenty-two. If you got no rifle bigger'n that, or none at all, come and get one here."

"I didn't know Reverend Peebles kept a supply of 'em handy," Cal Partridge said, and there was a ripple of laughter.

"He don't now, but he's gonna," Bob said, "because every man jack of you with more than one rifle bigger than a twenty-two is gonna bring it here." He looked at Peebles. "Okay if we keep 'em in the rectory, Tom?"

Peebles nodded, dry-washing his hands in a distraught way.

"Shit on that," Orrin Campbell said. "I got a wife and

two kids at home. Am I s'posed to leave 'em with nothin if a bunch of cawpses come for an early Thanksgiving dinner while I'm on watch?"

"If we do our job at the boneyard, none will," Bob replied stonily. "Some of you got handguns. We don't want none of those. Figure out which women can shoot and which can't, and give 'em the pistols. We'll put 'em together in bunches."

"They can play Beano," old Frank cackled, and Bob smiled, too. That was more like it, by the Christ.

"Nights, we're gonna want trucks posted around so we got plenty of light." He looked over at Sonny Dotson, who ran Island Amoco, the only gas station on Jenny—Sonny's main business wasn't gassing cars and trucks— shit, there was no place much on the island to drive, and you could get your go ten cents cheaper on the mainland—but filling up lobster boats and the motorboats he ran out of his jackleg marina in the summer. "You gonna supply the gas, Sonny?"

"Am I gonna get cash slips?"

"You're gonna get your ass saved," Bob said. "When things get back to normal—if they ever do—I guess you'll get what you got coming."

Sonny looked around, saw only hard eyes, and shrugged. He looked a bit sullen, but in truth he looked more confused than anything, Davey told Maddie the next day.

"Ain't got n'more'n four hunnert gallons of gas," he said. "Mostly diesel."

"There's five generators on the island," Burt Dorfman said (when Burt spoke everyone listened; as the only Jew on the island, he was regarded as a creature both quixotic and fearsome, like an oracle that works about half the time). "They all run on diesel. I can rig lights if I have to."

Low murmurs. If Burt said he could, he could. He was an electrician, and a damned good one . . . for a Jew, anyway.

"We're gonna light that place up like a friggin' stage," Bob said.

Andy Kinsolving stood up. "I heard on the news that

sometimes you can shoot one of them . . . things . . . in the head and it'll stay down, and sometimes it won't."

"We got chain saws," Bob said stonily, "and what won't stay dead . . . why, we can make sure it won't move too far alive."

And, except for making out the duty roster, that was pretty much that.

Six days and nights passed and the sentries posted around the island graveyard were starting to feel a wee bit silly ("I dunno if I'm standin' guard or pullin' my pud," Orrin Campbell said one afternoon as a dozen men stood around a small cemetery where the most exciting thing happening was a caterpillar spinning a cocoon while a spider watched it and waited for the moment to pounce) when it happened . . . and when it happened, it happened fast.

Dave told Maddie that he heard a sound like the wind wailing in the chimney on a gusty night . . . and then the gravestone marking the final resting place of Mr. and Mrs. Fournier's boy Michael, who had died of leukemia at seventeen—bad go, that had been, him being their only get and them being such nice people and all—fell over. Then a shredded hand with a moss-caked Yarmouth Academy class ring on one finger rose out of the ground, shoving through the tough grass. The third finger had been torn off in the process.

The ground heaved like (like the belly of a pregnant woman getting ready to drop her load, Dave almost said, and hastily reconsidered) well, like the way a big wave heaves up on its way into a close cove, and then the boy himself sat up, only he wasn't nothing you could really recognize, not after almost two years in the ground. There was little pieces of wood sticking to him, Davey said, and pieces of blue cloth.

Later inspection proved these to be shreds of satin from the coffin in which the boy had been buried away.

("Thank Christ Richie Fournier dint have that trick," Bill Pulsifer said later, and they had all nodded shakily—many of them were still wiping their mouths, because almost all of them had puked at some point or other during

that hellacious half hour . . . these were not things Dave
Eamons could tell Maddie, but Maddie guessed more than
Dave ever guessed she guessed.)

Gunfire tore Michael Fournier to shreds before he could
do more than sit up; other shots, fired in wild panic, blew
chips off his marble gravestone, and it was a goddam wonder someone on one side hadn't shot someone on one of
the others, but they got off lucky. Bud Meechum found a
hole torn in the sleeve of his shirt the next day, but liked
to think that might have been nothing more than a thorn
—there had been raspberry bushes on his side of the boneyard. Maybe that was really all it was, although the black
smudges on the hole made him think that maybe it had
been a thorn with a pretty large caliber.

The Fournier kid fell back, most of him lying still, other
parts of him still twitching.

But by then the whole graveyard seemed to be rippling,
as if an earthquake was going on there—but *only* there, no
place else.

Just about an hour before dusk, this had happened.

Burt Dorfman had rigged up a siren to a tractor battery,
and Bob Daggett flipped the switch. Within twenty minutes, most of the men in town were at the island cemetery.
Goddam good thing, too, because a few of the deaders
almost got away. Old Frank Daggett, still two hours away
from the heart attack that would carry him off after it was
all over and the moon had risen, organized the men into a
pair of angled flanks so they wouldn't shoot each other,
and for the final ten minutes the Jenny boneyard sounded
like Bull Run. By the end of the festivities, the powder
smoke was so thick that some men choked on it. No one
puked on it, because no one had anything left to puke up.
The sour smell of vomit was almost heavier than the smell
of gunsmoke . . . it was sharper, too, and lingered
longer.

And still some of them wriggled and squirmed like
snakes with broken backs . . . the fresher ones, for the
most part.

"Burt," Frank Daggett said. "You got them chain
saws?"

"I got 'em," Burt said, and then a long, buzzing sound came out of his mouth, a sound like a cicada burrowing its way into tree bark, as he dry-heaved. He could not take his eyes from the squirming corpses, the overturned gravestones, the yawning pits from which the dead had come. "In the truck."

"Gassed up?" Blue veins stood out on Frank's ancient, hairless skull.

"Yeah." Burt's hand was over his mouth. "I'm sorry."

"Work y'fuckin gut all you want," Frank said briskly. "But get them saws while you do. And you . . . you . . . you . . . you . . ."

The last "you" was his grandnephew Bob.

"I can't, Uncle Frank," Bob said sickly. He looked around and saw at least twenty men lying in the tall grass. They had swooned. Most of them had seen their own relatives rise out of the ground. Buck Harkness over there lying by an aspen tree had been part of the cross fire that had cut his late wife to ribbons before he fainted when her decayed brains exploded from the back of her head in a grisly gray fan. "I can't. I c—"

Frank's hand, twisted with arthritis but as hard as stone, cracked across his face.

"You can and you will, chummy," he said grimly.

Bob went with the rest of the men.

Frank Daggett watched them grimly and rubbed his chest.

"I was nearby when Frank spoke to Bob," Dave told Maddie. He wasn't sure if he should be telling her this—or any of it, for that matter, with her almost halfway to foaling time—but he was still too impressed with the old man's grim and quiet courage to forbear. "This was after . . . you know . . . we cleaned the mess up."

Maddie only nodded.

"I'll stop," Dave said, "if you can't bear it, Maddie."

"I can bear it," she said quietly, and Dave looked at her quickly, curiously, but she had averted her eyes before he could see the secret in them.

* * *

Davey didn't know the secret because no one on Jenny knew. That was the way Maddie wanted it, and the way she intended to keep it. There had been a time when she had, in the blue darkness of her shock, pretended to be *coping.* And then something happened that *made* her cope. Four days before the island cemetery vomited up its corpses, Maddie Pace was faced with a simple choice: cope or die.

She had been sitting in the living room, drinking a glass of the blueberry wine she and Jack had put up during August of the previous year—a time that now seemed impossibly distant—and doing something so trite it was laughable: She was Knitting Little Things (the second bootee of a pair this evening). But what else *was* there to do? It seemed that no one would be going across to the mall on the mainland for a long time.

Something had thumped the window.

A bat, she thought, looking up. Her needles paused in her hands, though. It seemed that something was moving out there in the windy dark. The oil lamp was turned up high and kicking too much reflection off the panes to be sure. She reached to turn it down and the thump came again. The panes shivered. She heard a little pattering of dried putty falling on the sash. Jack was going to reglaze all the windows this fall, she thought stupidly, and then: Maybe that's what he came back for. Because it was Jack. She knew that. Before Jack, no one from Jenny had drowned for nearly three years. Whatever was making them return apparently couldn't reanimate whatever was left of their bodies. But Jack . . .

Jack was still fresh.

She sat, poised, head cocked to one side, knitting in her hands. A little pink bootee. She had already made a blue set. All of a sudden it seemed she could hear so *much.* The wind. The faint thunder of surf on Cricket's Ledge. The house making little groaning sounds, like an elderly woman making herself comfortable in bed. The tick of the clock in the hallway.

It was Jack. She knew it.

"Jack?" she said, and the window burst inward and

what came in was not really Jack but a skeleton with a few mouldering strings of flesh hanging from it.

His compass was still around his neck. It had grown a beard of moss.

The wind blew the curtains out in a cloud as he sprawled, then got up on his hands and knees and looked at her from black sockets in which barnacles had grown.

He made grunting sounds. His fleshless mouth opened and the teeth chomped down. He was hungry . . . but this time chicken noodle soup would not serve. Not even the kind that came in the can.

Gray stuff hung and swung beyond those dark barnacle-crusted holes, and she realized she was looking at whatever remained of Jack's brain. She sat where she was, frozen, as he got up and came toward her, leaving black kelpy tracks on the carpet, fingers reaching. He stank of salt and fathoms. His hands stretched. His teeth champed mechanically up and down. Maddie saw he was wearing the remains of the black-and-red-checked shirt she had bought him at L.L. Bean's last Christmas. It had cost the earth, but he had said again and again how warm it was, and look how well it had lasted, even under water all this time, even—

The cold cobwebs of bone which were all that remained of his fingers touched her throat before the baby kicked in her stomach—for the first time—and her shocked horror, which she had believed to be calmness, fled, and she drove one of the knitting needles into the thing's eye.

Making horrid, thick, draggling noises that sounded like the suck of a swill pump, he staggered backward, clawing at the needle, while the half-made pink bootee swung in front of the cavity where his nose had been. She watched as a sea slug squirmed from that nasal cavity and onto the bootee, leaving a trail of slime behind it.

Jack fell over the end table she'd gotten at a yard sale just after they had been married—she hadn't been able to make her mind up about it, had been in agonies about it, until Jack finally said either she was going to buy it for their living room or he was going to give the biddy run-

ning the sale twice what she was asking for the goddam
thing and then bust it up into firewood with—
—with the—

He struck the floor and there was a brittle, cracking
sound as his febrile, fragile form broke in two. The right
hand tore the knitting needle, slimed with decaying brain
tissue, from his eye socket and tossed it aside. His top half
crawled toward her. His teeth gnashed steadily together.

She thought he was trying to grin, and then the baby
kicked again and she thought: *You buy it, Maddie, for
Christ's sake! I'm tired! Want to go home and get m'dinner! You want it, buy it! If you don't, I'll give that old bat
twice what she wants and bust it up for firewood with my—*

Cold, dank hand clutching her ankle; polluted teeth
poised to bite. To kill her and kill the baby.

She tore loose, leaving him with only her slipper, which
he tried to chew and then spat out.

When she came back from the entry, he was crawling
mindlessly into the kitchen—at least the top half of him
was—with the compass dragging on the tiles. He looked
up at the sound of her, and there seemed to be some idiot
question in those black eye sockets before she brought the
ax whistling down, cleaving his skull as he had threatened
to cleave the end table.

His head fell in two pieces, brains dribbling across the
tile like spoiled oatmeal, brains that squirmed with slugs
and gelatinous sea worms, brains that smelled like a wood-
chuck exploded with gassy decay in a high-summer
meadow.

Still his hands clashed and clittered on the kitchen tiles,
making a sound like beetles.

She chopped . . . she chopped . . . she chopped.

At last there was no more movement.

A sharp pain rippled across her midsection and for a
moment she was gripped by terrible panic: *Is it a miscarriage? Am I going to have a miscarriage?* But the pain left
. . . and the baby kicked again, more strongly than before.

She went back into the living room, carrying an ax that
now smelled like tripe.

His legs had somehow managed to stand.

"Jack, I loved you so much," she said, and brought the ax down in a whistling arc that split him at the pelvis, sliced the carpet, and drove deep into the solid oak floor beneath.

The legs, separated, trembled wildly . . . and then lay still.

She carried him down to the cellar piece by piece, wearing her oven gloves and wrapping each piece with the insulating blankets Jack had kept in the shed and which she had never thrown away—he and the crew threw them over the pots on cold days so the lobsters wouldn't freeze.

Once a severed hand tried to close over her wrist . . . then loosened.

That was all.

There was an unused cistern, polluted, which Jack had been meaning to fill in. Maddie Pace slid the heavy concrete cover aside so that its shadow lay on the earthen floor like a partial eclipse and then threw the pieces of him down, listening to the splashes, then worked the heavy cover back in place.

"Rest in peace," she whispered, and an interior voice whispered back that her husband was resting in *pieces,* and then she began to cry, and her cries turned to hysterical shrieks, and she pulled at her hair and tore at her breasts until they were bloody, and she thought, I am insane, this is what it's like to be in—

But before the thought could be completed, she had fallen down in a faint that became a deep sleep, and the next morning she felt all right.

She would never tell, though.

Never.

She understood, of course, that Dave knew nothing of this, and Dave would say nothing at all if she pressed. She kept her ears open, and she knew what he meant, and what they had apparently done. The dead folks and the . . . the *parts* of dead folks that wouldn't . . . wouldn't be still . . . had been chain-sawed like her father had chain-sawed the hardwood on Pop Cook's two acres after he had gotten the deed registered, and then those parts— some *still* squirming, hands with no arms attached to them clutching mindlessly, feet divorced from their legs digging at the bullet-chewed earth of the graveyard as if trying to run away—had been doused with diesel fuel and set afire. She had seen the pyre from the house.

Later, Jenny's one fire truck had turned its hose on the dying blaze, although there wasn't much chance of the fire spreading, with a brisk easterly blowing the sparks off Jenny's seaward edge.

When there was nothing left but a stinking, tallowy lump (and still there were occasional bulges in this mass, like twitches in a tired muscle), Matt Arsenault fired up his old D-9 Caterpillar—above the nicked steel blade and under his faded pillowtick engineer's cap, Matt's face had been as white as cottage cheese—and plowed the whole hellacious mess under.

The moon was coming up when Frank took Bob Daggett, Dave Eamons, and Cal Partridge aside.

"I'm havin a goddam heart attack," he said.

"Now, Uncle Frank—"

"Never mind Uncle Frank this 'n' that," the old man said. "I ain't got time, and I ain't wrong. Seen half my friends go the same way. Beats hell out of getting whacked with the cancer-stick. Quicker. But when I go down, I intend to *stay* down. Cal, stick that rifle of yours in my left ear. Muzzle's gonna get some wax on it, but it won't be there after you pull the trigger. Dave, when I raise my left arm, you sock your thirty-thirty into my armpit, and see that you do it a right smart. And Bobby, you put yours right over my heart. I'm gonna say the Lawd's Prayer, and when I hit amen, you three fellows are gonna pull your triggers."

"Uncle Frank —" Bob managed. He was reeling on his heels.

"I told you not to start in on that," Frank said. "And don't you *dare* faint on me, you friggin' pantywaist. If I'm goin' down, I mean to *stay* down. Now get over here."

Bob did.

Frank looked around at the three men, their faces as white as Matt Arsenault's had been when he drove the dozer over men and women he had known since he was a kid in short pants and Buster Browns.

"I ain't got long," Frank said, "and I only got enough jizzum left to get m'arm up once, so don't you fuck up on me. And remember, I'd 'a' done the same for any of you. If that don't help, ask y'selves if *you'd* want to end up like those we just took care of."

"Go on," Bob said hoarsely. "I love you, Uncle Frank."

"You ain't the man your father was, Bobby Daggett, but I love you, too," Frank said calmly, and then, with a cry of pain, he threw his left hand up over his head like a guy in New York who has to have a cab in a rip of a hurry, and started in: "Our father who art in heaven—*Christ,* that hurts!—hallow'd be Thy name—oh, son of a *gun,* I—Thy kingdom come, Thy will be done, on earth as it . . . as it . . ."

Frank's upraised left arm was wavering wildly now. Dave Eamons, with his rifle socked into the old geezer's armpit, watched it as carefully as a logger would watch a big tree that looked like it meant to fall the wrong way. Every man on the island was watching now. Big beads of sweat had formed on the old man's pallid face. His lips had pulled back from the even, yellowish white of his Roebuckers, and Dave had been able to smell the Polident on his breath.

". . . as it is in heaven!" the old man jerked out. "Lead us not into temptation butdeliverusfromevilohshitonit-foreverandeverAMEN!"

All three of them fired, and both Cal Partridge and Bob Daggett fainted, but Frank never did try to get up and walk.

Frank Daggett intended to *stay* dead, and that was just what he did.

Once Dave started that story he had to go on with it, and so he cursed himself for ever starting. He'd been right the first time; it was no story for a pregnant woman.

But Maddie had kissed him and told him she thought he had done wonderfully, and Dave went out, feeling a little dazed, as if he had just been kissed on the cheek by a woman he had never met before.

As, in a way, he had.

She watched him go down the path to the dirt track

that was one of Jenny's two roads and turn left. He was weaving a little in the moonlight, weaving with tiredness, she thought, but reeling with shock, as well. Her heart went out to him . . . to all of them. She had wanted to tell Dave she loved him and kiss him squarely on the mouth instead of just skimming his cheek with her lips, but he might have taken the wrong meaning from something like that, even though he was bone-weary and she was almost five months pregnant.

But she *did* love him, loved *all* of them, because they had gone through a hell she could only imagine dimly, and by going through that hell they had made the island safe for her.

Safe for her baby.

"It will be a home delivery," she said softly as Dave went out of sight behind the dark hulk of the Pulsifers' satellite dish. Her eyes rose to the moon. "It will be a home delivery . . . and it will be fine."

Wet Work

BY PHILIP NUTMAN

Corvino, pulling the trigger . . .

. . . *and the film loop turns again. Twenty years the same image; slight variations, but ultimately the same: blood, death.*

The bullet takes the Negro straight between the eyes, exiting the back of the cranium, spraying bone, blood, cerebral matter over the wall.

A professional assassin, his aim is true. A dead shot.

The body of the janitor lies on the floor, legs splayed open in a V pattern. What is left of the head lolls to the left. Above the corpse, a crimson skid mark.

Corvino, exhaling.

So easy. Squeeze a trigger, snuff out a candle. Another life taken.

He steps between the disorganized desks that clutter the classroom, proceeding to check the supply cupboard.

Empty.

From down the hallway the sound of breaking glass; three rapid-fire shots.

The brain, Harris. The brain.

Silence hangs heavy in the still atmosphere.

(. . . the white room in the apartment block overlooking the Potomac. Simple, Spartan, befitting an assassin. The two abstract paintings in the style of Pollack. One composed of blue and orange slashes, paradoxically both dynamic and tranquil. The other a red arc on white, like a seppuku mat . . .)

Harris's aim is deteriorating under the stress of the past week.

(. . . his room, his retreat from the insanity of the world's war zones, where only his eye for accuracy had

kept him alive . . . Vietnam . . . the Middle East . . .
Nicaragua . . .)

They call him One-Shot, or Mr. Trigger. Dominic
Corvino, the most reliable wet-work operative the Department owns. Guns are his friends. In the art of killing he is
a master craftsman.

Now the stakes have changed.

(. . . his sanctuary defiled . . . the shadowy figure
suddenly appearing in the doorway . . . the hiss of a sup-
pressor . . . and a white-hot poker of pain piercing his
chest . . .)

Now it is all down to basics.

He sits on a desk, pulling a Camel from his chest
pocket, lights it, and exhales. The stench of death an old
companion, the taste of a cigarette rare pleasure. Smoke
catches at the back of his throat. Too dry, the tobacco
stale. Corvino grinds it out with the heel of his right boot
as he stands, checking the clip in his .45 automatic.

In life only one thing is certain: change.

The whole apple cart has fallen; not to the left or the
right but straight down on its axle, spilling the load in
every direction so there is no escape from the fallout.

Strange times in Casablanca.

All the same: the streets and suburbs of the world's
cities awash with blood. Friend against friend, brother
against sister.

(. . . followed instantaneously by a suffocating weight
of blackness . . .)

Survival instinct overriding sentiment. There is no time
to care, just the will to survive.

Corvino catches sight of his reflection in the window,
the encroaching darkness defining the face that stares back
at him, illuminated from above by cold electric light.
Shadows pool his dark brown, deep-set Italian eyes,
framed by his thick, black brows, the pallor of his skin
wan and mottled in the unnatural light. His mouth is a
faint, terse red slash. The nature of his work, the index of
his experiences, do not encourage levity; he is a serious
man who performs serious tasks with irrevocable results.

He scratches at his jawline, his fingernails grating

against the fringe of stubble that coats his cheeks. Layers of dry skin adhere to the nails. He flicks them away.

Lack of proper nourishment.

Corvino steps into the corridor. To his left, Skolomowsky and Lewis stand outside their respective classrooms, the latter's navy blue jacket splashed with dark patches. Skolomowsky smiling. Cordite and the copper aroma of blood drift in the stale air of the high school. Corvino looks to the right. No sign of Harris. As he is about to move toward the room, Harris appears.

"Clear," he states in his harsh Brooklyn accent.

Corvino nods, turns to Skolomowsky and Lewis.

"Ditto," says the Pole.

Corvino pulls the radio from its holster as he replaces his Colt automatic in its sheath under his left arm.

"Alpha to Cleanup. Fourth floor sweep and clean complete. Start bagging them."

He signals visual confirmation to the bag boys in the parking lot from the wide windows next to the stairwell. Ten men in teams of two, each with a body bag, trot in formation up the steps and through the open doors.

"Are there any other rooms in this building that have not been swept?" He addresses the question to Lewis, but Skolomowsky answers.

"No," the big man replies. "Every inch of this place that's worth checking has been covered. We've got them all."

Corvino nods slowly. "Any resistance?"

"Nope," Lewis says.

Corvino notices a bullet hole on Lewis's jacket, fringed by a brown stain.

"Nada," mutters Harris.

"Not enough," Skolomowsky adds, smiling. "Too easy."

Corvino looks penetratingly at the Pole. Skolomowsky's passion for bloodletting threatens to cloud his professionalism again.

(. . . Tehran . . . Juzl dead . . . Lewis wounded . . . Skolomowsky's cock-up? . . . mission aborted . . .)

Skolomowsky: professional killer; professional sadist.

He distrusts the Pole, who has perverse tastes.

(. . . Nashville . . . Skolomowsky . . . the remains of a prostitute . . . skinned alive . . . the motel room awash with blood . . . unnecessary . . .)

Skolomowsky continues to smile at Corvino.

"Something wrong?"

Before he responds, the first duo of bag boys appear at the top of the stairs.

"Where?" one inquires.

"Each room. . . . No," he says finally to the Pole. "Check weapons, then return to the parking lot."

Corvino turns his gaze to the window, aware Skolomowsky is still staring at him. On the horizon small pockets of fire pulse in the South Washington suburbs. He looks down at his gun, pulling it free from the velcro strap, pops the clip, and replaces the cartridge with a full one.

Just in case.

A second duo run up the steps. He points to the nearest classroom. Lewis, Skolomowsky, and Harris file past him, heading to the first floor.

He has dispelled the question of what is happening. Like any good government employee he obeys orders; speculation is for the Think Tank, a foot soldier merely carries out orders.

Below him Lewis, Skolomowsky, and Harris gather in the parking lot next to the two gray armored vehicles. Bag boys and Beta team emerge from the school entrance to join them.

Corvino pulls the cigarette pack from his pocket without thinking, places a smoke between his dry lips, pauses, removes it, replaces it in the box.

He screws up the pack and tosses it to one side.

A sharp chill has settled in the air. Lewis paces by the truck, his M16 slung over his shoulder; expression calm, his movements indicate his internal feelings: stress, too many sleepless nights, and the psychological aftershock of what the Hit teams refer to as AZ—After Zombification—clearly taking their toll on his flayed nerves. Corvino can see he is a prime candidate for postoperation crack-up.

"Hey, Lewis," the Pole says. "Lewis. I'm talking to you."

Lewis does not respond.

"Lewis. You're slowing up. You hear me?"

Corvino is walking across the parking lot as Skolomowsky speaks.

". . . I said you're losing it. Just like in Tehran."

"Sweep complete?" Hutson, the Beta team leader asks Corvino.

As he is about to answer, a movement at the right corner of his field of vision: Lewis swinging the butt of his M16 in an arc to connect with Skolomowsky's jaw. A crunch as the Pole backflips to the tarmac. Lewis shrieks, diving on his downed partner, his mouth wide.

Corvino pulls the .45 from his holster, squeezing the trigger as the barrel comes into line with the side of Lewis's head: Lewis, at Skolomowsky's throat, tearing out the soft flesh and chewy esophageal tract. Dark blood fountains in the night air.

He's missed!

The thought frags his concentration as he squeezes off a second shot. That, too, goes wild. But the third finds its target and the right side of Lewis's head explodes. Lewis deflates over the Pole's still twitching body.

Corvino's mind is out of sync.

He's missed.

One-Shot Corvino, Mr. Trigger, has actually missed.

The Pole is still moving. The squeal he made as Lewis ripped out his trachea ceases, replaced by a harsh, rasping wheeze as his lungs draw in oxygen directly through the gaping throat wound. The Pole heaves the corpse off him, sits up. The wheezing increases, his shrunken eyes retreating farther into the withered sockets. Like a stunned yet still enraged bull, he lumbers to his feet, his face a rictus of rage.

Harris opens fire with his .357 magnum.

The first bullet catches the Pole in the groin. He bucks to one side but continues standing. The second catches him in the chest, exiting with a sound like snapping branches. The third takes his right arm off at the elbow.

What the fuck is Harris playing at?

The head, always the head; Corvino aims and fires . . .

. . . and the Pole's face disappears, the body sagging to the ground with a wet thud.

Corvino turns to Harris. The team member's face is a blank chalkboard, his features an unwritten text.

"Once we get back to Capitol Hill you're off duty, Harris."

Harris says nothing. He stares with empty eyes, his magnum smoking in his fist.

Corvino moves away from the vacant assassin to face Beta team, all of whom have their guns up.

"Clean this mess up," he nods in the direction of Skolomowsky and Lewis. "Let's load up and get this chuck wagon back to the White House. The president needs fresh meat."

Two members of Beta place their M16s against the nearest truck and pull fresh body sacks from the vehicle's rear.

In the space of one minute, total change.

It begins with a crescent of muzzle flashes and a thunderous roar.

Fifteen seconds: As Corvino turns, a bullet catches Hutson in the throat; he gags, blood spurting from his mouth as he stumbles back; two bullets take Corvino in the stomach, spinning him around; five Cleanup members fall; some begin blasting back with their M16s at the gunfire that comes from the perimeter of the parking lot; Corvino's .45 jerks in his hands as he pulls off five rapid shots: blood pumps from his stomach where a section of small intestine bulges from the large hole in his combat jacket; behind him, a figure tries to stand as more bullets rip into its torso; others drop to the ground.

Thirty seconds: Popping the spent clip from his pistol, Corvino speed-reloads, continues to fire, oblivious to his damaged internal organs. A bullet grazes his forehead, sending a stream of red into his eyes; he fires blind, tugging another cartridge from his ammo belt as he goes into a crouch that pushes his viscera through the now gaping hole; brains leave a head; the downed men writhe on the gore-soaked ground as wave upon wave of bullets tear into their bodies.

Forty-five seconds: Corvino keels over, his gun spinning

from his hand: He twitches spastically as he tries to crawl toward a truck. The parking lot is a firework display; as if punctuating the performance, one of the trucks (the one toward which Corvino crawls) explodes as a stray shell hits the gas tank, sending a fireball up up into the darkness, flaming gasoline spraying his smashed body.

Fifty-seven seconds: Corvino continues to crawl, his intestines uncoiling snakelike as his body burns. He is dying for the second time. There is no pain.

Sixty seconds: Corvino fades to black.

Nick Packard pulled the clip from the Ingram. His ears were ringing. Someone shouted, but whatever was called did not register against the pealing bells sounding out in glorious jubilation inside his head.

The young policeman, who had joined the Washington force only six months before, had hardly ever used a gun. Now the Ingram felt like an extension of his right arm. And hot shit, did it feel good!

Captain Stipe waved to the group composed of cops and civilians to advance. The flaming truck illuminated the carnage. Several gore-slicked zombies thrashed on the ground like maggots. One was trying to lift an M16 with a broken arm, so Packard fired a quick burst at the creature's head.

Take that, you friggin' sonofabitch fuck-faced flesh-eater!

"No more shooting!" shouted Stipe. Packard's ears were beginning to clear.

"Okay!"

There were thirty of them: seven cops and a ragged assortment of men and women, their ages ranging from late teens to mid-fifties. All were armed to the teeth with a wide selection of handguns, rifles, axes, pitchforks, a couple of crossbows, and numerous knives. One kid, a zit-covered geek, even had a homemade flamethrower, a Hudson sprayer/blow-torch combo that, despite its primitivism, could really kick ass.

"Packard," Stipe signaled to the young cop. "You're keen to wipe these things out, so finish 'em off."

"Fuckin' A."

Packard fired three short bursts and the last of the dead
meat stopped moving. All but one.

What remained of Dominic Corvino rolled over, a final
twitch of the death nerve. Packard plucked his .38 special
from his hip holster and fired twice into the burning head
of what had once been Dominic Corvino.

Hell, you couldn't be too careful these days.

Stipe walked over to a bullet-riddled body that lay face
down on the tarmac. The police captain pushed it over
with his foot. "Government assholes."

"Say again?" Packard said as he drew near.

"These are government dicks. I recognize this one."

"So what?" Packard hawked up a ball of phlegm, which
he spat on the creature's face. "They're still fuckin' zombies. Dead scum." He kicked the body, his boot breaking a
rib.

"Yes, but these were organized, right? They were working together, not running rampant. I mean, if some of
these things are retaining intelligence, we're in deeper shit
than we think." Stipe wiped the back of a hand across his
forehead.

He went to the back of the truck that was not on fire
and unzipped a body bag. It contained the corpse of a
small child, a little girl about seven, shot through the
chest, her once rosy cheeks dotted with chickenpoxlike
splashes of dried blood.

The child had been normal.

"Sheeit!" Packard's eyes widened. "This still gets to me,
especially the kids. So what do you reckon?" He continued to look at the dead girl, her dimpled cheeks frozen
marble under the light of the police captain's torch.

Stipe turned to him, his lips pursed.

"I think it's time we visited the White House."

A Sad Last Love
at the Diner
of the Damned

BY EDWARD BRYANT

There once was a beautiful young woman with long hair the russet gold of ripe wheat. Her name was Martha Malinowski and her family had lived in Fort Durham for three generations. Martha was nineteen and had spent her entire life in the border area where southern Colorado shades subtly from browns and tans to the dark green mountains of northern New Mexico.

Martha's eyes were a startling blue that deepened or paled according to the season and her mood. Her temperament had begun to darken with the onset of early winter snows, and so her eyes began to reflect that. Now they appeared the color of the road ice that formed on the headlights and steel bumpers of the pickups lining the parking strip beside the Diner.

She waited on tables for one, sometimes two long shifts each day at the Cuchara Diner. Occasional tourists speculated aloud that the Diner was more properly called the Cucaracha. Henry Roybal, the owner, would gesture at the neon tablespoon suspended in the front window. That made little difference to the tourists who rarely understood Spanish. The locals around Fort Durham simply referred to the place as the Diner. The Diner itself was a sprawling stucco assemblage that had been added to many times over the decades. Its most notable feature was Henry Roybal's pride and joy, an eight-foot-high neon

EAT that flashed from red to green and back again while a blue arrow pointed down at the Diner's front door.

Martha Malinowski's fair features haunted the illicit dreams of many in the community. She was largely oblivious to this and to the dreamers themselves. She ignored the ones she did notice. Her cap was set for Bobby Mack Quintana, the deputy sheriff. Bobby Mack was always cordial toward her, but that seemed to be about it. Martha wondered if he was just too shy to express his feelings.

Then there was Bertie Hernandez who openly lusted after Martha. Crude, rude, and vital, his buddies and he were among Henry's best customers. Martha was never glad to see them coming into the Diner. But a job was a job, and business was business in this world of sage, scrub grass, endless horizons, and Highway 159. Someday Martha would have saved enough cash to leave this place. Or if Bobby Mack wanted her, then perhaps she would stay. She was practical about romance, yet still maintained her dreams.

The men watched the little old ladies tap and scratch ineffectually against the Diner's thick plate-glass front window, their clawed fingers fluttering like the wings of injured birds.

"Don't look too mean to me," said Billy Gaspar, a strapping young man in a red plaid lumberjack shirt.

"You don't know squat about zombies," said Shine Willis, who was a few years Billy's senior and half a head taller. "I was up to the Springs last week when a bunch of 'em came boilin' out of a Greyhound bus downtown. They're faster than they look, and stronger too. Especially if they been eatin' good." He chuckled.

Billy looked a bit livid. "People."

"Yeah," said Shine. "People."

Bertie Hernandez glanced up from his breakfast plate. "Gimme another side of bacon, Martha," he said. "Have Henry make it good and chewy." The radio above the cash register was blaring out the Beat Farmers' cover of "Sweet Jane." "An' turn off that shit. I want to hear something good."

"Like what?" someone said from down the formica counter.

"Conway Twitty," said Bertie. "Good shit."

The radio stayed where it was set. The Beat Farmers' record segued into Joe Ely's "Crazy Lemon."

"Better," Bertie said.

"What we gonna do about the old ladies?" said Shine.

"Where'd they come from?" Billy Gaspar said. His fingers twitched around the handle of an untouched mug of cooling coffee.

"Eventide Manor, most like. The nursing home." Shine grinned mirthlessly. "Musta found a zombie in the woodpile sometime in the night, I'd judge."

"We gotta kill 'em?" said Billy.

"Too old to fuck," said Shine. "Too tough to eat."

Billy's complexion seemed to slide from white to greenish.

Somebody closer to the window said, "See the second from the left? That's ol' Mrs. Davenport, Kevin's grandma."

"The one in the center," said Bertie Hernandez, "is my mother. Fuck her. Let's do it." He swung around on the counter seat and stood in one fluid motion. He slid the big .357 magnum out of its holster and checked the cylinder.

"Nice piece," said Miguel Espinosa.

"Six old ladies," said Bertie. "I figure I can handle them."

"You want some help?"

Bertie shook his head. "Not unless they take a chunk out of me. Then shoot me quick." It all sounded matter-of-fact.

"Why don't all of you wait for Bobby Mack?" said Martha.

"Bobbee May-ack," Bertie mimicked her. "Your fag cop heartthrob? Fuck him. Let him find his own zombies to blow him."

Nose level with Bertie's Adam's apple, Martha looked up at him. "Don't say things like that. Not ever."

Bertie looked at her steadily for a moment. "Just watch what I do to the deadheads, darlin'. If it makes you wet enough, maybe I'll take you over to Walsenburg tonight for a movie show and then the Motel Six."

"Bertie," said Henry Roybal. "There's no call for talk like that." The Diner's owner had stuck his head out of the kitchen. "And don't get any mess on the window. I washed it just yesterday."

"They're smearin' the glass, right enough," said Shine. "Pus, blood, all sorts of shit."

"Okay," said Bertie, looking away from Martha toward the old ladies beyond the window.

Martha stood rigid. Then she turned toward Henry, whose corpulent body was still wedged in the kitchen doorway. "Can you get hold of Bobby Mack?"

Henry shook his head. "Tried. Can't raise nothing on the base station or the phone. Sheriff's number is busy. I figure everybody's calling to report a zombie or two. Sorry, *muchachu.*"

"Back me up," Bertie said to Shine. "Just in case." The other man nodded and hefted his Remington pump. Bertie smiled at Martha. "Kiss for good luck? No?" He shrugged and called to the men lined along the counter, "Somebody decoy the fuckers long enough for me to clear the door."

At the end of the counter, a weathered cowboy in boot-cut jeans and a pearl-snap shirt strolled over to the front window. He stared into the faces of the zombie women for a moment, then he turned, skinned down his pants and mooned them. The zombies crowded toward the pressed ham.

"Gross," said Martha.

Bertie flipped the latch on the front door and crunched out onto the gravel. Shine relocked the door. "Don't nobody get in my way if he needs help."

"It's all yours, buddy," said Miguel Espinosa. "I don't want none of those ladies."

The zombies had evidently figured out that fresher meat was now outside and within chewing distance. Still, it took all six a few moments to lurch around vaguely and fix on Bertie Hernandez. Bertie held the magnum in the proper two-handed position and sighted down the barrel.

"Bertieee—" The squeal of expelled breath was loud enough even to hear inside the Diner. Bertie's mother lunged at her son. The muzzle of the .357 belched flame and the back of Mrs. Hernandez's skull exploded outward, the spray of blood and tissue coating the face of the zombie close behind her.

Inside the Diner, Billy said, "I didn't think they were supposed to remember anything human."

Miguel shrugged. "Reflexes, I'll bet. You know, like chickens when you pull off their heads."

Billy looked dubious.

Bertie blew away the faces of the next two zombies; ducked a fourth that had the smarts to flank him; then practically stuck the muzzle in the mouth of a fifth creature. The exiting slug nicked one front corner of the Diner's roof.

"Dios!" yelled Henry. "Be careful!"

Bertie had taken his eyes off the craftiest of the zombies. While he was watching the sixth go for him, the other survivor got in close enough to grab his gun hand. Then the last zombie wrapped her spindly arms around his lower leg and began to gnaw one Fry elephant-hide boot.

"Shit!" said Shine Willis, flicking the latch and pumping in a round as he slammed open the door. He had a clear shot at the zombie Bertie was fighting off with both hands. The old woman's head simply disintegrated and the body flopped backward, twitching as it hit the graveled parking apron.

"Jesus," Bertie cried. "I'm fuckin' deaf!"

Shine reversed the pump and swung the stock into the skull of the remaining zombie chewing on Bertie's boot. It took three blows before the creature's jaws stopped champing.

"Christ," said Shine, panting. "She's worse'n a Gila monster."

Bertie kicked free of the zombie's doubly dead body. "Shit, man, I had her—I had 'em both."

"Yeah, sure." Shine wiped the bloody stock of the pump on an old lady's flowered dress. "If I was a second longer, you'd be zombie jerky and I'd be obliged to blow your fuckin' head into the Arkansas."

Bertie said nothing; just thumbed some shells out of his right front pocket and began reloading the magnum.

When he was done, he said, "Okay, bud, you got one on me. Let's go back in and I'll buy you a coffee."

"I need somethin' stronger than that," Shine said.

They both froze a moment when they heard the siren.

The county car slewed off the blacktop and into the gravel. Both Bertie and Shine jumped to avoid the spray of rocks. Bobby Mack Quintana got out of the car with his service revolver drawn. "What's going on here?"

"Fuck you," Bertie said. "Henry'll fill you in." He turned and walked back into the Diner, Shine following with the barrel of the Remington propped against one shoulder.

Bobby Mack stared after them. "Zombies?" he called.

"No shit, Sherlock."

The deputy took out a notebook and a ballpoint. He gingerly flipped over a body with his booted toe. He recognized the piece of face that remained.

Martha watched from inside. The body Bobby Mack was identifying was old Mrs. Hernandez. Martha had known her since she was a little girl. Mrs. Hernandez had read to her from the collection of P. G. Wodehouse books that had furnished Bertie's name.

Martha felt a sudden lurch in her belly. She barely made it to the ladies' room. As she hunched over the stool and heaved up her breakfast, she heard Bertie Hernandez complaining at the counter.

"Hey, Henry, get your buns out here. This bacon's *way* too done!"

"Bobby Mack, I want to talk to you," said Martha. Bertie and his friends were out back of the Diner in an open field, piling up the bodies of the six zombie ladies, dousing them with unleaded, and then holding out chilled masculine palms, calluses to the heat.

The deputy had reminded them about the recent state law. " 'You kill 'em, you burn 'em,' " Bertie had repeated somewhat derisively. "Sure enough, Deputy Dawg, we're good citizens. We'll have a little zombie roast . . . work up a healthy appetite for lunch."

"I can't wait around for this," whined Miguel Espinosa. "I gotta go to work down to the Quik-Lube."

"Just shut the fuck up," said Bertie. "We'll do it," he said to Bobby Mack. The deputy watched for a few minutes, then went back into the Diner.

When Martha asked to speak with him, he hesitated. "Official business?" he said.

Martha sighed. "You've got to be kidding. I just want to take a minute."

Bobby Mack looked doubting, then shrugged. "Okay, I can talk."

"Not here." She called to Henry in the kitchen, "Hey, boss, I'm taking my break." Without waiting for an answer, she led Bobby Mack out the door.

A cold autumn wind followed them a hundred yards across the highway and up a forested rise. The greasy black smoke curled over their heads. Martha wrinkled her nose. Bobby Mack Quintana looked fine in his tan uniform and Stetson. The black leather at his trimly belted waist didn't hurt.

"Just wanted to talk," she said, turning to face him. She had to tilt her face up to meet his dark eyes.

"Figured," Bobby Mack said. He smiled.

Shyly, she thought. Martha took a deep breath. "Would it be too bold," she said, "to ask why you don't like me?"

Bobby Mack looked stunned. "Don't like you? I *do* like you, Martha. Truly I do."

"You don't ever show it." She had amazed herself with her boldness. She knew she should be tongue-tied, but the words tumbled out anyway. "I want you to feel kindly toward me, Bobby Mack."

The deputy started to say something, but stuttered the words. He took a breath and started over. "I don't want to overstep what's right. I figured you and Carl Crump—"

"Carl Crump?" she said incredulously. Just what did Bobby Mack think was going on between her and the high school principal's son? "He's just a—just a horny jerk, just like—" His father, she started to say, but clipped off the words in time. No use aggravating things. She knew the Crumps square-danced with Bobby Mack's folks on Friday nights. *"Carl?"* she said again. "Why do you think he and I—?"

Bobby Mack seemed to be blushing. "Well, he was saying . . ."

"Who—Carl Crump?" The deputy nodded. "No way," said Martha. "I may not make much money at the Diner, but I've got some standards."

"And pride," Bobby Mack almost whispered.

"That too." Martha reached out and lightly grasped his hands. Their fingers touched warmly. "Any other gossip you want to ask me about?"

Bobby Mack met her eye. "No," he said.

She could have called him a liar, but didn't want to. She didn't want to think about it, but knew there were men in the town who talked about her, speculated, perhaps even claimed to have touched her in the dark, in the backseats of their cars, in the balcony of the movie theater in Walsenburg, on the grass along the bank of— "Okay," she said. It had never happened. But God knows, she had turned them down. They had said all the things that seemed harmless on the surface, but she knew meant something else if examined closely enough.

"Nice day," he said, as the shifting wind whipped corpse-smoke through the trees and into their faces.

Martha started to laugh and cough at the same time. When she could speak, she said, "No, it isn't."

Bobby Mack laughed too. "No, you're right. It's a bad day, a rotten day, except for this." His fingers tightened on hers.

She screwed up her courage. "Bobby Mack, do you think you might like to go out tonight and do something?" Smoke from the pyre curled over their heads and up into the pine branches. His fingers tightened so fiercely, she feared he'd bruise her. Yet she didn't mind.

"Yes," said Bobby Mack. "I get off patrol at six. Yes," he said again.

After a long moment they both smiled and began to walk back toward the Diner. The day was sufficiently overcast, Henry had turned on the neon sign. EAT, it flashed. EAT, EAT, EAT.

Bobby Mack checked in the county Ford by six and picked up Martha at the Diner in his Suzuki Samurai.

"How about the Lanes?" he said, glancing at her and then back at the road.

"Sure. That's fine."

"We can't bowl tonight," he said.

"I heard on the radio. The meeting's at seven."

"We should have time to eat."

"You want to stay for the meeting?" she said.

"I've got to. Sheriff's orders."

"Oh," she said.

"Shit!" Thump-*thump.* The Samurai bounced over something lying humped on the road. "Sorry about my language, Martha."

She ignored that. "What was it?"

"Looked like a dog." With a hunk taken out of its head. That's what he didn't say. "It was already dead."

"Poor thing." She stared out the side window. "It was all curled up the way Mrs. Hernandez was this morning."

Bobby Mack didn't say anything.

"This morning," Martha said, "is that how it's going to have to be from here on out?"

"I wish I knew." Bobby Mack's words were clipped. "The word from the legislature is that Bertie can do that sort of thing. Anyone can. They're looking at what happened back East. You don't argue with zombies. You just shoot them in the head."

"They can't all be bad," said Martha. "There have to be some that remember being alive."

"Maybe they do," answered Bobby Mack. "Maybe that's why they're so pi—irritated."

Martha was clearly not satisfied. "I don't think I could kill one if it was somebody I'd loved."

"Hard to say." Bobby Mack swung the Samurai off the blacktop. "I reckon we'd do most anything if we were pushed." The parking lot of the Chama Lake Lanes wasn't crowded. He parked by the row of elms bordering the near side of the lot.

"Not if I loved him," Martha muttered.

"Huh?" said Bobby Mack. "Sorry, I wasn't listening."

"Nothing. Let's go eat."

* * *

The cheeseburgers and fries were what she could have eaten anytime at the Diner, but these were prepared by a different cook. They tasted terrific. A Coke apiece. Hot fudge sundaes for dessert.

By seven o'clock the bowling alley had started to fill with the citizens of Fort Durham and the surrounding countryside. It was clear there would not be enough chairs in the area on the riser behind the alleys, so old MacFarland, the owner, handed out pairs of bowling shoes to the later arrivals. They had to seat themselves on the polished hardwood of the lanes.

"Looks like most everybody's here," said Bobby Mack. "Sheriff's over there, so's the mayor, most of the county commissioners."

Martha had noted all those, but also Carl Crump, both junior and senior, not to mention Father Sierra and Pastor Beecham, the latter accompanied by his wife. Both the pastor and the priest had come onto her—at least that was what she'd suspected. She was unsure how else to interpret their words and actions on separate occasions. It seemed tragic to her, sadder, somehow more shocking than something like the propositions of Principal Crump or his son. But the weirdest thing— She hardly wanted to think about that at all. The true strangeness was the overture she had received from Mrs. Beecham, the pastor's wife.

For an entire semester after that, the final term of her senior year, she had attempted to dress even more conventionally than she had before. It didn't seem to work. She could still interpret the smirks and smiles.

Mayor Hardesty levered his plump self upright behind the lectern. "Let's get this called to order, folks. Sooner we get started, the sooner we can get home and do whatever we need to do." The room quieted. "I figure you all pretty much know what's going on from listening to the TV and radio, and after hearing the Health Department lady at the meeting last week."

"Nobody believed her," said Bobby Mack in a low voice.

Martha knew that was true. At the time, the zombie

stories on the hourly KNBS news had been just that—
stories. It was like a war in Central America or a volcano
blowing up in Asia. You just couldn't believe in some
things unless you actually saw them. Otherwise they
weren't real.

The zombies were real enough now. The morning had
proved that. Mayor Hardesty mentioned the massacre at
Eventide Manor and briefly outlined Bertie's morning ex-
ploits at the Diner. "We all have to be heroes like that,"
said the mayor. "We've got to watch out for each other
and do more than just our share."

"And arm civilians with automatic weapons," Bobby
Mack said sarcastically into Martha's ear.

. The mayor went on. It was an attempt at being inspira-
tional. Then the time for questions came. Someone spoke
up from the rear of the snack area.

"How long's this zombie thing gonna last, anyway?"

"Probably about as long," said the mayor, "as it takes
for the army to get mobilized, come on in, and kick some
butt."

"After what happened out at the old folks' home, what
about maybe putting up some roadblocks? You know, like
a quarantine."

The mayor smiled politically. "You folks probably saw
the news shows tonight. Both Denver and Albuquerque
are in pretty bad shape. But fortunately for people out in
the sticks like us, the zombies don't drive much."

"Somebody got here and wiped out Eventide Manor."

The mayor looked as if he were strenuously attempting
to think on his feet. "Maybe it was a virus or something."
He shrugged. "Something in the air or the food we been
getting—"

"Not a good move," said Bobby Mack, voice low. "He's
just blowing smoke. Zombies can't infect you by sneezing
or letting you use their towels. They've got to bite you."

Martha shivered and laid her hand across his.

The room started to dissolve into chaos. People shouted
questions and opinions, paying no attention to the mayor's
gavel. "Let's get out of here," said Bobby Mack. He kept
hold of her hand and led her toward the door.

Martha saw stares following them, appraising expressions. Neither of the Crump men was smiling. Nor was the priest or the pastor and his wife. They hate me, she thought, somewhat startled by the epiphany. They want me, but they hate me too.

Outside, the chill night air took away the sweat and the stale cigar smoke. There was no need out here for them to hold hands, but they did it anyway. About halfway across the parking area, Bobby Mack let loose of her fingers and trotted on ahead.

"Hey! What the hell are you guys doing?"

When Martha caught up to him, she realized that Bertie Hernandez and his cronies were having some fun.

"We're havin' a tailgate party," said Bertie. "What's it look like? That we're stringin' us up a zombie?"

That was, indeed, what it looked like. Billy, Miguel, Shine, and the rest were gathered around Bertie's jacked-up old red Chevy pickup. The truck was parked under the elms. The tailgate was down, and on it stood a thoroughly bound man Martha didn't recognize. But then he would have been hard to identify in any case. One ear dangled freely, barely attached to a tattered strip of gray skin. Dark liquid hissed and frothed from ragged lips. Several twists of shiny barbed wire, wound around his head the long way, from crown to jaw, kept the man's mouth shut.

Bertie saw them both looking at the wire. "Gotta keep him from biting. This here's a zombie, *comprende*?"

"You're going to lynch him?" said Bobby Mack. "That's murder."

"Gotta be alive to be a murder," said Shine Willis, grinning.

"Mutilating a corpse, then," said the deputy.

"Come on, Bobby Mack, get off it," said Bertie. "You know as well as me that there ain't no laws at all protecting these things. It isn't like they're endangered species or whatever. They just gotta die, that's all."

"Who—who is he?" said Martha.

"The guy who got to the old folks' home," said Bertie. "I guess he was the one who was supposed to deliver the butt paper and towels. From the Springs, probably. Me and the boys went up to the home to check it out after lunch. We found this guy down in the basement munching down the last of Doctor Jellico's feet. There were pieces of some of the other people in the home too."

"He was a fag," said Shine.

Martha and Bobby Mack stared at Shine.

He shrugged. "Dunno really. But all the bodies he'd been chewin' on were men. Let the ladies go after he killed 'em. That's why they were all down to the Diner."

"Enough of this shit," said Bertie. "Bobby Mack, you gonna interfere, or can we get on with it?"

"I guess the governor says you can kill him if you burn him. But hanging's not going to do any good, is it?"

"It is," said Bertie, "when you use piano wire for the noose." He banged on the Chevy's fender. The driver gunned the engine, then popped the clutch. The truck lurched forward, leaving the zombie kicking.

With the creature's weight, it didn't take but for a few seconds before the wire loop twanged into a knot and the zombie's head and body took separate falls. The head bounced a few feet away, the eyes blinking. Miguel Espinosa gave it a hard rap with an irrigation shovel.

"Hey, Martha," said Bertie. "You still want to go on over to Walsenburg with me tonight?"

"I never said I wanted to go."

Bertie walked over to stand in front of them. "You gonna go out for a ride in the deputy's rice-burner?"

"I'm going to give her a ride home," said Bobby Mack.

"See that's the only ride you give her."

"Bertie—" Martha started to say.

"I mean it." Bertie showed a toothy smile. "It's the best for you or nothing, you know?"

"Go burn your corpse," said Bobby Mack. The two men stared at each other. Bertie lowered his eyes first.

Over beneath the tree, the men were playing kickball with the head.

Bobby Mack took Martha home the long way. "Probably shouldn't use the gas," he said. "Don't know when the tankers'll stop coming here. But I don't want to call it a night yet."

"Me neither," said Martha. The Samurai had bucket seats, but she did her best to lean into his shoulder.

They drove south, almost to the New Mexico line, stopping short and turning around when they saw the police flashers and the leaping flames from something burning on the road.

"It's either their state patrol or ours," said Bobby Mack. "I'm off duty. I figure they've got it under control, whatever it is. Those boys have firepower."

He drove north again, taking the county road south of Fort Durham that wound into the hills to the west of town. Headlights, one out of adjustment and too bright, paced them. Bobby Mack squinted at the glare, then pulled off on a hilltop turnout to let the other vehicle by. A black Ford quarter-ton roared past. "Looks like Billy Gaspar," Bobby Mack said. "Wonder what the heck he's doing up here?" The sound of the truck diminished.

They stayed in the Samurai and looked down at Fort Durham's scattered lights.

"It always looks bigger at night," Martha said.

"Lot of things do. I guess that's why most folks think the dark's scary. When I was a kid, I used to wake up in the summer around three, four in the morning. I'd set a mental alarm. Then I'd sneak out of the house and just explore around the ranch. The greatest thing was the milk cows. They'd be just standing there in the moonlight, big and quiet and warm."

Martha looked sidelong at him. "There weren't any zombies then."

"Not here, at least. I expect there were the first zombies, back down in Jamaica or wherever they come from."

"Radio says these aren't the same thing. I was listening to NPR—"

"You listen to public radio?" He sounded surprised, yet pleased. "Me too."

"I'm not stupid, Bobby Mack. Yes, I was listening to NPR. They had a voodoo priest on who was really mad about his people being blamed for the zombies."

"Can't say as I'd blame him."

She hugged herself. "I don't want to talk about zombies."

"It's pretty much all anybody's gonna want to discuss

for a while. Biggest thing to happen in this town since I don't know when."

A long minute went by.

"Bobby Mack, do you ever think about getting out of here? Going somewhere else?"

"I did that," he said. "I went away to college."

She laughed, but gently. "A couple hundred miles to Fort Lewis College in Durango isn't a long way."

"You didn't say *long* way."

"You know what I meant."

After a while, he said, "I don't know if I'd like it anywhere else."

"I know what you mean." Martha unhugged herself. "But sometimes I wonder what it would be like to find out."

"To go to California or something," he said, "it'd get lonely if you were by yourself."

"Yes," she said quietly. "I get lonely right here."

He sounded surprised. "You were always the prettiest girl around. Lonesome?"

"You don't know much about me, do you?"

"Reckon I was scared to find out," he said.

"No reason for that." Martha gently touched the side of his face. "No reason at all."

He shrugged slightly. "Like I told you, I heard things."

"They were wrong."

He touched her hair, her face, her lips. "I need to think about this."

"Do you?" she said, looking at him steadily in the glow from the dash lights.

"Yes, I do."

She touched his cheek with her lips. "There may not be much time."

"What's that mean?"

"I don't know," she said. "Just a feeling."

"One way or another," he said, "there'll be time." He leaned forward and flicked on the headlights. "I'd better get you home. I don't want your folks to raise Cain."

"Bobby Mack," she said, amazed again at her boldness. "Just one hug? One kiss?"

He nodded, and then held her and kissed her. And drove her home.

"That's funny," said Martha as they drove into the Malinowski yard four miles north of town.

"What?" Bobby Mack coasted the Samurai up near the house and turned off the lights.

"Yard light's off. Dad just replaced the bulb last week."

"Maybe he turned it off."

"Never does that when he figures I'm going to be late." She shrugged. "Maybe he expected I'd come home right after the meeting."

"Don't get jumpy," said Bobby Mack, grinning. "You're with the deputy sheriff, remember?"

"I remember." Martha got out of the Samurai. Bobby Mack started around the front of the vehicle to meet her. The night was only a day removed from the new moon, and the darkness was deep.

"Give me your hand," said the deputy. "I don't want to break a leg. I figure you know the terrain."

At the front step, Martha fumbled in her handbag for a key. "What with the zombies, Dad said he was going to start locking up at night." Once she had key in hand, Martha leaned up toward him. "Good night, Bobby Mack."

Whatever he was going to say was lost as they both heard the sound of something heavy, lurching and crunching in the gravel behind them. An indistinct shape loomed out of the darkness.

"GRRROARRRR!"

Clawed hands reached for him.

"Sweet Jesus!" said Bobby Mack, trying to get in front of Martha and reaching at the same time for his holstered pistol. Arms grabbed him from both sides and he was held immobile in the night. The creature in front of him staggered close and Bobby Mack smelled alcohol.

"Evenin', Deputy Dawg." It was Bertie Hernandez.

"Hey, man! It's okay, it's okay." Billy Gaspar's voice in Bobby Mack's ear. "We just didn't want you shootin' no one." He let loose of Bobby Mack's right arm. Someone else set free the left.

"You bastards!" said Martha. "What are you doing?"

"Just checkin'," said Bertie. "We're the PDA monitors, just like in high school. Wanta make sure the neckin' don't go too far, unnerstand?"

Bobby Mack said angrily, "I ought to—"

"Oughtta what, college boy? Just a little joke." Bertie turned heavily away. "Just a little joke. Okay, guys, let's go."

Bobby Mack started for him, but Martha grabbed his arm. "No, Bobby Mack. This isn't the time."

Bertie and the others were laughing uproariously by the time they piled into Billy Gaspar's black Ford. It had been parked around the angle of the house. Billy floored the pedal and the truck whined away toward the blacktop. The night swallowed the laughter.

Bobby Mack and Martha stared after them. The deputy realized his fingers were still clamped to the flap of his holster. He took his hand away.

The yard light went on, bathing the whole area in mercury vapor glare. Mr. Malinowski stood framed in the doorway, yawning and rubbing sleep from his eyes.

"Hey, you kids! What the hell's going on out there? Some of us are tryin' to sleep."

Martha and Bobby Mack exchanged looks. She reached up and touched his lips. "I'll see you at the Diner."

Talk at the Diner in the morning centered around two things, football and zombies. The preseason game between Denver and the Seattle Seahawks had been canceled just before kickoff. The rumors mentioned locker-room atrocities and half-devoured tailbacks.

"Musta been Seattle zombies," said Shine Willis grimly. " 'Bout the only way they could beat the Broncos." No one contradicted him.

"Okay, ace," said Bertie. "Listen up. I got a little question for you."

Everyone listened up, especially Shine.

"So can animals bite you and turn you zombie?"

"You mean like dogs?" said Shine. "Get bit by Cujo? Beats the shit out of me."

No one knew, but everyone had an opinion.

"I was wonderin'," said Bertie, " 'cause when I come out of the trailer this morning, the Jergensons' mutt came for me and I had to put him down. He looked like he'd already been dead a couple days."

Billy Gaspar looked glum. "Cripes, all we need is for every critter to be set against us."

"I wouldn't worry," said Shine. "The Jergensons' dog always looks like twenty pounds of shit. Probably just didn't like your looks. You shower this morning?"

The men along the counter laughed. A bit nervously, Martha thought. She dispatched the plates of hotcakes, eggs, potatoes, bacon, toast. Poured the coffee. The real stuff. No one here drank decaf.

A rough hand gripped her wrist. The coffee pot sloshed. "No more for me," said Bertie. "I'm tryin' to cut down."

"Let go," she said.

He sat there; she stood waiting. A silent tableau. The men stared, then went back to talking. But glances kept flickering toward Martha and Bertie.

"Tipped a few with Carl Crump real late last night," said Bertie casually. "He talks real interesting."

"I doubt that," said Martha. "Now let me go."

"No." The thick fingers did not relax. "He says you got a little mark under your left titty. Looks like a bird. That true?"

"No." Martha switched the steaming coffeepot to her right hand. "Let me go right now or you're going to get this all down your front."

In the sudden silence, the radio playing John Hiatt's "I Don't Even Try" seemed to blare out. The men at the counter no longer pretended to look away.

"If you'll go down for Bobby Mack," said Bertie, "then how come you won't do nothing for me?"

"Carl's a liar," said Martha evenly.

Bertie looked into her eyes intently. "Sure," he said, and let her wrist go. "Maybe tonight we can go to Walsenburg?"

She didn't know why she said it. "I'd sooner fuck a zombie." She said it so low, no one heard but Bertie. He stared at her.

Martha turned away and walked back to the kitchen,

trying to move straight and true, and not bolt. Once out of sight of the dining room, she rubbed at the quick tears. She felt a raw pain. Her wrist. She turned it over and saw the angry-looking black-and-blue marks. They looked like the wings of a bird.

Bobby Mack didn't come into the Diner for his mid-morning coffee stop. About eleven Martha called to Henry Roybal, "Hey, anything on the scanner? What's going on out there? Anybody hear tell of Bobby Mack?"

"Nary a word about your young man, Martha. Lots of other stuff, though."

She balanced a tray of dirty dishes and flatware into the kitchen. Jose, the dishwasher, took it away from her, grunting as the load clattered and splashed into a steel sink full of soapy water.

"What do you mean, other stuff?"

"Don't know, really. Lots of code things, like when they know people are listening and the sheriff don't want anything to hit the grapevine right away."

As if on cue, the police scanner crackled and hissed around a call: "Sheriff central, this is patrol three."

"Patrol three, come in."

"Hey, affirmative. Kenny and me, we got a confirmed patch of veggies just off county one-fiver at the Centennial Ditch. Must have been holed up in the First Baptist. We're gonna take actions as ordered."

"Veggies?" said Martha.

Henry Roybal nodded. "All mornin'."

The scanner crackled. "Patrol three, don't do nothing stupid."

"Central, can you send us backup?"

"That's a negatory, patrol three. Things are jumpin' all over the county."

"We copy, central. Do what we can. Got my old AK47 in the trunk. Worked on Charlie. Figure it'll harvest a whole row or two of veggies."

"My God," said Martha.

"Repeat, patrol three. Stay cool. We already lost a coupla harvesters this morning."

There was a silence on the scanner. Then the voice of

patrol three said, "We know that, central. This one's gonna be for Dale and J.B."

Henry Roybal expelled a long breath. Martha looked at him. They both knew exactly whom the voice was talking about. Town cops. They hadn't come in for coffee either. Bobby Mack, she thought, staring intently at the scanner. Say something. Report in. Please.

"Hey, central, we got civilians back of us. It's Reverend Beecham and some others." There was a pause, and then the voice got fainter as though the speaker were sticking his head out the car window. "Hey, Pastor! You need some help? The cavalry's here—"

A strangled scream filtered through the scanner.

A second voice shouted, "Central, they're veggies too—" A crackle of shots. Another scream. Indistinguishable noises. Scratching. A sound like something chewing on the microphone. Silence.

"Patrol three, what's goin' down? Report, patrol three—"

Martha rushed from the kitchen, trying to blank the sounds from the speaker. Bobby Mack. At least he wasn't patrol three.

The radio on the shelf was playing Nick Cave's cover of "Long Black Veil."

"Why don't you give us some news!" Martha cried at it.

"Mayor Hardesty don't want none of us to panic," said Bertie Hernandez. His pals and he had evidently entered the Cuchara Diner in the last minute or so. They'd tracked in some of the thin skiff of snow that covered the Diner's parking lot. Brown water pooled on the tile floor.

"I think maybe *I'm* about ready to panic," said Martha candidly. "I want to know what's going on."

"Don't worry, darlin'," said Bertie. "We'll take good care of you, somethin' happens."

"You didn't see Bobby Mack out there this morning, did you?"

Bertie and Shine Willis exchanged glances. "Not lately," said Bertie. "He's a smart boy. I 'spect he's okay, but probably real busy. You won't see him before tonight."

"Just what's going on out there?" said Martha. "For God's sake, tell me!"

"It's the zombies," said Billy Gaspar.

"They're spreadin' faster'n AIDS," said Shine.

"Yeah," said Bertie. "Looks like maybe all they got to do is bite you, not even kill you. The bastards are all over town, lotta people you and me both know."

"We killed a bunch of them," said Billy Gaspar. "But there's so many—"

"Now," said Bertie, "we got to hole up and rest. Diner's as good a place as any. Anyhow, I figure we got to have lunch. What's the special?"

"Meat loaf," said Martha.

Billy Gaspar groaned. "I don't think my belly can take that."

"Eat or be eaten," said Bertie with a grin.

"This is KHIP," said the radio, "the kay-hip country voice of the southern Colorado empire. Pueblo to Durango, we bring you the absolutely latest news. . . ."

"Shut up," said Martha tightly. "Just tell me what's going on."

The recorded opening trailed off, and there was a moment of dead air. The announcer, when he came on, sounded dead tired and scared shitless. "This is Boots Bell at the kay-hip studios north of Fort Durham. I've got a whole raft of announcements and they're most all life and death, so listen up."

"We're listening, goddamn it," said Bertie Hernandez, sounding as tightly wound as Martha. "Get to it." The boys hadn't gone out much during the afternoon. They'd stayed close to the Diner, bringing in weapons from their trucks and drinking a lot of beer. A few of the other regulars had drifted in. There was very little traffic on 159.

Boots Bell riffled some papers over the radio. Then he said, "The main thing is, stay indoors. Lock your houses. Anybody comes to your door, check 'em out good. All of a sudden, there's dead folks walking everywhere. This is no joke, no test of the emergency broadcast system, nothing like that. It's the real thing."

"Damn straight," said Shine Willis.

"If you've got weapons," said Bell, "keep them loaded

and handy. Shoot for the head. That's about the only way to kill a zombie."

"Hey, what about fire?" said Shine.

"—or burn 'em," Bell continued. "Remember they're quicker than they look, and real strong. They generally run in packs. If you see one, there's probably another ten sneaking up behind you."

Jose dropped a pan in the kitchen and half the guys at the counter twitched.

Bell said, "Here at the station, we've received word that the National Guard'll be moving in as soon as they finish mopping-up operations in Walsenburg." He hesitated. "Reckon that'll come after they clean up the Springs. And in Denver—well, we don't have much word at all." Papers rattled for a few moments. "We're keeping a map at the station of all sightings, so if you spot a zombie, give us a jingle and we'll pass the news along." There was a second voice, indistinguishable. Then Bell said, "We've already got so many reports of zombies, we can tell you it isn't safe to be anywhere outdoors in Fort Durham. Period. Sheriff and police officers are doing what they can, along with community volunteers. But if you don't have to be out, then don't go out. Not for any reason." Bell's voice cracked slightly. "The station manager just told me something, and I agree with it. If we stick together, we'll come out of this okay. Remember that."

In the Diner, the men with guns held them tight and exchanged looks.

"More news when it comes in," said Bell. "Now let's listen to some music." The speaker began to twang the opening chords of Tammy Wynette's "Stand by Your Man."

"At least," said Billy Gaspar, "they're not playing the Grateful fucking Dead." He tried to grin, but the effect was ghastly.

Martha set her tray down on the counter and went to the phone behind the cash register. She dialed her parents' number, knowing *of course they're all right,* but just wanting the reassurance. All she got in the earpiece was the soft buzz of a dead line.

* * *

By three o'clock, the first zombie appeared in the Diner's parking lot. It was Mrs. Dorothy Miller, who had been the head cashier at the Stockman's Bank.

"For Chrissake, kill her," said Bertie, waving Shine and Billy toward the door. "They're probably like ants, sending out scouts. We don't want the rest to know there's all sorts of food here."

The men nodded and went outside, Shine first. Billy put the butt of the 30.06 deer rifle against his shoulder and slowly squeezed off a round. The bullet went squarely through Mrs. Miller's left eye. The zombie flung out its arms and spun around. Shine raised his Remington pump at close range and blew Mrs. Miller's head completely off.

Shine and Billy dragged the body around the corner of the Diner and out of sight; then they came back in and shared a pull off Miguel Espinosa's flask of home brew.

Martha hardly noticed. She kept listening to the radio and badgering Henry Roybal to keep close track of both the CB base station and the police scanner. "Anything?" she'd say on her trips into the kitchen.

"Nothing," Henry would answer. "Listen, Bobby Mack's probably way too busy to use his radio. Try not to worry."

In the dining room, KHIP was playing Gordon Lightfoot's "Wreck of the Edmund Fitzgerald."

"Christ," said Shine, "who picks the music? I wish to hell Henry had a jukebox."

"But he don't," said Bertie. "We're just gonna have to make our own entertainment." He caressed the rifle lying across his lap. Then he looked up toward Martha and held out his cup.

Martha stared at him and started to turn away.

"Please?"

She thought about it a moment and then brought the pot over.

His expression was earnest. "Listen, Martha, if we all get out of this, think maybe we can start over?"

"No." She resisted the impulse to start laughing hysterically. "We can't start over what we never began in the first place."

Something seemed to smolder in Bertie's eyes. "I'm really on my best behavior now."

"I know that," she said quietly. "But I'm being honest with you."

"Me too," he said. "I really want you to be my girl."

She shook her head.

"Final word?" he said.

—*dangerously,* Martha thought. *He sounds like he'll do anything.* She nodded. Yes.

"Well, shoot," said Bertie. "I guess the only thing left is to fuck you till you can't see straight. Or walk straight, neither."

"Try it," said Martha, "and I'll kill you."

"And I'll come back," said Bertie. "And keep fucking you. Bet it doesn't do no good to kick a zombie in the nuts. What do you think?"

"I think you're disgusting." Martha held the handle of the coffeepot tightly. The temptation to blister his face so that it looked like a basic zombie visage of torn and rotting flesh was nearly irresistible. She turned away.

"I'll wait," said Bertie toward her back. "After you're done waitin' for Bobby Mack, I'll still be good and hard."

Without turning, she said, "I can wait too."

"Not long enough for the Deputy Dawg."

She whirled. "What do you *know*?"

Bertie ostentatiously licked his lips.

By six o'clock it was getting dark. Henry Roybal came out of the kitchen and switched on the EAT sign.

"Think that's a real good idea?" said Shine.

"You think zombies can read?"

"They could when they were alive," said Billy.

"They're animals," said Henry Hatly. "Beasts. Probably color-blind too."

Nobody pushed the issue. The neon on the roof fizzed and crackled. The glow on the snow outside the window cycled from red to green.

"Maybe we should make a break for it," said Miguel Espinosa. "Head for New Mexico."

"Doubt there's anything different there," said Bertie.

"May as well stay where there's lots of food and booze."
He winked at Martha. "And a pretty lady."

"I got a full tank of gas," said Billy to Miguel.

"How come *you* don't leave?" Bertie said to Henry.

The owner of the Diner answered without hesitation.
"My daddy stopped here in Fort Durham while he was on
his way to California during the Dust Bowl. He loved this
place." He shrugged. "I like it too. I been here for floods
and droughts, blizzards and tornadoes. I'm not going to be
driven off by a passel of flesh-eating sons of bitches."

The radio intermittently delivered repeats of the afternoon messages. There seemed to be few developments.
The warnings continued. Stay indoors. Lock the doors.
Load the weapons. Aim for the head. Boots Bell finally
added a new one. Save a round for yourself.

The men in the Diner talked and drank. Bertie Hernandez mainly drank. By eight o'clock he was chasing shots
of tequila with mescal rather than beers. Shine Willis
wasn't far behind him.

At nine-oh-seven by the Hamm's clock beside the radio,
Bertie hurled his glass against the far wall. It shattered
below the mounted head of a twelve-point buck Henry's
father had shot sometime around Pearl Harbor.

"I think," said Bertie, grinning horribly at Martha, "it's
time for some real entertainment."

Miguel and Shine had moved into position to either side
of her. Martha glanced at them, then back at Bertie. He
stood up and played for a moment with his Peterbilt belt
buckle.

"What I propose," said Bertie, "is to screw this little
girl until my pecker comes out her asshole. Is there anybody here with an objection?"

"I don't think I can let you do that, Bertie," said Henry
Roybal.

"Didn't think so. You're a good man, Henry." Bertie
drew the .357 magnum from its holster and shot Henry
Roybal through the heart. The impact threw the old man
back against the kitchen doors. They flopped open as the
body fell backward. The doors swung shut again, but now
dappled with butterfly wings of blood.

"Anyone else?" said Bertie, surveying the silent men.

No one said anything. Not everyone looked wholly enthusiastic, but there were no objections voiced.

"Okay, then." Bertie set the pistol down on the table, then bent and grunted as he tugged his boots loose. His belt buckle followed.

Martha bolted. She was not quick enough to elude Shine's grasp. She struggled, trying to knee him, bite him, crush his instep— Miguel slugged her across the back of the neck and she sagged toward the floor.

She heard Bertie say, "Let's see some pussy."

She felt hands ripping her brown waitress dress down its buttoned front. Rough fingers hooked her pantyhose and rolled them down off her hips, along her legs, clear to her feet.

Martha opened her eyes and glared at Bertie. He had taken off his pants and briefs and stood there in his long-tailed blue work shirt and socks. She suddenly noticed that his socks were slightly mismatched—black and dark blue. "Bertie —" she said. "Don't do it."

He smiled almost cheerfully as he loomed over her, fingering his balls. His penis jutted out and up like a construction crane. Apparently all the alcohol he'd drunk hadn't done a thing to his erection.

"Martha," he said, sounding almost gentle. "I've *got* to." He spat into his hand and slicked up the head of his penis. "You know what's going on out there. This may be our only chance."

She didn't know how to answer him in a way that would mean anything.

Bertie smiled. "Oh," he said, "don't worry about a last-minute rescue by good ol' Bobby Mack Quintana."

She finally confronted what she suspected. What she didn't even want to *think*. As calmly as she could, she said, "What did you do to him?"

"It's not what *I* did to him," Bertie said, walking forward to stand between her spread legs. "It's what the Jergensons' Dobie did to him. I just put him out of his misery. It was a favor." Bertie laughed in a way that was almost a giggle. "Woulda done the same for a dog."

Martha felt the tears, willed them back. No time. Suddenly the radio came through, as though the sound were piped directly to her ears. KHIP was playing "Poor Poor Pitiful Me."

Bullshit! She arched her back, suddenly whipping her right leg up into Bertie's crotch.

Bertie twisted surprisingly fast, turning the blow on his thigh. He put one socked foot on her left ankle. Shine took her right.

Miguel snickered from up beside her head. "Make a wish."

"No gratitude in this pussy," said Bertie conversationally. "I expect there will be." He started to kneel down between her legs.

—as Bobby Mack Quintana came through the front door.

He didn't open it. He just came through it in a crash and chaos of shattered glass and yells from the men along the counter.

"What the fuck?" said Bertie, springing to his feet and lunging for the magnum on the table.

Men cursed and someone screamed, and everyone scattered to get out of Bobby Mack's path. He stood there for a moment and Martha could see he was not alive. He wore his uniform, but no hat. His khaki shirt was soaked with crusted blood that had obviously cascaded down much earlier from the shredded ruin where his throat had been. There were three black holes across his chest where large-caliber bullets had punched in. A fourth bullet had creased his face, laying open one cheek and setting his nose askew. Corruption had already set in. The flesh around his mouth seemed to be rotting. Fluids oozing from tatters in his face gleamed in the glow of the fluorescents.

"Christ, Bobby Mack," said Bertie, holding his pistol out in two shaking hands. "How many times I got to kill you?" The fire and noise reached out, slamming Bobby Mack backward, staggering his body but not felling him.

The zombie turned slightly to look at Martha still on the floor. Its mouth opened, and somehow sounds gurgled up through the torn throat. "Mar-thhha . . ."

Bobby Mack turned back toward Bertie, striding forward before the man could pull the trigger. The dead deputy reached down and grasped Bertie's penis, fingers wrapping around the thick base and the scrotum. With one powerful yank, he pulled back and up, the flesh giving way, tearing like rotten fabric.

The zombie's arm came up and Bertie's abdomen and stomach opened like someone had jerked the seam on a full Ziploc bag of lasagna. Viscera spewed across the dining room. If Bertie screamed, it was drowned out by the sounds of all the other men either frantically grabbing for their weapons or diving for a door.

Bertie's arms windmilled, spasming. Blood sprayed across the overheads and the light suddenly filtered red.

No one was holding onto Martha now, and she tried to scramble to her feet. Bobby Mack had turned to Shine and Miguel, digging fingers into the former's face and shoving the latter back into the glass shards protruding from the door frame. The zombie tossed Shine's face away as though it were a discarded Halloween mask and lurched toward Billy Gaspar.

"I didn't do it!" Billy screamed. "It was them. It was *them*—" Bobby Mack pulled off Billy's left arm and then pulped his head with the hard-muscled limb.

It suddenly seemed very quiet in the Diner. It was inhabited only by the dead and the dying. And Martha. She crouched back by the counter as Bobby Mack turned and came to her. They confronted each other and she stared sickly at his mutilated face.

He reached out jerkily, but his fingers were gentle as they touched her hair. He tried to say something, but the destroyed throat wouldn't let him.

"You too," Martha said, tears finally coming now. "I love you too."

Then she heard the screaming from outside.

Men were dying in the parking lot. In the glow from EAT—EAT—EAT, Martha could see the survivors of the Diner being torn apart by shadowy knots of zombies.

She turned toward Bobby Mack and took his hand. The skin felt as loose as an oversized cotton work glove. "We've got to get out of here," she said. "Come on."

He didn't move. Bobby Mack stared behind her. Slowly, unwillingly, she looked too.

Martha recognized most of the faces.

Some had recently fed—strings of meat hung slack and bloody from the corners of pursed-lip mouths. They were all there. Her nightmares: Carl Crump, Sr., dead eyes alight behind the smashed lenses of a pair of precariously balanced tortoise-shell glasses. Pastor Beecham, his clerical collar and black jacket streaked with gore that looked just as black, except that it glistened wetly in the light. Mrs. Beecham's red bouffant was in disarray, sodden ringlets hanging around her ears. Her gray A-line dress hung in tatters off one shoulder. Father Sierra's head was turned askew on the stalk of his neck by about forty-five degrees. He looked like an owl staring at its prey.

Carl Crump, Jr., reached out toward Martha, and Bobby Mack batted the blood-clotted nails away from her. The younger Crump wore a Maui shirt and ridiculous tropical flower-print jams.

He must be freezing, thought Martha irrelevantly. She realized she couldn't count all the zombies that were crowding into the Diner. Teachers, the night clerk from the 7-Eleven, some of the volunteer firefighters, the county librarian, her doctor. It looked like half the population of Fort Durham.

Carl Crump, Jr., groaned out something Martha couldn't understand. His father stirred beside him. Both zombies put their hands to their crotches like an obscene joke version of the see-no-evil, hear-no-evil monkeys.

She realized they both had enormous erections.

"No!" she said, huddling close to Bobby Mack. The dead deputy gurgled something and put one arm around her.

And then the zombies went for them.

There simply wasn't much maneuvering room, and so the mob surge did little good until the tidal force of corpses swung toward the Diner's front window and the glass exploded outward into the parking area.

Martha found herself on her back, both hands around Mrs. Beecham's neck, attempting to keep the snapping, pit-bull teeth from her own throat. Then a kick from

Bobby Mack's boot caught Mrs. Beecham under the collarbone and the zombie twisted away.

Carl Crump, Sr.'s, fist slammed into Bobby Mack's mouth, crumbling teeth and disappearing up to the wrist.

"Bobby—!" Martha screamed.

The elder Crump's hand reappeared, the fingers dripping with blood, nails squeezing cartilage and gray matter. Bobby Mack's body began to spasm, arms jerking away at bizarre angles. Crump licked his own nails.

The crush of dead, writhing bodies bore Martha down into the freezing gravel. A clawing hand snatched away her bra and part of her right breast. At first she felt no pain—just the cold air on her nipples.

She saw the wild tangle of henna-red hair descend toward her crotch, felt the cold lips and icy tongue violate her vagina, tried to draw back against the unforgiving gravel as rotting teeth ground into her flesh. Mrs. Beecham's face, slick with Martha's blood, lunged against her repeatedly, until her husband shoved his wife aside.

Pastor Beecham mounted her as Martha raked at the vacant eyes. Other arms grabbed at her and she felt her left shoulder twist and separate. Her right arm flailed, fingers searching for any purchase at all among her attackers.

The clergyman's penis slid deep into her like a rod of absolute-zero ice. Then Carl Crump, Jr., was at her, rolling her on her side and shoving his erection up into her anus. Martha felt the tissues tear. This time there was no merciful shock. This *hurt* and she screamed.

As Carl, Jr., pushed at her from behind, the movement seemed to excite Reverend Beecham. He shoved back, bubbles of saliva and stale air grunting from his blue lips. Martha could see Carl's father and the others waiting like patient customers in a post office queue.

The pain was a grinding, broken-glass agony that drew out the cells of her brain, sucking them into infinity. "Damn you!" Martha cried. "Damn you *all*!"

The intrusions of the others within her inexorably pounded toward some sort of vanishing dead climax. At first Martha watched, increasingly distant. A frozen calm began to narcotize her. Then she realized how close Bobby

Mack's mercifully inert body lay, twisted into the complex lovers' knot her body composed with the thrashing ministrations of Beecham and Carl Crump, Jr.

She could reach his holster flap with her right hand. Her fingertips touched the cold, still-bright leather. Surely one live round must remain in the cylinder of his .38 Police Positive. *Please.*

Carl Crump, Sr., squatted down above her face, runneled fingers moving back and forth along the purpling length of his erection.

Martha's numbed fingers twitched at the holster flap, tugged, pushed at the snap. The catch clicked free. She could feel the knurled walnut butt of the pistol. *Thank you, Bobby Mack.*

The zombies inside her grunted and heaved. Martha sensed others, many more, crowding around her. Dead eyes looked at her, but none of them *saw.* They never had. Her vision grayed.

The zombies kept coming—

—and coming—

Just one bullet, Martha thought.

There was.

Bodies and Heads

BY STEVE RASNIC TEM

In the hospital window the boy's head shook no no no. Elaine stopped on her way up the front steps, fascinated.

The boy's chest was rigid, his upper arms stiff. He seemed to be using something below the window to hold himself back, with all his strength, so that his upper body shook from the exertion.

She thought of television screens and their disembodied heads, ever so slightly out of focus, the individual dots of the transmitted heads moving apart with increasing randomness so that feature blended into feature and face into face until eventually the heads all looked the same: pinkish clouds of media flesh.

His head moved no no no. As if denying what was happening to him. He had been the first and was now the most advanced case of something they still had no name for. Given what had been going on in the rest of the country, the Denver Department of Health and Hospitals had naturally been quite concerned. An already Alert status had become a Crisis and doctors from all over—including a few with vague, unspecified governmental connections—had descended on the hospital.

Although it was officially discouraged, now and then in the hospital's corridors she had overheard the whispered word *zombie*.

"Jesus, will you look at him!"

Elaine turned. Mark planted a quick kiss on her lips. "Mark . . . somebody will see . . ." But she made no attempt to move away from him.

"I think they already know." He nibbled down her jawline. Elaine thought to pull away, but could not. His touch

119

on her body, his attention, had always made her feel beautiful. It was, in fact, the only time she ever felt beautiful.

"You didn't want anyone to know just yet, remember?" She gasped involuntarily as he moved to the base of her throat. "Christ, Mark." She took a deep breath and pushed herself away from him. "Remember what you said about young doctors and hospital nurses? Especially young doctors with administrative aspirations?"

He looked at her. "Did I sound all that cold-blooded? I'm sorry."

She looked back up at the boy, Tom, in the window. Hopelessly out of control. No no no. "No—you weren't that bad. But I'm beginning to feel a little like somebody's mistress."

Some of the other nurses were now going into the building. Elaine thought they purposely avoided looking at the head-shaking boy in the window. "I'll make it up to you," Mark whispered. "I swear. Not much longer." But Elaine didn't answer; she just stared at the boy in the window.

There was now a steady stream of people walking up the steps, entering the hospital, very few permitting themselves to look at the boy. *Tom,* she thought. *His name is Tom.* She watched their quiet faces, wondering what they were thinking, if they were having stray thoughts about Tom but immediately suppressing them, or if they were having no thoughts about the boy at all. It bothered her not knowing. People led secret lives, secret even from those closest to them. It bothered her not knowing if they bore her ill will, or good will, or if for them she didn't exist at all. Her mother had always told her she cared far too much about what other people thought.

"I gather all the Fed doctors left yesterday afternoon," Mark said behind her.

"What? I thought they closed all the airports."

"They did. I heard this morning the governor even ordered gun emplacements on all the runways. Guess they left the city in a bus or something."

Elaine tried to rub the chill off her arms with shaking hands. The very idea of leaving the city in something other than an armored tank terrified her. It had been only a few months since the last flights. Then that plane had come in from Florida: all those dead people with suntans strolling off the plane as if they were on vacation. A short time later two small towns on Colorado's eastern plains—Kit Carson and Cheyenne Wells—were wiped out, or apparently wiped out, because only a few bodies were ever found. Then there was another plane, this one from Texas. Then another, from New York City. "It's hard to believe they could land a plane," had been Mark's comment at the time. But there were still more planes; the dead had an impeccable safety record.

"I'm just as glad to see them go," Mark said now. "Poking over that spastic kid like he was a two-headed calf. And still no signs of their mysterious 'zombie virus.'"

"No one knows how it starts," she said. "It could start anywhere. It could have dozens of different forms. Any vague gesture could be the first symptom."

"They haven't proven to me that it *is* a virus. No one really knows."

But Denver's quarantine seemed to be working. No one got in or out. All the roads closed, miles of perimeter patrolled. And no zombie sightings at all after those first few at the airport.

The boy's head drifted left and right as if in slow motion, as if weightless. "I missed the news this morning," she said.

"You looked so beat, I thought it best you sleep."

"I *need* to watch the news, Mark." Anger had such a grip on her jaw that she could hardly move it.

"You and most everybody else in Denver." She looked at him but said nothing. "Okay, I watched it for you. Just more of the same. A few distant shots of zombies in other states, looking like no more than derelicts prowling the cities, and the countryside, for food. Nothing much to tell you what they'd really be like. God knows what the world outside this city is really like anymore. I lost part of it—the reception just gets worse and worse."

Elaine knew that everything he was saying was true. But she kept watching the screens just the same, the faces seeming to get a little fuzzier every day as reception got worse, the distant cable stations disappearing one by one until soon only local programming was available, and then even the quality of that diminishing as equipment began to deteriorate and ghosts and static proliferated. But still she kept watching. Everybody she knew kept watching, desperate for any news outside of Denver.

And propped up in the window like a crazed TV announcer, young Tom's head moved no no no. At any moment she expected him to scream his denial: "No!" But no words ever passed the blurring lips. Just like all the other cases. No no no. Quiet heads that would suddenly explode into rhythmic, exaggerated denial. Their bodies fought it, held on to whatever was available so that muscles weren't twisted or bones torqued out of their sockets.

His head moved side to side: no no no. His long blond hair whipped and flew. His dark pebble eyes were lost in a nimbus of hair, now blond, now seeming to whiten more and more the faster his head flew. His expressionless face went steadily out of focus, and after a moment she realized she couldn't remember what he looked like, even though she had seen him several times a day every day since he had been admitted into the hospital.

What is he holding on to? she wondered, the boy's head now a cloud of mad insects, the movement having gone on impossibly long. His body vibrated within the broad window frame. At any moment she expected the rhythmic head to levitate him, out the window and over the empty, early-morning street. His features blurred in and out: he had four eyes, he had six. Three mouths that gasped for air attempting to scream. He had become a vision. He had become an angel.

"It's going to take more than a few skin grafts to fix that one," Betty said, nervously rubbing the back of her neck. "My God, doesn't he ever stop?" They were at the windows above surgery. He'd been holding on to a hot radiator; it had required three aides to pull him off. Even anesthetized, the boy's head shook so vigorously the surgeons had had to strap his neck into something like a large dog collar. The surgeries would be exploratory, mostly, until they found something specific. It bothered Elaine. Tom was a human being. He had secrets. "Look at his eyes," Elaine said. His eyes stared at her. As his face blurred in side-to-side movement, his eyes remained fixed on her. But that couldn't be.

"I can't see his eyes," Betty said with sudden vehemence. "Jeezus, will you look at him? They oughta do something with his brain while they're at it. They oughta go in there and snip out whatever's causin' it."

Elaine stared at the woman. *Snip it out. Where?* At one time they had been friends, or almost friends. Betty had wanted it, but Elaine just hadn't been able to respond. It had always been a long time between friends for her. The edge of anger in Betty's voice made her anxious. "They don't know what's causing it," Elaine said softly.

"My mama don't believe in 'em." Betty turned and looked at Elaine with heavily-shadowed eyes, anemic-looking skin. "Zombies. Mama thinks the zombies are something the networks came up with. She says real people would never do disgustin' things like they're sayin' the zombies do." Elaine found herself mesmerized by the lines in Betty's face. She tried to follow each one, where they became deeper, trapping dried rivers of hastily applied makeup, where pads and applicators had bruised, then covered up the skin. Betty's eyes blinked several times quickly in succession, the pupils bright and fixed like a doll's. "But then she always said we never landed on the moon, neither. Said they filmed all that out at Universal Studios." Milky spittle had adhered to the inside corners of Betty's mouth, which seemed unusually heavy with lipstick today. "Guess she could be right. Never read about zombies in the Bible, and you would think they'd be there if there was such a thing." Betty rubbed her arm across her forehead. "Goodness, my skin's so *dry*! I swear I'm flakin' down to the *nub*!" A slight ripple of body odor moved across Elaine's face. She could smell Betty's deodorant, and under that, something slightly sour and slightly sweet at the same time.

That's the way people's secrets smell, Elaine thought, and again wondered at herself for thinking such things. *People have more secrets than you could possibly imagine.* She wondered what secret things Betty was capable of, what Betty might do to a zombie if she had the opportunity, what Betty might do to Tom. "Tom's not a zombie," she said slowly, wanting to plant the idea firmly in Betty's head. "There's been no proof of a connection. No proof that he has a form of the virus, if there is a virus. No proof that he has a virus at all."

"My mama never believed much in *coincidences,*" Betty said.

Elaine spent most of the night up in the ward with Tom and the other cases that had appeared: an elderly woman, a thirty-year-old retarded man, twin girls of thirteen who at times shook their heads in unison, a twenty-four-year-old hospital maintenance worker whose symptoms had started only a couple of days ago. As in every other place she'd worked, a TV set mounted high overhead murmured all evening. She couldn't get the vertical to hold. The announcer's head rolled rapidly by, disappearing at the top of the screen and reappearing at the bottom. But as she watched she began thinking it was different heads, the announcer switching them at the rate of perhaps one per second. She wondered how he'd managed the trick. Then she wondered if all newscasters did that, switching through a multitude of heads so quickly it couldn't be detected by the average viewer. She wanted to turn off the TV, but the doctors said it was best to leave it on for stimulation, even though their charges appeared completely unaware of it. Dozens of heads shaking no no no. Heads in the windows. Heads exploding with denial. Heads like bombs.

Two more nurses had quit that day. At least they had called; some had just stopped showing up. All the nurses were on double shifts now, with patient loads impossible to handle. Betty came in at six to help Elaine with feeding some of the head shakers.

"Now buckle the strap," Elaine said. She had the "horse collar," a padded brace, around the old woman's neck, her arms around the woman's head to hold it still. Betty fiddled with the straps.

"Damn!" Betty said. "I can't get it to buckle!"

"Hurry! I can't hold her head still much longer." Holding the head still put undue pressure on other parts of the system. Elaine could hear the woman's protesting stomach, and then both bladder and bowel were emptied.

"There!" Elaine let go and the old woman's head shook in her collar. Betty tried to spoon the food in. The woman's body spasmed like a lizard nailed to a board. Sometimes they broke their own bones that way. Elaine held her breath. Even strapped down, the old woman's face moved to an amazing degree. Like a latex mask attached loosely to the skull, her face slipped left and right, led by an agonized mouth apparently desperate to avoid the spoon. Elaine thought it disgusting, but it was better than any other method they'd tried. The head shakers choked on feeding tubes, pulled out IVs, and getting a spoon into those rapidly moving mouths had been almost impossible.

"I know it's your turn, but I'll go feed Tom," Elaine said.

Betty glanced up from the vibrating head, a dribble of soft brown food high on her right cheek. "Thanks, Elaine. I owe you." She turned back, aiming the spoon of dripping food at the twisting head. "I don't know. If I had to be like them . . . I don't know. I think I'd rather be dead."

Tom had always been the worst to feed. Elaine fixed a large plastic bib around his neck, then put one around her neck as well. He stared at her. Even as the spasms pulled his eyes rapidly past, she could see a little-boy softness in those adolescent eyes, an almost pleading vulnerability so at odds with the violent contortions his body made.

She moved the spoon in from the side, just out of his peripheral vision. But every time the metal touched the soft, pink flesh of the lips, the head jerked violently away. Again and again. And when some food finally did slip into the mouth cavity, he choked, his eyes became enormous, the whites swelling in panic, and his mouth showered it back at her. It was as if his mouth despised the food, reviled the food, and could not stand to be anywhere near it. As if she were asking him to eat his own feces.

She looked down at the bowl of mushy food. Tom reached his hand in, clutched a wet mess of it, then tried to stuff it into his own mouth. The mouth twisted away. His hand did this again and again, and still his mouth rejected it. Eventually his hands, denied the use of the mouth, began smearing the food on his face, his neck, his chest, his legs, all over his body, pushing it into the skin and eventually into every orifice available to receive it. He looked as if he had been swimming in garbage.

Tom's face, Tom's eyes, pleaded with her as his hands shoved great wet cakes of brown, green, and yellow food up under his blue hospital pajama top and down inside his underwear. Finally, as if in exasperation, Tom's body voided itself, drenching itself and Elaine in vomit, urine, and feces.

Elaine backed away, ripping off her plastic gloves and bib. "Stop it! Stop it! Stop it!" she screamed, as Tom's head moved no no no, and his body continued to pat itself, fondle itself, probe itself lovingly with food-smeared fingers. Elaine's vision blurred as she choked back the tears. Tom's body suddenly looked like some great bag of loose flesh, poked with wet, running holes, some ugly organic machine, inefficient in input and output. She continued to stare at it as it fed and drained, probed and made noises, all independent of the head and its steady no no no beat.

She ran into Betty out in the corridor. "I have to leave *now*," she said. "Betty, I'm *sorry*!"

Betty looked past her into the room where Tom was still playing with his food. "It's all right, kid. You just go get some sleep. I'll put old Master Tom to bed."

Elaine stared at her, sudden alarms of distrust going off in her head. "You'll be okay with him? I mean—he didn't *mean* it, Betty."

Betty looked offended. "Hey! Just what kind of nurse do you think I am? I'm going to hose him off and tuck him in, that's all. Unless you're insisting I read him a bedtime story, too? Maybe give him a kiss on the cheek? If I could *hit* his cheek, that is."

"I'm sorry. I didn't mean . . ."

"I know what you meant. Get some rest, Elaine. You're beat."

But Elaine couldn't bear to attempt the drive home, searching the dark corners at every intersection, waiting for the shambling strangers who lived in the streets to come close enough that she could get a good look at their faces. So that she could see if their faces were torn, their eyes distant. Or if their heads were beginning to shake.

Mark had been staying in the janitor's apartment down in the basement, near the morgue. The janitor had been replaced by a cleaning service some time back as a cost-cutting measure. Supposedly it was to be turned into a lab, but that had never happened. Mark always said he really didn't mind living by the morgue. He said it cut the number of drop-in visitors drastically.

Elaine went there.

"So don't go back," Mark said, nibbling at her ear. He was biting too hard, and his breath bore a trace of foulness. Elaine squirmed away and climbed out of bed.

"I have to go to the bathroom," she said. After closing the bathroom door, she ran water into the sink so that she would be unable to hear herself pee. People reacted to crisis in different ways, she supposed. Mark's way was to treat all problems as if they were of equal value, whether it was deciding what wattage light bulb to buy or the best way to feed a zombie.

Elaine looked down at her legs. They'd gotten a little spongier each year; her thighs seemed to spread a little wider each time she sat down. Here and there were little lumps and depressions which seemed to move from time to time. Her belly bulged enough now that she could see only the slightest halo of dark pubic hair when she looked down like this. And the pubic hair itself wasn't all that dark anymore. There were streaks of gray, and what had surprised and confused her, red. By her left knee a flowery pattern of broken blood vessels was darkening into a bruise. She tried to smell herself. She sometimes imagined she must smell terrible.

It seemed she had always watched herself grow older while sitting on the toilet. Sitting on the toilet, she found she couldn't avoid looking at her legs, her belly, her pubic hair. She couldn't avoid smelling herself.

She stood up and looked at herself in the mirror. She looked for scars, bruises, signs of corruption she might have missed before. She pretended her face was a patient's, and she washed it, brushed her hair. As a child she'd pretended her face was a doll's face, her hair a doll's hair. She'd never trusted mirrors. They didn't show the secrets inside.

"I have to go back," Elaine said coming out of the bathroom. "We're short-handed. They count on me. And I can't let Betty work that ward alone."

But Mark was busy fiddling with the VCR. "Huh? Oh yeah . . . well, you do what you think is right, honey. Hey—I got us a tape from one of the security people. The cops confiscated it two weeks ago and it's been circulating ever since." Elaine walked slowly around the bed and stood by Mark as he adjusted the contrast. "Pretty crudely made, but you can still make out most of it."

The screen was dark, with occasional lighter shadows floating through that dark. Then twin pale spots resolved out of the distortion, moving rapidly left and right, up and down. Elaine thought of headlights gone crazy, maybe a moth's wings. Then the camera pulled back suddenly, as if startled, and she saw that it was a black man's immobile face, but with eyes that jumped around as if they were being given some sort of electrical shock. Frightened eyes. Eyes moving no no no.

But as the camera dwelled on this face, Elaine noticed that there was more wrong here than simple fright. The dark skin of the face looked torn all along the hairline, peeled back, and crusted a dark red. A cut bisected the left cheek; she thought she could see several tissue layers deep into the valley it made. And when the head moved, she saw a massive hole just under the chin where throat cartilage danced in open air.

"That's one of them," she said in a soft voice filled with awe. "A zombie."

"The tape was smuggled in from somewhere down South, I hear," Mark said distractedly, moving even closer to the screen. "Beats me how they can still get these videos into the city."

"But the quarantine . . ."

"Supply and demand, honey." As the camera moved back farther, Elaine was surprised to see live, human hands pressing down on the zombie's shoulders. "Get a load of this," Mark said, an anxious edge to his voice.

The camera jerked back suddenly to show the zombie pressed against gray wooden planks—the side of a barn or some other farm building. The zombie was naked: large wounds covered much of its body. Like a decoration, an angry red scar ran the length of the dangling, slightly paler penis. Six or seven large men in jeans and old shirts —work clothes—were pushing the zombie flat against the gray wood, moving their rough hands around to avoid its snapping teeth. The more they avoided its teeth, the more manic the zombie became, jerking its head like a striking snake, twisting its head side to side and snapping its mouth.

An eighth man—fat, florid, baggy tits hanging around each side of his bib overalls—carried a bucket full of hammers onto the scene and handed one to each of the men restraining the zombie. Then the fat man reached deeper into the bucket and came out with a handful of ten-penny nails, which he also distributed to the men.

Mark held his breath as the men proceeded to drive the nails through the body of the zombie—through shoulders, arms, hands, ankles—pinning it like a squirming lizard on the boards.

The zombie showed no pain, but struggled against the nails, tearing wider holes. Little or no blood dripped from these holes, but Elaine did think she could detect a clear, glistening fluid around each wound.

The men stared at the zombie for a moment. A couple of them giggled like adolescent girls, but for the most part they looked dissatisfied.

One of the men nailed the zombie's ears to the wall. Another used several nails to pin the penis and scrotum; several more nails severed it. The zombie pelvis did a little gyration above the spot where the genitals had become a trophy on the barn wall.

The zombie seemed not to notice the difference. The men laughed and pointed.

There were no screams on this sound track. Just laughter and animalistic zombie grunts.

"Jesus, Mark." Elaine turned away from the TV, ashamed of herself for having watched that long. "Jesus." She absentmindedly stroked his hair, running her hand

down his face, vaguely wondering how she could get him
away from the TV, or at least to turn it off.

"Damn. Look, they're bringing out the ax and the
sickle," Mark said.

"I don't want to look," she said, on the verge of tears.
"I don't want *you* to look either. It's crazy, it's . . . por-
nographic."

"Hey, I know this is pretty sick stuff, but I think it tells
us something about the way things *are* out there. Christ,
they won't show it to us on the news. Not the way it *really*
is. We need to know things like this exist."

"I know goddamn well they exist! I don't need it rubbed
in my face!"

Elaine climbed into bed and turned her back on him.
She tried to ignore the static-filled moans and giggles coming from the TV. She pretended she was sick in a hospital
bed, that she had no idea what was going on in the world
and never could. A minute or two later Mark turned off
the TV. She imagined the image of the zombie's head fading, finally just its startled eyes showing, then nothing.

She felt Mark's hands gently rubbing her back. Then he
lay down on the bed, half on top of her, still rubbing her
tight flesh.

"They're not in Denver," he said softly. "There's still
been no sightings. No zombies here, ma'am." The rubbing
moved to her thighs. She tried to ignore it.

"If there were, would people here act like those red-
necks in your damn video? Jesus, Mark. Nobody should
be allowed to behave that way."

He stopped rubbing. She could hear him breathing.
"People do strange things sometimes," he finally said.
"Especially in strange times. Especially groups of people.
They get scared and they lose control." He resumed rubbing her shoulders, then moved to her neck. "There are no
zombies in Denver, honey. No sightings. All the news
types keep telling us that. You *know* that; you're always
watching them."

"Maybe they won't look the same."

"What do you mean?"

"Maybe they won't look the same here as they do everywhere else. Maybe it'll take a different form, and we won't

know what to look for. They think it's a virus—well, viruses mutate, they have different forms. Maybe the doctors and the Health Department and all those reporters aren't as smart as they think they are. Christ, it might even be some form of venereal disease."

"Hey. That's not funny."

"You think I intended it to be?" She could feel her anger bunching up the shoulder muscles beneath his hands. She could feel all this beginning to change her; no way would she be the same after it all stopped. If it ever stopped.

"I know. I know," he said. "This is hard on all of us." Then he started kissing her. Uncharitably, she wondered if it was because he'd run out of things to say to her. But she found her body responding, even though her head was sick with him and all his easy answers and explanations.

His kisses ran down her neck and over her breasts like a warm liquid. And her body welcomed it, had felt so cold before. "Turn out the light, please, Mark," she said, grudgingly giving into the body, hating the body for it. He left silently to turn out the light, then was back again, kissing her, touching her, warming her one ribbon of flesh at a time.

In the darkness she could not see her own body. She could imagine away the blemishes, the ugly, drifting spots, the dry patches of skin, the small corruptions patterning death. And she could imagine that his breath was always sweet smelling. She could imagine his hair dark and full. She could imagine the image of the zombie's destroyed penis out of her head when Mark made love to her. And in this darkness she could almost imagine that Mark would never die.

His body continued to fondle her after she knew his head had gone to sleep.

Mark's kiss woke her up the next morning. "Last night was wonderful," he whispered. "Glad you finally got over whatever was bothering you." That last comment made her angry, and she tried to tell him that, but she was too sleepy and he'd already left. And then she was sorry he was gone and wished he would come back so his touch would make her body feel beautiful again.

She stared at the dead gray eye of the TV, then glanced at the VCR. Apparently Mark had taken his video with him. She was relieved, and a little ashamed of herself. She turned the TV on. The eye filled with static, but she could hear the female newscaster's flat, almost apathetic voice. ". . . the federal government has reported increased progress with the so-called 'zombie' epidemic . . ." Then this grainy, washed-out bit of stock footage came on the screen: men in hunters' clothing and surplus fatigues shooting zombies in the head from a safe distance. Shooting them and then moving along calmly down a dirt road. The newscaster appeared on the screen again: silent, emotionless, makeup perfect, her head rolling up into the top of the cabinet.

It was after four in the morning. Betty had handled the ward by herself all night and would need some relief. Elaine dressed quickly and headed upstairs.

Betty wasn't at the nurse's station. Elaine started down the dim-lit corridor, peeking into each room. In the beds dark shadows shook and moved their heads no no no, even in their dreams. But no sign of Betty.

The last room was Tom's, and he wasn't there. She could hear a steady padding of feet up ahead, in the dark tunnel that led to the new wing. She tried the light switch, but apparently it wasn't connected. Out of her pocket she pulled the penlight that she used for making chart notations in patients' darkened rooms. It made a small, distorted circle of illumination. She started down the darkened tunnel, flashing her small light now and then on the uncompleted ceiling, the holes in the walls where they'd run electrical conduit, the tile floor streaked white with plaster dust, littered with wire, pipe, and lumber.

She came out into a giant open area that hadn't yet been divided into rooms. Cable snaked out of large holes in the ceiling, dangled by her face. Streetlight filtered through the tall, narrow windows, striping piles of ceiling tile, paint cans, and metal posts. They were supposed to be finished with all this by next month. She wondered if they would even bother, given how things were in the city. The wing looked more like a structure they were stripping, demolishing, than one they were constructing. Like a building under autopsy, she thought. She could no longer hear the other footsteps ahead of her. She heard her own steps, crunching the grit under foot, and her own ragged breath.

She flashed her light overhead, and something flashed back. A couple of cameras projected from a metal beam. Blind, their wires wrapped uselessly around the beam. She walked on, following the connections with her light. There were a series of blank television monitors, their enormous gray eyes staring down at her.

Someone cried softly in the darkness ahead. Elaine aimed her light there, but all she could see were crates, paneling leaned against the wall and stacked on the floor, metal supports and crosspieces. A tangle of sharp angles. But then there was that cry again. "Betty? Tom?"

A pale face loomed into the blurred, yellowed beam. A soft shake of the face, side to side. The eyes were too white, and had a distant stare.

"Betty?" The face shook and shook again. Betty stumbled out of a jumble of cardboard boxes, construction and stored medical supplies breaking beneath her stumbling feet.

"No . . ." Betty's mouth moved as if in slow-motion. Her lipstick looked too bright, her mascara too dark. "No," she said again, and something dark dripped out of her eyes as her head began to shake.

Elaine's light picked up a glint in Betty's right hand. "Betty?" Betty stumbled forward and fell, keeping that right hand out in front of her. Elaine stepped closer thinking to help Betty up, but then saw that Betty's right arm was swinging slowly side to side, a scalpel clutched tightly in her hand. "Betty! Let me help you!"

"No!" Betty screamed. Her head began to thrash back and forth on the litter-covered floor. Her cheeks rolled again and again over broken glass. Blood welled, smeared, and stained her face as her head moved no no no. She struggled to control the hand holding the scalpel. Then she suddenly plunged it into her throat. Her left hand came up jerkily and helped her pull the scalpel through muscle and skin.

Elaine fell to her knees, grabbed paper and cloth, anything at hand to dam the dark flow from Betty's throat. After a minute or two she stopped and turned away.

There were more noises off in the darkness. At the back of the room where she'd first seen Betty, Elaine found a doorless passage to another room. Her light now had a vague reddish tinge. She wondered hazily if there was blood on the flashlight lens, or blood in her eyes. But the light still showed the way. She followed it, hearing a harsh, wet sound. For just a moment she thought that maybe Betty might still be alive. She started to go back when she heard it again; it was definitely in the room ahead of her.

She tried not to think of Betty as she made her way through the darkness. *That wasn't Betty. That was just her body.* Elaine's mother used to babble things like that to her all the time. Spiritual things. Elaine didn't know what she herself felt. Someone dies, you don't know them anymore. You can't imagine what they might be thinking.

The room had the sharp smell of fresh paint. Drop cloths had been piled in the center of the floor. The windows were crisscrossed by long stretches of masking tape, and outside lights left odd patterns like angular spiderwebs on all the objects in the room.

A heavy cord dropped out of the ceiling to a small switch box on the floor, which was in turn connected to a large mercury lamp the construction crew must have been using. Elaine bent over and flipped the switch.

The light was like an explosion. It created strange, skeletal shadows in the drop cloths, as if she were suddenly seeing *through* them. She walked steadily toward the pile, keeping an eye on those shadows.

Elaine reached out her hand and several of the cloths flew away.

My god, Betty killed him! Betty killed him and cut off that awful, shaking head! The head was a small, sad mound by the boy's filthy, naked body. A soft whispering seemed to enter Elaine's ear, which brought her attention back to that head.

She stopped to feel the draft, but there was no draft, even though she could hear it rising in her head, whistling through her hair and making it grow longer, making it grow white, making her older.

Because of a trick of the light the boy's—Tom's—eyes looked open in his severed head. Because of a trick of the light the eyes blinked several times as if trying to adjust to that light.

He had a soft, confused stare, like a stuffed toy's. His mouth moved like a baby's. Then his naked, headless body sat up on the floor. Then the headless body struggled to its feet, weaving unsteadily. *No inner ear for balance,* Elaine thought, and almost laughed. She felt crazed, capable of anything.

The body stood motionless, staring at Elaine. Staring at her. The nipples looked darker than normal and seemed to track her as she moved sideways across the room. The hairless breasts gave the body's new eyes a slight bulge. The navel was flat and neutral, but Elaine wondered if the body could smell her with it. The penis—the tongue— curled in and out of the bearded mouth of the body's new face. The body moved stiffly, puppet-like, toward its former head.

The body picked up its head with one hand and threw it out into a darkened corner of the room. It made a sound like a wet mop slapping the linoleum floor. Elaine heard a soft whimpering that soon ceased. She could hear ugly, moist noises coming from the body's new bearded mouth. She could hear skin splitting, she could see blood dripping to the dusty floor as the body's new mouth widened and brought new lips up out of the meaty darkness inside.

The sound of a wheelchair rolling in behind her. She turned and watched as the old woman grabbed each side of her ancient-looking, spasming head. The head continued its insistent no no no even as the hands and arms increased their pressure, the old lady's body quaking from the strain. Then suddenly the no no no stopped, the arms lifted up on the now-motionless head, and pulled it away from the body, cracking open the spine and stretching the skin and muscle of the neck until they tore or snapped apart like rotted bands of elastic. The old woman's fluids

gushed, then suddenly stopped, both head and body seal-
ing the breaks with pale tissues stretched almost to trans-
parency.

The new face on the old woman's body was withered,
pale, almost hairless, and resembled the old face to a remarkable degree. The new eyes sagged lazily, and Elaine
wondered if this body might be blind.

The old woman's head gasped, and was still. The young
male body picked up the woman's dead head and stuffed it
into its hairy mouth. Its new, pale pink lips stretched and
rolled. Elaine could see the stomach acid bubbling on
those lips, the steadily diminishing face of the old lady
appearing now and then in the gaps between the male
body's lips as the body continued its digestion. The old
woman's denuded skull fell out on the linoleum and rattled its way across the floor.

Elaine closed her eyes and tried to remember everything
her mother had ever told her. Someone dies and you don't
know them anymore. It's just a dead body—it's not my
friend. My friend lives in the head forever. Death is a
mystery. Stay away from crowds. Crowds want to eat you.

She wanted Mark here with her. She wanted Mark to
touch her body and make her feel beautiful. No. People
can't be trusted. No. She wanted to love her own body.
No. She wanted her body to love her. No. She tried to
imagine Mark touching her, making love to her. No. With
dead eyes, mouth splitting at the corners. No. Removing
his head and shoving it deep inside her, his eyes and
tongue finding and eating all her secrets.

No no no, her head said. Elaine's head moved no no no.
And each time her vision swept across the room with the
rhythmic swing of her shaking head, the bodies were
closer.

Choices

BY GLEN VASEY

[1]

Provisional Center for Disease Control
Puerto Nuevo, Florida
Interoffice Memorandum #57–608
From: Kenneth J. Howell, Acting Director
To: Malcolm Foley, Director of Research

Malcolm,
This just came into my hands today. Rather than take the time to edit it, and risk omitting something you might find useful, I had Marcie type it just as I received it. I added only one note, near the end where the writing changes hands. I still have the original. It is in a travel-worn spiral notebook, the kind you used to be able to pick up new at any five-and-dime. If you think it could help in any way, send word and I'll see it gets to you. It is, by all appearances, authentic.

The primary point of interest is the final dozen pages or so.

I have included a map of the general location where it was picked up. You may want to have your people investigate, if that is possible. Maybe even bring some of these people in for examinations or something. If I can be of any assistance, just holler.

I don't know if this will be a help to you, or simply another distraction. I know how understaffed and overworked you are, but I figured that a shot in the dark is better than holding your fire at times like these. My shot in the dark is sending this your way, relatively risk free. Yours will be deciding what, if anything, to do with it now. Not so easy a choice, either way.

I don't suppose it helps much for me to say that I
don't envy your position, but I'll say it anyway. This
is probably the second time in history that it has been
less harrowing to be a bureaucrat than a scientist.
The first was during the Spanish Inquisition.
Oh, for the good old days!
Keep the faith,
Ken

For a moment Ken Howell almost smiles at the brief
witticism with which he has concluded the memo. Then
he nearly weeps.

Earlier in the day he had found his secretary weeping.
He had tried to comfort her. Had offered her a few lame
words of solace. In so doing he had discovered one of life's
weary truths: there are no words of solace that do not
point out and accentuate the very cause of our need for
solace.

She had continued crying, so he'd left her office for his
own. He did not want her tears to weaken him. There was
no percentage in that.

I AM NOT CRYING

He is in a position of responsibility. One that requires
him to display strength and unclouded judgment. He cannot let the others come to doubt him. He cannot allow
himself the luxury of doubt.

I AM NOT CRYING

No. He will not weep. Not now. Not even here, alone.

I AM NOT CRYING ALONE

A disembodied voice echoing through the corridors of
his brain. Nostalgic. Memorial. Elegiac. Foreign and forever unknowable.

I AM NOT ALONE!!

He hears Marcie moving restlessly in the adjoining office. He knows that she is ready to leave.

Soon he will go to her.

Soon they will leave the building together and walk
across the compound to their living quarters, as they always do.

Just as soon as he can find the strength to cease his
weeping.

[2]

The silence of the June dusk was underscored, rather than interrupted, by the fluttering thrash of the spiral notebook as it flew through the air toward the highway. Branches rustled softly as they parted for it. Pages fanned and rippled in the breeze of its passage. There was a muffled thump as it landed at the base of some thorny-looking scrub brush, not twenty feet from the deserted road.

That was all. Brief. Temporal. Quickly past. Then silence reigned again, all the more tyrannically for having been thus emphasized.

Dawson drew his legs up so that his chin was resting upon his knees. He wrapped his arms around his shins and pulled inward. Pulled harder still.

I AM NOT CRYING

Pulled until his thighs pressed into his chest so vigorously that every muscle in his body bloomed with pain.

I AM NOT CRYING

Pulled harder still. Back, ribs, neck, jaw, arms, legs, buttocks. Every muscle clenched willfully.

I AM NOT CRYING ALONE

His will: to become a well of pain. Physical pain. Ephemeral pain. Consciousness-distorting pain. Pain he could control. He had only to relax and it would abate.

I AM NOT ALONE!!

Unlike the pain of his ineptitude. The pain of loss, despair, loneliness and fear. Unlike the pain of words.

Earlier his head had been filled with words. Somehow he had thought that they were dying to get out. Somehow he had believed that he might be able to use them to escape his other pains, to make some sense out of his utterly senseless situation. But when he had tried to use them, the words had fled. Only the primal scream had remained, and that had been but little help. Having vented that scream in a scrawl that had covered one single page, he had thrown the book away into the dusk.

He had risked his life for that book.

Had risked his life, and feared he yet might lose it, on the chance that words might help him stay alive.

To escape such thoughts he pulled harder on his legs, then relaxed himself completely and luxuriated in the brief pleasure that washed through his body. Then he sighed and gently pulled his shirt away from his left shoulder to examine the deep red scratch there.

He thought about infections. About the virus, germ, bacteria, fungus—whatever the hell it was—that had changed the world so drastically.

Shivering and sweating simultaneously, he found himself hoping that they were both symptoms of fear rather than fever. Even psychosis would be preferred.

Had that been a sound, or the thought of a sound? He sat frozen with immediate alertness, words and chills and sweats forgotten. Listening.

I WILL SURVIVE!

Not wanting them to find him. Not wanting to die.

I WILL TO SURVIVE!

Not wanting to die like that.

It wasn't precisely a will to live, but it was something.

Though I don't know why.

And it was all that he had left.

The night's darkness had become complete before Dawson was able to convince himself to move again. Whether the sound had been real, or made of mind, he knew then that it presented no immediate threat. It had not been repeated. It was not advancing on him.

He knew, too, that though he was far too weary to continue traveling, he could not permit himself the luxury of sleep. To sleep would be to invite them to approach as closely and incautiously as they wished.

He rose and scrambled down the wooded slope toward the highway. On his knees he thrust his hands into the thorny brambles and groped until he found his prize. When he withdrew the notebook, his hands were bleeding from a dozen minor cuts. He didn't notice them. His eyes were blurred with fresh tears.

Again he heard a sound. This time he was certain of it. Worst of all he could even place the direction from which it had come. It had come from up the slope. From somewhere near the spot that he had left his backpack leaning up against a tree.

He cursed himself for seven kinds of fool and peered through the darkness, searching for movement. He saw nothing.

He waited, listening again. Again he heard nothing further. He wondered if this new silence were a ploy, an attempt to catch him off his guard. An attempt to lure him back to the tree. Back to the backpack that he could not leave without.

He told himself that the dead were not so canny, then immediately reminded himself that there were others.

He waited what seemed a very long time, clutching the notebook to his chest, before he finally made his way, slowly and cautiously, back up the slope. He was standing beside his backpack, just beginning to breathe again, when his heart was stopped by the sound of an owl in a nearby tree.

Then there was silence.

Darkness had made his previous words invisible to him. He was grateful for that kindness. He knew them by heart and had neither the need nor the desire to be reminded of them.

I AM NOT CRYING

He didn't need light. He knew that he could write by feel. If only words would come to him. Something other than the primal scream. Something to retain his interest and attention. Something to keep him awake.

He set the notebook and pen aside and got his first-aid kit out of his backpack. He wet a piece of cotton with some alcohol, then pulled his shirt away to clean the scratch on his shoulder. He rubbed hard, causing a warm, raw, stinging sensation to spring up. The scratch did not seem to be infected.

"Does not *seem* to be," he murmured.

"Not yet."

He rubbed harder, moving his lips in silent prayer, uncertain to whom the prayer was addressed. His mind drifted back then. Re-envisioned the scene. The origin of this particular concern.

* * *

The early afternoon had been hot and humid. Brilliant. Satanically sunny. His head had throbbed, pounded, screeched, and screamed with a headache whose magnitude he would have deemed neither possible nor survivable even a day earlier. He was staggering along the shoulder of a highway weakened by hunger, thirst, weariness and pain. He was wishing that his backpack really was as heavy as it felt, that it held more than it did of both food and water.

On the back of his pack hung a cardboard sign, with letters ten inches high. The sign proclaimed no destination, but rather a state of being.

ALIVE, was all it said. He hoped that it would give passing motorists pause. Particularly those with guns. It had seemed a good idea when he had first conceived it two weeks before, but on this golden afternoon he was no longer certain of the sign's veracity. His headache was distorting everything: sight, sound, thought and feeling.

"Do they know that they are dead?" he had wondered. "How do they know?"

He stumbled and shambled gracelessly along the shoulder of the road thinking, "I have seen enough to know that this is how they move. Is this how they feel? How they perceive things?"

His eyes were rigid, his face contorted in an agonized squint. He was blinded by sunlight and by pain. Dizzy and weak, all of his senses were drowned by the excruciating immediacy violating his temples, his scalp, his retinas and the base of his skull.

A sign loomed before him. He stopped walking and tried to focus on it. Tried to attempt to divine its meaning.

It bore a name. The name of a town, he was certain, though he could not place it.

He felt, vaguely, that this should mean something to him and sat down abruptly upon the gravel of the shoulder, determined to wait out enlightenment. He knew immediately that he should have left the road. Should have accepted the modest concealment that the weeds and wildflowers would have offered him. But he could not bring himself to rise.

"A town," he thought, "probably small, but a town nonetheless.

"There will be a concentration of them. That's it! That's the meaning. A concentration of them. I have to skirt the town. Don't draw too close. Don't let them sense me."

But he had continued to feel that some part of the sign's message was still lost to him, that there was something yet he should be thinking about. So he remained seated, continued swimming in place through his pain.

Suddenly a car sped by, racing toward the town. At first it had merely startled him, but a moment later the incident disturbed him far more profoundly. The car had approached from behind him. Despite its considerable noise he had been wholly unaware of it until it had been virtually on top of him. His headache had completely obliterated his senses.

"That's the message," he staggered to his feet.

"Need something to stop it, bring me back. Can't skirt the town, gotta go in."

He knew that the townies would sense him. Would converge on him as soon as they did. Would devour him and turn him into one of them, if they got the chance. But walking the highway half-blind, half-deaf and three-quarters senseless was not a viable option.

Once in town a sense of exultation began to filter through the mass of pain he had become. Finally engaged in a definite activity with an immediately foreseeable conclusion, adrenalin had kicked into his blood, juicing him high. When he had marked the first of his slow and clumsy pursuers, it was a thrill of confidence in competition that raced through him, rather than a sense of deadly fear.

"I *know* I am not one of them," he had shouted, "They do not feel like *this!*"

Though his pain had not diminished, his mind and senses had grown more acute, his limbs incredibly agile. He found it easy to outsmart and outdistance the townies.

When he spotted the drug store's smashed plate-glass

door, he darted through it without breaking stride. Inside, he moved rapidly up one aisle and down the next, his head pivoting, his eyes searching. His hand was reaching for the box of analgesics within the same second that his eyes had found them. In the space of another second he had turned to retrace his steps and make his exit.

Then he heard the sound of something shuffling through the broken glass at the front of the store.

"Don't panic," he told himself quickly.

"Get that thing away from the door first."

He moved to the center aisle to gain an unobstructed view of the entrance.

The thing he saw shambling toward him had once been a slender, elderly man. Now its face was a bloated blue-green mask, as soft and swollen as the face of a drowning victim. Even at a distance its stench was stultifying to Dawson's adrenalin-enhanced sense of smell. It wore a fishing vest, dark green trousers, and hiking boots, all of which were caked with dried gore. As was its mouth, its cheeks, chin and neck.

Dawson thought that he could beat the ghoul to the door by simply moving swiftly to one of the vacant aisles and making a run for it. But he wanted to be certain, and he knew that his chances would improve if he held his own ground just a little longer, letting the thing draw nearer to him.

He looked around quickly for something to use as a weapon. Instead his eye was caught by a stack of brightly colored spiral notebooks. On an impulse wholly ungoverned by thought he stooped and picked one up.

When he stood again, he saw that the broken door framed yet another of the ghouls, this one a portly woman in a once-white waitress uniform.

Now his panic rose. How many would there be? Enough to trap him in the store? Enough to track him in the aisles?

He permitted the first to draw closer than he had originally intended, to insure that the second, too, would pursue him down the center aisle.

When he thought that she was far enough from the door, he made his move. He spun to his right, took two strides, hooked a quick left, and went racing down the far aisle.

In spite of his haste his eyes managed to register, and his brain to comprehend, the existence of a display of writing instruments hanging on the wall to his right. It shouldn't have made any difference to him, but before he could stop it, his right hand was reaching out, making a quick stab at a package of pens.

The package caught on its metal hanger and would not come free. So he committed the most foolish act of his life. He skidded to a halt and made a second lunge for the pens. They remained just out of reach.

"Idiot!" he screamed. But he took one more step back and freed them from the rack.

His mind was a chaos of imprecations and death visions, but when he made it to the end of the aisle, he saw nothing in the doorway and bolted through it.

The hand that clamped down on his shoulder and arrested his movement was the vise of death itself.

The face that the hand belonged to had, not long since, been that of a teenager. Now it was blistered by acne turned to rot. It was the face of leprosy, far advanced. The neck of the thing was half eaten away. Maggots writhed in that hellish wound.

Dawson screamed and drove his feet against the ground with bruising force. His shirt tore, and he felt a burning streak of pain trace a line across his shoulder.

He had freed himself, in spite of his idiocy.

[3]

I am well concealed. The night is quiet. I am safe for the moment.

Safe?

For the moment. They are incapable of stealth. I think.

The others, the random violent gangs of those yet living, seem to refuse stealth. They are always making noise. Perhaps it is obsessional. An attempt to scare off death. To scare off their awareness of what has happened to this world. A way of converting everything into one big perpetual Saturday-night bar brawl.

Am I any different? Trying to write as if the world knew, or cared, that I was still going on? As if it might ever be read by anyone? Am I really trying to confront this, sort it out? Or am I merely trying to avoid the issue in my own way? Making my own kind of noise? My own banging of pots and pans against the eclipse?

Does it really matter?

He sighed then and leaned his head back against the rough bark of the tree. He closed his eyes and heaved a deep, shuddering breath.

He had forced his hand to write, his mind to concentrate upon the act, to avoid remembering the afternoon and, in some way, to justify the awful risks he had taken. But the writing was a failure. Instead of stifling thought it had brought the questions back to haunt him again. The same questions that had run through his mind repeatedly and incessantly over the course of the past two weeks.

Where am I now?

How far have I to go?

How long have I to live?

What are my chances?

What are my options?

Will the living ever have the world again?

Does it really matter?

Any of it?

Questions that were so familiar that their presence had very little power to irritate him any further. He had long since lost faith in the existence of answers, and that had rendered the questions impotent. They were not enough, even, to keep him awake.

He came awake abruptly, feeling hands upon his arms and legs. Hands upon his shoulders and his chest. Hands pulling him in all directions at once.

He screamed and hands came up to cover his mouth, stifling the sound. He bit these hands and was shocked as the pain raced up his arm and spine to electrify his brain.

The hands on his mouth were his own. They were real. The others had been phantoms. Creatures invented by his own stress and incaution.

He shuddered as he sat up. His eyes darted rapidly about, trying to pierce the surrounding darkness.

There were no further sounds.

He was alone.

I AM NOT ALONE!!

Blessedly alone.

   I have a goal.

In the past keeping a journal had helped Dawson to sort things out. Had helped him to get through trying times with some portion of his sanity intact. Had provided him with a constructive escape from the immediacy of his various dilemmas. Had helped him to cope. Now those times were long ago and a world away. Coping had become a new thing. He was no longer balancing an awkward relationship, a career decision, financial concerns or the unexpected death of a close friend. Now writing was a way to avoid sleep. Avoiding sleep was a way to avoid death. A way to avoid the hands that would, the next time certainly, find him vulnerable.

The line that he had just scrawled at the top of the new page had seemed a good beginning, but he had no idea what should follow it.

Finally he decided to trace it back. To try to go back to the moments at which he had made his decision, had chosen his goal. Back to the time when the idea of the goal seemed one of hope, rather than desperation.

   Time was, when I—and I was not alone in this— took for granted that the cataclysm, the great world crash course in catastrophe and death, would be nuclear annihilation. That it would be unannounced and just sudden enough to eliminate any possible thought of escape. That there would, really, be no time in which to make choices. Or, perhaps, that two choices would remain for those lucky souls who had survived the initial blast:

1) Grab your ass and run, until you can run no further.

2) Hunker down on that selfsame ass and pretend at bravery, pretend at some last vestige of defiance by making it clear that they no longer had the power to make you run.

Of course neither choice would make much difference. At best it is the choice of the Christian facing the lion: flee, only to be chased, caught, and eaten; or refuse to flee, robbing the spectators only of the chase. A question more of stance and personality than of principle or wisdom. The bloody outcome the same, in either case.

Not a good situation, surely, but at least that much would have been clear from the start. There would be no room for self-delusion. There is something reassuring about a situation in which all choices are equal, even if they are all equally bad. One is absolved of any personal responsibility.

Then God, in his infinite mercy and wisdom, pulls the big switch on us. Throws us a curveball—no, a knuckler—when we were all geared up for the heat, and no doubt busts a gut laughing as we tie ourselves in knots trying to hit it.

Oh, yes! He left us lucky survivors with a veritable plethora of choices. And, lo! they do not all lead unto death! No, not by a long road. In fact, the great majority of them lead to something considerably worse —though only after a long and painful march, of course. I assume that it's all very purgative.

So his sacred prerogative of free will remains intact, as ever, propelled by fear and buoyed by false hope.

Dawson paused to wipe sweat from his forehead, but his mind never left the stream of his composition. He was wholly unaware that he had achieved the level of escape and absorption that he had once dared to hope for. He was writing with the intense concentration that he had known in his midteens, when he had wanted to be the new Thoreau. With the lack of self-consciousness he had achieved somewhat later, when he was keen on being the second coming of Kerouac. With the lack of constraint he knew only in his late twenties and early thirties, when he had long since given up any thoughts of literary fame and kept a journal simply for the therapy and joy that it provided.

Escape, immersion, involvement achieved, he became very much awake.

> For the hope that he has offered us is not "the thing with feathers" that Emily Dickinson once knew.
> No!
> His hope is the thing with teeth. It is the hope of survival. The hope that one might prolong one's personal experience of horror and deprivation. The foolish but stubborn hope that somehow, after day upon day of terror and pain, he might smile down upon whoever remains and lift his awful curse.
> We are all drowning. A drowning man cannot easily discern the difference between a timber and a straw. A desperate man cannot distinguish between a hope that is never likely to pan out, and one that *cannot* under any circumstances.
> Yet these are the choices we must make.
> These are the hopes he has left us.
> I have a goal.
> Straw or timber?
> A desperate man grasps at what he can.

Dawson paused, breathing deeply. He cast his head back to look up through the tangle of branches and noticed that the sky was beginning to dismiss its darkness.

He listened. There were no disturbing sounds. Only birds, making virtually the same noises that birds have made through all the ages of mankind.

[4]

> A godsend.
> I hope.
> Godsend or self-activated trap, it hardly matters. I

cannot survive forever without sleep. Real sleep. I will stay the night. I have chosen the likely death of staying in one place and submitting to unconsciousness, over the certain death of attempting to continue on through my exhaustion.

I am hoping that I am not too grossly underestimating their abilities to sense and to seek. Never before have I felt so claustrophobic. Never before have I had so excellent a reason to.

The small, boxlike house was neither wide nor long, though it stood two stories. It had given Dawson the impression of a retreat, a hunting or fishing camp where an urbanite might escape his lot for a couple of weeks and a half-dozen weekends each year. It was almost out of sight from the road, and Dawson felt that if he hadn't been moving slowly, and on foot, he would have missed it altogether. He found that thought to be a friendly one.

It hadn't been the thought of sanctuary that had given him the necessary courage to investigate, it had been the hope of finding food. Any food to supplement his godweary and diminishing rations of dried fruit and nuts.

Once he had assured himself that the place was truly deserted, he lost no time in reaching his decision. He quickly set about constructing makeshift barricades for the door and windows on the first floor. He knew that the simple restraints that he was building would not keep them out for long, if indeed they should discover him, but he hoped that they would prove substantial enough to give the ghouls some difficulty. If they were enough to delay the beasts, and to increase the amount of noise that any entry would create, they would have served the purpose they were built for.

Only later did he search for food.

The pantry turned out to be a pleasanter surprise than he'd have dared to hope: canned ham, tuna, stew and a variety of canned vegetables, all in great quantity. There were two full five-gallon plastic water bottles and, prize of prizes, an unopened bottle of whiskey and one of rum. These final items presented him with a dilemma that he

knew he'd have to work out later, but he could not deny
the pleasure that their presence had inspired in him.

He filled his arms and made his way upstairs, to the
larger of the two small bedrooms.

> I know that drinking in this situation is foolish. I
> must remain alert. But to take advantage of the posi-
> tive aspects of my circumstance, it is imperative that
> I sleep. To sleep I must curb my anxieties, my sense
> of being trapped. No other method seems to be forth-
> coming, so I will drink. Only in moderation, of
> course. Just enough to help me sleep.

Later, in a sloppier hand, he wrote:

> I cannot stop wondering how long I have. How
> keen, how far-reaching are their senses? How near
> are they now? Will I waken in the middle of the night
> to find them hammering on the door? Worse? Will I
> waken with their godawful hands and teeth
> STOP!
> I know I may be drinking my death in this godfor-
> saken trap
> ENOUGH!
> Does it matter? Does any of it matter? Why pre-
> tend? Ultimately there is no escape, just stays of exe-
> cution. I die tonight, tomorrow, some other day or
> night.
> I die.
> That is what it all boils down to. Why pretend
> otherwise? The world is theirs now. We are all
> doomed. No escapes remain, only choices.
> I have chosen to die drunk in this bed, trapped
> inside this house. If I wake tomorrow, I may choose
> another way to die.
> These are the only choices that remain to me. This
> is how I am permitted to utilize God's sacred prerog-
> ative.

[5]

Long rays of late-morning sunshine suffused everything
in the room into a single golden haze. Dawson closed his
eyes against the gentle glow and stretched.

"Bear of a hangover," he muttered.

He glanced over toward the nightstand to check the
time.

No nightstand.

No time.

It all came back very suddenly.

> They have not found me.
> Yet.
> But I do not feel capable of traveling now. The
> drink was a stupid mistake. Letting it get so out of
> hand. Like on a fucking holiday.
> Perhaps that's what I needed, though. Release.
> Oblivion. If the delay it has caused doesn't kill me, I
> think I will consider the episode less harshly.
> I will try to spend another night here. I prefer to
> travel by daylight and have already missed much of
> today's. I will not drink tonight.
> I am hoping that their absence now indicates that
> they are all too far away to sense me. Straw or tim-
> ber?
> I will spend the time I have here writing. It is the
> only safe peace upon which I can draw.

Three weeks earlier Dawson had been fooling around in
the kitchen of his suburban bachelor flat, drinking beer
and putting the finishing touches on a mammoth pizza,
preparatory to sliding it in the oven. Mike, who had been
his closest friend for better than fifteen years, was in the
kitchen with him, keeping him company and offering expert advice on pepperoni placement. Scott, a new acquain-
tance more Mike's friend than Dawson's, was in the living
room watching the Dodgers and Mets play the Saturday
afternoon Game of the Week.

That evening the three of them intended to catch the local heroes in person. "A real game," both Mike and Dawson had chided Scott, "an American League game."

It had been a beautiful day. Their moods were excellent.

"Mike, Daws—get in here! Quick!!"

Scott's voice accosted them with such ridiculous urgency that Dawson had rolled his eyes while Mike scrinched up his face and answered, in a lilting falsetto, "Coming, dear."

"Hurry dammit!"

Dawson picked up the pizza.

"Go ahead Mike, no need for both of us to miss the earth-shattering replay. I'll be right in, you can tell me all about it."

As Mike left the room, Dawson carried the pizza over to the oven and wondered how Scott could get so worked up over nothing. Not only were the two teams in the wrong league, but they were the easiest two teams in that wrong league to root against.

"Well, what can you expect of a Los Angelino?" he muttered, and left the kitchen to join his friends.

The strange looks on their faces told him that something was drastically wrong. The voice from the tv set was not the bubbly effulgence of an inane sportscaster filling dead air. Instead it was the deadly serious, but somehow comically urgent, drone of a tv newsman. A bulletin of some sort.

"Either the missiles are in the air, or the president has another migraine," he thought.

Then he began to listen in earnest.

"You changed the channel, this is part of a movie, right?"

"No."

"A spoof then, like the War of the Worlds broadcast . . . 'We interrupt this meaningless mundane broadcast to bring you . . .'"

"No, man. This is serious."

"What sort of judge are *you*? You thought the Mets and Dodgers were serious."

"Shut the fuck up!"

They listened.

They watched.

The talking head in the box apprised them of the most incredible things. Then it was gone, and they watched some grown men playing with a ball on a green field.

Then the head came back, speaking even more urgently. This time he had film clips to show them too. Eventually the network stopped trying to go back to the game.

That's when Dawson knew that things were really out of hand.

The three of them sat in Dawson's living room for an unknowable period of time, mesmerized by phosphor dots, incomprehension and fear. They were subjected to a veritable parade of talking heads: reporters, so-called experts, and the seemingly inescapable man on the street.

The advice of the experts was, at best, difficult to fathom:

—Stay where you are. Secure it. It is unsafe to venture out.

—Seek a federally sanctioned shelter. Emergency personnel will be on hand to aid you. Stay tuned for a complete listing of government-run emergency shelters in your area.

—Stay clear of all federal and state-run shelters. Communications to many are down. Many have been overrun.

—Call this HOTLINE for expert advice and up-to-the-minute details of the situation in your area.

So they watched the horror unfold, increase in complexity, and develop new facets and twists of terror, in the proverbial comfort of Dawson's own home. It was being vigorously covered on television, thereby abridging any need for them to be anything other than spectators. The tv gave the experience a distinct air of unreality.

Dawson had the strange feeling that he had seen it all before in bits and pieces. The language of the television was the same as it had always been. Even the experts with their dry faces, excitable voices, and competing "facts" seemed only like so many salesmen delivering their eternal pitches:

"Act now . . ."

"Don't delay . . ."

"Operators are standing by . . ."

"Over fifty locations to serve you . . ."

So the three of them continued staring, as each had done for uncountable hours in the course of their lives, at the strange blue phosphorescent glow of the tube.

It didn't occur to them to do anything else.

It didn't occur to them that there was anything else to do.

Eventually Mike roused himself sufficiently to go to the phone and dial the HOTLINE.

He listened to the phone ring.

Twenty times.

Then fifty.

Seventy-five.

Then he returned to the sofa, to sit and listen to the experts a little longer.

The next decisive action that any of them took was when the screen went blank. It was Scott who rose then and fiddled with the set until he found a station that was still broadcasting.

Mesmerized.

Phosphor dots and fear.

Maybe it was simply the fact that someone was knocking on the door. Surely that was a startling enough development itself. Not that the knocking frightened us, we were too far gone for that. Our fear had become abstract, incapable of approaching us in such a fashion. That, in fact, was our real problem at the time.

Besides, in the world we were used to—and had refused, to that point, to divorce ourselves of— knocks on the door were, at worst, annoyances, never threats. So even though we had all been informed that the world outside my apartment had changed drastically, I think we shared an instinctive rationale that death would never be polite enough to knock.

Perhaps it was the effect of seeing real people,

made of actual flesh and actual blood, after so many hours of serious, soulless electronic faces.

But I think it was something more than either, or both, of these things.

As soon as he opened the door, Dawson recognized the people on his doorstep, not as individuals, but as a class. He recognized their paraphernalia—their books and magazines and tracts—but most of all their hand was tipped by the patented, vacuous, God's-gracious-grins they wore.

For a moment Dawson was seized by a wave of vertigo. Everything seemed suddenly normal again.

It was a natural. One moment he had been sitting with friends watching God-knew-what on the tube, and in the next he was opening the front door to the local chapter of God's militia. Both were basically reliable components of his mundane Suburban-American existence.

He opened the door wide and smiled broadly at the four of them. Their spokesperson, an attractive black woman in her early thirties, launched her well-rehearsed spiel. Her voice was dripping with rapt sincerity and eagerly earnest goodwill.

Dawson began to laugh. It was a reed-thin laugh, pitched far too shrilly.

The woman stopped speaking.

Two of her companions moved back a step.

Dawson's laughter diminished, and the woman launched her spiel a second time.

"You have come to ask me," he interrupted, "if I have made my peace with God. Is that it?"

He glared at them maniacally.

One of them gave an uncertain nod.

"Then let me assure you," he went on in a voice made half of whisper and half of shout, "that He and I have never quarreled."

He beamed into their uncomprehending faces.

"In fact," he added, "I never even met the man!"

He slammed the door on them and turned to face his companions. He started laughing again, that same hysterical, high-pitched squeal.

"Can you believe it?" he shouted, "Jehovah's Witlesses, out on a day like this!"

He continued laughing until he collapsed, weeping, to the floor. A shuddering mass of confusion and nothing more.

It was several minutes before Mike moved to help him to his feet. Then Mike guided him back to his chair in front of the television.

What I think it was, was the realization that there were still people in the world. People making choices. People choosing to continue to live, not merely to survive, as we were doing almost in absentia. It seems to me now that that is the difference between living and surviving: the making of choices.

Scott and Mike and I hadn't made a conscious decision since the news had first interrupted our routine. Though, by mere luck, we had survived, we had ceased to be alive. We were merely zombies waiting for the ghouls to find us. How many were there like us? How long did any of them last?

The only thing that had saved us to that point was the fact that ghoulism—or whatever one might wish to call it—was not yet so widespread as it is now.

The only thing that saved us from that point on, I am now convinced, is the fact that the Witnesses found us first and woke us up.

They showed us that there were choices to be made simply by pursuing their own choice, which   pie in the sky or no—they must have known to be tremendously dangerous.

So perhaps they were out doing God's good work, if it is neither vain nor ridiculous for me to think that our personal fate could possibly matter to a God who had permitted these horrors.

Scott was a Vietnam veteran, the kind who maintained a belief that the war had been right and just, and that the United States had wimped out in the end. His choice was to steal a car, his own being unavailable at the time, and make his way to the nearest army installation so that he might re-enlist.

Neither Mike nor Dawson tried to talk him out of this decision, though Scott was forty-four years old and had not kept himself in the best of shape.

Mike, who had grown up within a mile of Dawson's residence, chose to seek the sanctuary of his old grade school. Though Mike had often complained that he had been scarred and victimized by the twin voices of God and discipline during his parochial school career, and though he had often claimed that the most terrifying presence he had ever encountered had been the enormous mass of his third-grade teacher, it was there, and to her in particular, that he felt compelled to turn in his greatest need of guidance and protection.

Dawson didn't try to explain to Mike that, according to his own descriptions of the woman, she had been an ancient and obese heart-attack candidate those many years ago and was now, quite certainly, many years dead.

Sometimes the choices we make, especially under unbearable stress, don't make any coherent sense. We will not allow another man to tell us that. It is the case of the drowning man attempting to mount the straw. Certainly it is imbecilic, but in such situations reason holds little sway. Even if you overcome the drowning man's initial anger and make him understand, you will have succeeded only in robbing him of hope and making him more miserable yet. Unless you have a timber to offer him.

How could I have dissuaded either of them? What had I to offer them in place of their thin straws?

I let them both go.

Even Mike whose choice was, by far, the most foolish.

Even Mike whom I have loved like a brother for better than fifteen years.

Only when he was alone in the house was Dawson able to make his own choice. Once he had, he made his preparations rapidly and left. He did not bother to turn off the TV.

The only choices we are ever really left with are these three: be a leader, be a follower, or be an individual.

Many find security only where the self is given up, subsumed. Where Authority makes the decisions. Where rules are clear and strict. Where orders create Order and are not to be questioned.

Others find it only where they are themselves the Authority and Order that fashions the rules and makes the decisions.

Scott may be safe now, following some well-armed, battle-wise sergeant or lieutenant amidst a throng of like-minded companions. But I doubt it.

Mike may be safe in the darkness of his old school, with his phantom Order protecting him from very real chaos. But that is even easier to doubt.

The Witnesses may still be knocking on peoples' doors, waking people up, protected by some heavenly umbrella. But that, I find, is hardest to believe.

More likely by now they have knocked on one too many doors. Have made the big change. Are still out there making converts, but of a different sort. Their teeth revealed no longer by their God's-gracious-grins, but by the godawful grimace of a hellacious hunger.

Yes. That I find easier to believe, but not to think about.

And I . . . ? I have a goal. Straw or timber? How much farther? Can I make it? What will I find? Does it really matter?

[6]

"You know, a man can make it as far as he's gotta go, if he knows how to handle time.

"A man can hold on the rungs of a tank-car ladder for better'n five hundred miles if he ain't got no choice; if there ain't no way for him to crawl to a better position, and the train don't make no stops to allow him to relocate himself.

"But to do it he's gotta get it straight in his head that no time is gonna pass while he's hangin' there."

An eighteen-year-old Dawson looked on, listening closely. Incredulous, but wanting to believe.

"Now I'm not sayin' that it's gonna be easy, not by a long road, but it's when things ain't easy that a man's gotta learn to assert his control. It's when the world isn't offerin' any respite that a man's gotta manufacture some of his own.

"Sure, when he's hangin' there, his hands and arms and legs and back aren't about to start believin' him. They'll be keepin' their own kinda time. But that ain't where the battle's gotta be fought.

"I figure if a man can't keep his head from gettin' bossed about by his muscles, well . . . we'd have been better off just stayin' in the trees.

"But he can, and there's the rub. If a man has a mind to, he can learn to keep his head still in time. And if he keeps time from passin' up here," dark, leathery fingers tapped a sunburned forehead, "then he can keep himself from givin' his arms and legs the message that they are right: that he *has* been hangin' on too long, that he *does* have too far left to go, that he *might as well* give up the ghost and let himself just slide on down beneath them merciless wheels.

"You see, the thing to remember about muscles is that they gotta get some message from the brain before they can do just about anything. So if a man can keep himself from believin' his muscles' complaints, he can keep himself from givin' in to them. If he can keep his brain from believin' that time is passing, he robs time of its meaning, and it stops altogether.

"Time ain't nothin' but a man-thought thing anyway, so if a man refuses to think it, it don't happen for him."

The weathered face flashed a mischievous smile.

"Course when the train finally does stop and that man finally does get off, it's not just his muscles as'll be arguin' the case against him. Every man-clock at the place he

lights will chime in at callin' him a liar. But that man's
still got his ace card up his sleeve. He gives it any thought
he'll know there weren't no human possible way that he
coulda hung onto that ladder for upwards of six or seven
hours, whatever it took to get him where he is. And that
alone oughta put the proof to it. It's gotta be the clocks
and muscles that are wrong, cause there he is and still
alive. He'd found a hole in time and slipped through that,
'stead of slidin' down beneath them wheels a good bit
back.

"And knowin' that it works that way just makes it that
much easier the next time he finds himself in that kinda
spot."

And Dawson found he could believe, needed to believe.
He shook back his long hair and nodded in vigorous affirmation.

> Leader, follower, or individual?
>
> I like to think I made my choice when I was eigh-
> teen, and have simply deferred its actualization all
> these years.
>
> Only once in my life did I experience a setting in
> which a person could be an individual while main-
> taining the advantages of living in a group. It was a
> marriage of independence and interaction, of freedom
> and support.
>
> It was a brief stay. Afterwards I somehow allowed
> myself to fall back into the ways for which I had been
> trained and educated all my life. I permitted myself
> to accept a position in the lower echelon of the rat
> race I claimed to despise. I let myself be distracted
> from the truths I had claimed I had learned through-
> out that summer turning into fall.
>
> I tell myself now that those truths, my belief in
> them, merely slept and did not die. I tell myself that I
> am now the prodigal son, hoping that some family
> remains for me to return to.

One week after his graduation from high school Dawson was farther from home than he had ever been before.
His backpack and sleeping bag were slung on his back, his

right thumb was pointing to the horizon behind him, and his left hand held a sign that simply read: FURTHER.

By early August he had found himself staying at a hobo camp, "among members of America's forgotten tribe," as he was to record passionately in one of his many journals of the period. Like most Americans he had assumed that hoboism had long since dwindled and died. This was not the only illusion that these people would shatter, or drastically reshape, during his brief stay.

He discovered that not all hobos were hopelessly flawed individuals, failures incapable of living within the society that their lifestyles defied. Some of them were outcasts, surely, but many of them were escapees; people too proud and willful to consign themselves to the strictures and constraints of a more "acceptable" American existence.

Flawed? Certainly. Each in his own way. But no more so than many whom Dawson had met in other walks of life.

Failures? Not at the lives that they had finally chosen for themselves, whatever failures and incompatibilities might have led them to this choice. Therefore, perforce, their choice had been a wise one.

On the whole they were flexible, tolerant and compatible beyond any other class-group in his experience. They combined the habits of self-reliance and selfless cooperation in a way that Dawson had always suspected was too idealistic to be practiced in any real-world setting. And he felt that there was no setting based more in the real world than theirs.

It was there that he met Hoagie.

Hoagie was the most remarkable individual that Dawson had ever met. In his presence Dawson sometimes wondered if he had ever *really* met an individual before.

Hoagie was, by every evidence, only a handful of years older than Dawson, though the ruggedness of his appearance made it difficult to ascribe to him any particular age. He was an educated man, though he had adopted a manner of speech that required one to pay careful attention to the thoughts he was conveying in order to divine that fact. He was a man who had found contemporary American society wanting—"wanting far too much," he would say

—and so had discarded it as best he could. He was a man, so Dawson felt, of unparalleled wisdom, integrity and compassion.

All of this had quite an impact on Dawson at the time. He was, after all, a young man of semisheltered upbringing who had yet to have any of his personal wisdoms put to the acid test of living-it-out.

So Hoagie became a sort of hero to him.

He also became a steadfast friend.

Hoagie taught Dawson how to pick a freight; how to read the coded lettering on the flanks of the individual cars, so that he'd know where they had originated and where they were heading. He taught him how, and when, to mount a train; how to ride one; how to disembark; and what to do and where to go once he had done so. He taught him how to recognize and avoid the peculiar hazards of particular trains, railyards, and towns. And he taught him, without ever putting it into words, how to read the signs of another man's intentions during an initial confrontation.

By Hoagie's side Dawson learned how to live without money, how to live without food when he had to, and how to get both when he could without compromising his integrity. He also learned that integrity was an extremely personal thing, separate from any rules or strictures that had ever been imposed from without, and that each man had to discover its composition for himself.

Dawson learned about the Network. Something Hoagie referred to as "the only functional anarchy existing in the United States."

"All it is," Hoagie had told him, "is folk lookin' out for folk, knowin' that the favor'll be returned somewhere down the line. Some folks call it karma, some call it castin' your bread upon the waters, some just say 'what goes 'round, comes 'round.' Just simple cooperation is all, but so few really live that way, that when they see it work, they think it's some remarkable achievement.

"Think about it: You don't need no Bill of Rights if there ain't nobody tryin' to interfere with you."

* * *

Hoagie taught Dawson about hardship and freedom.
And Hoagie taught Dawson about time.

I can almost believe that it is all over. That the
horror has finally ceased. That I have traveled forward or backward in time, to a period when the
threat does not exist.

Such thinking is dangerous. I cannot permit myself
to believe such things. But it is difficult.

For twenty-four hours I have not been threatened.
Looking out this window I am confronted only by
grass and trees, shimmering in the complacent afternoon sun. There is a stream too. Not large enough for
trout, but certainly supporting a thriving population
of minnows, crayfish, frogs, salamanders, dragonflies
and water-skaters.

Everything within my range of vision is so tran-
quilly unaffected.

And then there is me.

Wondering if I am insane.

Yet.

Wondering if the horror is really ended.

I cannot entertain such thoughts. I might begin to
consider staying yet another day. And, if that day
was uneventful, yet another.

Eventually they would find me.

My time here is limited. If I do not impose that
limit, they most certainly shall.

Two men alone on a hillside, lying motionless among
tall grasses that obscured them from the vision of the
world, just as surely as it obscured the world from their
own sight. A warm September sun was running gentle
fingers over their weary muscles, inducing them to lazi-
ness and introspection. Occasionally from the base of the
hill rose the sound of a passing train. To them the sound
was unintrusive, even welcome. It was an affirmation of
their freedom, and of the infinite multiplicity of choice. In
all other ways the afternoon was silent.

Softly, dove-voiced, one of the men spoke.

"You know, all this was underwater once. Prehistoric fishes and sharks swimmin', right up over our heads. Maybe even that first fish that got so adventurous. The one that crawled up onto the shore to check things out or to get away from the sharks. The very one that started that long and weary march. That march that started turnin' fish into reptiles, and reptiles into birds and mammals, and some of them mammals into something like men. That march that we're continuin' whether we will or no.

"And maybe the reason that he got so damn adventurous is that he looked down here below him, and saw us lyin' in the tall grass in the sun, and it looked good to him.

"Better'n dodgin' sharks, anyway.

"Or maybe he just saw us, and recognized the fact that if somethin' like us was ever gonna happen, then someone somewhere along the line was gonna have to do a heap of adventurin'. Maybe he decided that it might as well be him as got the ball started rollin'.

"Or maybe he saw the next thing. The thing we're frayin' our fins into hands to become, without our ever knowin' it.

"Do you see 'em up there, swimmin' about?"

There was a significant pause before the second man replied. When he did, his voice was shaded faintly with a tone of loss, regret.

"No . . . no, I don't. Not really."

"Well I can. Know why?"

Silence.

"Cause they're there, right now, swimmin' 'round just like they was a million years ago. Just like they always was, and always will be.

" 'All at once, is what eternity is.'

"That's what The Poet told us. And he was right. He was right about alot of things. But most people just don't see it."

"Which poet?"

"The Poet. The only Poet. And I don't mean Shakespeare, or Milton, or Too Sad Eliot. Naw, none of them they teach at schools. Schools won't touch him, cause he got too much of it right. They don't want to deal with that. That's why I walked away a half-dozen credits shy of my B.A."

Another brief silence.

"Want an example?"

"Sure."

"Hear that train comin'?"

The second man listened, but heard nothing. He waited a moment before making his reply. As he opened his mouth to speak, his ears did pick up the sound, so faint and far as to be nearly indiscernible.

"Yes! I hear it."

"Okay, that's a start. Think with me now. Together we'll go back. Not nearly so far back as them fish, just a short hop. About a hundred years or so should suit.

"Think of it: the nineteenth century, the age of steel, the birthing and bursting Age of Industrialization, the heyday of the Iron Horse. Yeah, that very train is one of the things them fishies worked their fins to fingers for, or so the vanity of man would have you believe.

"The West's still wild, the slaves but lately freed, and a handful of Indians ain't laid down and given up the Ghost Dance yet.

"You got all that in your head now?"

"Yes."

"Good. Now you just think on that a space, and when that train gets 'round to comin' up beneath this hill, you just raise up and have yourself a peek. See if what The Poet said ain't true."

The first man closed his eyes and lay still.

The second man waited alertly, almost without breathing. He thought about what his companion had said. He listened intently, until he could almost feel himself becoming one with the slowly increasing sound of the train. He was soon convinced that something was different, that something had changed, but was uncertain whether the change he felt was within himself or without.

The train was a long time coming. When he was certain that it had reached the base of the hill, he rose up on his knees and peered downward over the tall grasses.

Then he drew in his breath and held it, as a wave of vertigo washed over him.

He was watching a huge, black, nineteenth-century steam engine pull a sooty tender, and an equally dated line of passenger cars, along the shining double line of the rails. His eyes lingered on the mixture of smoke and steam pouring out of its stack, trailing down the entire length of the train and dispersing gently in the still summer air.

When the train had passed from sight, he sat back down and stared at his companion, who seemed to have fallen asleep. Puzzled, he laid himself back in the grass, his eyes searching the sky above him.

A voice floated gently over him, as if his friend were chanting softly in his sleep.

"Swim, little fishy, swim.

"Crawl, little fishy, crawl.

"Build, little fishy, build.

"Fly, little fishy, fly.

"Then blow it all to hell, and die."

Later Dawson would come up with any number of logical, and unsatisfying, explanations for what had occurred that afternoon. But the magic of those moments would never diminish, or recede from his memory.

So I will leave at dawn, grateful for my brief reprieve.

I have gathered everything that I intend to carry with me, into this one room. I have left the window open for two reasons: to allow in the breeze, which is gentle and kind; and to allow in any sounds from below, which might not be.

A small bureau is pushed up against the bedroom door. I know that it might slow down my escape, if things should take a certain turn; but it might also buy me some valuable time, if things should twist a slightly different way.

My pack is stuffed, as full as I can get it, with the food and water that I have found. I am also taking the bottle of rum. Perhaps this is foolish, but I tell myself that I have no other form of anesthetic. Foolish or not, it is the choice that I have made.

At dawn I will set out, once again, for the Hub.

Hoagie told me once that I could find him, if I ever really needed him.

I need him now.

If anyone knows how to survive this horror, and still remain alive, it is him.

"If you ever need to find me, this is the place to start. It's like the Network is a nervous system, and the Hub is the brain. A word dropped here at nightfall will be travelin' six different directions by noon the next day. By noon the day after that, you couldn't tabulate all the places it's gone. And the word'll reach its man, sure as rain, if he's still on the Network, no matter where on the continent he may be. You can count on it.

"So if you ever need me, start here. If I ain't around, just put out the word and wait. You'll get me, or my message, before too long."

That November had started out cold. Dawson pulled his tattered overcoat more tightly around his body, shuffled his feet and nodded.

"I'll be back," he said softly, making a pretense of adjusting the straps on his backpack. Then he looked into his companion's eyes, nodded more firmly, and spoke with greater resolution.

"Yeah. Probably in the spring."

He was startled by his friend's laughter.

"Oh yeah. I got you pegged, brother. Fair-weather sort, eh?"

Though the assertion was made good-naturedly enough, Dawson felt his face color. He opened his mouth to speak, but no words came out.

Hoagie just shook his head, slowly letting his smile give way to a more sober expression.

"Yeah, you're a fair-weather sort, for now at least, but that's okay. You're young yet. Life hasn't burned you. The cradle hasn't cramped you up too bad. But you'll grow."

He raised a hand to Dawson's shoulder, gripped him hard.

"Maybe I'll see you next spring, and maybe not. You'll make that decision when the time comes. Either way, remember this: someday, when you wake up and realize what a mess you're in—what a goddamn mess the whole of the civilized world has got itself in, draggin' you along to boot—and you decide you just don't wanna stay caught up inside that mess anymore . . . just remember you ain't gotta be. You got choices, and nobody's got a right to make them choices for you, or to tell you which is right and which is wrong.

"There's alot worse ways to live than this, even if a bunch of them ways are easier and a bit more comfy. There ain't no reason you gotta live and die in any of them worse ways.

"It's up to you."

[7]

A muffled thumping sound, followed by a faint scraping.

The same sounds repeated. Clumsy. Erratic. Intermittent. Persistent.

A similar series of noises rising from a slightly different location.

The noises doubled.

Trebled.

Dawson's heart was racing even before he opened his eyes. This time there was no luxurious forgetfulness, no vagrant searching for the nightstand and the clock. He was immediately aware of his desperate situation.

Dazed, he listened.

There was the sharp crack of wood splintering. Then a grating sound, as if a heavy object were being pushed across the wooden floor downstairs.

Somehow, he could not bring himself to move.

The first emotions he became conscious of were anger and indignation. They were invading his *sanctum sanctorum*. They were proving his sense of security to be false. They were proving him for a fool.

Then came the fear, and all other emotions became meaningless.

He was trapped.

Judging by the sounds, there were already too many at the entrance downstairs. Too many *in* the entrance. There would be no escape through the narrow confines of the house. Clumsiness notwithstanding, their sheer numbers would overwhelm him.

Where had they all come from so suddenly?

Finally he bolted from the bed and thrust himself toward the window to look out.

Darkness.

Within the darkness, five darker shapes—no, seven—shambling about, moving vaguely toward the broken entrance of the house.

Eight—no, nine.

A sound behind him indicated that the first one had stumbled onto the base of the stairs. It was on his scent.

Eleven outside.

He wrestled his arms through the straps of his backpack, cursing his own clumsiness, then lurched back to the window. More were coming through the trees. Several had disappeared around the front of the house.

He thrust his legs out the window and bent awkwardly at the waist to get his head through. When he tried to sit up straight on the windowsill, his backpack struck the underside of the window, nearly causing him to fall. He ducked again, this time low enough to clear the backpack, and perched there, peering into the darkness below.

One of the ghouls in the yard looked up at him and made a wretched sound. Another turned toward it, then followed its gaze to the window.

Behind him Dawson heard the bureau being pushed slowly across the floor.

He leapt.

A moment of freedom.

Falling.

Movement through the night's damp air.

A sensation of speed.

PAIN!

Ankles legs spine stomach ribs PAIN. White/black PAIN. Red/white PAIN. Everything PAIN. Nothing but PAIN.

Then a thought crept in:

"Can't walk can't run can't escape."

Then, in answer:

"If I can't walk, they cannot make me be like them. Not like that. A predator."

A small victory. A minor success. He told himself to savor that at least. Then he opened his eyes.

Dark shapes swayed before him, looming ever nearer. Shadowed, contorted, vacant faces, shattered slavering mouths tight and shrill with horrific exhilaration.

"NO!!!"

He pressed hard against the pain and gained his feet, spun away from the approaching figures and lunged into something heavy, putrescently soft and yielding.

A grunt of air, not his. Hot, fetid breath pushing against his cheek. He screamed and swung his elbow in a high arc, felt it strike deeply into the soft thing's substance as it knocked the beast down. He kicked once, futilely, at the wretched face and nearly fell on top of it.

He screamed and ran.

As dawn began to filter through the trackless woods through which he moved, he believed that he was still running.

He was not. His staggering, lurching gait carried him no faster than an old man's ambling morning walk. It was the best that he could muster. Simply continuing onward demanded the utmost of his effort and his will, but he would not stop to rest.

Eventually he noticed the light growing bright around him. He decided then to leave the cover of the trees for the easier going of the roadside.

Later he heard a sound.

Some portion of his mind believed that he should be able to place that sound. That he should recognize it easily. But he was incapable of that.

Most of his mind was still trapped in the darkness of time, witnessing and reliving the moments when his hands were shoving putrid flesh away from his own face while, behind him, other hands were reaching out to draw him close. He could feel them there, behind him, getting closer, reaching out, about to grab him.

"NO!"

He shuddered.

Then he whimpered, "no."

He stared a moment at the sun, now well above the horizon, and wondered if it held any meaning for him. Whether there was anything he could learn or deduce from its existence or position. Then the sound came back to him, and he remembered what it meant. It was the distant hum of a car. It was approaching from behind him.

He turned to look down the road just as the vehicle became visible around a distant curve. It was a blue Ford pickup, and it was moving fast.

He stared at it a moment. Then with great effort, and a sense of trepidation he did not fully comprehend, he extended his right arm and opened his palm to it. Beseeching it to stop. Beseeching it to save him.

Within moments it was close enough for him to see clearly the muzzle of a shotgun protruding from the passenger window. It was aimed directly at him. He threw himself upon the ground just as the thunderous sound enveloped him.

Pain jarred him. He wondered if he had it in him to rise again, or if he would simply lie there and slowly bleed to death. Then he realized that the pain was not so localized as it ought to be. It was everywhere at once. He had not been shot, he had simply re-wrenched every injury that he had received when he leapt from the window.

He cursed his assailants, wept for himself and lay there in a heap.

When he finally rose to continue on his way, he was surprised to find—not ten feet beyond the spot where he had flung himself to the ground—a body sprawled across the shoulder of the road. It's shattered skull oozed fluids that bore only a cursory resemblance to human blood. Its blue-green skin marked it even more clearly for what it was. It had not been there when he had turned to hail the truck, of that Dawson was certain.

He understood then, that he had not been the target. Not of the people in the pickup at least. They had actually saved his life.

He hurried on.

[8]

"Just try to relax. We don't live far from here. Just out on Pitney Road.

"Oh, but that's so stupid of me. I mean, you're not from around here, are you? You wouldn't know . . . I mean, Pitney Road doesn't mean a thing to you, does it?"

Dawson didn't respond. He could hear the woman beside him, but it stopped there. He was incapable of listening to, or comprehending, her words. Beyond even caring. His mind was shattered, scattered in a million fragments.

The woman was in her early thirties. She looked as if she had once been stunningly attractive, in a pristine sort of way. Perhaps even very recently. But hers was not the sort of face to wear much trial and turmoil gracefully, and recent experiences had left their mark upon her.

Dawson hadn't even noticed this much. He was absorbed in the kaleidoscopic spectacle of the fragments that had once been his soul. For each fragment he saw a dark hand reaching out, threatening to crush it into even smaller pieces.

He was shivering. Staring out the open window of the car. A car that he had not even beckoned to, but had merely withdrawn from along the roadside to watch warily as it passed. It had stopped anyway. But the moving fragments, and the moving hands, they did not stop. They were all that he could see. They required his full attention.

"It's a nice area. . . . I mean, it was. It's set off a bit, and we've got it secured real good. I did it myself, and though I've never exactly been a wizard with tools and all, I can guarantee that it *is* safe. George would be real proud of me. . . . I mean, he will be real proud of me when he sees it."

There was a brief silence.

"We have guns, too. George was always big on hunting, so we had some guns around the house. I've gotten pretty good with them, I practiced alot right away and . . . well, since then I've had a couple of occasions when I needed to use them, so I know that I can handle them if the need arises."

Another pause as she spares a glance at Dawson's vacant face.

"What I'm trying to say is that it's safe there. I mean, you'd be safe, you know, if you decided that you wanted to stay with us awhile. I mean, until you're recovered or whatever. I mean, it's safer than being out on the road like I found you, and you look like you could use some time to recuperate. It really wouldn't be any trouble. Would it, Kirsten?"

The six-year-old girl, blond like her mother, sat silently in the backseat sucking her thumb and staring intently at the back of the stranger's head.

Her mother hadn't expected a response and didn't wait for one.

"It gets kind of lonely, just the two of us up there waiting for her Daddy to come home. It'd be kind of nice to have a visitor for awhile. It'd be nice to have another grown-up to talk to for a change. You know what I mean?"

Again the woman looked at Dawson, then turned back to her driving, biting her lip.

"It's just . . . you know . . . I mean I don't pick up hitchhikers, that is, I never did until now, because . . . well, things are different now. I could tell you were alive and I just thought: what if George was walking down some road trying to get home, would I want somebody to pass him by just because they didn't know him? No. I'd want them to stop and help him out if they could.

"I mean, with all of the people that have died, and the way everyone else seems to have gotten themselves all scattered out, if you have to wait for someone you know to come along and help you, you'll be waiting an awful long time. Just being alive has come to mean so much. It means that we're in the same situation and all, so we should be able to help each other out. Should at least be willing to try, don't you think?"

Tears welled in her eyes as she turned toward him, her face bunched tightly.

"Dammit!" she spat. "Why don't you say something?"

Dawson turned to look at her and blinked.

She looked back at the road, her own eyes blinking rapidly, the fingers of her right hand coming up to swipe roughly at her cheeks.

"I'm sorry," he said, and though his voice sounded hollow, it somehow managed to convey sincere and deep regret.

"No, no it's me," she countered, "it's just that . . . oh . . . I don't know."

"We're here."

She set the emergency brake, then leaned across the car toward Dawson. He pressed back into his seat nervously, perplexed by her movement. When she popped open the glove compartment and withdrew a pistol, he understood and relaxed.

She peered around the car.

"I don't see any signs of them now, but you never know. We'll have to be careful when we go in. I always leave the front door unlocked when we go out for supplies like this."

She turned toward Dawson.

"Does that seem dreadfully foolish of me?"

Dawson shook his head once, uncertain if it was the correct response but wanting to give her something.

"I just figure that if Kirsten and I aren't there, then there's nothing to draw them in. Don't you think that's true? That somehow they sense us and pursue us, and if we're not there to sense, they'll leave the place alone?

"And I keep thinking: What if George does come back and he doesn't have his key—I mean, a man can hardly be expected to hang onto his house key at a time like this—and what if he finds the house all locked up and he thinks we're gone or dead, and he gives up and goes away forever?

"Or, what if they're after him and he needs to get into the house right away, but it's locked and . . ."

She let her voice trail off as she gazed once more at the world surrounding the car.

"And I don't want to leave a note on the door. That seems too dangerous. I don't think they can read, but

. . . others can. The others that are still alive, and I know that some of them . . ."

She looked at Dawson.

"Well, I don't trust everyone is what I mean. I can't."

She looked back toward the house.

"So I left a note on the refrigerator, so he'll be sure to wait for us if he comes back while we're gone."

She cast her eyes down to the gun lying in her lap and began, again, to blink back tears.

Dawson's eyes had not left her face for a long time. But it was at this moment that suddenly, as if with the throwing of a switch in some long disused chamber of his being, he first saw her. Despite the ravaged weariness of her features, she was instantly very beautiful to him. He wanted to reach out to her, or speak, but found that he could do neither.

"I'm sorry," she said. "I must sound like an idiot babbling on like this. It's just that . . ." She cut herself off.

"We'd better go in."

She got out of the car, watching all around her for any sign of movement. Dawson and Kirsten did the same.

They moved to the back of the car and gathered up several packages that had been stowed in the trunk.

"We'll have to make a room-to-room check, once we get in and put these down," she told him, "that's always the worst part. Though I haven't found any surprises yet."

Dawson followed the woman mutely into the kitchen and set his parcels down on the counter. Kirsten lagged behind, taking a seat on the living-room couch where she could still be seen by the two adults. Her movement and posture gave Dawson the impression that it was all part of a familiar and unvarying procedure. Once seated the child remained very still, sucking her thumb and watching her mother and the stranger.

"It seems like no one's been here," the woman's eyes scanned the kitchen methodically, coming to rest on a note held to the refrigerator by a magnetic banana.

"Neither friend, nor foe." She sighed at this, but smiled wanly at Dawson. He noticed that her shoulders did not slump, as he had expected. If anything, her stance seemed more confident, more self-assured and determined than before. She was home now. She was safe. Ready to recharge and to do whatever needed to be done.

Dawson was amazed, both by the change in her and its apparent source. He wondered when it had last occurred to him that the concept of home could have any real meaning to anyone. He watched her closely as her tensions unwound, as her face took on a less drawn and haggard appearance, and she became beautiful to him again. More so than before.

As she heaved a deeper sigh, he felt himself breathe with her. He felt his own tensions relaxing under her sterling example. Felt the dark hands recede a bit, and the strange inner workings of an arcane reconstruction going on within his deepest and most private places.

She looked upon him, her eyes both solemn and bright.

"I still have to check the other rooms. Will you come with me?"

Staring into her eyes, he nodded.

She smiled. "Thank you."

He dropped his gaze and saw the pistol in her hand. He shuddered, thinking of the frightening state the world had come to. It was several moments before he could raise his eyes to meet hers again.

A heavy sound from the top of the staircase, like someone dropping a five-pound bag of sugar, was followed immediately by Kirsten's inane scream of incomprehensible glee.

"Daaaddeeee . . . !!"

"Kirsten! Wait!"

Dawson turned in time to see the child bolt off the sofa and streak out of sight in the direction of the stairs. Then the woman shot past him in pursuit of her child. Dawson followed her, but after three quick strides was forced to halt just inside the living room, to avoid colliding with her. The woman's body had gone rigid. He followed her gaze to the staircase.

The ensuing moments passed like hours, giving Dawson the unwanted opportunity to absorb every detail.

On the staircase stood a thing that had once been a man. Its hands were closed upon the shoulders of the child. Kirsten, overwhelmed by the fear of realization, kicked and screamed, struggling vainly to be free as the ghoul hoisted her toward its grotesquely twisted mouth.

The woman raised the pistol with both hands, trembling violently.

"Stop!" her voice hysterical. "For God's sake, stop!"

Teeth ripped into the soft whiteness of the girl's neck. A spray of crimson pulsed across the ghoul's face and splashed onto the wall beside it. The child's scream gurgled to a halt just as the first shot sounded.

A deep burgundy rose opened on the ghoul's forehead, jerking its face away from its prey, forcing the thing to stand erect. A look of dumb puzzled shock leapt from its eyes in the moment before they rolled back to show only whites.

The pistol sounded again. Chunks of cheekflesh and bone splattered against the wall.

Again. The thing collapsed backwards on the stairs, the child landing heavily upon its chest. Kirsten's body rode the ghoul's in a gruesome parody of father-daughter play, as it slid slowly and erratically down the stairs, arms and legs akimbo.

Again the pistol sounded. Again and yet again. The body shuddered from the impact of the bullets. Then there was only the recurring click of the pistol's hammer falling upon empty chambers. Two times. Five times. Seven.

The pistol fell to the floor, rapidly followed by the woman.

Dawson felt a scream beginning in his bowels, fighting, fluttering, ricocheting upwards in panicked flight, seeking an escape but unable to find one. He whimpered and tore his eyes away from the blood-mottled grotesquerie of flesh upon the stairs. He looked upon the woman lying at his feet.

The side of her face rested heavily upon the carpet. Her eyes were closed. Her limbs were sprawled haphazardly. He watched her back rise and fall erratically with the discordant rhythm of her breathing.

Then he uttered some pitiable, bizarre ululation and, with great heaving strides, rushed for the exit.

Outside he knelt in her garden vomiting, for what

seemed a very long time. When he was empty, he spared one final glance toward the house before hurrying away.

[9]

Dawson panicked at the sound of the approaching car, but there was nowhere to hide. On his right was a rocky slope, too steep to climb swiftly. On his left a metal guard-rail and a precipitous drop.

Whimpering, he pressed himself against the rocky slope and covered his eyes to avoid being seen.

The sound grew until it covered everything and enveloped him in fear. The fear blossomed, brightened into fireballs, at the sound of brakes. Then it vibrated, leapt, and danced, as he heard the car door open and shut.

"Nononononononono . . ." he believed that he was shouting, but the voice that emerged was weak and strained and sickly.

Then another voice spoke. Smooth and strong. Commanding, deep and gentle.

"No." Dawson's shout was, again, barely audible. It did nothing to stop that other voice. He felt rage against that voice, so cool, so firm, so unyieldingly soft.

It drew closer. Very near indeed.

Dawson's hands scrambled frantically against the wall before him, came up with a fist-sized rock. He spun quickly, opening his eyes just as the rock left his hand, hurtling toward the source of the voice. His aim was very wide. The voice's face smiled kindly.

"You'll die. I'll kill you."

They were the first words Dawson had spoken, though he had been in the car for more than an hour. He had spent that time not looking at the man, staring instead out the window to his right, fighting off a sickening sense of *déjà vu*. He knew only that he didn't want to remember. Not anything.

The man beside him recognized Dawson's words as a potential crack in his effortful armor, but he prodded very gently. He knew very well what he was up against. What the two of them were up against. Calmly and unhurriedly, he posed his question.

"Now, why would you do that?"

Then he waited patiently through Dawson's silence.

"I won't *do* it. It will be done. Not by my hand but by my presence. I will bring it on, cause it. I will be responsible."

"Try to tell me why you feel this way."

For the first time since getting into the car Dawson turned to look at his companion. He was a broad-faced man with dark hair and several days' worth of beard. Glasses would have looked at home on his face, but he wore none. They would have made him look more like a preacher, too. Hadn't the man said he was a preacher, earlier in the ride, perhaps years ago? Well he looked the part, even without the glasses, despite the bright blue short-sleeved shirt and the casual work pants.

Dawson looked back out the window before responding.

"Everyone I know is dead. Everyone that I ever met, before or after. It doesn't matter. I meet them, they die. I want to die instead, but I'm just a carrier. I'm immune. I can only watch the others."

The man waited a moment, to be sure that Dawson was finished, then spoke again.

"You probably don't want to hear me say that I've heard people say that before, or that it's a common delusion these days and was never terribly uncommon. People felt that way even before . . . the change, or whatever you might want to call it. But whether you *want* to hear it or not, it's true, and it's exactly what you *need* to hear. It's what you need to be thinking about right now. You are not alone."

Dawson turned quickly to look at the man who also turned to meet his gaze. The crack in the armor was visibly wider.

"Tell me about it," the preacher said, "tell me everything you can remember. Even the things that you're trying so hard to forget."

And after awhile, after a bit more gentle probing and respondent opening up, Dawson did just that.

* * *

"These are terribly trying times, friend."

The car was parked behind an old mill, near a wide and glistening creek. The two men were sharing a cup of luke-warm coffee from a thermos that the preacher, whose name was Richard, had produced from beneath his seat. Richard handed the cup back to Dawson and went on.

"Oh, I know that just sounds like so much pious-preacher-happy-horseshit, the kind of platitudes I mouthed so often for people who only *thought* their world was falling apart, but you can't deny that no one alive was ever prepared for what has happened to this world. We were unprepared physically, tactically and spiritually—for which I'll accept my share of the blame, being in the pro-fession as it were."

Richard smiled and Dawson passed the cup back to him, pleased by the smile but unable to return it.

"But worst of all," the smile went away, "we weren't prepared psychologically. All of our carefully learned tac-tics and procedures for dealing with life in this world be-came useless to us. That was the most devastating thing. We lost our rules, our codes, our coping mechanisms. Since nothing was predictable anymore, there was nothing that we could believe in, so we lost our faith. In losing faith we lost both self-esteem and will."

Dawson stared at his palms, lying open and upturned in his lap.

"I cannot share your faith, Richard. I cannot believe in your God. Love and mercy, they told me. He'd never have let this happen, no matter how fucking mysterious his ways."

"I don't blame you."

Dawson looked up at his new friend, listening intently.

"I don't buy the list of hocum anymore either. But that's not the kind of faith I'm speaking about. And as for sharing, you don't need the kind of faith that could ever possibly be shared. You need the kind that is yours alone. Something from within you, compounded of what you've been and seen through all your days."

Richard took another drink from the cup, handed it to Dawson, then started the engine. They drove.

When night took full possession of the surrounding landscape, they were still driving, the car's headlights pushing away the darkness in front of them. They had spent the bulk of the evening talking about the different kinds of faith that existed in the world. Even in a world such as theirs had become. They had discussed exhaustively the connection between faith and will, and between will and the ability to survive.

Richard claimed that while events had destroyed his faith in an omnipotent and merciful deity, they had reawakened and renewed his faith in his original purpose and his sense of mission.

"I came to the calling, or so I told myself at the time, to serve the people. To save them. A worthy mission. The only mission any servant of a kind, compassionate godhead should ever aspire to. But I think sometimes that God . . . no, not God, but the image of God and all the attached dogma, get in the way of such folk. It did in my case, anyway.

"Well, since the change, the deluge, whatever, I feel that my original purpose has been rekindled. Perhaps I've really focused on it for the first time ever. And now that purpose is my faith. My will. It is how I have learned to survive."

Then he told Dawson about his new work. About how he had spent the past few weeks traveling as extensively as possible, trying to find survivors. Trying to help them in any way that he could. Mostly by talking to them about purpose and will. Trying to inspire them.

"So you see, I haven't really changed jobs," he had smiled, "just employers. I really don't talk religion much anymore, not unless someone else has a need. I feel I'm doing more for folks now that I ever did before. And now's just when they need it most. It's a good feeling. Even makes this living hell worth living in."

So, as darkness shrouded the low hills through which they passed, Richard tried to direct Dawson's mind toward an acceptance of life, rather than death. Tried to find the carrot that Dawson might be persuaded to pursue.

Dawson found that he liked the man. He believed in Richard's wisdom and wanted to please him. He wanted to hope. Wanted to hope out loud. But he was hesitant. Each time that he reached for that double-edged emotion, he drew back, remembering past hurts. He wasn't sure if he was ready yet, or ever would be.

It was well into the night when he screwed up sufficient courage to make the plunge. He would hope, whether it was safe or not. He would live, no matter how desperately.

"I *do* have a goal," he declared in a very firm voice.

Richard took his eyes from the road to smile encouragingly at his companion at the very same moment that the bullet smashed the windshield.

Dawson was thrown violently against the door as the car suddenly swerved. Then he was thrust backwards into his seat as Richard regained control and tromped on the gas.

Turning quickly to look behind, Dawson saw two figures emerge from the shadowy trees that lined the road. He saw two bright orange flashes as he heard two more shots ring out, but neither shot found its mark. Then the car swung around a curve, obscuring his view of their assailants, while preventing any further shots from threatening his and Richard's escape.

"They wanted the car, didn't they?" Dawson blurted out, inexplicably more excited than frightened by the narrowness of their escape.

He turned to congratulate his friend for his heady driving, but froze before he could speak again.

A dark stain, already large, was rapidly spreading across Richard's chest.

"Oh God!" was the best that Dawson could manage.

Knuckles white, face pallid and rigid with pain, Richard maneuvered the car along the winding road at dangerous speeds for five more minutes. Dawson neglected the road entirely, felt no threat from speed or obstacle, and stared hard at the preacher's face.

Richard brought the car to a complete stop before allowing himself to slump backwards in his seat. Even then he held his neck and head rigidly upright. His lips moved slowly, with precise determination.

"I am going to die, Dawson. But it is *not* your fault.

"In fact, you can save me, after a fashion. Do me one final favor."

Dawson was never certain whether Richard smiled or winced then, before he continued in a more strained voice.

"No. Two.

"First: live. Determine now to live. Make my going worth that much. Take the car. Reach your goal. Don't let them get it."

Dawson nodded, though the preacher's eyes were closed.

Then Richard's eyes flew open as he searched for the door handle, opened the door, and let himself fall out onto the road.

Dawson lurched across the seat in a vain attempt to grab his friend and haul him back into the car.

Blood trickled from the corners of Richard's mouth as he looked into Dawson's eyes and shook his head. His breath came in gasps. When he spoke again, it was with a voice made half of gravel, and half of bubbling blood.

"Second favor . . . glove box . . . pistol . . ."

Dawson just stared.

"Get it!"

Richard began to cough, spraying blood on the open car door, his hands and clothes. Recovering somewhat he spoke again, his voice sounding worse by the moment.

"Shoot me . . . the head . . . don't want to walk . . . like that."

Dawson continued to stare.

"Put me out."

Their eyes locked, and for a moment Dawson believed that he could do just as his friend had requested.

Then Richard's eyes shut, with his last gurgling exhalation.

[10]

I am grateful that the last stages of my journey are lost to me, obscured by a fog of combined remorse and fear. Remorse at and fear of precisely what, I cannot say. I will not subject myself to so thorough an examination. At least not yet.

In more general terms I know that the remorse is caused by who and what I have proved myself to be. The fear by what I might discover if the fog dispersed and I was forced to confront the actions and scenes that I have so willfully forgotten. I am glad that I proved incapable of recording the events of that period here. If I had written, I would refuse to read it.

Hoagie tells me that none of it matters anyway. We drank the rum last night, and he said that nothing from the past, whether personal or collective, really matters anymore. Things are different. I am alive. I am here.

"You are a new being," he told me, "just begun today. Just this instant. How can you judge yourself harshly, when you have done nothing in this new life? There is nothing to judge. How can you know your limitations, when you have yet to test them? You've got a clean slate. The learning process must begin again. You are who you are *right now.* You are, and can be, no one else. Make it be who you want it to be."

I want to believe him.

This place is considerably different than it was. More permanent. Less nomadic. They have constructed shelters, which are crude and primitive, but far more substantial than anything that stood here in the past. They are no longer a transient tribe. Their primary means of transportation is lost to them. It is not that the trains no longer run, because they do, but now they are so rare and so well guarded that it is death to approach one. Only government trains. The soldiers' orders are pretty clear.

Most of the people here (I think there are more than twenty of us) carry guns. I wondered briefly how the others had come by theirs, but that thought threatened to make me remember how I came by my own. I was able to curtail such thoughts just before the fog would have lifted to let me see.

Maybe, one day, I will let myself remember. Some day when I feel stronger than I do now. Some day when I feel stronger than I can ever imagine myself feeling.

Hoagie and several others set out this morning on a hunting expedition. I asked him what they hunted around here, but for reasons I cannot begin to fathom he became uncharacteristically brusque.

"Meat. Food. Anything that'll give us the strength to survive another day. Anything whose death will help preserve us so that, maybe someday, some of us will have survived long enough to see the end of this."

His manner disturbed me. I had never seen him so agitated. But, true to form, when he saw that I was taken aback by the tone of his response, he smiled and softened. It was a sad smile, world-weary and resigned, but I couldn't remember the last time I had seen a smile of any kind, so I did my best to smile back.

"Thought for the day," he said: "All the rules have changed. Everything you ever knew is wrong. All mores have been abolished. Never confuse mores with morals."

He smiled at me again, but this time there was a grimness about the smile that made it impossible for me even to try to return it.

I am confused again. But I suppose that, with all that Hoagie has been through in the past few weeks, I shouldn't expect to understand his every action and gesture.

As the hunting party returned that evening, most of the members of the camp stopped what they were doing in order to greet them. Dawson was lashing some branches together to improve the lean-to he had constructed. He finished the knot he was working on, then rose to join the others.

His stomach constricted in grief when he saw the two dead men the hunters were bearing back to camp. Somehow it had not occurred to him that the hunting expedition would prove so hazardous.

"Of course, you idiot," he reprimanded himself silently, "like Hoagie says, it's a different world out there. More dangerous. That's probably why he acted so strangely. He was afraid he might not be coming back."

When the full implication of that thought struck him, Dawson felt the onset of panic. He pressed roughly into the crowd to get a closer look at the two dead men. It struck him as odd that there were no exclamations of grief surrounding him. Only quiet, iron-voiced conversations, in the grim tone of men discussing disturbing but necessary work. Were the Hub's inhabitants so inured, he wondered, that they couldn't whip up any feeling for their own?

Then the words began to register:

". . . not long dead, by the look of 'em . . ."

". . . two, four days each, should be half-palatable . . ."

". . . best we can hope for, considering . . ."

". . . what I wouldn't give for a side of fucking beef . . ."

". . . venison . . ."

". . . a Big-fucking-Mac . . ."

When he gained a vantage point, he lost all ability to be confused by these half-caught phrases. There was something familiar about one of the corpses. Not the familiarity that he had feared, but something irreconcilably worse. The fog that had obscured his recent past vanished in an instant. He could not take his eyes off the bright blue, short-sleeved shirt with its huge, dark stain of dried blood, except to look up at half of the man's familiar face. The half that had not been destroyed by one or more of the hunters' bullets.

There was no doubt left in him. Though he sorely wished there was.

Hoagie's voice cut sharply through the others.

"Rory, Mojo, Harrison—you clean and dress 'em. Greg, build up that fire and get the rig set up."

Dawson doubled over and vomited where he stood.

> I leave this place at dawn, though there is nowhere in this world that I can go.

"Listen to me, dammit! You can't stop the fucking world from bein' the way it is. The world's got a helluva lot more momentum than you or me or every goddamn soul in it could ever fucking muster. You gotta accept that first.

"After that, you got two choices: you quit the world by dyin', since that's the only way out that works; or you give in to the momentum and live as long as you can, hoping against hope that the world is gonna get better. 'Cause if you don't give in to that momentum, you're quittin' whether you say so or not, 'cause the world's gonna roll right over your sad old bones. It's gonna crush you, baby."

Hoagie's face was red and tight. His voice a controlled fury. Dawson refused to look at him.

"You walk outta this camp tomorrow and you're quittin'. Quittin' help and hope and any chance you might have of even thinkin' you might live long enough to see the end of this thing.

"And all over what?

"You say it's a matter of principle, but it's not. Principles are based on morals, and what you freaked out on ain't morals, it's a breaching of your basic cultural training. That's all. Training you received in order to get along in a culture that is now dead. It died weeks ago, man. Might as well be years. Might as well be centuries, for all the good your stickin' by its learnin' is gonna do you. Dead is dead. Let it go, man."

Hoagie took a deep breath, trying to calm himself a little.

"Try to think of it this way:

"The world you grew up in had mechanisms to teach you how to deal with all of the compromises it demanded. You learned so well that most of the time you never even knew that you were compromisin' your silly ass off. When that world died, everything became new, different, more demanding. The compromises became obvious because they weren't the same ones you had lived with every fucking day of your life. There weren't no mechanisms anymore to teach you how to accept them, either.

"Okay, the world sucks. Everything you knew is wrong. But you can deal with it so long as you adapt. Adapt or die. That's what it comes to."

There was a lengthy silence.

"You getting any of this?"

A longer silence.

"Fine. Make your own choice, man. I've made mine."

Hoagie turned to walk away, but Dawson's meek voice arrested his movement.

"It scares me Hoag."

Hoagie turned to look back at his friend. Dawson's eyes were pained.

"You're inviting whatever it is that did this to them, made them walk again and all, into your own systems. What if it's a virus, a bacteria, an infection of some sort. It could kill you. It could make you like them."

Hoagie shook his head.

"If we don't eat, we die. Then we'll be like them soon enough. Some of us have been eatin' like this for two weeks or better, and we ain't lost no one yet. At least not like you mean."

Dawson let his gaze fall back to the ground.

"I don't know. I just can't . . ."

He left the phrase unfinished.

I am weak. A coward. I have proven this in everything I've done. I don't know where to go. I am not even strong enough to maintain my own resolve.

If I stay. If I choose, even, to eat with them. Am I choosing, out of some reserve of strength, to adapt; or more simply, out of weakness, choosing not to die?

Are such distinctions real, or am I merely tormenting myself as Hoagie insists?

Morals? Mores? Are any distinctions ever real? Do we ever, really, encounter any choices we are capable of making?

It has been days since I could bring myself to write. I see, now, that it serves no purpose. Probably never did.

Alot like my life, that way.

I see this now as the journal of a dying man, as dictated to his murderer. Cause of death: betrayals. First his betrayals of others, finally his betrayal of himself. The fogs have lifted completely. I can now see all of it. It is only by the grace of that fog that I have lasted this long.

Excuse me: that *he* has lasted this long. This is an obituary, I must remember to keep it impersonal.

His betrayal of the woman—leaving as he did, when he could have stayed and saved at least her— wounded him severely. His betrayal of the preacher —again in leaving when there was something yet that needed to be done, one final favor begged but never granted—wounded him further.

But he was finished off by his betrayal of himself, ironically, in not leaving when he should have.

As further irony his cause of death will be assumed, by others, to be starvation. And all because of the betrayal that he refuses to commit.

Let his epitaph read:

WEAKNESS
brought him to death's door
STRENGTH
gained him entry.

I thought I would not write again, but there is no more solid solace to be had this night.

Hoagie is dead.

A hunting trip. One got up behind him somehow. Tore most of the back of his neck away before the others shot it.

He died before they got him back to camp.

I asked them, angrily I must admit, why they had brought him back. I implied, all indiscreetly, that they intended to make a meal of him, as well as of the beast that killed him.

Harrison slapped me hard for that. Several others hit me even harder with their eyes.

Can't say as I blame them. I was not the only one who loved the man, nor the only one who relied upon his love.

"We are not cannibals," I was told. And, though I wouldn't admit it at the time, I understand the distinction.

They have not put him down yet. Have not immobilized him. They have a ritual, it seems, in which they must wait for him to rise before they shoot him. I suppose that this is done in the hope that he will not rise, making the shooting unnecessary.

I understand this on a gut level, though pragmatically it seems a needless extension of the anxiety.

They have been courteous enough to grant my request for the vigil. All of it. Though I gather that this sort of thing is usually done in shifts.

I can't really explain why I want to be the one that finally puts him down, except to say that I feel I owe him this much, at least. Owe it to the preacher and the woman and myself.

I guess that I still have something to prove. That I am not all weakness and betrayal. That I can, at least once, do right by those who have done right by me.

The camp sleeps. Only the perimeter guards and I remain awake.

I am waiting

It should not be long now.

Twenty-four hours since his death, and the vigil continues.

It is amazing.

I allowed Harrison to relieve me at dawn, but made him promise me the watch again tonight, if it is necessary.

I pray that it is. If anyone that I have ever known deserves to rest in peace, then it is Hoagie.

Tomorrow at dawn we will bury him, regardless.

Harrison tells me that Hoagie might not rise. That this happened once before, in the days just preceding my arrival. The man had died in a similar manner, but he never rose or walked again. They buried him not far from here, and his grave lies undisturbed.

Mojo, who claims he is a reincarnation of some famous Aztec shaman, says that ingesting the spirits of one's enemies frees you from their power after death. That the habit of eating the ghouls has protected Hoagie from the "demons of the other world" that otherwise would have possessed him and made him walk with them.

He also claims that such protection can be had simply by eating their hearts.

I don't buy that, any more than any of Mojo's other stories, but it makes me think.

I am thinking of something I once said to Hoagie about viruses, infections and contagion. I am thinking about acquired immunities and built-up tolerances. About vaccines and anti-bodies. Life-saving poisons.

I am not a biologist, but it makes more sense to me than voodoo.

I am also thinking about coincidences. About rare, but natural, immunities. Wondering how likely it might be to have two such cases in so small a community. I have heard of and witnessed no cases like this anywhere else, but my experience—statistically speaking—has been too small to base reliable conclusions upon.

I am also learning how to pray.

We buried Hoagie this morning.

At his wake I broke my fast.

I understand, now, what he was trying to tell me about choices, but for me it is not continuing life that seems so important. It is the chance to refuse to rise again, after my inevitable death.

That is my determination.

My choice.

I am willing to make the necessary compromise.

The stew gagged me, though the meat was made as inconspicuous as possible. Harrison tells me that that is a common first reaction. He also says that the stew is less strong when fresh.

I am getting better at prayer.

It occurs to me that word of this possible cure must get out. Perhaps, with this information as a starting point, some vaccine might be distilled or manufactured.

But how to get the word out? To whom? Who is left to utilize or broadcast this information?

Government trains still run, so some portion of the government must remain, at least, semifunctional. Clearly the military still exists, but what else?

The Center for Disease Control in Atlanta should have been a priority, but were they quick enough to save it? If not, some other facility? If so, where?

I will not leave here on a wild-goose chase, not knowing where to go, or what my chances of getting there might be.

If there is any chance at all, it is the trains themselves. The men on the trains, or certainly their superiors, would know what options were available. They can best get this information to a place where it might do some good.

I will give them the entire journal. As much of my story as I have down, to convince them of my earnestness. To show them some portion of what I have been through.

I have need of it no more.

I am becoming whole again.

My mind is clear.

[Transcriber's note:

This final portion is written in a hand sufficiently

distinct from the rest of the text, as to allow no
doubt of separate authorship.   -K.H.]

They shot him dead.

He made the mistake of callin out to them guys
bout what he got and how important it was for them
to take it. Tried to run right up long side that train
and hand it right up to them.

They shot him dead at twenty yards.

I was watchin.

Its to bad to cause I liked him. Never even got to
tell him I was sorry bout hittin him that time. So I
picked the watch I thought hed come up on.

I was right.

So ether hes wrong bout that immuzation stuff he
was talkin bout, or he didnt eat with us long enuff.

Im glad if he had to come up he come up on my
shift tho. Someway its easier when you liked a guy.
You dont want no body else puttin him back down.
You want to do it yourself.

Got to talk to him that way to. Got to say my
sorrys. Told him Id rite his obit here and get his goddam book on the next train thru some goddam way.

You get a funny feelin like that. That somthin in
the guy can still here you. Like maybe itll help some-
ways.

Ill be more carful than him tho. Ill toss it on the
train from cover somewhere.

Aint gonna let them shoot me dead.

Not whiles I got a choice.

The Good Parts

BY LES DANIELS

In life, he had been huge but hardly menacing; his four hundred and eighty-three pounds had been all fat and no muscle. It had actually been hard for him to move.

But now it was hard for almost everyone to move. Their muscles, their tendons, their bones, all were soft as slime, soft as rot, soft as his.

But he was bigger.

Instead of hunting with the pack he hunted behind it, waiting till they brought a victim down and only then moving in to help with the kill. The others in the pack never seemed to notice what he did, never fought against him as he shouldered them aside with his bloated bulk. They only had eyes for the meat, and they fell where they were pushed when he leaned down into the crimson trough and went for the good parts.

If there was any thought at all left in his jellied brain, it would have been expressed in those three words: the good parts.

He had always liked the good parts, even when he was alive. He had liked them in his books and he had read them over and over again, marking the margins in red so they would be easier to find next time. And he had liked them in his movies. Actually he never went to the movies (the seats were too small), but that didn't matter since he had his VCR. He could sit in the dark and watch the good parts over and over again. Forward and back, forward and back. In and out. Up and down. And while he watched, he ate.

He had books like *High School Gym Orgy* and *Hitchhiking Harlots,* he had films like *Romancing the Bone* and *Debbie Does Dallas,* and he had magazines like *Eager Bea-*

vers and *Hot to Trot.* In a way the magazines were the best: if he found one with the right kind of pictures, there was nothing in it but good parts.

But all that had been back in the days before civilization had collapsed, before the dead had risen to devour the living. Now he was even better off. Once he had only stared at the good parts and stuffed himself, but now he had achieved his destiny. He was eating the good parts.

He didn't realize how safe he was; he didn't understand that being big and slow kept him out of the firefights till they were over and the living ones were down. The good parts were hard to reach, but that was lucky too: the quickest hunters were still pulling at extremities, arms and legs and heads, when he lumbered up and bulldozed his way toward the good parts. Sometimes he had to settle for a breast or a buttock, but most of the time he got what he really wanted. His favorite food tasted like a fish and cheese casserole basted with piss: no one had time to take a bath.

His yellow teeth were matted with pubic hair and mucous membrane; he never brushed.

He might have been a sexist when he was alive, but all that was behind him now. Anybody's good parts were his meat.

He was a virgin.

There wasn't much to do but eat and look for more to eat. One day he lurched into the Naughty Nite Bookstore, and he almost remembered it. A few of the usual crowd were there, bumping into the walls and moaning with dismay because no food was in the place. They left, but he lingered. He picked up a magazine called *Ballin'*. He couldn't read the title, but he could see the pictures, and he was still looking at them when he walked out of the store and found himself in a small apartment in the back. The couch looked cozy. He sat down on it for a few minutes to look at his magazine, and then went out to look for food, but later he came back again. He had to go somewhere.

He had a home.

Once in a while some of his friends followed him home (they had to go somewhere too), but after milling around for a few minutes they decided that nothing was happening there and went away. Nobody understood him.

A meat shortage developed. Sometimes it hardly seemed worth getting up. He had quite a collection of magazines after a few months, and he was losing his teeth. Some of his fingers fell off.

Still, a guy's gotta eat, so sometimes he would haul himself up and look for lunch. Everyone he saw on the street looked sad. The city echoed with their howls. Some tried munching on each other, but the meat was rotten and the trend never caught on.

One day a female followed him home. He might have looked like he knew something, and he certainly looked well fed. In fact, he was a mountain of maggots, and he let her eat some. It was better than nothing.

Her clothes had rotted clean away, and he noticed that he could see her good parts. She looked like a picture in a magazine. Well, close enough. Some instincts never die.

He had an inspiration, and then he had a wife.

She didn't seem to mind. When he pulled away from her, vaguely confused, he left his penis inside of her. He never really missed it. It was too far gone to eat in any case.

After that they hunted together. The pickings were slim. Once he got a few bites out of a leg, which wasn't what he felt like having that night, but it was better than nothing. He didn't notice that she was getting fatter even though they hardly ever ate.

One day she took him to the Stop 'n' Shop, a place she knew almost as well as he knew the Naughty Nite Bookstore. She showed him how a can opener worked. He wasn't really interested, and he didn't care much for the food, but she was wolfing it down as if it still was hot and fresh.

Of course he didn't know that he would be a father soon.

After all, who knew what a zombie could do?

The human scientists who studied them had other things to think about than the possibility of zombie sex. The zombies seemed to be too busy working on oral gratification for anyone to worry about their genitals. Nobody had their minds in the gutter anymore; they had their bodies there instead.

But the female was pregnant. She was expecting. She was what used to be called full of life. And you know it could have happened, because it did.

The female began making regular trips to the Stop 'n' Shop, coming back home with all the cans that she could carry. He didn't get the point, but he began to go along to help her. It was something to do.

Their friends thought they were crazy.

Actually, they didn't see that much of their friends anymore. A lot of them were falling apart, especially the skinny ones. Decay was in the air. Parts of bodies lay in the streets. Some were moving and some were not. Being fat became suddenly fashionable: it made it easier to stay in one piece. Bulk was beautiful.

When the day finally came, the birth was unorthodox. The baby simply crawled out through its mother's bloated belly, and after that the female had trouble getting around. In fact, she came apart at the waist, and she would have died if she had been alive. He propped her top half up in a closet and gave it food from time to time, but it lost interest and disintegrated.

The child was a girl, and it was human.

When he first realized that, he almost took a big bite out of her, but suddenly he noticed that something was wrong. Her good parts weren't really good enough to eat yet. She wasn't ripe.

It was tempting, no doubt of that, but for all he knew this was the last fresh food that he would ever see. He wanted to wait. He wanted to care for her. He wanted the perfect banquet for his last meal. Not only would she be riper, but she'd be bigger, too. He might even invite some people over for a party.

They didn't wait for invitations. Only a few days later, while he was stuffing some concentrated chicken noodle soup into his daughter's little pink mouth with some of his stumps, he heard the old gang shuffling through the bookstore, their voices rising in a ravenous chorale. It was just like them to spoil his surprise.

He was protective of his only child, and he was still the

biggest man in town. He shut the door that led into their little home and leaned his massive bulk against it. Of course the zombies tried to break it down, but most of them broke up instead. Their arms and legs snapped like spaghetti strands. Some of them crawled away as best they could, and some of them didn't even bother, but none of them got in. They just rotted and liquified and merged with the floorboards of the Naughty Nite Bookstore.

The little girl was fine. She grew stronger as the days and weeks and months sped past, and it was just as well she did, because her father was growing steadily weaker. Pages fell from the calendar, and pieces fell from him. He was still waiting, but the truth was that he had waited for too long. Now she was the one who opened up the cans and gave the food to him. His teeth were gone, and in fact there wasn't much left of his mouth, but she cheerfully packed what she could into his dripping, reeking, gaping maw. He couldn't move. He was trapped on the couch, a festering mountain of pus, and after dinner she would climb into his lap and turn the pages of his favorite magazines so they could enjoy them together. She liked the funny pictures, and they were pink the way she was.

Daddy was gray and green.

We can't go on like this, he would have said, but he couldn't speak, and he couldn't think much either. Of course that was nothing new, but he sensed dimly that things were getting out of hand when she perched on his knee one night and sank into it up to her armpits. She laughed and clapped her hands at Daddy's little joke, and in response he gave a sort of sigh, but that was about it.

The next morning, when she woke up, Daddy had soaked through the couch and spilled onto the carpet. At first she thought he might be kidding, but a few days later she decided she would have to face the facts. She'd been wondering about him for some time, but now there could be no doubt in her mind.

Daddy was history.

She stuck around for a while just to make sure, noticed that her supply of food was running low, cried for a few minutes, and then toddled toward the door. Armed only with her can opener, she went forth naked into the world.

There were some bones and puddles lying around, but nothing moved. She would survive, and perhaps she would find others like her, new humans born of dead desire. They might be living near a porn store, where only the will was wanted. There might even be, in time, an outbreak of new life.

She had seen her father's books, and she knew what to do with the good parts.

Less Than Zombie

BY DOUGLAS E. WINTER

People are afraid to live on the streets of Los Angeles. This is the last thing I say before I get back into the car. I don't know why I keep saying this thing. It's something I started and now I can't stop. Nothing else seems to matter. Not the fact that I'm no longer eighteen and the summer is gone and it's raining and the windshield wipers go back and forth, back and forth, and that Skip and DJ and Deb will soon be sitting with me again. Not the blood that splattered the legs of my jeans, which felt kind of hot and tight, as I stood in the alley and watched. Not the stain on the arm of the wrinkled, damp sweater I wear, a sweater that had looked fresh and clean last night. All of this seems meaningless next to that one sentence. It seems easier to hear that people are afraid to live rather than Skip say "This is real" or that song they keep playing on the radio. Nothing else seems to matter but those ten, no, eleven words. Not the rain or the cold wind, which seemed to propel the car down the street and into the alley, or the faded smells of marijuana and sex that still flow through the car. All it comes down to is that the living are dying and the dying are living but that people, whether alive or dead, are still fucking afraid.

It's actually the weekend, a Saturday night, and the party by this guy named Schuyler or Wyler was nothing and no one seems to know just where Lana is having her party and there's nothing much else to do except go to a club, go to a movie, go to the Beverly Center, but there aren't any good bands playing and everyone's seen all the movies and we went to the Beverly Center last night so I've been driving around and around in the hills overlooking Sunset and

Skip is telling me that we've got to score some crystal meth. DJ does another line and he's running his finger over his teeth and gums and he asks Skip whatever happened to his friend Michael and Skip says "Really?" and DJ laughs and Skip pushes in my Birthday Party tape and twists up the volume and Nick Cave starts to scream.

I light a cigarette and remember something, a dream maybe, about running down the streets of Los Angeles, and I pass the cigarette to Skip and he takes a drag and passes it back to Jane and Jane takes a drag and passes it back to Skip. DJ lights a cigarette of his own and just ahead a billboard reads Your Message Here and beneath it is an empty space. A car is stopped at the next light, a silver Ferrari, and when I pull up next to it, I turn my head to see two guys inside wearing sunglasses and one of them looks at me and I look back at him and he starts to roll down his window and I drive fast out of the hills and back into the city. The rain is pouring harder and the sidewalks are empty and the streets shine like black mirrors and I start thinking about last summer and I make a couple of wrong turns and end up back on Sunset.

Summer. There is nothing much to remember about last summer. Nights at clubs like Darklands, Sleepless, Cloud Zero, The End. Waking up at noon and watching MTV. A white Lamborghini parked in front of Tower Records. The Swans concert, DJ pissing in the aisle at the Roxy in the middle of "Children of God." A prostitute with a broken arm, waving me over on Santa Monica and asking me if I'd like to have a good time. Breakfast at Gaylords, Mimosas with Perrier-Jouet. Lunch with my mother at the Beverly Wilshire and then driving her to LAX for the redeye back to Boston. Dinner with Deb and her parents at R.T.'s, blackened mahimahi, Cobb salad, Evian water, and feeling Deb up under the table while her father talked about the Dodgers. The new S.P.K. album. Going to Palm Springs with Skip over Labor Day weekend and getting fucked up and watching a lizard crawl along a palm tree for about an afternoon. Jane's abortion. Monster billboards of Mick Jagger grinning down on Hollywood Boulevard like the skull of a rotting corpse. Clive getting busted, DWI and possession, and his father getting him off and buying him a new 380SL. Hearing the Legendary Pink Dots on AM radio. And, oh yeah, the thing with the zombies.

It's ten P.M. and I'm sitting at the bar in Citrus with Skip and DJ and Jane and the television down at the end is turned to MTV but the sound is off. I order a Stoly straight up and DJ orders a Rolling Rock and Jane orders a Kir and Skip orders a champagne cocktail and Jane changes her mind and orders a champagne cocktail. We look at the menus for a while but we're not very hungry since we did a half a gram at this guy Schuyler's or Wyler's party so we sit at the bar and we talk about new videos and this girl I don't know comes up to me and thanks me for the ride to Bel Air. Jane digs in her purse and I think she takes some Quaaludes and I look down the bar and out the window and I see nothing at all. "What are we going to do?" I ask no one in particular. "What are we going to do?" Skip asks back and he gives me a matchbook and shows me the handwritten address on the back, some place in the Valley, and he tells the bartender that we'll take the check.

I drive to Jane's house. Nobody's home. Jane forgets the security code and Skip is telling her to try typing the year, it's always the year, and she types one nine eight nine into the little box and the red light goes green and the front door's open and we're inside. We walk through the darkness of the hall to get to the kitchen and there's a note on the table with the telephone number of the hotel where her mother and father, or her mother and her mother's lover, are spending the holidays. There's a stack of unread newspapers and a can of Diet Coke and an empty box of Wheat Thins and then the three videotapes.

"Deal with it" Skip says and he picks up the videotapes and he walks into the living room and he starts on the vodka and tries to turn on the television. I sit on the floor with DJ and Jane, and her parents have one of these big-screen TVs, forty-five inches maybe, with a pair of video-

tape machines on top, and Skip finds the right buttons and
the first tape is rolling. I think that maybe DJ got the
tapes or probably Jane, she was at Claremont for a while
and had a friend who knew some guy whose brother
worked one time at a video store, a film student, and this
guy stuck them away when the lists came out, and Jane
maybe balled him and got the tapes, so we're watching
them, all in a row, three of them, lying on the floor of this
high-ceilinged living room with this antique furniture and
this print by Lucian Freud and Jane keeps telling us that
she's seen all these movies before even though she hasn't.
Skip is sitting with the remote control in his hand and he
doesn't say a word, he keeps flicking the fast forward,
jumping ahead to the best scenes, and the first one is called
Dawn of the Dead and right away this zombie's head gets
blown apart by a shotgun blast and this other zombie gets
its head chopped off and the next one is just called *Zombie*
and the last one I can't remember much about except the
part where this doctor blew away this little girl, she was a
zombie, and he put the pistol almost right to her head and
the pieces of head and brains and blood went spraying
away across the inside of an elevator and just for a moment you could see right through the space where her
brain used to be and I look at Jane right after this happens
but she isn't looking at me, she's looking at Skip and DJ,
and I guess she knows what she wants, don't we all?

An hour later, there's no more vodka and there's no more
beer and the television is turned to MTV and Jane just
lays there on the floor of her parents' living room, staring
at the ceiling, while DJ fucks her for about the third time.
Skip is on the telephone in Jane's bedroom, trying to score
some meth from a dealer in the city, and after a while I'm
in there with him, looking at the poster of The Doors and
the poster of The Smiths and listening to him say "Deal
with it" over and over before he slams the telephone back
onto the cradle and rolls his eyes at me and looks at the
posters and says "Strange days and strange ways" and
then he starts to smile and I think I get it.
    The telephone rings and Skip answers and it's Deb. Skip
sighs and waves me to the phone and I say hello and she

says hello and asks me what I want for Christmas and can she talk to Jane. I tell her I don't know and that Jane can't talk right now and she says that's okay, she's coming over, don't go, she'll be right there and I say okay and good-bye and she says good-bye. I watch Skip go through the drawers of Jane's desk. He stuffs a pack of cigarettes and a lighter into his pocket and hands me a Polaroid picture and it's Jane when she was a little girl and she's standing in front of a fat birthday cake with eight blue-and-white candles and she is smiling a big smile and I don't tell him that that's me standing next to her, the little blond kid with the burry haircut and the thick black glasses. He isn't looking at the photograph anyway, he's looking at me, and all he says is "You faggot" and then he has his hands on the buckle of my jeans and he's pulling me onto the bed on top of him.

Afterward, we smoke a couple of cigarettes and I follow Skip back downstairs. DJ has found another bottle of beer somewhere and he's sitting on the couch watching MTV. Jane is still lying on the carpet, staring at the ceiling, and the fingers of her right hand are moving, clutching into a fist, flattening, then clutching into a fist again. Skip walks over to her and unzips his jeans and says that Deb is on her way and doesn't anybody know how we can score some meth. Jane's right hand flattens, then curls into another fist, then flattens again, and she looks up at Skip and says "Well?" and DJ looks up from the television and says "Well what?"

Another video flashes by. Another. Then another. Love and Rockets has no new tale to tell by the time Deb shows up. She's wearing a silk blouse and a brown leather miniskirt that she bought at Magnin's in Century City. "Love you" she says to no one at all. She kisses DJ on the cheek and sticks out her tongue at Skip and Skip acts like he doesn't notice and keeps on fucking Jane. She says hello to me and I say hello back and she tries on my sunglasses. She walks across the room and starts searching through a stack of CDs. She holds up an old album by Bryan Ferry, puts it down, and picks up one by This Mortal Coil. She says "Can I play this?" and when nobody answers, she slides it into the player and punches a few buttons and cranks the stereo up loud. DJ is watching MTV and Skip is watching MTV while he's fucking Jane and Jane is still looking at the ceiling and I'm trying not to look at Deb. She is singing along with Elizabeth Fraser, swaying back and forth in a kind of dance. I dreamed, she is singing, you dreamed about me. Then she sits down in front of the fireplace and slips a joint out of the pocket of her skirt and she takes off my sunglasses and squints her eyes and she looks a long time at the joint before lighting it. "Song for the Siren" winds down and there's a moment of silence and Skip is pulling himself off Jane with a sound that is hot and wet.

"Next" he says, and he looks first at Deb, then at me.

I dream, but I dream about me. I see myself walking through the streets of downtown Los Angeles and the day is cloudy and the sun goes out and it starts to rain and I start to run and I see myself start to run. In my dream I am chasing myself, running past the Sheraton Grande, past the Bonaventure, past the Arco Tower, and for a minute I think I am going to catch up but the streets are slippery with rain and I fall once, twice, and when I stand again I can't see anyone but this teenager at the opposite corner of the intersection and when I look again it's me, a younger me, and he's fifteen years old and he turns away and starts to run and I start chasing him and now he's thirteen years old and he runs and I run and now he is eleven years old and he is getting younger with each step, younger and smaller, and now he's nine years old and he's eight years old and he's seven years old and I've almost caught him and he's six years old and he turns into this alley and I'm right behind him and he's four years old and it's a dead-end street and he's three years old and he can just barely run and I catch him and he's two years old and I pull him up into my arms and I'm at the end of the alley and he's one year old and I'm standing on the porch of our house, the house where I grew up in Riverside, and he's six months old and I'm knocking on the door and I can hear footsteps inside and he's three months old and

my mother is coming to the door and I can't wait for her
to see me and he's just a baby and he's getting smaller and
he's disappearing and the door is opening and my mother
is looking out and he's gone and I'm gone and then there's
nothing. Nothing at all.

It's midnight. Still raining. Jane's parents live in the
Flatlands, next door to the French actor in that new CBS
sitcom, and his dog is barking as we get in the car and
Skip shows me the matchbook and the handwritten address and gives me some directions. I drive toward West-
wood and take a right onto Beverly Glen and somewhere
in the hills I stop at a liquor store for some cigarettes and
a bottle of Freixenet and then I'm back at the wheel and
I'm driving onto Mulholland and into the Valley and onto
the Ventura Freeway and I look at Skip and he acts like
he's smiling, his left hand keeping beat on his leg and it's
right on target, one two three four, one two three four, but
I don't know the song on the radio, I've never heard it
before. I look into the rearview mirror and I see that Deb
is all over Jane and I see that DJ is watching them and I
see that Deb's tongue is in Jane's mouth and I look at Skip
and I see that he is watching me while I'm watching DJ
who is watching Deb and Jane and I still don't know the
name of that song.

Skip taps me on the shoulder and we're coming up on the
exit and he has just popped something into his mouth and
he downs it with the last of the Freixenet. He drops the
black bottle onto the floor and opens his palm to me as if
to say "Want some?" and I look at the little yellow pill
and I wonder if I could use some Valium. The music is
loud with guitars, it sounds like the Cult, and Skip is
pounding out the big electric beat on the window, harder
and harder, and spiderwebs are running across the glass
and he hits the window one more time and it shatters and
he shows me his hand. Little cuts run along his knuckles
but he hasn't started bleeding and the song ends and the
commercial begins and he turns the volume back down.
We go to the Lone Star Chili Parlor in Hidden Hills and

sit there drinking coffee and wait awhile because we're early and then we go back to the car.

The Valley at two A.M. Van Nuys Boulevard out farther than I thought it went. The moon is curled and shiny and I pull into the parking lot and for some reason Skip seems nervous and we pass the empty theater twice and I keep asking him why and he keeps asking me if I really want to go through with this and I keep telling him that I do. Jane is digging around for something in her purse and Deb is saying "I want to see" and DJ is trying to laugh and as soon as I step out of the car and I look at the line in the shadows, I tell him again.

The mall is no Galleria, not even a mall, just a hollow horseshoe, a curve of little shops, the theater, a drugstore, a pizza place, a karate club, and lots of empty windows lined with whitewash and old newspapers and printed signs that say Commercial Space. There's a chubby kid sitting in a lounge chair in front of the theater, wearing Vuarnets and reading *The Face* and taking ten dollars from each person who wants to go inside. He doesn't even look up as we walk by. DJ pays him and Deb takes my hand and we're inside and the hallway is lined with torn movie posters and shattered glass and spray paint and Skip nods at me and points to the handwritten sign that reads Club Dead.

The lobby looks something like an attic and it's dark and crammed with furniture. Some guy at the back, the manager maybe, is dealing dollar bills to a pair of policemen. He nods at Skip and he nods at me and he lets us through and this girl in the corner winks at me and tries to smile, pale white lipstick and her tongue licking out, and she knows Skip and she says something that I can't hear and Skip gives her the finger.

Inside the lights are bright and it takes my eyes a while to adjust. The place is crowded but we find a table and five chairs and DJ orders a round, four Coronas and a Jack Daniels, straight up, for Deb. "Black Light Trap" is playing over the sound system and the bar is lined with boys trying to look interested in anything but what's about to go down. No one is looking at Jane, plain Jane. Some are looking at Deb and some are looking at these other girls smoking clove cigarettes and standing or sitting in little groups. Skip points out his friend Philip, standing in the back and wearing sunglasses and a black Bauhaus T-shirt.

I get up from the table and go to the bar and then outside with Philip and it's raining and I can hear Shriekback from inside singing that we make our own mistakes and I score from Philip and then I go to the bathroom and lock the door and stare at myself in the mirror. Somebody knocks on the door and I put my foot back against it and say "Deal with it" and lay out three lines and do them and take a drink from the faucet and decide I need a haircut.

It's hot back in the theater and I hold my Corona up to my face, my forehead. There's a man sitting at a table next to us whose eyes are closed so tight that he is crying. The girl he's sitting with is tugging at the crotch of her Guess jeans and drinking a California Cooler and she's fourteen if she's a day. When the man opens his eyes, he looks at his Rolex and he looks at the stage and he looks at the girl and for some reason I'm relieved.

That's when the music goes down and the lights dim and there's some applause, scattered, and the music revs up again, something by Skinny Puppy, and at long last it's showtime. There are video screens set in a line over the stage and I look up and they shoot on one by one and it's a clip, just a short sixty seconds or so, from one of the films we saw, a grainy bootleg copy of a copy of a copy with subtitles in some foreign language, Spanish I think, and the zombies are loose inside a shopping mall and Skinny Puppy is pounding on and the singer's voice is barking deep down trauma hounds and the film clip jumps and now it's from some place back east, you can tell by the trees, and this is from television, from the news last summer, before they stopped talking, before the lists came out, and these soldiers are sweeping through a little town and the buildings are burning and the air is filled with smoke and they're moving house to house and they're blasting the doors and firing inside and now there's a pile of bodies and it's on fire and now it's that commercial, that public service announcement, whatever, and the Surgeon General is saying that the dead are alive, they're coming back to life, but we're killing them again, it's okay, it's all right, and somebody told me he's dead, all those guys are dead, and now the film clip jumps again and the colors roll over and over and the picture steadies and there's a test pattern. Skip says "This is it" and a new picture fades in and then this real tinny music, more like muzak, and it's a video, a home video, something shot with a Handycam maybe, and the picture is a basement or a garage, just bare walls, grey concrete, and after about a minute shadows start walking across the walls and then the first one's out on stage.

The music is gone and there's nothing but silence and a kind of hum, the tape is hissing, and the camera goes out of focus and the picture breaks up and then it's back in focus and she is looking at the camera. She's recent, blond and tall and sort of cute, and she's wearing a Benetton sweatshirt and acid-wash 501 jeans and it's hard to believe she's dead.

"This is real" Skip says to me and he turns to DJ and Deb and Jane and he says "For real." It's quiet in the club, quiet except for the hissing tape, and on the tape the girl is staring at the camera for a long time and nothing else happens. The floor behind her is covered with plastic trash bags and what looks like newspaper and there's a thin wooden cot and there's a worktable in the corner and I wonder why there's a power saw on the table and it does seem warm and I reach for my Corona and the bottle is empty and I look around for the waitress and everybody is watching the screen so I do too. This guy comes into the picture with a coil of rope and he's wearing this black hood and she sees him or hears him and she starts to turn his way and she stumbles and her legs are caught, there are chains on her ankles, and now there's another guy and he's wearing a ski mask and he's coming up behind her and he's carrying a chain and something like a harness, a leather harness, and I look at Deb and Deb looks at me and now they're hitting the girl with the chain and she falls to the ground and they're hitting her some more and now the rope is around her and the harness is over her face and I look at Deb and Deb is touching herself and I look back at the video and they're cutting her clothes and now they're cutting her and I look at Deb and Deb looks at me and she reaches to touch me and now they loop the rope around her neck and Deb's hand is moving up my leg and now the first guy is gone and Deb's hand is moving and now he's back and Deb is squeezing me and he's got a hammer and he swings it once and he swings it twice and Deb is squeezing me harder and now the rope is fastened overhead and someone in the audience says "Yeah" and Skip's arm circles Jane and he pulls her close and says "For real" and now they are yanking the rope and the noose is tightening and her feet are off the floor and Deb's hand is moving and squeezing and I tell her to slow down and she stops and says to hold on a minute and I try and I look back at the screen and now they have a set of hooks and Deb's hand is moving again and the hooks connect to chains and her hand is moving faster and the chains go taut and faster and there's a sound like a scream and faster and her head is bent back and faster and now they have a dildo and faster and they're fitting it with nails and faster and faster and faster now they have a boy, faster a little naked boy, and faster now they have a blowtorch and faster now they have a power drill and faster now they have and now they have and now they and now they and now and now and now the picture is gone and my crotch is wet and Deb reaches over and hands me a napkin.

It's four A.M. and it's getting cold and we're still sitting in the club and Skip is picking lint from my sweater and telling me that he wants to leave. The Clan of Xymox fades to Black and it's a wonderful life, the singer is singing, it's a wonderful, wonderful life. Jane is vomiting in the corner and the lights are dark and red and for a moment I think it looks like blood. DJ is turned away, watching two boys wet-kissing in the shadows beyond the stage and taking deep pulls on another Corona. Deb is out back fucking this guy from U.S.C., bleach-blond and tan and wearing a white Armani sweater. Skip is telling me that we ought to leave real soon now. The music clicks off and it's smoke and laughter and broken glass and the sound of

Jane spitting up and then the live band saunters onto the stage and the band is called 3 but there are four of them. The bass player has a broken right hand and Skip says "The bass player has a broken right hand" and slides a clove cigarette from his shirt pocket. The four-man band called 3 starts playing a speed metal version of "I Am the Walrus" and Deb is standing in front of me and she kisses me and tells Skip she's ready and Skip is saying that we have to leave and DJ is pulling Jane by the arm and Jane is still bent over and I wonder if I should ask if she's okay and my eyes meet Skip's and he cuts them to the exit and the next thing you know, we're gone.

Skip says Jimmy has a camera and I drive over to Jimmy's house, but Jimmy, somebody remembers, is either dead or in Bermuda, so I drive to Toby's place and this black kid answers the door wearing white underwear and a hard-on. A lava lamp bubbles red in the living room behind him. "Toby's busy" the black kid says and shuts the door. I take the Hollywood Freeway to Western Avenue but it's not right and I take the Hollywood Freeway to Alvarado but it's not right and I drive downtown and I take an exit, any exit, and I see the Sheraton Grande and I see the Bonaventure and I see the Arco Tower and I think it's time to run. Skip says to stop but it's still not right and I turn the corner and now it's right and so I stop and Skip tosses Jane out the door and she's facedown in the gravel and it sounds like she's going to vomit again.

"You didn't have to do that" somebody says but I don't know who. DJ is sitting up in the backseat and he pulls his arm from around Deb and shrugs and looks down at Jane. Skip starts to laugh and it sounds like choking and he turns up the radio and it's the New Order single and Jane is crawling away from the car. Skip is pulling something from under his jacket and his door slams and I check the rearview mirror. I look at the reflection of Deb's eyes for a moment and I don't say anything more.

The car is stopped in the middle of the street, at the mouth of an alley, and I see now that it's the alley from my dream, a hidden place, a perfect place, and Jane is crawling away from the car and Skip is walking toward her and he's taking his time and there's something in his hand, something long and sharp, and it glows in the glare of the headlights and his shadow is streaking across the brick walls of the alley and I think I've just seen this. Skip is standing over her and I see Jane start to say something and Skip is shaking his head as if he's saying no and then he's bending down toward her and she just watches as he cuts her once, then again, and she rolls onto her back and he flicks the knife past her face and she doesn't blink, doesn't move, and now the back door slams and DJ and Deb are out of the car and walking down the alley and now I'm walking down the alley and when we get there Skip shows us the knife, a thick military job, and Jane is bleeding on her arms and hands and a little on her neck and DJ says "Make it like the movie" and Skip says "This is the movie." He looks at DJ and he looks at Deb and he looks at me and he looks at Jane and he slides the knife into her stomach and the sound is soft and she barely moves and there isn't much blood at all, so he slides the knife into her stomach again, then into her shoulder, and this time she shudders and her back arches up and she seems to moan and the blood bubbles up but it isn't very red, it isn't very red at all. Deb says "Oh" and Skip tosses the knife aside and Jane rolls onto her stomach and I think she's starting to cry, just a little, and he looks around the alley but there's nothing there, garbage cans and crumpled papers and the burned-out hulk of an RX-7, and he finds a brick and he throws it at her and she curls up like a baby and DJ picks up the brick and throws it and Deb picks up the brick and throws it and then it's my turn and I pick up the brick and throw it and hit her in the head.

    We kick her for a while and then she starts to crawl and there still isn't much blood and it's the wrong color, almost black I guess, and it isn't very shiny and it's just like dripping, not spraying around or anything, and she is almost to the end of the alley and the street ends and there's a curb and there's a sidewalk and there's a wall and there's a light from somewhere beaming down and she crawls some more. Her head is in the gutter and Skip looks at DJ and he is saying "This is real" and he pulls at Jane's hair and her head is bent back and her mouth is open and he's dragging her forward and then he's pressing her face against the curb and her upper teeth are across the top of the curb, her lips are pulled back into a smile and it looks like the smile in the Polaroid, Jane is eight years old, and her head is hanging there by those upper teeth and I look at Skip and I look at DJ and I look at Deb and Deb is looking down and she's smiling too and Skip is saying "Real" and he puts his boot on the back of Jane's head and he presses once, twice, and that smile widens into a kiss, a full mouth kiss on the angle of concrete, and then he stomps downward and the sound is like nothing I have ever heard.

The sound is on the radio. I'm listening to the radio and it echoes along the alley and it plays song after song after song. I'm sitting on the curb with Skip and DJ and Deb, and DJ is smoking another cigarette and the stubs are collecting at his feet and there are seven or eight of them and we've been here an hour and it's nearly light and we've been waiting but now it's time to go.

"Okay, Jane" Deb says and she is standing and she is jabbing Jane with her foot and she is saying "We gotta go." Skip is standing and DJ is standing and Deb is looking at her Swatch and she says "Get up" and then she says "You can get up now." She is jabbing Jane with her foot and Jane isn't moving and Skip is wiping his knife and looking at Jane and DJ is smoking his cigarette and looking at Jane and I'm just looking at Jane and then I think I know. No, I do know. I'm sure I know.

"She's coming back, right?" Deb is saying and she's looking at Skip and she's looking at DJ and then she's looking at me. "Bret?" she is asking me and she is crossing her arms and she isn't smiling now. "She's coming back, isn't she?" Deb is saying "I mean, we're all coming back, right?" Skip is putting the knife in his pocket and DJ is finishing his cigarette and I am standing and she is saying "Right?"

People are afraid to live on the streets of Los Angeles. This is the last thing I say as I walk away from Skip and

DJ and Deb and get back into the car. I don't know why I keep saying this thing. It's something I started and now I can't stop. Nothing else seems to matter.

I sit behind the wheel of the car and I watch the windshield wipers go back and forth, back and forth, back and forth, and the city blurs, out of focus, beneath the thin black lines. I want to say that people are afraid. I want to say that people are afraid of something and I can't remember what and maybe it's nothing, maybe it's a dream and I am running, I am running after something and I can't remember what, I can't remember the dream, and the windshield wipers go back and forth, back and forth. People are afraid of something and in my dream I am running and the radio is playing and I try to listen but it is playing the song I do not know. The windshield wipers go back and forth. The doors open and close and then I drive away.

Like Pavlov's Dogs

BY STEVEN R. BOYETT

[1]

"*Good* morning, happy campers!" blares the loudspeaker on the wall above the head of Marly Tsung's narrow bed. "It's another beautiful day in paradise!" A bell rings. "Rise and shine!"

Marly the sleepy camper slides out from her pocket of warmth. "Rise your own fucking shine," she mutters as she rises from her pallet and staggers to the computer screen that glows a dull gray above her desk. The word UPDATE pulses in the middle of the monitor; she flicks it with a finger and turns away to find the clothes she shed the night before.

"Today is Wednesday, the twenty-ninth," says her recorded voice. "Today marks the three hundred seventy-second day of the station's operation." Marly sniffs and makes a sour face at how pleasant her earlier self sounds. How *enthused*. "Gung ho," she says.

"The structural integrity of the Ecosphere is ninety-nine point five percent," the recording continues brightly, "with indications of water-vapor leakage in panels above the northern quadrant of the Rain Forest environment."

"Christ," says Marly, hating the daily cheerfulness of her own voice. She slides into faded, baggy jeans, then scoops on peasant sandals.

"Unseasonal warm weather in this region of Arizona has increased the convection winds from the Desert environment, and as a result the humidity has increased in the Rain Forest environment. Rainfall may be expected in the late afternoon. Soil nitrogenating systems are—"

Marly puts on a T-shirt, sees the neck tag pass in front of her, pulls the shirt partway off, and turns it around.

Leaving, she pauses at the door and looks back. Computer console on oak desk, dirty laundry, precariously stacked pop-music cassettes, rumpled bed. If someone were to come in here, someone who knew Marly but wasn't on Staff, would they be able to figure out who lived here?

She looks away. The question is moot. The only people in the entire world who know Marly are the Ecostation personnel.

She slides shut the door on her own voice and heads down the narrow hall to one of the station's two bathrooms.

FLUSH TWICE— IT'S A LONG WAY TO THE KITCHEN is scrawled in black felt-tip on the wall facing her. It's been there a year now. More recently—say, ten months ago— someone wrote, below that, EAT SHIT. And below that— with a kind of prophetic irony—WE'RE ALL IN THIS TOGETHER.

Marly never did think these were very funny.

She flushes— once—and heads for the rec room and the inevitable. Her waste heads for reclamation and the (nearly) inedible.

Four of the other seven station personnel are in the rec room ahead of her. Billtheasshole stands on the blue wrestling mat. He's wearing his gray UCLA sweat suit again. If clothes could get leprosy, they'd look like that sweat suit. On a leather thong around his neck is a silver whistle. Marly thinks her usual idle morning thought about what it would feel like to choke Billtheasshole by that lanyard. She imagines his stern face purpling, his reptilian eyes dimming. Watching his tinfoil colored eyes staring at the door, Marly invents Tsung's law: The biggest shithead and the person in command can usually be shot with the same bullet.

Pale Grace sits glumly at an unplugged gaming table, drumming her nails against the dark glass tabletop. Marly shakes her head. A year now, and Grace still looks like someone desperate for a cigarette. She catches Marly watching her and ducks her head and twitches a smile.

Marly thinks of just staring at her to drive her even more crazy, but what's the point?

Slumped against the heavy bag in the corner like a determined marathon dancer is Dieter. He smiles sleepily at her and scratches his full, brown beard. "Grow me coffee," he says in his pleasant Rotweiler growl, "and I will unblock your pipes for the next year."

She smiles and shakes her head. "No beans," she replies. This has become their daily morning ritual. Dieter knows what that headshake is really for: He's unblocked her pipes enough already, thank you.

Sitting barefoot in lotus on the folding card table is little carrot-topped Bonnie. She smiles warmly at Marly, attempting to get her to acknowledge the spiritual kinship that supposedly exists between them because Bonnie is into metaphysics and Marly is Chinese.

Marly makes herself look inscrutable.

In walk Deke and Haiffa, a mismatched set: him burly, her slight; him hairy, her smooth; him Texas beefeating good-ole-boy-don't-shoot-till-you-see-the-black-of-their-skin, her Israeli vegetarian educated at Oxford. Naturally they are in love. Marly pays them little mind beyond a glance as they walk in holding hands like children and sit on the unraveling couch; Deke and Haiffa return the favor. They have become Yin and Yang, a unit unto themselves, outside of which exists the entire rest of the world. Proof again that there is such a thing as circumstantial love, love in a context, love-in-a-box.

Last in is Leonard Willard. Marly still spells his name LYNYRD WYLLYRD on the duty roster, long after the last drop of humor has been squeezed from the joke, which Leonard never got anyway. Leonard is the youngest staff member, always compensating for his inexperience with puppyish eagerness to please. But despite the fact that Leonard could have been one of the original Mouseketeers, Marly takes his constant good cheer as an indication of his bottomless well of self deception. The Ecosphere station is his world; everything outside it is . . . some movie he saw once. In black and white. Late at night. When he was a kid. He really doesn't remember it very well.

Predictably, Billtheasshole blows his whistle the moment the last person walks in. "Okay, troops," he says. "Fall in." He likes to call the staff members "troops." He would still be wearing his mirrored aviator sunglasses if Marly hadn't thrown them into the Ocean.

She falls in behind the others as they line up on the wrestling mat to begin their calisthenics. Or, as Billtheasshole calls them, their "cardiovascular aerobic regimen."

[2]

Sweetpea spits gum onto low-pile, gray carpet. "Flavor's gone," she explains.

Doughboy laughs. Shirtless, his hairy belly quivers. "Where you gonna get some more, girl?"

("Sailor?" someone calls from the stacks upstairs. "Goddamn motherfucker—*Sailor!*")

Sweetpea just shrugs and turns her back on Doughboy. She goes to join a group gathered behind one of the tall bookshelves. 0900: American History. One of the group pulls a book from a shelf and heaves it, then gives the finger to someone Doughboy can't see. The hand is snatched back as a return salvo is launched from Engineering. The book tumbles across the floor and stops facedown like a tired bat near Doughboy's left boot. *Alloy Tensile Strength Comparisons.* He doesn't attempt to interpret the title, but bends down, picks up the book, and pulls Sweetpea's gum from where it has stuck against a page that shows a graph. He brings fingers to chapped lips and blows. Fingers in mouth, then out, and wiped against blue jeans that have all the beltloops ripped loose. "Dumb bitch," he says, and chews.

A loud slap from above. Doughboy looks up to see gangly Tex being thrown against a tall shelf. The shelf tips, but does not fall. Books do.

"What the fuck you *yelling* for, man?" Sailor stands above Tex, who has set a hand to his reddening cheek. Sailor remains there a moment, looking down at Tex with hands on hips, then bends and pulls Tex to his feet. He dusts him off and pats his shoulder. "Look, I'm sorry I hit you, man," he says. "Only, don't run around *yelling* all the time, okay?"

"Sure," says Tex. His hand leaves his inflamed cheek, and he glances at his palm (for blood? wonders Doughboy). "Sure. But, I mean, I was just wonderin', y'know? I mean—" He looks around the library. "What're we gonna find here?"

Sailor frowns. He looks around. One hand tugs at the face of Mickey Mouse hanging from his right ear. When he looks back at Tex, he's smiling wryly.

"Books," he says.

Doughboy nearly chokes on his gum, he thinks this is so goddamn funny.

"What are *you* laughing at?" from above.

Doughboy only shakes his head.

Sailor shakes his head, too, but for completely different reasons. "Fuck," he says. "I used to *go* to this school." He comes down the stairs with two hardcover books tucked under one arm. "Yoo of A."

Doughboy angles his head to see the titles; Sailor hands him the books. Doughboy holds one in each hand before him. His lips move. Furrows appear in his forehead.

Sailor taps the book in Doughboy's left hand. *"Principles of Behavior Modification,"* he supplies. He taps the thicker in Doughboy's right. *"Radiation and Tissue Damage."* He clasps his hands behind him and rocks back and forth, beaming.

"You taking a test?"

Sailor shakes his head. "Nope. Deadheads are. I think I can teach them to find food for us. *Real* food."

Doughboy makes a farting noise. "Shit. *We* can't find real food; how you expect them to?"

"The name 'Pavlov' ring a bell?"

"No."

Sailor sighs. "Why I stay with you limpdicks I will never know," he says.

Doughboy stacks the books. "But how you gonna get—"

"God damn you, nigger!"

They turn at the shout from Engineering.

"That *hurt,* motherfucker!"

"Why you didn't move, then, home?" replies American History. "What you been throwing at *me* the last—"

Shouts, something heavy thrown against a wall, a bookshelf falling against a bookshelf, scuffling, and cheers as American History and Engineering begin beating the living shit out of each other.

Sailor walks over to break it up. He takes his time, wondering why the hell he's bothering in the first place. He oughta just let evolution sort 'em out. Well, he's there now; he might as well do something to split 'em up.

It's Cheesecake and Jimmy. Figures. Cheesecake's got the upper hand, which is no surprise, and with no more than two or three blows he's already made a mess of Jimmy's face. White boys never could fight.

He leans forward to grab Cheesecake's teak arm as the knotted fist at the end of it rises, but something stops him. Around them

("You gonna let that nigger put a hurt on you, boy?")

are scattered newspapers. One lies spilled like a dropped deck of cards

("Fuck 'im up! Yeah! Yeah!"),

fanned out to expose the Local section.

Dull slap of bone-backed meat on softer meat.

Sailor bends to pick up the paper.

("Cheese, man, ease up. C'mon, man.")

       'Space
       Breaks

("Motherfucker hit me on my head with a book. A big book, motherfucker!")

Sailor turns the paper over.

       Station'
       New Ground

He unfolds the paper.

("Ah! Fucking nigger! I'll kill you, fuckin—")

       'Space Station'
       Breaks New Ground

Sailor frowns. An artist's conception accompanies the article.

"Let him up," Sailor says mildly, and they stop.

(Tucson)—Official groundbreaking ceremonies were held Monday morning in a tent 60 miles north-west of Tucson, to mark the beginning of construction on Ecosphere—a self-contained "mini-Earth" environment that may prove a vital step in mankind's eventual colonization of other planets.

Budgeted at a "modest" $30 million, according to project director Dr. William Newhall of the University of Arizona Ecological Sciences division, Ecosphere will be a completely self-sufficient, 5-million-cubic-feet ecological station. The station will contain five separate environments, including a tropical rain forest, a savanna, a marshland, a desert, and a 50,000-gallon salt-water "ocean," complete with fish. There will also be living quarters for the Ecosphere staff, scientific laboratories, livestock, and an agriculture wing—all on two acres covered by computer-controlled "windowpanes" that regulate the amount of sunlight received. Even Ecosphere's electrical energy will come from the sun, in the form of arrays of solar-power cells.

"Ecosphere will be a sort of model of our planet," says chief botanist Marly Tsung. "We'll have a little of everything"—including several thousand types of trees, plants, animals, fish, birds, insects, and even different kinds of soil.

If all goes well after Ecosphere is constructed and stocked, eight "Ecosphereans" will bid goodbye to the outside world and enter the station's airlock, and they will remain as working residents of this model Earth for two years.

Designed to reproduce and maintain the delicate balance of the Earth's ecosystem in the midst of a hostile environment—presently the Arizona desert, but conceivably Mars by the end of the century—Ecosphere will also serve as an experiment in how future interplanetary colonists might get along working in close quarters for long periods. However, Grace Havland, team psychologist, does not foresee any problems. "We're all self-motivated, resourceful, problem-solving people," she says. "But we're also very different from one another, with widely varied interests. I think that will help. That, and the fact that the station itself provides a lot of stimuli."

What could go wrong? In the first place, Ecosphere's delicate environment could suffer a

(turn to page 16D)

"I remember this," says Sailor as the others gather around to see what's got him so interested. Jimmy mops his face with his torn, white T-shirt. "They started building it when I was in school." He turns to 16D. "They interviewed a bunch of these assholes before they went to live in it. There was this Chinese girl with blue eyes." He whistles appreciative recollection and lowers the paper. Suddenly he frowns and hands the paper to Florida, who scans the article and studies the cutaway drawing of the Ecosphere (which is not a sphere at all). Florida's dark eyebrows flex toward his hairline. One big-fingered, skull-ringed hand strays to his scarred leather hunting vest. He passes the paper around for the others to read and scratches the back of his neck under the red elastic band that holds his long pony tail.

Ed the Head squints at the article as if it is out of focus. His lips move as he reads, then he turns bleary eyes to Sailor. "So they, like, built some kinda space station in the middle of the goddamn desert. So fuckin' what?"

"So now you know why no one lets you do the grocery shopping," says Sailor. "You wouldn't recognize an opportunity if it gave you a whip-cream enema."

Ed fingers his matted beard. "Chill out, dude. Ain't nobody fuckin' with *you.*"

Sailor shakes his head. "It's all just one big mystery to you, isn't it?" He looks around at the group. "Jesus," he says, and takes back the paper before leaving them.

"What he mad about?" Cheesecake rubs cut knuckles with two ragged-nailed fingers.

Florida folds his Popeye arms, making himself look twice as big as he already is. "That space station's set up to go for years without any help from outside," he says in his surprising melodic baritone. He pulls off his silver ear cuff and massages the outside curve of his ear. "They control their environment. They grow their own food. They raise their own livestock. Get it now?" His arms unfold. "Apples. Oranges. Chicken. Eggs. Bacon."

"Oh, man . . ." from someone behind Jimmy.

"Aw, those dudes're wasted by now," says Ed the Head.

"Reefer," adds Florida.

Ed the Head straightens. "No shit? Hey, Florida, man, you wouldn't fuck with me, now. . . ."

"How we know they still there?" demands Cheesecake. "They be walkin' around dead and shit, by now."

Florida smiles and replaces his earcuff. "We don't know," he says. He glances at Sailor and raises an eyebrow. "Yet."

"Doughboy. Hey, Doughboy!"

Doughboy turns with a finger still up his nose. "Yo, Sailor," he says mildly. He twists, pulls out—

"We still got that baby?"

—and puts the finger in his mouth. He withdraws it with a wet smack and shrugs. "I dunno. Maybe. You wanna go to the zoo an' see?"

Outside the hurricane fence at the juncture of Optical Sciences and Physics: Sailor and Doughboy peer about the corral.

"I don't see it," says Sailor. "Maybe they ate it?"

"Nah. They don't do that, much. Somehow they know the difference." He bangs the fence with both palms.

Shambling figures turn.

"Hey," shouts Doughboy. *"Hey, you deadhead fuckheads!"* He bangs harder. " 'Course," he says, more conversationally, watching their stiff approach, "they coulda tore it up. They're kinda dumb that way."

Watching them shuffle toward him and Doughboy, Sailor suddenly begins to giggle. He bends forward and his mouth opens, as if he has been kicked in the stomach. The giggle expands and becomes full-throated. He can't control it. Eventually he drags a bare, anchor-tattooed forearm across one eye, saying "Oh, shit . . ." in a pained way, and wipes the other eye with the other arm. "Oh, Jesus. Whose idea was *this*?"

Doughboy grins and rubs a palm across sparse blond billy-goat beard. "You like it?" The hand lowers to hook a thumb in a front pocket of his Levi's. "Florida ran across a T-shirt shop in the Westside Mall. He brought back a shitload of 'em. And a bunch of us got the deadheads outta of the zoo one at a time and put 'em on 'em."

Sailor shakes his head in amazement.

A little old lady deadhead reaches the fence ahead of the others. Part of her nose is missing, and the rest flaps against one wrinkled, bluegray cheek in time with her sleepwalker's gait. She runs face-first into the fence, then steps back with a vaguely surprised look that quickly fades. Hanging shapelessly about her upper body is a ridiculously large, blue T-shirt. I'M WITH STUPID, it reads, with an arrow pointing to her left.

Sailor begins to laugh again.

Doughboy is laughing now, too.

The dead old lady is joined by an enormous Hispanic deadhead with the figure of a bodybuilder. His skin is the color of moss. A strip of bone shows above his ear where a furrow of scalp has been ripped away. His arms and chest look overinflated. He wears a tight, red maternity blouse. Centered over his bulging pectorals is:

BABY
↓

The deadheads make plaintive little noises as they reach like sad puppies for Sailor and Doughboy, only to regard the fence that blocks their hands as some kind of miraculous object that has inexplicably appeared in front of them.

There are twenty of them clustered around the fence now, purpled fingers poking nervelessly through the wide mesh.

"No baby," says Doughboy. "But it wouldn't be here anyway. Can't walk yet."

"Walk?" Sailor frowns. "It probably never will." He regards the hungry drowned faces as he speaks. "I wonder if they age?"

Doughboy's eyes narrow. "Baby doesn't have to have

been like that from the start. Coulda been born after everything turned to shit, then died an' gone deadhead."

"Yeah, but still—how would we know? Do they get older as time goes by?" He nods toward the fence. "Can a deadhead die of old age?"

Doughboy shrugs. "We'll find out someday," he says.

Sailor looks away from the fence. "Are you an optimist or what?"

Doughboy only snorts.

"Who's the one by himself back there?" Sailor points. "He doesn't move like a deadhead."

"Whozzat? Oh, Jo-Jo? Yeah, he's pretty fuckin' amazing, ain't he? He's a regular Albert fuckin' Einstein—for a deadhead, I mean. Quick, huh?"

The figure standing alone turns to face them. He wears a brown T-shirt with white letters that spell out HE'S DEAD, JIM.

Sailor's frown deepens. "He's *watching* us."

"They all do that, man. We look like those big ol' steaks in the cartoons."

"No, I mean . . ." He squints. "There's something going on in that face. His *tabula* ain't quite *rasa.*"

"Yeah, what you said. Here—" Doughboy leaves the fence and goes to a plastic milk crate. He pulls out a disk that glints rainbow colors. "Cee Dee," he says, grinning, and holds it up. "Michael Jackson. *Thriller.*"

In his other hand is a rock.

He steps to the left of the knot of deadheads who still claw vaguely toward them. He glances at Sailor and angles the compact disk to catch the sunlight.

"Jo-Jo," he calls. "Hey—Jo-Jo!" He jumps *(light on his feet, for a jelly-belly,* thinks Sailor) and lobs the rock.

"Jo-Jo!"

hunger me jojo they call jojo and throw at me without hurt only eat and i with move them to jojo from their meat mouths i reach to hunger with light of hot above with bright the fence the hunger-others grab and pull but shining outside they hold the shining thing and forward i into the fence grab against press into my face and raise my hands in hun-

ger not to the shining thing but to the hand that holds it in
hunger jojo they say and i will eat

"He," declares Sailor, watching the deadhead toss the
rock it has caught from hand to hand, "is smarter than the
average deadhead."
Doughboy nods. "Fuckin' A, Boo-Boo."

[3]

Bill hangs around after the others leave, sweating from
their cardiovascular aerobic regimen. They will disperse to
attend to the many jobs that await them each day; maintaining the Ecosphere is a full-time job for eight people.
And keeping those eight people in shape and responsive to
the needs of the ecological station, maintaining their *esprit
de corps,* making them understand their responsibilities to
the station's investors, to science—indeed, to the human
race—is quite a burden. That's why Bill is glad that he is
the one in charge—because, of the eight, only he has the
discipline and organizational abilities, the qualities of *command,* to keep them functioning as a unit. And—*as a unit*
—they will persevere. He imagines he is a lifeboat captain,
forcing the others to share their labor and rations, sometimes extreme in his severity and discipline. But when rescue comes, they will all thank Bill for running his tight
little ship. Yes they will.
He goes to a locker and removes a French fencing foil.
He tests the grip, slides into stance, and holds his left hand
loosely above and behind his head. *En garde.* Blade to
quarte. Block, parry, riposte. Lunge, *hah!* He is
D'Artagnan; the wine of his opponent's life spills upon the
wrestling mat. *Touché.*

The pigs in their small pen near the corner formed by
the human habitat and the agricultural wing are slopped
by Grace. Of all the dirty work in the station she must
perform (even though it is not her job to), the team psychologist finds working with the pigs almost pleasurable,
and certainly less troublesome than working with Staff.
Grace is a behaviorist, and a behaviorist will always work

better with pigs than with people. The pigs in their un-
complicated Skinner box of a muddy pen are easier to
direct and adjust than those upright pigs in their bigger,
labyrinthian pen.

The ground darkens around her and she looks up at a
cloud passing in front of the sun, distorted by the triangular glass panes above. She idly wonders how long it's been
since she went outside the station. She shrugs. What difference does it make?

She bends to pat Bacon's globular head. She has named
the pigs so that she will remember their prime function, to
prevent her from becoming too sentimentally attached to
them: Bacon, Fatback, Pork Chop, Hot Dog, Sausage, and
Hambone. The pigs are wonderful: not only do they clear
the quarter acre of land devoted to raising vegetable crops,
and fertilize it as well, but they are astonishingly gregari-
ous, affectionate, and intelligent animals. Which any farm
girl knows—but Grace has devoted her life to the exacting
science of manipulating human beings, and has only recently become devoted to the emotionally admirable pig.

If only the staff were as easy to manage. Humbly she
tries to tell herself that she's only doing her job, but, truth
to tell, if they hadn't had someone to keep them psychologically stable all this time, she doubts they'd have lasted
even this long. She thinks of the other staff members one
at a time as Pork Chop and Sausage nuzzle her calves. She
maintains a file on each one of them and updates it every
day with her observations and impressions of their sessions together. Luckily the sessions have diminished in
importance, which is as it should be, since everybody is so
mentally healthy. So goddamned healthy. So *enormously*
adjusted.

Pork Chop squeals, and Grace realizes she has been
squeezing his poor ear as hard as she can. She lets go and
pats his thick head. "There, there," she says. "There,
there."

She thinks again of the book she will write when all this
is over. It will sell well. She will be on Phil Donahue.
Holding an imaginary pen, she practices signing her name.

* * *

Bonnie is not far from Grace; she works, shirtless in the early-morning sun, on her knees in the three tall rows of cornstalks. The agricultural wing is like the playing board of a child's game, with squares devoted to corn, potatoes, beans, peas, squash, carrots, and tomatoes. She wishes they had watermelon, but it would require far too much water to be ecologically justifiable. But at least there's the fruit grove by the wall, there—right beside the vegetables —with apples, oranges, and lemons. The soils are as rich as possible, having originally been procured from all parts of the United States.

Is it *still* the United States? Bonnie wonders. Surely somewhere it *must* be.

She returns to her work, examining stalks and peeling back husks to check for insects. There are screen doors in the narrow access corridors between the agriculture wings and the Environments, but still, insects manage to get through. Despite their productive yield the Ecosphere is actually never very far away from starvation, and the loss of a single crop to insects could be—well, it just didn't bear thinking about.

Bonnie likes to work with plants. Not in the same way that Marly does— that appraising, sterile, *scientific* way— but in a sort of . . . *holistic* way. An *organic* way. Yes, that's right: organic. She smiles at the word. Bonnie feels a kinship to the plants, with the interrelatedness of all living things. She likes to feel the sunlight on her bare, freckled skin because it reminds her of the ironic combination of her specialness and insignificance. The sun is an indifferent ball of burning gases ninety-three million miles away, yet without it there could be no life. "We are all made of the same star-stuff," Carl Sagan used to say. Well, Bonnie feels that stuff in her very cells. It sings along the twined strands of her DNA.

She certainly doesn't miss sex. She doesn't need sex. She hardly ever even *thinks* about sex.

She sits up and shuts her eyes. She breathes deeply. *Om mani padme om.* Who needs sex when there is such passion in as simple an act of life as breathing?

She finds a bug in a cornhusk and crushes it between thumb and forefinger.

Leonard Willard takes everybody's shit every day. He puts it in phials and labels it and catalogs it; he analyzes it and files the results. He operates and maintains the waste-reclamation systems and biological and mechanical filtering systems. It's a dirty job, but someone has to do it. If no one did it, the Ecosphere wouldn't work. Leonard likes to think of himself as the vital link in the Ecosphere's food chain. Filtration is his life. Ecosphere gives him an abundance of opportunity to feel fulfilled: there are filtration systems in the sewage facilities, in the garbage-disposal units, in the water-reclamation systems; there are desalinization units between the Ocean and the freshwater marsh; there are air filtration units, and air is also cleaned by pumping it beneath the Ecosphere and allowing it to percolate through the soil from several areas.

Leonard loves to purify things. To take a thing that is unusable in its present form, and by passing it through buffers and barriers and filters, distill a usable, needed thing—that makes him feel useful. Needed. Staff couldn't breathe without him. Staff couldn't drink without him. Without Leonard, staff couldn't take so much as a healthy shit. Without Leonard, the shit would never hit the fans.

Leonard has Hodgkin's disease, a cancer of the lymph system. Years ago radiation therapy made all his hair fall out and stabilized his condition enough that he could be put on chemotherapy, which only made him stupid and violently ill for two days out of every month. He began putting on weight again, and his hair grew back in, even thicker than before, and the doctors felt encouraged that his condition had stabilized. Somehow his body learned to live with the disease.

Or, from a different perspective, he thinks (reaching a gloved hand into a water conduit to withdraw what looks like a dirty wet air-conditioning filter), the disease has allowed his body to live. So that it can continue to feed. This is why Leonard rarely worries about the things that roam the Outside, the things Bill has dubbed carnitropes. He doesn't worry about them because his body is being eaten from the *in*side. Or, to distill it in a very Leonard-like way, there is shit in his blood, and he can't filter it out.

He shakes the wet filter over a plastic sheet. Ropy black strands drip down. Leonard cleans the filter with a compressed-air hose, returns it to the conduit, then bundles and twist-ties the plastic sheet.

Walking with it dripping to the lab, Leonard realizes that there is nowhere else on Earth, anymore, where he could perform his job. Leonard feels he is the most realistic of all the Staff—and he knows what it's like outside their brittle little environment. Though he helps maintain the station, and therefore the illusion the station represents, he understands intuitively that his reasons for doing so are quite different from theirs. They maintain Ecosphere as a denial of what has changed Outside. He maintains it as a triumphant affirmation of the same. As above, so below. None of the others, being physically fit, can appreciate this. Therefore none of the others can adequately appreciate Leonard.

But he keeps up a cheery façade. It's important to him that he do this.

In the lab he unbundles the plastic and breathes deeply. *That* is the stuff of life, and don't let anyone tell you otherwise.

Deke and Haiffa are fucking on the thirty-foot beach. Deke and Haiffa are always fucking somewhere. "Oh, look," Haiffa says. She points, and their rhythm halts. Deke rolls his head to look out on the water, not minding the sand that grinds into his brush-cut hair.

"Don't see nothin'," he says.

"A fish," she says. She sets her hands on his chest and resumes.

"Fish on Friday," he says. "Maybe I'll hook 'im. What's today?"

"I don't know." Her accent, which used to charm him, is invisible to him now. "Wednesday."

"Anything-Can-Happen Day," he says, and arches his back as he begins to come.

* * *

Above them on the roof, Dieter the marine biologist watches through the glass. Sometimes the Ecosphere to him is a big aquarium. He watches Deke and Haiffa not from a need to accommodate voyeurism so much as from a desire to alleviate boredom. The first couple of months, everybody went at everybody else in various combinations, then settled into a few pairings that dissolved, either from attrition or from entropy, and now everybody is more or less an environment unto his or her self. In this they are like the scientific wonder in which they all live, but which none calls home.

Dieter is supposed to be cleaning solar panels. Dust from the Arizona desert accumulates on the Ecosphere's glass-and-aluminum roof, and when it is thick upon the solar cells, the station's power supply is diminished. But there are a lot of solar-power cells, and it is a hot July day in the Arizona desert. Dieter takes frequent water breaks.

Below him Haiffa and Deke seem to be finished, and he looks away. He stands and puts his hands on his hips, turning to take in the gleaming, sloping geometry of glass and aluminum that is the station. Ecosphere is built into the side of a gently sloping hill; the rain forest uphill is forty feet higher than the desert downhill, which is also nearly six hundred feet distant. Hot air rises from the desert and flows uphill; condensers in the rain forest cool the air and separate the moisture. It actually rains in the indoor rain forest.

Dieter looks at the terraced Aztec pyramid of glass and aluminum that caps the rain forest. What would it feel like, he wonders, to jump from the top? A sense of freedom, the exhilaration of weightlessness, and then the ground, stopping all thought. All worry. All pain. All fear.

But an eighty-foot fall might not kill him. And even if it did, he'd just get back up and start walking around again. No, a bullet in the brain is about the only way to go, he thinks laconically, bending to pick up his rags and economy-size bottle of Windex. Shame Bill had to have the foresight to lock up the guns they obtained on that one expedition to Tucson, a year ago.

He looks left, over the edge and down at the parking lot behind the human habitat. The Jeep Cherokee and the Land Rover are still there. It would be so goddamned easy. Just get in, crank up one of those babies—might need to juice up the battery, but there was plenty of that to go around—put her in gear, and fucking *go*.

He'd do it in a minute, too, if there was someplace to fucking go *to*.

And Marly. She climbs down from a tree, drops her pruning shears, unties her harness, and lets it fall at her feet. She mops her brow. It is amazingly humid in here. "Tropical" is such a misleading word, she thinks, conjuring mai tais and virgin beaches. In the higher branches of the tree she has been pruning it is not so bad; the eternal trade wind from the downhill desert is cooling. On the surface, though, the breeze is broken up by the thick foliage, and the climate is dank and wet.

She watches a squirrel dart along branches. They've been having trouble with the squirrels. They're dying out, and no one is sure why. Marly was against their presence from the start; they're filthy little rodents that carry disease and live by stealing whatever they can get their grubby little paws on. Everybody likes them because they have neotenic characteristics: big heads in relation to the body, big eyes in relation to the head. They look, in other words, like babies, and *everybody* likes babies. Well, small-scale evolution is taking care of the little shits, so Marly guesses she showed them. Nobody would listen to her because she's a botanist, which everybody knows is just a fancy word for gardener. Have you met Miss Tsung, our Chinese gardener—oh, I *do* beg your pardon: *Ms.* Tsung, our *Asian botanist.*

She wipes palms on denim and walks from the rain forest to the sparse growth near the beach. She pulls open a screen door and walks down an access corridor, then out the screen door at the far end. Bare-breasted Bonnie waves to her as she cuts across a corner of the Agricultural wing. Marly ignores her and enters the Supply section of the human habitat.

"Supplies, supplies!" she says.

From a closet whose door is marked EXT STORES she takes the two-man tent and a sleeping bag.

Walking toward the front door she meets Billtheasshole walking in. He stops in front of her, eyebrows rising, and does not get out of her way. "Again?" he says, looking at the blue nylon tent bag and rolled sleeping bag. "I don't know that I altogether approve of this antisocial behavior, Marly. Everybody needs his privacy—or *her* privacy—but you are *actively segregating* yourself from us."

She holds the camping supplies before her like a shield. Her mouth forms an O as she mimics sudden recollection. "Oh, I *am* sorry," she says. "We were having the Tupperware party tonight, weren't we? Or were Haiffa and Deke going to sell us Amway? I forget."

"Grace tells me you didn't show up for your last two scheduled sessions." He rubs his jaw (tending toward jowls) with the span of thumb and forefinger. Of the four men on Staff, only Bill continues to shave—his badge of civilization endeavoring to persevere. Striking a blow for *homo gillette.*

She laughs. "Who has? I don't have time for her bullshit. She's more fucked-up than the rest of us. Just tell her it was my bad toilet training, okay?"

"I am merely attempting to express my concern over your lack of cooperation," he says with the mildness of psychotic conviction. "Everyone has to contribute if we're going to pull through—"

"Pull through? Pull *through,* Bill? What is this, some *phase* the world's going through? Going to grow out of it, is that it?"

"I think I understand your resentment toward authority, Marly, but you must see that some sort of hierarchy is necessary in light of—"

"Authority?" She looks around, as if expecting a director to yell "Cut!" "Why don't you do me a favor, Bill, and fuck off?" She shoulders past him.

"This will have to go into my report," he warns.

She opens the door. "More demerits!" she wails to the vegetable crops. "Golly. I'm—I'm so *ashamed.*" She turns back to smile meanly, then tries to slam the door behind her. The hydraulic lever at the top hisses that she'd better not.

A last swipe with a dirty rag, and Dieter grins at his reflection. "I can *see* myself!" he says.

He collects the dirty rags scattered around him on the glass. Waste not, want not: the Golden Rule of the Ecosphere. He stands and surveys the surrounding Arizona desert. As an experiment in maintaining an artificial environment in the midst of an alien one, Ecosphere is immensely successful: They are an island of glass on the rusted surface of Mars.

He stretches cramped muscles and breathes in the dry Martian air. Dieter Schmoelling, naked to the alien plain, the only human being able to withstand—

He frowns. Wipes sweat from his brow. Shades his eyes, squints, bends forward.

A tunnel of dust, a furrow in the desert. A giant Martian mole burrowing toward the invading glass island. A Martian antibody come to attack the invading foreign cell.

A car.

[4]

Marly is pitching her tent in the downhill desert when the P.A. sounds an electronic bell: *Bong!* "All personnel to the fruit grove," commands Billtheasshole. *Bong!* "All personnel report to the fruit grove immediately." And clicks off.

What confidence, what assurance! The son of a bitch just *knows* that everybody will show up there, *bong!* Marly thinks of not showing up, just to remind him that his authority lies entirely in their acquiescence, but curiosity gets the better of her. Despite her dislike of him, she knows that Bill wouldn't call them together in the middle of their working day for no good reason. But what Bill thinks of as a good reason is not necessarily dreamt of in her philosophy.

Marly sighs, pulls up stakes, and walks around the bluff, past scrub, into savanna, beside the ocean, into the southern access corridor, across croplands, and into the fruit grove.

The others are already there, except for Bill. Their backs are to her as they look out the windows. "I suppose we're all wondering why he called us here," says Marly.

Dieter turns and beckons her over. She pulls an apple from a tree and heads toward them. She bites into the apple and Dieter frowns. She grins and offers it to him, Chinese Eve. His frown deepens, and she laughs at his seriousness.

He makes room for her and points to the ruler-straight desert road, but he really doesn't need to. Marly can see the car heading for them. It's only three or four miles away.

"Should've baked a cake," she says, but inside she feels a pang, something tightening.

Bill joins them, holding a double-barreled shotgun. Her heart slams, and for a moment she is certain Bill is going to kill them all. This is it; she knew it would happen some-day—

Deke steps forward and takes the shotgun from Bill's hands. Bill is so surprised by this . . . this *usurpation,* that he allows him to.

Deke breaks the shotgun and removes the corrugated red plastic shells. He returns shells and broken shotgun to Bill, shakes his head in contempt, and steps back.

"They'll probably pull into the parking lot," says Bill. "I'm going out on the roof, in case they try anything." From a back pocket he pulls out a slim walkie-talkie. He hands it to Dieter. "I'll call you if I need you," he says. He turns to Leonard. "Talk to them over the P.A. in the monitor room," he orders. "Find out what they want and get them out of here. Ladies—"

"We'll make coffee," suggests Marly.

"I want you to keep out of sight."

"I want a gun."

Bill shakes his head. He turns away and heads for the human habitat, where the airlock is. They follow him, since the monitor room is at the north end of the human habitat anyway. Marly catches up to Bill. "Then give me the key to the armory," she persists. "You're not taking it out of here so you can get your ass shot off on the roof."

He frowns, but cannot fault her logic. He draws a many-keyed holder from a retractable line attached to his belt and selects a key. He gives it not to Marly but to Deke, then turns and trots ahead of them.

Marly glances back toward the apple trees. The car is perhaps two miles away.

Inside the habitat Bill veers right at a T intersection; the others veer left and climb a flight of stairs. They enter the monitor room—all but Deke, who grins at Haiffa, tosses the armory key, catches it, and hurries down the hall.

Camera One already stares unblinkingly at the asphalt parking lot. Leonard activates Camera Two and sends it panning. The others cluster at his chair.

"Check, check," says the walkie-talkie in Dieter's hand. "Do you read me? Over."

"Loud 'n' clear, man," replies Dieter. He rolls his eyes.

"I'm on the roof, making my way toward the agricultural wing where the cover's better. Over."

"Right. I mean, yeah . . . over?"

Leonard turns from the control panel. "I'm guh-guh-*going* to test the puh-puh-P.A. Ask him if he c-c-can *hear* it."

Dieter relays the message, and Leonard says "T-testing wuh-wuh-one t-two three," into the microphone.

"Loud and clear," says Bill. "Listen, if there's any—here they are. Over and out."

The car is a dusty black El Camino. They watch on Monitor One as it pulls into the asphalt lot, slows, and parks beside the Land Rover. The driver waits for the dust to clear. Over the speakers they can hear the engine idle, can hear it knocking after it is switched off.

The driver opens the door and steps out holding a pump shotgun. He turns, says something to a passenger (there isn't room for more than two in the El Camino), and straightens. He shuts the door and approaches the Ecosphere.

He is the first live human being they have seen in over a year.

"Hello?" he calls. Squeak of feedback, and Marly

winces. Leonard adjusts the gain. "Hello, is anybody there?"

Leonard pushes a button and Camera Two zooms in.

He is young—early twenties. His hair is dark, straight, shiny, tied in a pony tail, to his waist. Faded gray jeans with white-threaded holes in the knees below a long, unbuttoned, black-and-white-checked shirt with rolled sleeves. Earring dangling from right earlobe.

"Hello?" he calls again.

Leonard thumbs the mike switch. He clears his throat self-consciously and the man steps back. The shotgun comes up.

"Wuh-wuh-we *hear* you," Leonard says.

The man looks around for the source of the voice.

Leonard glances at the others. "Wuh-wuh-*what* do you want?" he says into the mike.

The shotgun dips, lowers. "Food. Just—food. Me and my wife are . . . we haven't eaten in a while—"

Deke arrives carrying an armload of rifles and ammunition. Silently he gives one to each of the other six, continually glancing at the monitor.

"—and our baby is pretty sick. We just want some food; we'll leave you alone, after."

Bonnie refuses a rifle. Deke shrugs. "Your funeral," he says.

"If we give them food now they'll only come back for more later," says Grace.

"Prob'ly with friends," adds Deke, handing Marly a rifle.

Leonard fiddles with the monitor controls. Camera Two pans left, centers on the El Camino, and zooms. Leonard adjusts the focus. There is a young woman in the car, holding a bundle that might be a baby.

Leonard looks at Dieter, who shrugs.

On Camera One the man waits.

Leonard frowns and thumbs the mike again. "How did you nuh-nuh-*know* we w-were here?"

A breeze billows the tail of the young man's shirt. "There was an article in the paper," he says. "In the Tucson library. I thought maybe you were still here." He looks around and wipes his brow. "Hot out here," he says.

"Suffer, bud," says Deke. Marly glares at him.

Dieter goes to stand beside Leonard. "Maybe we should, like, tell him to get his wife out of the car," he says.

Leonard glances up. "W-w-what if he won't?"

"What if *she* won't?" adds Bonnie.

"Hey, beggars can't be choosers," Dieter replies. "They'll do it."

Leonard turns back to the mike. "Tell your w-w-*wife* to step out of the cuh, car," he says.

"You didn't say please," murmurs Marly.

"She—our baby's pretty sick," says the man. "I don't . . ." He seems indecisive, then turns toward the car and walks from Monitor One to Monitor Two. He opens the passenger door and leans in. He glances back once or twice as he speaks.

Leonard fiddles with the gain knobs.

"—ust do it. No one's going to hurt you. . . . I don't care what the little fucker feels like, just do it. And keep your cakehole shut."

The passenger door opens and a girl gets out. She wears khaki pants, sandals, and a dirty white T-shirt. She is perhaps seventeen years old. She wears a lot of make-up and bright red lipstick. The breeze tugs her tangled hair.

She holds a bundle before her. A little hand protrudes from it, grabs air, finds her breast, clasps.

"All right," says the man. "Now, please—can you spare us some food?" Leonard pulls back Camera One until he's in view again. They watch him gesture expansively. "You have a lot; we just want enough for a few days. Just enough for us to drive across the desert. We're trying to get to California."

Again Leonard glances at the others. "Cuh, Cuh, California? What's there?"

"My brother."

"I'll just bet he is," mutters Grace.

"Hold on a m-m-minute," says Leonard, and kills the mike. He swivels in his chair with a questioning look.

"I don't like it, man," says Dieter.

"Not one bit," says Deke.

"Maybe just some apples, or something . . ." says Bonnie.

Marly pulls back the bolt of her carbine and begins feeding little missile shapes to the breech.

"Sure," says Deke. "You wanna take it out to 'em?"

"Belling the cat," muses Grace.

"Dieter? Dieter, do you read me?" Bill's voice, a loud whisper.

Dieter lifts the walkie-talkie. "Roger . . . Bill."

At the console, Leonard suppresses a giggle. Behind him on the monitors, the man, the girl, and the baby await their reply.

"Keep it down; I don't want them to hear me up here. Don't tell them we'll give them any food. Over."

"We were just voting on it," says Dieter.

"It's not a voting issue. They don't get any."

Marly finishes loading her rifle and slaps the bolt in place.

"Just a couple of apples?" asks Bonnie.

Marly glares at her, hating her every milquetoast fiber.

"We have to remember the Ecosphere," continues Bill's tinny voice. "We can't upset the balance. We can't introduce anything new or take anything away. We can't breach the integrity of the station."

Marly shoulders her rifle and leaves the room.

"Hey, listen, Bill—" begins Dieter, but Bill is still transmitting.

"—ink of what this station represents: we're a *self-contained* unit. We grew that food ourselves. We live on a day-to-day basis."

"They're not asking for very much," mutters Bonnie. She sits in a chair and stares sullenly at the television monitor.

Dieter thumbs the "send" button. "We think it's a bad idea for other reasons," he says. "Grace feels that if we feed them, they'll just, like, come back for more. Probably they'll tell others, y'know? Uh . . . over."

"Exactly! And *they'll* tell others, and we'll be barraged. We'll be like a . . . a free McDonald's out here."

"Golden arches," says Haiffa solemnly, and steeples her hands. Deke pinches her butt.

"We've got a consensus, then?" asks Dieter.

"Tell them no," says the walkie-talkie.

"They don't look too hungry to me," says Deke. "Get 'em outta here."

"Still," mutters Bonnie, "it seems such a shame. . . ." She watches the monitor and does nothing.

"Hello? Hey, hello?"

Leonard activates the mike. "Wuh-wuh-we're still here," he says. He seems much more confident now that a decision has been made for him. "Listen, we . . . we've taken stock of our, um, *situation* here, and we've talked it over, and examined the, uh, *parameters* of our food-intake quotients. You have to understand: we're rationed out ourselves. A meal for you means a meal less for someone here." His tone has become warm, congenial. "I'm sure you understand."

"You're saying no?" The beggar seems incredulous.

"I'm saying I'm sorry, but we've analyzed your situation with regard to ours, and we simply can't . . . *accommodate* you at this time."

"I don't fucking believe—you won't give us three days' food?" He keeps glancing around, as if persuasive arguments lie around the asphalt parking lot. "What about my wife?" he asks. "What about our *baby*?"

"I'm very sorry," says Leonard. He does not sound very sorry. He sounds, in fact, glad to be in a position to refuse something to someone, for a change. Like a hotel manager effusively sympathetic because there's no room at his inn. "But you come here asking a favor," he continues stutterlessly, "and you don't have any right to blame us for declining to grant it."

"Favor?" The man raises the gun. "You want a *favor*, you god—"

"Hold it *right there*, son." Bill's voice, over the speakers.

The young man hesitates.

"Don't do it. I don't want to shoot, but I will." Bill doesn't sound reluctant to shoot. He sounds very excited. "Now, you've asked for help and we can't give it. We would if we could. My advice to you is for you and your wife to get back in your car and head out of here. Don't head for California; head for Phoenix. There's bound to be food there, and it's only a few hours' drive."

"But we just *came* from—"

"Then head south. But you can't stay here. You got that? We don't have anything for you."

"We'll *work* for it!"

"There's no work for you here. This is a highly sophisticated station, and it takes a highly trained staff to operate it. There are a lot of us, and we're all armed. We need everything we have, and there isn't enough to go around. I'm sorry, son, but that's life in the big city. I—"

Bill breaks off. The young man and his wife look at something off camera.

"Get back inside!" yells Bill. "Back inside, now! That's an *order*!"

Leonard pans Camera One as close as it can come to the airlock entrance, which is below it and to the right. He shakes his head and gives a low whistle.

"Well," says Dieter. "Fuck me."

[5]

The rifle is braced on its strap on her shoulder. Her finger is on the trigger. In the other hand she holds a wicker basket. She's not nervous as she heads toward them—in fact, she's surprised how calm she is. Behind and above her, Billtheasshole yells for her to get back inside. She ignores him, but she feels a curious itching between her shoulder blades—probably because Bill is more likely to shoot her than they are.

They don't look as good off camera. A scar splits his eyebrow; another runs the length of his upper arm, bisecting a blue-gray anchor tattooed on his muscular biceps. He's not thin, but he looks undernourished. Vitamin deficiencies.

And the girl looks . . . well, *worn* is the only word Marly can think of. Used up. Her eyes are dull and unresponsive.

The hand gropes again from the bundle the girl carries. She presses it protectively to her, and Marly glimpses mottled flesh when the baby tries to suck the girl's nipple through the cotton of her T-shirt.

Marly stops ten feet from the man and sets down the basket. The girl glances down and holds the baby farther from her body.

The man and Marly stare at each other for a moment. "What's it like?" asks Marly. She inclines her head to indicate the Arizona desert. "Out there."

"Pretty rough," he says.

She nods a few times. "Well . . ." She indicates the basket and steps back from it. "I'm sorry I can't do more. There's fruit, some vegetables, a little meat. A can of milk for the baby—what's wrong with it?"

"I don't know."

"Well, none of us is a medical doctor," she says. "But you might want to try a pharmacy whatever town you go through next. Or a doctor's office. If it's an infection, try ampicillin. If it's some kind of disease . . . well, antibiotics shouldn't hurt anyway. But keep her—him?" They don't say; Marly raises an eyebrow and continues. ". . . on liquids, and get her out of this heat."

Since setting down the basket she's been backing toward the airlock. The man comes forward. Instead of picking up the basket, he glances at the roof of the habitat.

"No one's going to shoot you," says Marly. "Just take it and go. And don't come back."

He lifts the basket and backs toward the El Camino. The girl is already behind the open passenger door, and now she eases into the cab. He sets the basket next to her, gets in, and shuts the door.

The man studies Marly. He nods, slowly. He starts the car and backs out. He backs up until he is out of the parking lot, then turns around and drives away.

For several minutes Marly watches the settling of the receding rooster tail raised by the car, and then she goes inside.

"Just who the hell do you think you are?"

"I'm one-eighth of this station, same as you, and I grew that food as much as anybody else did."

"You defied a direct order—"

"From someone with no authority over me. You know as well as I do that the hierarchy depends on the nature of the crisis."

"We put it to a *vote,* damn you—"

"Nobody asked for mine. How about you, Grace? Haiffa? Leonard? Bonnie?"

"Did you give any thought whatsoever to the repercussions this might have on us? You've just sent ripples through a very small pond."

"For Christ's sake, Bill, I gave them enough food to last them three *days*—if they're careful."

"We're not much more than three days from food depletion ourselves. *Every* change affects *all* of us. You of all people should know that, Marly. The experiment can't continue if outside—"

"The experiment ended over a *year* ago, Bill! Along with the rest of civilization! Why don't you fucking wake up!"

"All the more reason for us to hold out. Maintaining this station *is* maintaining civilization."

"But not humanity."

"Hey, Marly—the guy's just tryin' to say that, y'know —sometimes hard decisions have to be made. I'm sure he didn't like turning them down. Did you, man?"

"Of course not."

"Oh, Christ! Look, I'll *skip* a meal a day for three days, to make everything nice and even, all right? Will that make you happy?"

"*I* thought we should give them some food."

"Yeah, Bonnie. But you didn't do shit."

[6]

"*Motherfuckers.*" Sailor has the pedal to the metal. "Those mother*fuck*ers, man. I thought we'd just grab some food from them, you know? As an excuse to case the place. See how many of them are left, see how good their security is, all that shit. But, goddamn, I never thought they wouldn't give us any food. Fuck, *we'd* have given us food, I know we would've. We've *done* it before! Sons of fucking bitches." He bangs the steering wheel. "They wouldn't feed a goddamn *baby,* man!" He glances at Sweetpea. "You *believe* that?"

Sweetpea is holding the baby at arm's length, staring at it with loathing. "It was chewing," she says dully.

"Of course it was chewing; it's a goddamn—"

She drops the baby and begins batting her hands about her as if fighting off wasps. "It was *chewing,* it was *chewing,* it was *trying to eat me through my shirt,* its *mouth* was on me, oh, God, and it was moving, and I thought, that poor baby, and then I *realized*—"

Sailor grabs her arm and yanks. The El Camino swerves. "Calm down. Calm fucking *down.*"

She stares at him wide-eyed. On the floorboard the baby paddles air like a roach on its back. Half out of its swaddling, the skin around its neck blues where the make-up leaves off, its left arm missing, ripped from the socket some unknown time ago. Its right arm reaches; its toothless mouth opens and closes. Its eyes are like flat plastic.

Sweetpea pulls her legs up to the seat.

"We have to drive straight out of here," says Sailor. "We can't give them any reason to think something's not right. Just stay calm until we get over the rise, there, all right? All right?"

"I want it out of here."

"In a minute." He seems amused at her revulsion. He snorts. "Just close your eyes and think of England."

Huddled on the seat, she turns to look at him. A mile later she says, "You wanna know why I fuck all the others and not you?"

Sailor gives her a you-can't-be-serious look. "Because I don't *want* to fuck all the others?" he asks innocently.

She ignores him. "Sometimes the others are nice to me, you know? They give me things, they show me things. They take me where good things are. You give me the fucking creeps. You're like a fucking deadhead; you live inside your brain all the time and hardly ever come out, and when you do, it's fucking creepy. You got maggots in your brain, or something. I wouldn't fuck you if you were the last man on earth."

"Well, gosh," Sailor says meanly. "There can't be many more to go." He sighs. "Maybe someday . . ."

She slits her eyes and he laughs.

They top the rise. On the other side Sailor pulls off the road and fishes out his .45 semiautomatic from under the seat. He works the action and turns off the engine. He takes the keys, not about to leave them with her. He goes to her side and opens the door. He picks up the baby and turns to face the desert.

Its head lolls. Its mouth works. Its single hand grabs gently at the hair on his forearm. Its mouth opens and closes, opens and closes.

He holds the baby at arm's length, puts the barrel of the pistol against one unblinking flat-plastic eye, and fires.

[7]

hands: remember other hands of other food that touch and make the hunger go without the need of food from her *a* her *i remember but the hunger and without her now the hunger still but her* hands

[8]

Marly takes soil samples from the savanna. She must determine whether the recirculated air is percolating properly throughout all the environments; she suspects blockage in places.

Dieter leans against a mangrove tree, arms folded, left leg crossed over right.

"Hey, I'm not saying that you did the wrong thing," he is saying. "I'm just playing devil's advocate here. I mean, from Bill's standpoint, you've violated the integrity of the Ecosphere. You risked possible contagion; you depleted a carefully regulated—"

She stands with a metal scoop and a dripping, mud-filled plastic baggie in hand. She turns away from him and squishes toward another section of mangrove. She squats and gropes in the stagnant water.

Other than their brief sexual liaison in the first months of the station's operation, Dieter and Marly have something in common: They both helped design environments for the EPCOT Center at Walt Disney World in Florida.

Under contract from Kraft, Marly worked on a pavilion called The Land, which raised its own crops in various experimental ways, including hydroponics and alternate-gravity centrifuge environments. Dieter helped stock a million-gallon, walk-through ocean called The Living Seas, complete with sharks and dolphins.

Marly wonders how ol' Walt Disney World is faring these days. The personnel and guests probably look and act pretty much the same. Down & Out in Tomorrowland, same as her.

Now, a week after reality so rudely impinged upon their own little world, Marly is trying to sever all connections with Staff as best she can, under the confined circumstances. She has slept in a tent in the desert every night. She has eaten only food she picks and prepares herself from the Agriculture wing. She does not report for morning exercises with Bill, psychiatric consultation with Grace, the weekly Staff gripe sessions, or the twice-weekly operations reports. She receives all environmental updates from the computer. She stands night watch on the monitor screens when scheduled to—a duty increased since what she has come to think of as the Food Incident.

So now Dieter stands around, dragging the Incident out into ridiculous academic discourse, and the jissum of his mental masturbation falls all over her. She wants to spill his alleged brains with her garden trowel, but what she does is continue working and ignore him. It's not very difficult. Thinking about it, Marly realizes that she's already spent over a year in solitary with these seven people.

For the others it's life as normal—as normal as they can make it, which is very normal indeed, if you apply a now-anachronistic standard. The Food Incident was simply an unplanned-for contingency; they tap its pertinent minutiae into their data banks and schedules and allotments; they compensate, and adjust, and otherwise act as though it were no different than any of the other minor inconveniences that must be dealt with to keep the Ecosphere going.

Marly knows better. She knows their heads are in the sand. She knows that, one day, the real world will show up and kick them in the ass.

But Marly also knows that it's a lot easier to get by in here than Outside. She is torn: she certainly does not want to leave the station, but she is not sure how much longer she can tolerate these whitebread martinets. Self ostracism is her temporary compromise. She's on hold. She is a weather vane, shaping herself around the direction of the wind.

[9]

"Again."

Florida turns on the flashlight. Sailor watches as Jo-Jo's hands, knotted in the T-shirt (HE'S DEAD, JIM), extend before him. Jo-Jo trudges toward the source of the light like Frankenstein's monster.

Florida clicks off the light and Jo-Jo stops. He looks confused. Through the fence Sailor extends a broom handle from which dangles a fresh piece of cat. Jo-Jo grabs it and begins gnawing, string and all.

"How are the others coming along?"

Florida shrugs. "Not as good. Jo-Jo's still smartest. We can get 'em to go for the light, though, as long as we give 'em munchies after. They'll follow a piece of meat anywhere, particularly if it's alive. It's got so that every time they see a light, they expect food. But Jo-Jo's the only one you can get to carry things. Got him to open a door, a couple times."

One deadhead (SHIT HAPPENS) trips over a lounging deadhead whose shirt proclaims that she is BORN AGAIN.

Sailor shakes his head. "Pretty fucking stupid."

Florida nods. "Don't see what good all this is gonna do us."

"They taught pigeons to run machines by pecking buttons. Deadheads are as smart as pigeons."

"Not by much."

"No," Sailor agrees. "They're like plants that turn to follow the sun. Only they follow live meat. But we can redirect that impulse to get them to go after something else if we give them meat as a reward. Clustered stimuli and delayed gratification. They used to do the same thing to get people to quit smoking."

Florida laughs and scratches a muscular arm. "Dead? Call Schick! But Sailor, what do we need 'em for? We do all right by ourselves."

Sailor shrugs. "I want to use them," he says simply.

"You're still pissed at those techno-weenies out in the desert? Fuck 'em, bud. Let 'em rot. Ain't nothing those peckerwoods got that we can't get ourselves."

"There's more to it than that," Sailor mutters.

"You're taking this pretty personally," says Florida.

Sailor turns on him. "They wouldn't feed a fucking *baby.*"

"Sailor, it was a deadhead."

"They didn't know that."

"So what? What possible difference can it make?"

"Aw, man, fuck you, all right?"

At the fence, finished with his bit of cat, cyanotic-tinged face against the broad steel mesh, Jo-Jo watches. Beside him now are the others, carnitropically attracted. They jostle and vie mindlessly, like teenagers before the gate at a rock concert. The upraised elbow of a deadhead (PARTY ANIMAL) strikes the temple of a skinny woman wearing a blank T-shirt that has a bumper sticker slapped onto it: I EAT ROAD KILL.

Sailor and Florida turn at the sound of approaching music. Cheesecake has a ghetto blaster the size of a suitcase on his muscular shoulder. Run D.M.C. are demanding that sucker emcees call them sire. How Cheesecake can walk and dance at the same time is a mystery to Sailor, whose musical taste always ran to Tangerine Dream and King Crimson anyhow. Well-ordered, hightech music. White boy stuff.

Cheesecake's eyes glint in the light from the building the others are burning down across the quad. His irises are bright, mirrored rings.

"Fuck," whispers Florida, and reaches for his holster.

Sailor stops him with a hand on his elbow. Florida glances at him, and Sailor shakes his head.

Cheesecake stops before them and sets the ghetto blaster down, dancing jointlessly.

"I thought you'd gone deadhead," Florida says mildly.

Cheesecake dances. "Say what?" The music is pretty goddamn loud.

"I nearly shot your nigger brains out!" yells Florida.

"Wha' for?"

Florida and Sailor glance at each other and laugh.

"Oh, man . . ." says Florida, shaking his head.

"Hey, you like these?" Cheesecake points to his eyes. "They bad, or what?"

"Where'd you get 'em?" yells Sailor.

"I dunno. Some building." He waves across the quad, where the building burns.

"Optical sciences," says Sailor.

"Yeah."

The song changes; the beat doesn't.

"You're gonna get your ass shot off with those on," yells Florida.

"Say what?"

Florida shakes his head and turns to Sailor. "I don't think the others are gonna be too enthused on coming down on that place, Sailor," he says. "No percentage in it."

Sailor nods. "Figured."

"I have to tell you, too." He watches Cheesecake dancing. "Sweetpea thinks . . . well, she wants some of the guys to split up, you know, and come with her. You aren't exactly Number One on her hit parade."

"She wants to leave, let her."

"Yeah, but . . . a lot of the guys'd go with her. You know how it is."

"There's girls at that station in the desert."

"Yeah?" Hearing this last, Cheesecake brightens. "Hey, yeah?"

Sailor nods, and begins to elaborate, but stops when he sees Florida staring at the zoo pen. He turns to look.

"Hey, Jo-Jo!" Cheesecake points and grins. "Check you out, bro!"

sounds they make i remember from boxes it made me move not toward *like food but* with *and sometimes with sounds and moving with* her

* * *

"Jesus Christ," Sailor breathes, watching Jo-Jo stiffly dancing. "He *remembers*."

Later that night Jimmy sees Cheesecake coming down the steps of the Student Union and blows his nigger brains all over the concrete. Engineering defeats American History.

"He was walkin' funny an' his eyes was all fucked an' shit," he tells Sailor. "What the hell was I *supposed* to think?"

"Fuck if I know," replies Sailor, certain now that it's time he moved on.

[10]

Leonard in the monitor room is drawing circles on a yellow legal pad. He draws them two lines tall and one after the other, circle beside circle. He is trying to teach himself to draw a perfect circle every time. He will not stop until he draws two consecutive rows of perfect circles.

At the end of each row he surveys the monitor screens. Cameras are placed around the station, along with an alarm system on the bottom row of glass panes around the perimeter.

Leonard does not see the Ryder truck with its lights out glide to the base of the slope and stop several hundred yards from the south end of the Ecosphere. He does not see the driver's-side door open and close (without the cab light coming on), nor the black-clad driver hurrying to the back to raise the door. He does not see the masked Pied Piper with a flashlight beam lead a group of shambling figures toward the Ecosphere.

Leonard draws a row of nearly perfect circles and surveys the monitors. He looks directly at the Ryder truck at the bottom left of Monitor Five, but motionless in the dark it looks like the rest of the angular landscape and he returns to drawing circles.

He completes a perfect row, and is halfway through a second when the alarm goes off.

[11]

Marly awakens to the sound of a distant bell. It is dark inside her two-man tent. She slips out of her sleeping bag and pushes past the entrance flaps.

Stars shine in the Arizona sky above glass above desert built in desert.

She zips her coverall and tries to get her bearings. It's the general alarm; somebody on monitor watch must have hit it.

Monitor watch?

A chill clenches her stomach. She retrieves her carbine from the tent and heads down the bluff, then around the miniature oasis and toward the marshlands. Marshwater has begun to soak through her Reeboks when she hears the screams. She stops, and chill water saturates.

From the animal pens. She splashes toward the savanna and the nearest access corridor.

The sound of the pigs squealing in terror awakens Grace. Her room is right next to the animal pens, and she hurriedly throws on a robe and looks out the window. There is motion, but it is too dark to make out anything.

She leaves her room and hurries down the corridor, out the front door, and past the bean poles toward the animal pens. Only then does she notice that an alarm bell is ringing. Her feet are getting dirty and there is a cold draft blowing from the apple orchard. She should have thought to put on her slippers, at least, but no, if something's happened to Bacon, or Pork Chop, she'd want to get—

She stops. The cool breeze is coming from the end of the apple orchard. In the dim light she can see two triangular glass panes are missing from the wall past the trees. What could have caused that? It could have just . . . *blown* in —the difference in external air pressure, maybe, or even just a strong gust. Maybe *that's* what had upset the poor little piggies: the sound of breaking glass.

The squealing comes again, startling her. She rushes toward the pens, unmindful of cold air or dirty feet. "There, there," she calls as she opens the waist-high gate.

"Mommie's here. It's all right." She finds the switch for the bare bulb above the pigpen and flips it up. "Mommie's—"

Bacon is standing on top of a man. The man has arms and legs wrapped around Bacon. Bacon is gnawing on his shoulder. His round head tosses, tearing flesh and pulling tendon.

Beside them is the gutted body of Hambone. Grace is horrified to see that Hambone is still alive.

The man's head comes up. Bacon's ferocious gnawing does not seem to bother him. He opens his mouth and bites her neck. Pork flesh tears and blood gouts. Bacon squeals.

"What are you doing?" Grace is heading toward him before she knows what *she* is doing. *"You get away from her!"*

Bacon slips loose. Blood squirts rhythmically from her neck. The man stands amid snuffling pigs. He turns toward her. Pig blood streaks his Grateful Dead T-shirt. Bloodless flaps of flesh fold from torn fabric at his shoulder.

Grace is only beginning to register what it is that turns toward her. That heads toward her with vacant eyes and outstretched arms. That needs her as no one has. She backs up a step. "No," she says. "No, wait." Snuffling pigs nuzzle her calves. "You can't—you don't *belong*—"

She falls backward over Fatback. The frenetic pig tramples her stomach. The breath is knocked from her. Something tugs her foot. She looks up. Hot Dog's mouth is around her instep. She jerks back her leg. The pig makes a guttural noise like the growling of a dog. Its eyes are wide and dull in the light from the bare bulb.

She sits up. The intruder bends to her. He places a hand on either shoulder. He opens his mouth. Pork gobbets hang from green-coated teeth. She cannot get breath enough to scream. She pushes him away and tries to stand. Hot Dog tears into her calf. The intruder bends again. Her leg is burning. She kicks away. Hot Dog squeals and bites again. The intruder lowers his face to her breast. Ringing bells and squealing pigs. His teeth come together. It burns. He turns his head. It tears. She pushes

him away. Wetness warms her hands. Tatters of herself in
his mouth. Her fingers smear dark wet across his face.
Into his mouth. He bites. Bone crunches. She pulls back
her hand. Two fingers gone. Leg numb. Why so cold?
Vague pressures. Distant sound of chewing.

Burning white flashes as he feeds the pigs feed on rip of
meat stripped from bone pull tendons bitten tugged
snapped like hot strands of cheese that pulse the pulse that
beats that ebbs that slows and fades
  away.

[12]

Marly hurries along the access corridor, wet shoes
squishing. The Ecosphere is very dark; they do not like to
keep "exterior" lights on at night because they would be
visible for miles.

At the screen door leading to the agriculture wing she
pauses.

Pop. Pop-pop!—and breaking glass.

She unslings her carbine and opens the door.

Dieter jumps awake at the sound of the bell. He sits up
in bed and glances at the flashing computer screen on his
desk. INTEGRITY BREACH. He rubs his eyes, gets out of
bed, and puts on his clothes. He fastens his belt and opens
his closet to retrieve a .45 automatic in a shoulder holster
and the pump 30.06 Deke gave him the day of the Food
Incident.

He is halfway up the stairs to the monitor room when
he hears the screams from outside. He pumps the rifle,
chuk-chik! and hurries into the corridor, where he meets
Bonnie in her white kimono. They run for the front door.

The screams have stopped by the time they are outside.
Neither has a flashlight, and they stand in the darkness for
a moment, letting their eyes adjust. Bonnie gestures nervously toward the animal pens, and they head that way,
Dieter in the lead and Bonnie clinging close behind, both
trying to be silent but making a lot of noise.

At the low barrier to the pigpen they stop. The pigs are
gathered and snuffling, hind ends wiggling. Dieter vaults

the barrier and claps his hand against the rifle stock. The pigs scatter, and Dieter stops in his tracks. Spread before him is emptied Grace, and before her in the flesh kneels a real live dead carnitrope. The carnitrope raises its head and opens its mouth. A quivering strip of flesh hangs on its upper lip, then slides off.

Behind him Bonnie vomits.

Dieter levels his rifle and pulls the trigger. It will not depress. The carnitrope is getting to its feet. For some reason Dieter does not think to check the safety, but drops the rifle and pulls the .45 from its holster. The carnitrope shambles toward him, dragging a worn wing-tip shoe through Grace. Dieter thumbs the safety and pulls the trigger. The bullet makes a small hole going in and a large hole going out of the carnitrope's chest. The corpse staggers back under the impact, heel squirting something rubbery from beneath, then comes forward again. Dieter aims higher and fires twice. The back of the carnitrope's head sprays away, and behind it a pane shatters. The corpse slams backward to land in the remains of Grace.

Bill pops awake the second he hears the alarm bell. He's anticipated something like this, and he's ready. They'll never catch old Bill with his pants down. He pulls a Smith & Wesson .44 magnum from under his bed, snatches his brown coverall from across the back of the chair at his desk, where he has left it so that he can find it in the dark, and pulls it on without letting go of the enormous pistol. He goes to his door and raises the pistol alongside his head. Purple light flickers from his desk as the computer monitor screen comes to life. INTEGRITY BREACH, it reads, and begins blinking. Bill narrows his eyes and turns back to the door. He snatches it open and peers into the corridor.

Nothing.

The bell continues to ring.

He jumps into the corridor and lands in a policeman's firing stance, legs straddled, left hand around right hand holding the gun, back straight, arms a little bent. He didn't read *Soldier of Fortune* for nothing.

He turns quickly. The corridor is clear. He straightens and moves for the stairwell and the monitor room.

Leonard is puh-puh-panning cameras like mad, searching for any sign of motion, when Bill bursts into the room. He starts, then bolts out of his chair when he sees that Bill clutches the buh-buh-biggest pistol he has ever seen, aimed square at his chest. He glances at the monitors and Bill lowers the gun.

"You sounded the alarm?"

Leonard shakes his head. "Window buh-buh-broke. In the orchard."

Bill frowns, still looking at the monitors. "False alarm?" He sounds disappointed.

Leonard shrugs.

Bill peers forward. "Hold Camera Five," he says.

Leonard hits a button on the console. Bill leans until his face is five inches from the screen. "Bring it up."

"Do you mean zoom, or p-p-*pan* up?"

Bill glares. "Zoom," he says.

Leonard works the controls until Bill is staring at a Ryder truck not three hundred yards downhill from the desert environment. He turns to look at Leonard. He raises the gun. Leonard raises his hands as if to ward off bullets.

From outside they hear gunshots. *Pop. Pop-pop.*

[13]

Haiffa swims naked in cool tropical water. She cannot bear to open her eyes in salt water and so swims blindly, coming up for a breath and flipping back down again. Her long hair streams behind her; she is a mermaid. Or a Siren, perhaps, to torture the naked ears of Ulysses.

She likes to swim after making love. She likes to think of Deke lying spent on the shore, waiting for his Venus to emerge.

She swims out past the sandbar and surfaces. She waves toward the narrow shore, but Deke does not see her because he is facing the Staff Quarters to the west and scratching his head. She draws a deep breath and dives.

The bottom is less than twenty feet down, here; she grabs it with her hands. Grit collapses in her palms. Sometimes she has accidentally grabbed crabs here, or scraped herself against rock, or been startled when—

—something slides across her leg. She jerks, but of course it is only a fish, though for a moment it felt—

Her ankle is grabbed. The grip is cold and firm. She whirls and opens her eyes. Salt water stings. Dark water. She reaches. Her fingers brush the cloud of her hair. She kicks out, but encounters nothing. Her leg is tugged. She jackknifes to free herself from whatever holds her. Something with ridges. It feels like a *hand,* but that's ridic—

Agony as something rips along the blade of her foot. Air bubbles contain her scream, float to the surface, and pop without a sound. Haiffa curls up and grabs at her foot. Her hands encounter something round, with hair. A head. But it can't be a head, not down here. Her hands slide across it as her foot pulses into the cold water. Her fingers trace cold flesh and opened eyes.

Following her next scream is a short gasp. It contains water. She forces herself to check it. Salt water in her throat. She coughs. The little air that remained to her bubbles up. Her lungs feel scoured. Her foot throbs. Her leg is pulled in again. Two hard crescents press into her thigh, and press harder. In the sudden pain of tearing flesh she rips away a clot of hair in one hand. Thrashing now. She tries to scream, but there is nothing. Her mouth works to call, but the world lies above a veil of water she cannot part. The only sound is the beating of her heart.

The flailing arm that holds the hair is grabbed, is pulled. Her mouth stretches horribly as arm muscle is pulped and torn away. Mottled red tinges the darkness in her eyes. A tone builds in her ears, the sustained ringing of a distant underwater bell. Some threshold is crossed in her brain, a line of resistance past which the instinct to breathe defeats the knowledge that there is no breath to draw. She inhales. Her lungs fill with water. Relief floods into the midst of her pain. Coolness quenches the burning in her chest.

Something tears loose inside her. The ringing grows, her heartbeat slows. Red lace webs her vision. Pain spreads up her arm as she is drawn into a cold embrace, is held like a lover, is kissed with great passion, is consumed, while around her the water grows warm.

Deke rises from the beach at the sound of gunfire. *Pop. Pop-pop!* Pistol, sounds like. He brushes sand from his butt and turns toward the agricultural wing. He opens his mouth to improve his hearing, but there is nothing further to hear. He does not see the hand rise from the water behind him, wave a frantic goodbye, and sink again.

He picks up his jeans, shakes them out, and begins pulling them on. "Haiffa," he calls. "Haiffa!"

He peers forward, straining to see in the darkness. The Olympic-sized ocean is placid.

Been under an awful long time now. Prob'ly swam out past the sandbar, but she oughta be able to hear him call. Should check out that gunfire. Better make sure Haiffa's okay first.

He walks to the end of the beach and skirts the ocean to the west, where the savanna begins.

"Haiffa?"

Probably somebody finally had enough of ol' Billy-boy and did it to him. More than likely idjit did it to himself, way he handles a gun. Damn fool could screw up a two-car funeral on a one-way street. Three shots, though.

"Haiffa!"

Well, it'd probably take him three shots to find a brain in that head to blow out anyway, the stupid son of—

Something in the water there? Not big enough to be Haiffa, though. But what the hell *could* it be? Gator? Shee-it. Something else appearing beside it, something smaller. *Oh, forgot to tell you, man.* Dieter's voice in his head. *Put a little tiger shark in the ocean. Full stock, right? Scavengers of the deep, y'know?*

Splashing as something rises from the water. Dripping as it emerges.

"Haiffa . . ."

Reaches the smaller object in the water, grabs it, picks it up. Brings it toward itself. Heading toward him. Taking shape from the darkness. Wet figure. Woman. Not Haiffa. Pulls the object away from its head, dangles it by its side.

In silhouette he sees the object is a leg from ragged-ended knee to foot. Pulled in again. Piece ripped away.

Deke sprints toward the beach. Fucking pistol on the towel. He splashes through the muddy ground, hits soft, wet sand, heads to the dark square of towel. Yep, pistol's there. Smith and Wesson beats four aces, his daddy used to say. Take that to the bank. Bill had wanted the guns back. "Sure you can have it back," he'd replied, and repeats it now. "You take it from me, it's yours."

He wipes palms on jeans and grips the pistol firmly. On the sand he waits as the figure stumbles onto the beach, recovers, and gropes toward him. *Carnitrope.* What the fuck was *that* supposed to mean? Plant's *photo*tropic, Bill explained. Turn toward sunlight. Biochemical reaction. Stimulus/response. *Ding!*—slobber. *Carni* = meat.

Fuck.

He raises the pistol and thumbs back the trigger—

Carnitrope his goddamn ass. They can call it that if it makes 'em feel better, but his momma didn't raise no fools.

—sights down the long barrel—

"The only thing working is their hindbrains—the reptilian complex," Marly had lectured. *"They're like snakes that wait in one place all day for something to come along. The R-complex lets the carnitropes move, and the only reason they move is to get live meat."* Chink bitch. He may be just a glorified fucking janitor, but where did she come off—

—fires.

The figure staggers back and drops the leg onto the sand. It comes forward again.

"Cut off the R-complex—decapitation, massive neural destruction," Marly had continued, *"and the tropism is removed."* In memory Bill smiles. *"In other words,"* he elaborated, *"if you blow their brains out they have a motivation problem."*

"Blow your fuckin' brains out," breathes Deke. He cocks the hammer and fires again.

A sudden furrow glistens above the creature's left eye. The creature takes two more steps. Stops. Reaches up an inquiring hand. Fingers sink to knuckles. Hand lowers.

Another step. Front knee buckles, and it pirouettes to the sand.

Deke holds the gun on it for a few more seconds, then straightens and nears it cautiously. Yep. Dead for good.

Writing on its wet T-shirt. LIFE'S A BITCH, THEN YOU DIE. Different lettering beneath: THEN YOU COME BACK. Nipples beneath the wet fabric. Peekaboo.

Deke looks out over the little ocean. A little log, propelled by the eternal north wind, drifts toward the sandbar.

Crack! More gunfire. Rifle, this time. He better—

—searingblindwhiteness. Jesus *fucking*—

He sinks to his knees. His belly is turning warm. Somebody pushed a hot soldering iron through his chest. He looks down at his knees. Grit-ringed wet spots in the denim. *I hate that. Fuckin' cold spots when I walk*—

You never hear the one that gets you. Goddamn lie. Heard that one just fine. Oh, shit. He tries to rise, but something shudders to a halt inside.

[14]

Sailor lowers his nine-millimeter Ingram submachine gun. The man he has just shot arches his back and spasms once. God, he hates that. Like all the nerves are screaming at once. Gives him the fuckin' willies.

He turns away from the beach. Invisible in his black jeans and sweatshirt, he works rapidly but quietly from tree to tree, heading uphill from the palms on the beach to the dense foliage of the rain forest. At the north end vegetation meets slanting glass panes. He pulls a box from his nylon backpack, wedges it between two aluminum struts, and turns a Radio Shack wireless intercom to "receive." He hurries toward the west wall, where he places another box and attaches another intercom.

He pauses at the screen door to the access corridor that leads back to the agriculture wing, where he broke in ten minutes ago. Floodlights are on outside the staff quarters, illuminating neat rectangles of crops. Getting in there isn't going to be easy.

* * *

Bill looks from the carnitrope lying in tattered Grace to the missing panes at the end of the orchard. "All right, now, let's not jump to any conclusions," he says. "It could be that one just got in here and went for the pigs, and Grace found it."

"Right," says Leonard. "It ruh-ruh-*rented* a Ryder truck and d-d-*drove* on up here to see if it could buh, buy a bacon, lettuce, and tomato sandwich." He wipes a shaking hand across his mouth.

Bill narrows his eyes.

"It was eating her," Bonnie says flatly. She looks strangely calm, as if Grace's death at the teeth of a reanimated corpse is yet another factor to account for in the many trivial events that accrue during the normal operation of the Ecosphere. Yes, Grace is dead; now work schedules will have to be adjusted, and the sudden one-eighth surplus of food and water will have to be noted, and of course a new person will have to be appointed to moderate the weekly gripe sessions, not to mention someone else having to slop the remaining pigs.

Bill, Dieter, and Leonard regard her stonily. It is as if her casualness toward Grace's death is more repulsive than the fact and manner of Grace's death. There is something alien about it. If only she would go into hysterics, they would understand. That's what a woman is *supposed* to do when this sort of thing happens; they're *conditioned* by society. They can't help it. So why doesn't Bonnie just have a screaming fit and get it over with?

"I guess we shouldn't assume there aren't any more of them," Dieter says.

Bill nods. "Someone let them in here deliberately. An infiltration."

"Huh-who?" asks Leonard.

Dieter cradles his arms and rocks them, humming "Rock-a-bye Baby."

Bill frowns. He inclines his head, slowly. "We have to stay together," he says. "I don't want—"

Pop.

Their heads jerk.

Pop.

"Beach," says Leonard.

"Deke and Haiffa," says Dieter.

Bill brandishes his pistol. "Leonard, you come with me. Dieter, stay with Bonnie."

Bill trots away without waiting for Leonard, pistol in the lead.

Crack! Different sound from the beach. Bill stops. He glances back. "Leonard?"

Leonard swallows and cuh-cuh-catches up to Bill, his rifle held before him like a shield he doesn't trust.

[15]

Marly in the southern access corridor, trying to decide what to do. First three shots from near the agriculture wing to the northwest, and now three more from the vicinity of the beach. Which way should she go?

Well . . . assuming it's the same people shooting, she ought to head in the direction of the most recent shots.

She firms her grip on the carbine and turns back.

"I don't want to wait here."

Dieter looks at Bonnie as if suddenly remembering she is there. "We have to wait till they find out what's going on."

"I *don't* want to wait here." She glances toward the pen at the bodies of the two pigs, the carnitrope, and Grace. The other pigs snuffle and make nervous sounds, run into one another, trample the bodies, sometimes stop to nuzzle the freshly dead, and raise their piggy heads with piggy noses freshly red.

Dieter goes to the pen and bangs the low wall to calm the pigs, but they only bleat louder. "I'm gonna let 'em out," he decides. Bonnie says nothing, and Dieter opens the little wooden gate. The pigs do not bolt, so Dieter enters the pen and drives them out.

"I'm going inside," says Bonnie. "I'm going to my room. Until this is over."

"Hey, you can't do that. You heard what the man said."

"He's got no authority over me. There's no rank here. I

wouldn't have volunteered if there was. Fuck that supremist bullshit."

"I mean about the zom—the carnitropes." He walks from the pen, and they head toward the front of the staff quarters. "There are probably others in here," he continues. "And *someone* let them in. You don't even have a gun."

"I despise the things. They're *male* weapons. Extensions of the male sexuality. If you can't rape something, you exterminate it."

Dieter gives a moment's thought to exterminating Bonnie, but none to raping her.

"I'm going to my room," Bonnie continues, "and locking the door. No one will bother me there. I'm not going to be a party to you people acting out your primal hunting instincts. I am civilized, and I refuse to collaborate."

"You are one fucked-up asshole," says Dieter. "You know that? I use the word asshole because it is nonchauvinistic. Everyone has one, y'know?"

Bonnie opens the front door to the staff quarters and goes inside. Dieter shakes his head. He levels the 30.06 extension of his male sexuality and surveys the floodlighted area. He wishes he had a cigarette, the first such craving he has felt in a while. Or a joint. They had to give up cigarettes when they entered the Ecosphere, and bringing in marijuana seeds was out of the question, even though Marly claimed they'd grow fine in the tropics.

He stands stiffly and swiveling, trying to make his face hard. Dieter the Martian colonist standing sentry duty within the lone glass island, the only thing between safety and the living-dead invaders who threaten their very—

Something pokes his back. "Don't move." The voice is tight, as if the throat that produced it is constricted.

He begins to move anyway, then stops.

"Drop the gun. Now."

He lowers the rifle. Holds it at arm's length. Lets go.

Loud thud of a large-caliber handgun from somewhere near the ocean.

Someone shoves his shoulder. "That way. Inside."

Dieter attempts to walk normally. If he passes an opened door, a corner to scuttle around—

"Keep your hands up. I have a submachine gun, and you wouldn't get five feet without looking like an outtake from *Bonnie and Clyde*. Got it?"

He glances back despite himself. *"Bonnie and Clyde?"*

Poke in the kidneys. "Move, asshole."

"Where are we going?"

"Power room. Battery room. Whatever the fuck you people call it."

"I don't know how—"

"I don't care what you don't know. You take me to it. Fuck with me and I'll kill you. And I'll put the bullet in your heart so you come back, like my friends out there."

Dieter imagines himself an automaton: stumbling, agape, hands outstretched, eyes needy, drawn to living flesh. Turning left toward the power room, he finds himself wondering just how different it would really be.

[16]

"It's Deke."

"It got him? The, the carnitrope, it got him?"

Bill toes Deke's face-down body, which yields jointlessly. There is a small, nearly bloodless hole between the shoulder blades. Bill bends and turns the body over. The torso rolls, but the legs stay knee-down, body twisted at the waist.

That's how you know someone's dead, Leonard thinks. Because they don't care what position they're in.

Bill rolls the lower half of Deke's body as well. Out of some sense of decorum? Whatever; he squats before the big man's chest. A larger, more ragged exit hole exactly at the solar plexus. "Someone shot him in the back," Bill says.

Leonard glances around the beach. They're pretty exposed here. Something floats against the sandbar in the water. A sniper there, prone in the water? Too far, too dark, to tell. "Shouldn't we take cuh, cuh, *cover*?" he asks.

"Whoever shot him wouldn't remain in one position." Bill stands and goes to the corpse of the carnitrope. "They'd sweep the terrain, continue mobile. Tactical maneuvering. Offensive advantage. Search and destroy. Divide and conquer."

Leonard comes up beside him. "Took one with him," Bill observes.

They do not see Deke's body stir behind them.

"Lot of guh-good it did him," Leonard replies.

They do not hear it regain its feet and begin to slouch toward them.

Leonard maintains a respectful distance from the morbid X of the carnitrope. "So . . . w-what should we duh-do now?"

Bill never answers, because Leonard's shoulder is grabbed. He turns and finds himself face to face with Deke. At first he is relieved: They made a mistake and Deke is not duh-duh-dead after all. But realization floods in: Deke is wall-eyed and slack-faced. Thickened blood stains his chin. Sand clings to the right side of his face, to his eyelashes—Leonard can even see grains in his eye. But Deke does not blink. He does not breathe. He does not have any light of life in his eyes. His cold fingers curl on Leonard's shoulder, and pull. What do you want to say, Deke? What are you trying to tell me? Nuh-nuh-nothing. His mouth opens. Bill is shouting something, but Leonard is so fascinated by the sight of Deke back from the dead like some redneck Jesus that he doesn't really hear Bill. Deke the Resurrected pulls him nearer, and Leonard knows he ought to do something, but all he can do is stare. The rifle is a piece of wood in his hand. *Flesh of my flesh, good buddy.* That's what Deke would say if the front part of his brain was still working. *You gonna be baptised now! You gonna get the faith! The Holy Spirit gonna enter you! Whosogoddamnever believeth in me shall not perish, but shall dwell in the House of the Bored forever.*

But Deke the Saviour stops. He stares at Leonard in a kind of open-mouthed sorrow, a wistfulness like a child denied a sugary cereal on a trip to the grocery store with Mom. The hand still holds his shoulder, but no longer clutches with need, no longer pulls imploringly. A doglike, questioning look enters the dull eyes. Leonard feels a kind of stupid disappointment. He feels a sudden compulsion to reason with Deke, dead or no, to ask him just what

the heck is going on here, good buddy, you gonna eat me
or what? But the enormously long, black barrel of a pistol
enters the scene and taps Deke on the temple. Leonard
sees the hand curled around the handle, bite-nailed index
finger curved over the trigger, hammer cocked. Bill to the
rescue. Bill who nightly yearns for rabid dogs, broken-
legged horses, mortally wounded soldiers in a platoon pur-
sued by enemy soldiers. It is the proof of your grit to shoot
your own dog; it is the token of your humanity to put a
thing out of its misery. Bill has wanted to put something
out of its misery for as long as he can remember. An
unnatural and unsanctified reanimation stands between
Deke and his heavenly reward; Bill as God's agent shall
liberate his spirit.

The finger squeezes, the hammer descends, the bullet
flies, the locker of Deke's being sprays onto the sand. Father forgive them.

Marly ducks back behind the tree. Jesus Christ, they
killed him; they shot Deke—

No. No. Think. Piece it together. Deke was dead already.

All right. Then maybe Bill and Leonard knew what was
happening here, what this madness was all about.

Sweating in the artificial subtropic night, she steps out
from behind the tree. She lowers her rifle and waves.
"Hey," she calls.

Bill whirls and fires. The .44 magnum goes off like a
cannon. Behind her she hears the bullet slam into the tree.
A splinter strikes her arm.

She drops, rolls sideways, and ends up prone with the
butt of her carbine against her right shoulder, left eye
sighting. "It's Marly," she calls. "Drop your gun."

"Marly—" Bill heads toward her.

"Drop your gun, or Deke's gonna hold the door for you
on his way in."

He hesitates, possibly thinking about the independent
clause of Marly's sentence, but drops the gun. His left
hand goes to his wrist.

"You, too, Leonard."

"Listen, Marly, there's muh, muh, *more* of those things around here. I don't think it's such a g-g-good—"

She pulls the trigger. The rifle doesn't buck nearly as much as she thought it would. A plume of sand kicks up behind Leonard's right leg, and he drops his rifle. Marly stands and heads toward them. "Now what the hell's going on?" she demands as she approaches.

"Someone's b-b-broken into the station," Leonard says from the beach.

"Infiltration," adds Bill. "Carnitropes for distraction. Behind enemy lines. Liberating the soles in limbo. Tactical incursion, hit and run, select firepower for multienvironment guerrilla warfare. Strategic placement, Staff on alert." He is breathing heavily. His right wrist is swelling.

Marly looks at Leonard, who shrugs and looks momentarily worried. Bill, he seems to be indicating, is playing poker with a pinochle deck.

"Grace is dead," says Leonard, and Marly feels something with blades unfold in her chest. Not because she cared especially for Grace, to be quite honest, but because their hermetic group is irretrievably reduced. Change has been introduced into the system; ripples will spread from this splash. About fucking time.

She indicates the corpses on the sand behind Leonard. "One of them?"

He nods. "Huh-Haiffa, too, we think."

"I saw what happened with Deke. Why did he stop? He had you, but he just stopped."

"Because I liberated him," replies Bill. "I freed him, I cast him from limbo. Because I blew his goddamn brains out."

"Why did he stop attacking you before Bill shot him?" Marly firmly directs her question to Leonard, who shrugs.

"I don't know. One m-minute he was all over me, and the nuh, next it was like he'd smelled bad muh-muh-*meat,* or someth . . ." He stops.

Marly frowns.

"B-b-bad meat," says Leonard. "Oh, my God. That's it. Culls from the herd. Cellular awareness." He looks at Marly. "Jesus Christ, that's it." His stutter is much slighter.

"It's an extremely good pistol, actually," says Bill.

Marly ignores him. She is uncertain what to do. Now Leonard seems to be popping his excelsior, too.

"Hodgkin's disease," says Leonard, and thumps his chest. For a moment Marly thinks it's another *non sequitur,* but then she realizes.

"You son of a bitch," she says. "You never said—"

And the lights go out all over the Ecosphere.

[17]

Bonnie sits in lotus on her bed. *Om mani padme om. Om mani padme om.* She uses the litany as a kind of squeegee to wipe away the karmic scum she feels she has accumulated tonight.

She is just beginning to feel relaxed when the lights go out. She sits in darkness for a moment, waiting for her eyes to adjust.

She hears a faint noise like popcorn popping in the distance.

She debates whether she should stay in her room. What decides her is the realization that the air vents probably aren't working if the power is out. She'll want to be outside.

But . . . outside? The men are stalking each other, and probably Marly playing their adolescent army games along with them. Outside? No; let them get it out of their systems. Of course there are carnitropes out there, the reanimated corpses, but Bonnie feels no superstitious dread whatsoever toward them. They didn't *ask* to be what they are, and what they are is really not very different from plants. Hungry plants, mobile plants, but plants all the same. And Bonnie feels a kinship with plants. She certainly does not feel *threatened* by them, just as she does not feel threatened by the carnitropes. You could outrun them, outsmart them, out-anything them.

She gropes around her modular dresser until she finds a miniature Tekna flashlight. She twists the ridged section ringing the lens, and the light comes on. She slides the circle of light around her room and is reminded of a germ under a microscope. Light is the only weapon she needs.

She fixes the circle of light on her door and makes her way toward it.

"This is it." Dieter opens the power-room door and begins to enter.

"Stay right there. Turn on the light."

"I can't stay where I am and turn on the light."

"Turn on the light, asshole."

Dieter leans in and turns on the light. He takes short steps as he is prodded in. The door is shut behind him. He turns to look at his captor for the first time and is unsurprised to recognize the long-haired young man who came begging last week. Was it last week? He's not sure how long ago it was. Time flies.

"Yeah, it's me," says the young man. "You just stay right there. Lace your fingers and put your hands on top of your head. We're playing charades and you're a sequoia, got it?"

Dieter doesn't get it, but he nods anyway and does as he's told.

The man keeps the submachine gun trained on him as he shrugs out of a nylon daypack. He bends and unzips it, keeping the gun on him, then pulls out a box about the size of a cardboard pencil case. The box is olive-drab and curved like a hip flask. In upraised letters one side reads FRONT TOWARD ENEMY. He carries box and backpack toward power-convertor controls, circuit breakers, generator controls, voltmeters, regulators, and stacked banks of power-storage batteries. He sets the box face-down on a bank of controls, pulls out a little white box with square buttons that looks like a portable radio, connects it to the curved box, and trips a toggle switch. He sets another curved box against the battery bank. "Nice little ratbox you people have here," he says conversationally as he goes about his work. "All the comforts of home. Air conditioning. Barcaloungers. MTV."

"What do you want from us?" Dieter asks.

"Nothing." He glances at him. "Really." He shrugs. "Used to want a hamburger or two, but hey, that's life in the big city, now, isn't it?"

"Look, man, *I* wanted to give you some food. I *told*

them we should, that it was only the right thing to do. But they wouldn't—"

The man waves him to silence. "Water under the bridge," he says. "Let the dead past bury its dead, I say." He indicates the row of circuit breakers. "Main power switch?" he asks.

Dieter shrugs. "I'm a marine biologist," he says.

"Mmph. Chust followink orders, huh?"

Dieter says nothing. The man rises and goes to the row of circuit breakers. He throws a knife switch. Nothing happens. He pulls another one. Nothing. Another.

" 'S awright," he says. "They're doing something somewhere." He continues throwing switches.

The lights go out, and Dieter makes his move.

Sailor waits until he hears the door latch jerked down and the door snatched open. He fires a burst on full auto, sweeping the barrel in a tight crescent. The clip is empty in seconds. He thumbs the release, pulls out the empty, drops it, pulls a fresh one from his back pocket, and slaps it in. He bends and gropes until he encounters the backpack. He pulls out a penlight and switches it on, then attaches it beneath the squarish gun barrel with electrical tape and plays it around the room.

The body props open the door. Bulletholes in a slight diagonal to either side of the door frame. Sailor shoulders his pack and steps over the body. "One duuumb fucker," he says. He trains the penlight beam down. All back shots, a whole bunch of them. They don't count for shit in the long run, but that's all right. It's Sailor's party. The more, the merrier.

Flashlight beam guarded with one hand, he steps past the body and makes his way down the hall.

Bill doesn't waste a second: He knows where his gun is, and when the lights go out, he bends, scoops it up, and runs. He doesn't need light to find his way. Hyperacute kinesthesia. Night sense. Geared to register motion. Under siege. Trojan horse. Marly and Leonard calling, but he keeps running. Charlie's out there. In the bush. In the desert. In the marsh. In the fields. In their own back yard.

Gotta deploy. Gotta recon. Stay low. Hit and roll. Hit and run.

He reaches the screen door easily and negotiates the access corridor in a westerly direction. He emerges in fresher air and croplands. Out there. Waiting.

Footsteps. Running toward him. Breathing, low, from the ground. *Crawling,* sneaky sons of bitches. Pale figure coming toward him on hands and knees. He raises the magnum and fires. Pain stitches his sprained wrist. Tough shit. Gotta be tough, son. No pain, no gain.

Squealing, labored breathing. Stubby, flailing legs in front of him. A goddamn *pig,* for Christ's sake!

Wrist throbbing, he stalks the cornfields. There, *there,* two of the fucks. Zip, zip, good as dead. *Good as dead*—hah! Better soon.

He stalks. Three shots left? Let's see: one that liberated Deke, one that missed Marly, one for makin' bacon. Yep: three left.

They're turning for him now. Stupid bastards, not even brains enough to hide. Couldn't sneak up on a goddamn slug. He walks right up to the nearest. Gun against the nose. It grabs the barrel. "Say goodnight, Gracie," he says, and pulls the trigger—but the sonofabitch has grabbed around the *back* of the gun, and the hammer won't cock back. Bill tugs the gun and the creature merely follows. The other one is pretty close now. Bill puts a foot on its stomach and shoves. The gun slides free. Bill steps back. Too close to take time to aim. Head a hard target. Policeman crouch, good form, squeeze . . .

Boom! and the fucker slams backward like it's been sledgehammered by God himself. In the muzzle flash the T-shirt reads SAVE THE WHALES.

Bill ignores the pain in his wrist as he takes aim and fires at the second staggering figure. *Boom!* EAT ME, reads the shirt.

Bill laughs. "Eat *this,* shit for-brains!" He waves the magnum. His wrist is on fire. He is alive.

He runs for the staff HQ. Ten feet in front of it, the door is flung open. He fires automatically: last bullet, quick on the draw, and right in the goddamn *forehead,* yeah!

What's her T-shirt say? He bends, pulls a flashlight from the twitching fingers, shines it down.

No T-shirt. Kimono, parted to expose one breast. Doesn't say a thing. Germ circle of light slides up to dead eyes, drilled forehead, red hair.

Bonnie.

[18]

Leonard walks the forest of the dead. He is one of them and they leave him alone. He is tainted. He is taboo. He is *bad meat.*

Leonard laughs.

In the distance, gunfire.

Sweating he wanders smiling through lush tropics. He'll make it. They'll leave him alone. Leonard alone may run the gauntlet of the dead. The rejected cull triumphant. Darwin in reverse: Those who have not survived will allow the genetic undesirable to continue.

Another shot.

Leonard pauses. There is more to fear from the living, he realizes.

Then I shall climb a tree. I will sit in a branch and await the dawn. And then? I will be free. To do whatever I want. For as long as . . . as I have left.

He finds a tree and hoists himself up from the leaf-carpeted ground.

Marly thinks it's about time to abandon ship. At the first sound of gunfire she was acting out of concern for the Ecosphere and the safety of the others, but now she realizes that the Ecosphere has been a ghost ship for quite some time, Flying Dutchman in the Arizona desert, and the truth about her crew is that it's *always* been every man for himself. The current situation merely brings the point home.

Nope: too late to repair the leaks, to Band Together As A Unit; no returning to Those Golden Days of Yesteryear. Time to jump in a lifeboat and row for shore.

Marly exits the access corridor and crouches low near the glass. In her pocket is the key to the armory, taken from Deke's body on the beach. In the armory are the keys to the Land Rover, along with more guns and ammunition.

She runs forward, bent low, carbine ready. She nearly trips over the body of a pig. Half its head has been blown away.

Billtheasshole.

She hurries on toward the habitat. In the darkness every shape is a threat. Why didn't she think to grab a flashlight? Well, this wasn't exactly the sort of emergency they'd planned on.

But wasn't it exactly the sort of emergency they should have considered? Didn't crop blights sort of pale in comparison?

She heads toward the three tall rows of corn; from there she can survey her surroundings before proceeding.

Body among the stalks. Face up, face gone. SAVE THE WHALES beneath. She steps around it and puts some distance between it and herself, then kneels in the rich soil. Tang of nitrogenated fertilizers.

She looks toward the staff quarters. The door is partway open, propped by a body. She can see it only from the waist down; from the waist up it is inside the building. Too dark to tell who it is.

Cornstalks rustle.

Marly grows still. She strains to hear, but it is difficult because of the sound of her breathing, of her heartbeat in her ears. She turns her head slowly. The sound is approaching from her right.

She turns that way and steadies in a marksman's stance, right leg back and weight over the knee, left leg forward, left elbow on left knee, rifle steady.

There.

It lurches toward her almost drunkenly. It's moving pretty slowly; she has plenty of time. She steadies, sights, and fires. The rifle bucks slightly. The drunken figure staggers back, trips over the body behind it, and lands on its butt. It gets to its feet again.

Go for the head, Marly remembers. *The chest is the easier target, but the head is the only thing that powers it. Medulla oblongata.*

She slaps the bolt of the carbine with the heel of her hand and pulls it back. The cartridge spits out. She pushes the bolt forward, and it sticks. She pulls back, pushes again. No good. She glances again. Scarecrow approaching through the corn. *If I only had a brain.* She stands and turns—

—into the arms of another. It hugs her. Stink of rotten meat. Opens its mouth. Gold filling glints. Half-moon crescent in one earlobe where an earring has been ripped away. Its head bends toward her.

Marly gets an arm up and grabs it by the throat, forcing its head back. The flesh against her palm is loose and leathery cool, like touching the neck of a turtle. She bats her rifle against its side, but can get no room for a powerful swing. The creature bleats softly. Smell of stale air from dead lungs. Quiet, so quiet; absurdly, she thinks there ought to be more noise.

Her hair is tugged from behind.

She turns and the hungry thing turns with her, wedged now between her and the first one. She pushes against the unbreathing throat while the other tries to reach around the one holding her. She can't get loose.

Pop! like a champagne cork. The carnitrope not holding her cants to one side, balances on one leg like a street mime doing an obscure impression, and falls. The one holding her works its head from side to side and snaps its teeth to bite the hand it wants to feed it. *Clack-clack! Clack!*

"Turn it!" someone yells. "Turn it toward me! Goddammit—"

Marly strains. For a panicked moment she feels overbalanced, about to fall over with the creature on top of her, but she jerks a leg back, brings it up into the creature's groin, and pivots.

A loud riveting sound from her right. The creature's head peels away like a rotten plum. It holds her a moment longer, and she feels its dead fingers spasming against her. Then it drops, and she pushes it away and jumps back, turning toward the sound of the gunfire.

A flashlight, but who's behind it? Bill? Dieter? Leonard?

He walks closer. The light shines beneath the squarish barrel of his submachine gun.

"You . . . ?"

He nods. The light does not waver. He cups it with his left hand. "Get out of here," he says.

"But—I don't—"

"Go on. Party's winding down."

Marly considers him for a moment, then nods. "I was just leaving," she says.

"Good idea."

She starts to thank him, but stops. Thanks are not called for here. He hadn't thanked her for the basket, had he? She nods again. "I have to get ammunition and supplies."

"You have about ten minutes."

"The others," she begins. "I have to—"

"Fuck the others. Get your shit and get out of here."

Still she hesitates. "I—I'm a botanist. I can keep this place going. I know how. It can keep you and your wife— and your baby—"

"Wasn't a real baby." The light dips, then raises again. "Deadhead."

"Dead . . . ? Ohmigod."

"There's a lot of 'em out there, deadheads. But you wouldn't know. You've been in here."

She feels a clammy turning inside. World of dead babies, relentless crawling, toothless chewing. "You want the station," she says. "I understand that. But look, I know how to maintain it. It won't last without—"

"I don't want it to last. I want to bring it down."

"To . . ." She searches out his face above the light. Again she nods. "Yes," she says. "Yes, I guess so."

"Eight minutes." The light clicks off, and he's gone.

[19]

Bill with his Tekna light in the apple orchard. Gun in hand, swollen wrist. Incursion. Evasion. Stealth. Sentry removal.

There's one up ahead. HE'S DEAD, JIM. No shit, Sherlock.

* * *

*things on trees food once but no more smell i remember
made water in my mouth but nothing now is light toward
light for food with light she with light her hands would hold
the treefood would feed would let into my mouth and i
would eat the food of the tree but not the food that is her
hand that holds the light and behind the light is food and if
i reach the light i will eat and i will be and i will know*

Bill holds the flashlight in sprained right wrist and
raises the gun in his left hand. Marly unlocks the dark
storage closet-become-armory, takes a flashlight from a
shelf, plays it around the room, and begins cramming
boxes of ammunition into an orange crate. Dieter pushes
his bullet-riddled body from the floor and staggers down
the dark hall; behind him the power-room door thuds
shut. Bonnie grows cold half-in, half-out the front door of
the habitat. Leonard awaits the dawn on the limb of a
South American tree. Haiffa bobs gently on the ocean,
nuzzling the little sandbar. Sailor sets a final charge. Pigs
run blindly through dark geometry of cropland. Bill aims
and fires at the thing that gropes toward his light, bracing
for the recoil. Marly shoves packets of dried food into a
plastic garbage bag. *Click:* Bill stares in wonder at the
gun.   *the light i reach for behind the light is
always food*   Heading for the front door with
supplies and a slung carbine, Marly sees Dieter shambling
away from her down the dark corridor. Sailor pauses at
the air-lock door when he hears Bill's scream. He smiles,
he claps softly, he bows. He leaves; wait for the encore,
folks. "Dieter?" Marly ventures. Leonard stands in the
tree and peers into the lightening east. Dieter turns toward
Marly. Sailor trots down the hill and opens the driver's
door of the Ryder truck. Marly drops orange crate and
garbage bag, saying, "Shit." Dieter's eyes fill with something not recognition. Leonard drinks in the faint coral
tinge bleeding into the horizon. Jo-Jo drinks in tincture of
Bill beneath apple blossoms. Marly raises the carbine. Dieter's face is a rictus she remembers from orgasm. Sailor
turns the key, depresses the clutch, puts the truck in gear,
and eases onto the road. Bill stares unblinking at the infin-

ity of departing night above the glass roof of his little pocket of civilization. Marly lowers the rifle. Dieter reaches for her needfully. Leonard sits again on his leafy throne, feet dangling, to watch the sunrise. Marly picks up garbage bag and orange crate, turns, and steps over Bonnie holding the front door for her.   *light then food i move from sound not from the box but sounds i hear anyway and she holds out her hand*   Sailor drives a mile away and pulls off the road beside a low hill, turning the truck to face the Ecosphere. Sparkle of glass and aluminum by dawn's early light. Marly runs from the air lock, throws bag and crate into the back of the Land-Rover, sets carbine on passenger seat, slides key into ignition. Sailor glances into the long side-view mirror. He will wait until the sun clears the horizon. Faint buzz from under the hood: battery dead. *Shit.*   *and the sound louder and others move with and she looks at me with her hand out to me and her mouth opens and sound from it*   Leonard on high looks down on Marly opening the hood of the Land-Rover outside. Let her go; let them all go. Leonard knows who he is now; the death inside him has found the pure unfilterable fundament of death without. Sailor opens the door and gets out. The sun is a dome on the horizon, a frozen nuclear explosion, the Eye of God. Marly removes the battery and tosses it onto the asphalt. Spare in the back of the Rover; Bill is—was?—nothing if not redundant. Motion turns her head: A figure inside the Ecosphere presses against the glass, flattened dead features of its face above a T-shirt that reads RUGBY PLAYERS EAT THEIR DEAD. Sailor breathes in the cool morning air that blows across the desert floor. He pulls the elastic band from his hair for the breeze to have its way. He feels very alive. In the distance the Ecosphere gleams like a discarded toy. Marly slams down the hood, gets in the Land-Rover, and turns the key. Once, twice, and it starts. She squeals out of the lot, and Leonard waves good-bye.

[20]

The sun clears the crooked line of mountain-limned horizon. Sailor goes to the back of the truck and raises the door. He removes a box from the wood-slatted bed, and from it removes another box. He raises the telescoping antenna in back of this, and presses a button. A red light glows: CHARGE OKAY. He carries the box to the front of the truck and sets it on the high hood. He hoists himself up beside it, then sets it in his lap and throws another switch. Another red light winks on above the white-painted word ARMED. Sailor cracks his knuckles and looks to the framework of aluminum struts supporting triangular glass panels in the distance.

"It is a far, far better thing I do," he says, and flourishes a finger.

"Oh, no, you don't."

The finger pauses. He glances right. The wind blows his hair over his eyes. He shakes his head to move it out of the way. The Chinese woman stands on top of the hill, carbine trained on him. They stare at each other across the orange-lit slope. The rifle barrel traces a curt line to the right; Sailor sets the transmitter aside. She juts her jaw; Sailor eases down from the warm hood of the truck. She heads down the hill toward him; Sailor spreads his fingers and holds his hands away from his body.

"Have a seat," she says.

Sailor sits.

"Hands on top of your head."

Sailor puts his hands on top of his head. "You never let me have any fun," he says.

"What were you going to do," she asks. "After this?"

Sailor shrugs. "Don't know. Got a bunch of shit in back of the truck. Oregon, maybe. Find some asshole survivalist's nuclear bomb shelter, set up camp. I try not to think that far ahead anymore. How 'bout you?"

Her turn to shrug. "Yosemite, maybe."

He grins. "Bears and 'possums. Raccoon stew."

"This what I think it is?" She nods toward the transmitter on the hood.

"Ain't about to play no rock and roll, if that's what you mean."

"That's what I mean." She keeps the carbine aimed toward him and grabs the transmitter. The two red lights shine steadily: CHARGE OKAY. ARMED. And a button with no light: DETONATE.

She looks back to see him wincing under the vacant, one-eyed stare of the rifle. "Nervous?"

"We've got to stop meeting like this."

"I can't let you do it," she says. "I'm sorry."

"Why not?" Sailor lowers his hands. "You like the rest of those assholes? Are you *endeavoring to persevere*?"

"No." She lowers the rifle to the road and holds out the transmitter. She takes a deep breath. "Because *I* want to."

She extends her hand—

[21]

—Dieter exploring the aquarium of the dead, intrepid Martian explorer alone and yet accepted, finally where he belongs, cartographer of the damned—

—Bill reborn, rising with the dawn, finally at peace with the world, content at last with a single purpose and mission: to feed—

—Leonard arboreal, monument to Darwin descending; Leonard *Rex Mortura*, King of the Dead; Leonard with power at last, returning to earth enlightened to survey these his new people, this the new necropolis—

others but nothing for them i walk there is light past the treefoods i go near i press my face against the clear toward the light i shut my eyes and she is there with the soft of her hands and there is music and roger she says Roger come dance with me, and I take her hand, and I open my eyes, and there is music, and light, and I remember—

[22]

—and brings her finger down.

Saxophone

BY NICHOLAS ROYLE

The answers were those he had feared. It was practically impossible to obtain the necessary visas on behalf of another without leaving the country and engaging in dangerous, belligerent activities. Not that this came into conflict with his principles, for he had none. But it was hazardous. The pirate squads that roamed the purgatory of Yugoslavia were susceptible to incendiary attacks from both Eastern and Western forces. Hungarian troops patrolled in small units armed to the teeth with thermite grenades; and the American planes dropped napalm, because they were confident the casualties would be *mostly* Eastern, say 70 percent or so.

Hašek crawled back down the constricted steel-walled passageways he'd been forced to use to get to the visa information bureau. At a junction of three passages he stopped, rested his damaged back against the wall, and flexed his fingers, effortlessly twisting them into a breathless run up and down the keys he imagined to be there.

He emerged near the main square of old Tirana, facing one of Stalin's many decapitated statues. Four ragged figures huddled round a flickering screen under a corrugated shelter to his left. Two of them were smoking, impossible since inhalation and exhalation were beyond their capabilities, but old habits die hard. A third man lifted a bottle to his disfigured mouth and poured alcohol down his throat; again, a useless act given the absence of thirst and physical sensation. These men were not necessarily new here; some creatures had been here for months and still indulged their former desires out of habit rather than need.

Hašek had to see about joining one of the squads conducting sorties across the border and as far north as Belgrade. For this he had to get to the Shkodra region of the city, and to get there he needed transportation. There was no public transport, so he had to get his hands on some kind of vehicle.

"Three hundred lek," the old Albanian told him.

"Three hundred! You're joking!" He looked aghast at the clapped-out old three-wheeler. "That wouldn't get me to Durres, never mind Shkodra."

"It's a good vehicle. Three hundred lek. Very good price. Look elsewhere if you wish."

Hašek knew Kadare had him; there was nowhere else to go. The old man had a virtual monopoly in the city and therefore in the country, for the city had expanded to such an extent that the two were now the same.

"Two hundred," Hašek tried.

"Three hundred," was the reply, no hesitation. "The tank is full. The battery charged."

He drove most of the way one-handed. His left hand mimed the lower notes of "These Foolish Things" while the fingers of his right hand tapped out the high notes on the steering wheel. The sky appeared briefly between concrete walls and rusting iron roofs. Literally thousands of people were wandering about; war casualties, their Albanian hosts, and some of the American and European refugees who had fled the war and got in before visa controls were introduced.

The farther north he went, the more iron and steel dominated the ramshackle architecture at the expense of concrete and rough stone. The dead were everywhere, walking from one construction to another, visible also through gaps in the walls, sitting watching television and playing games.

Shkodra was close, just beyond lay Yugoslavia and his only chance of obtaining visas for Barton. She was waiting in West Berlin, checking every day at the replication unit where the documents would come through if Hašek was successful.

"Why do you want to join a squad?" they asked him, with some suspicion.

He'd decided against honesty. It would only create extra difficulties.

"I want something to do. I'm bored of the games."

"So it would be just a game for you?"

"No. Far from it. It's how we make our country rich. It's serious business." They just stared at him. "I want to be useful."

They knew he was lying. The dead never did anything for the good of anyone else—unless by accident. They acted purely out of self-interest. Slaves to instinct. But it seemed he'd said the right words.

"There's a squad leaving tonight, one man short. The fourth member finally lost all power of movement today. Sulphur mustard gas. Killed him some weeks ago, but left him able to move. Until today."

The man took out a small map of the vicinity and began drawing on it. "Look. This is where you should meet them."

It was like a gulch between two massive skeletal blocks of rough concrete apartments, built in the early days of the war when the first casualties were arriving by boat and pushing inland. The lights were purplish and glimmering. An ex-Yugoslav army jeep lurched up the rough road, throwing its two occupants about inside.

"Why did you want to join us?" asked the driver, a Russian called Varnov, who had been so badly burned he had no skin left apparent on his body. He wore a loose-fitting, torn-and-patched military uniform actually from the old Albanian armed services. He and Jensen, a tall, strong Danish woman with strange, mauve eyes and close-cropped, dyed-black hair, had picked up Hašek and another group member, Vollmer, a dark-skinned German, and were now jostling northwards minutes from the border.

"Something to do," Hašek replied without turning his gaze from the mountains. Even here the city climbed the slopes in iron and steel and prefabricated units, on which the endless lights shone thickly. The sky was spiderwebbed with reception aerials and radar warning systems. The defenses had so far proved impenetrable to military forces, though in fact little was known about the country outside of its own and Yugoslavia's borders.

They had no trouble at the frontier, thanks to the agree-

ment between the two states. Yugoslavia conducted corrupt arms deals for money and was living with both East
and West, while Albania persisted in isolationism. But
since many native Albanians had joined their leadership in
accepting the Greek Orthodox Church's offer to possess
and settle on Corfu, the people of Albania—the dispos-
sessed, the exiled, and in the greatest numbers, the dead—
often crossed to Yugoslavia to enjoy a share of that country's opportunities for exploitation.

Which was what Hašek was doing now. Varnov's squad
would cruise until they found living people who would be
especially vulnerable to their particular form of attack.
They were entering the outskirts of Titograd, where there
was no shortage of black-market traders—the people with
whom the squad would eventually do business—but their
numbers were constantly multiplying as more flowed into
the country, so that even with the death squads targeting
them, they were not significantly depleted.

Smoke issued from a side street and a vehicle exited
under its cover so suddenly that the squad's jeep had to
veer sharply to the right to avoid a collision.

The first they knew was a guttural scream from the
German, Vollmer, sitting in the back on Hašek's left. Two
spikes of a grappling hook pinned him to the jeep's
bodywork, one through the shoulder, the other through
his forehead and skull. A chain taut from the stem of the
hook disappeared into the smoke, stretching to the other
vehicle, still hidden but tracking the jeep. A second hook
thudded into the hood and dragged the jeep off course.
Varnov attempted to regain control, but the aggressor appeared to their left and smashed heavily into the side of
the jeep. This set the jeep back on its original course, and
as Hašek cut through the chain of the rear hook, and
Jensen, in the passenger seat, worked at the front hook,
Varnov regained power in his steering. Having done so,
using the element of surprise, he jerked the wheel to the
left and the nose of the jeep careened into the front right
side of the other vehicle, a Hungarian armored car. Hašek
and Vollmer, who had freed himself from the hook,
opened fire on the Hungarian unit. A grenade bounced off
their own bonnet and exploded away to the right. Jensen

engaged her weapon and delivered a sustained volley of automatic fire across the gap between the two vehicles. Although the side of the car was visible, its occupants were not. They were still active, however, shooting sporadically and with no great accuracy, though one bullet did tear through Hašek's upper arm, missing the muscle by millimeters.

Varnov passed something back to Vollmer, saying: "Use it. I can't aim while driving." Vollmer had a look; it was a thermite grenade. But before he had a chance to lob it over, his whole body jerked backwards, pivoting at the neck. Hašek twisted his head around. A man had jumped from the other car and was riding on the back bumper, holding onto a garrote around Vollmer's neck. The man's face trailed off halfway down: nose, mouth, and chin were gone, wiped out in some former conflict. Just tatters of flesh were left in front of his top vertebrae, which Hašek saw through the space where his throat should have been. Clearly the man was one of their own people, not a Hungarian soldier; but once engaged in hostilities, it was hard to let go. He freed one of his hands, took a pistol from his belt, and fired at Hašek. The Czech was thrown to the floor of the jeep with the force of the shot, which had lodged under his shoulder blade. He grunted, not with pain but with displeasure at being so unceremoniously floored by a man from the same side. He took aim with his own gun, but his stream of bullets hit air. The wire had sliced right through Vollmer's neck and spine, and the faceless attacker fell away, clutching the German's head. Meanwhile, Jensen had retrieved the grenade and skillfully threw it high so that it dropped in the armored car and exploded on impact. The thermite flashed brilliantly, silhouetting the remaining three dead men as they carbonated and were swiftly destroyed.

The men in the armored car had certainly been pirates, just like Varnov, Vollmer, Jensen, and Hašek, looking for the same thing but ending up mistaking the jeep's crew for some of their living, breathing targets. Now the three had to press on, without Vollmer; the remainder of his body still sat uselessly alongside Hašek.

Jensen and Varnov wouldn't think Hašek's reasons for

being there were any different from theirs: to plunder the
living for their special booty, which in Yugoslavia was
easily exchanged either for straight cash or for the techno-
logical hardware and luxury goods the new Albanians depended on.

They weren't in it for the general good, but because
personal instinct drove them on. And if a man had twelve
televisions, he probably wouldn't be able to watch them all
at the same time, so his neighbor could take one almost
without him noticing. In a land where the people had so
few desires, they were well served by what was basically
an anarchic system. All aspirations concurred.

Apart from a few exceptions. Hašek being one. He'd
been creative in his life, a man of music. The memories of
it haunted him. Even now his fingers were playing "An-
thropology" on the butt and barrel of his submachine gun
as the jeep rattled on.

They drove through another area of fires, keeping especially vigilant regarding the thick clouds of low smoke.

Hella Elizabeth Barton scanned the street behind her
before turning into Gothaerstrasse. Her suspicion was not
unfounded; she'd been under surveillance for some weeks
now, ever since meeting and forming an attachment to
Trefzger. A vociferous opponent of chemical and bacteriological weapons since before the war started, he had been
a marked man, officially, for years; branded a communist,
a pacifist, an anarchist, and generally a headcase, but a
dangerous one, he lived under the constant watchful eye of
military and civil authorities in West Berlin.

In the last few days, though, he had gone into hiding,
and Barton had been doing her best to conceal her movements. Making love by candlelight was preferable to sex
by torchlight, which they had endured in Trefzger's old
apartment, as the duty officers in the street and the building opposite played their torches constantly over his cur-
tained windows.

Barton ducked through the basement window and felt
her way around the decaying walls of the room to the door
at the far side. She worked the locks and shut the door
behind her. Down the steps, dripping moss and fungus,

and through another locked door at the bottom. She was in the derelict U-bahn tunnel—commissioned, built, and never used—and had to feel her way again. She always expected a train to come scraping along the rusted rails, but one never did, nor ever would.

Six knocks brought Trefzger to the door. He hustled her in before saying hello.

"You're getting very jumpy these days, Detlef," she reproached him.

"I should go and live in Albania," he replied, "where your Hašek is."

"He's not my Hašek. And anyway, Berlin is the perfect place. Your work would never reach anyone from down there."

"Of course it would," he said. "They have excellent communications. Probably the best in the world." He looked at her. "Let's go in."

Later, when they were lying on a deep rug and she was running a hand through his long blond hair, he asked: "How was your day at the replication unit?"

"You talk as if I work there," she said. "I only waited an hour. Nothing came through. No documents, no messages. Any day now though, I should think."

"He must really want you, Hella."

"No, I don't think so. I think he just wants something from me. Wants to use me. Same old story."

"You know," Trefzger said, sitting up, "you shouldn't pretend to be so cynical. I can see you still feel for him underneath."

"You're jealous," she said, gently scratching his back.

He laid a hand on her thigh. "No, I'm not jealous. You'll grow tired of me one day like you did of him."

"He died in a chemical attack a year ago."

"You left him long before that, Hella. Seven or eight years before. He no longer excited you, just as one day I will no longer excite you."

"That's not true." She sat up fully and threaded her hand around his waist, allowing it to drop to his crotch. "You excite me. He never did."

Trefzger knew it wasn't true, but rather than being a lie, it was a sort of code. He turned and kneeled between her legs. She drew his head closer and they kissed. He kissed her chin, her neck, her shoulders, and her breasts, gently biting. She threw her head back and tried to control her breathing. She opened her eyes to see if that would help. There was Detlef's desk, his computer, the monitor screen a pattern of green symbols. Papers, books, pens, pencils . . . It was no good, the catalog of mundanity could not distract her body. She trembled as he sucked at her breast and as she distinctly felt the pulsing of his blood between her thighs. Wheezing now, she ignored the pain and hitched her legs up a little.

"All right?" he asked her.

"Yes," between gasps for air.

"Your asthma?"

"Yes. Come on."

He didn't move, so she moved up farther, opened wider, and eased down onto his penis. He responded, thrusting up, and she yelped, then wheezed. Her breathing was a harsh rasp, but she urged him on, quicker still and harder. He came suddenly and she rode higher, then fell back, away, breathing quickly and noisily.

"Here." Trefzger had reached for her insufflator. She pressed and inhaled, twice.

"It's ridiculous," she said, between gulping for air. "You're meant . . . to grow out of it . . . I'm getting . . . worse every day. A doctor . . . the other day . . . told me if I didn't have this stuff . . . ," indicating the drug, "and I had a severe attack . . . it could be serious."

"I was wondering," Trefzger said, slowly, "why it should be getting worse. Then it came to me today. It's the germs. All the bacteriological stuff. Most of them are composed of tiny spores. Tularemia, anthrax, plague, all these things. They are acting as irritants. There's not enough in the air to kill, but plenty to exacerbate an asthmatic reaction. That's the case away from the most active war zones, anyway. That's why I don't think you should go down to Belgrade or Tirana."

"I have to," she said, breathing a little more easily. "He needs me. He wants to live again, and I'm the only person he's got to help him."

"You do care more about him than me." Trefzger sounded hurt.

"I don't," she shouted. "Don't you understand? He needs me for five minutes. It's not much to ask."

"You won't let me give you a child," he said bitterly. "You had one by him."

"You bastard!" She struck out, hitting him in the face. "Thanks for the memory." She stood up in a rage and stormed across to the far side of the room, where she stood for a moment, then slumped down in a corner.

Her son, whom Hašek had not seen since just after the birth, when she left, taking the baby boy with her, had died at the age of eight in a heavy bomb attack on Hanover.

Varnov's steel club thudded into the lieutenant's head, and the man fell with a resounding crash, taking several wooden chairs with him.

They were in Belgrade now, where they'd found themselves driving through and past endless groups of aimlessly wandering children, until they found what they wanted: a vulnerable unit of fit men. A group of American soldiers, wearing uniforms under heavy, dark coats, were completing a deal with a small party of Czechoslovakian rebels. The two groups froze on either side of the room with the pile of weapons in the middle, when Jensen broke the door down and Varnov and Hašek stepped through behind her. The American lieutenant pulled an automatic pistol from inside his coat and shot several times, hitting Varnov and Hašek, before Varnov clubbed him to the floor. Using his machine gun, Hašek dispatched the Czech who advanced on him, experiencing a flicker of recognition at the insignia on the rebel soldier's battledress. So, the man was a Czech, as Hašek himself had been, but it meant nothing; there was work to be done.

It was important to fire as little as possible, so as not to damage the vital organs, which was what they were after.

All Hašek, Varnov, and Jensen had to fear was an incendiary or explosive attack, something that would ravage their bodies to such an extent that they would be unusable. Also, whereas a few bullet wounds were neither here nor there, to be subjected to constant automatic gun-fire could theoretically destroy them. So when the Czechs ran to the weapons and seized the flamethrowers on top of the pile, Jensen and Hašek hurried to disarm them. But they were not quick enough. A blond, spiky-haired Czech, no older than seventeen, operated his weapon, and Jensen, whom the youth was facing, awaited her annihilation by fire. But nothing happened. The other Czechs experienced the same problem. The Americans had sold them dud weapons. The youth grabbed a repeating rifle and aimed at the Americans. Again nothing happened.

The Americans, meanwhile, seeing their popularity dwindling, were crowding into the corner, trying to open a door that, as a precaution, the Czech leader had locked earlier.

Hašek and the Czech youth, armed now with a working machine gun, bore down on the frightened Americans, one of whom opened fire, unwisely choosing Hašek as his target. The bullets passed uselessly through the dead man, and the Czech sprayed the men in the corner with gunfire. He was stopped by Varnov, who brought his club to bear on the backs of his knees, then, as he fell, on his kneecaps. The boy screamed, dropped his gun, and fainted.

While Hašek checked the Americans for any sign of life, Varnov held the Czechs, and Jensen systematically slit their throats, thus preserving all their organs.

"Hašek," Varnov said. Hašek looked up. "The boxes in the jeep."

Hašek understood and left the room. Returning with the boxed preservation cylinders he found Varnov and Jensen already at work on the corpses. Two sets of surgi-cal hardware lay open on the floor. Jensen replaced one instrument and took a small hacksaw. Hašek watched as she cut through the Czech youth's forehead and worked at his skull, being careful not to saw too quickly and damage the brain. Varnov was extricating a heart with maximum speed and mess: he had to keep wiping his scrawny hands on his coat to prevent the scalpel slipping in his grasp.

Hašek told them he was neither equipped nor experi-enced and would therefore sit out the operations. Neither replied, so he left the room. He went downstairs and sat in the jeep. There was no one around and no trace yet of any natural light in the sky. Belgrade's solid gray buildings had survived the war very well so far. Practically all were still standing. Varnov had parked the jeep between two imposing but essentially characterless examples, in juxta-position to which Hašek seemed almost to come alive.

His hands molded around his remembered saxophone and his fingers warmed up on a few scales before slipping into Sonny Rollins's "St. Thomas." He played this through, then slowed down the tempo and segued into "You Don't Know What Love Is." He'd played through six more tunes, with some lengthy improvisation, by the time Varnov and Jensen appeared, heavily laden with their boxes, at the entrance to the building. They came down the steps and walked over to the jeep.

They drove northwest a little way to Zemun, where Varnov had planned to rendezvous with Larry, an Ameri-can dealer. Larry, whose surname, if one existed, was known to nobody, did not discriminate on grounds of na-tionality: he'd accept anyone's organs, even an Ameri-can's, provided he had buyers lined up. Especially an American's, in actual fact, since he often liked to pitch his sales talk with the proud boast that this was not just any old kidney, this was an *American* kidney he was selling. Consequently, many of his buyers were American.

The electronically controlled gate swung open and Varnov stepped through, closely followed by Jensen and Hašek. Larry was waiting for them at the door, with his woollen plaid shirt and large, overhanging belly. They filed in and down a number of corridors.

The room they ended up in seemed to be the nerve center of Larry's operations. It was also his living room. A television set in the corner was tuned to American foot-ball. On the floor by the battered armchair facing the set were three cans of American beer and a dirty polystyrene food container. On the other side of the room was ranged a bank of monitors and computer terminals. One screen displayed up-to-the-minute details of relative currency changes throughout the world. Another gave the correct time in all major capital cities. Several preservation boxes stood waiting on a wooden bench.

"Well, come on, fellers," Larry said, picking his teeth. "Let's see what you got."

Larry examined the contents of the cylinders and announced he would take three kidneys, two livers, two sets of lungs, one set of testicles, and a brain.

"I hope it's an American brain," he said.

"Yes, it is," Jensen lied, holding up the cylinder containing the blond Czech youth's brain. All the Americans had received bullet wounds in the head.

"And the testicles, too?" asked Larry.

"Yes, American also," said Varnov, truthfully.

Larry explained he couldn't take the risk on the remaining viscera, since he could not predict how soon he would find more buyers. He paid them, in dollars, and returned to his chair to watch football and crack open a beer before they had even left the room.

Back in the jeep, Varnov distributed the money. Hašek noticed his share was slightly less and assumed this was accounted for by his nonparticipation in the eviscerations. He accepted the money—a large sum and more than sufficient for his purposes—without mentioning the discrepancy.

They returned to Belgrade, Varnov and Jensen to try to unload the unsold organs on another dealer and then to visit Petrovic, a Yugoslav, to see about subscription to a new satellite television and communications system; and Hašek, though the other two did not know it, to seek out Midgley, a corrupt British envoy to the Yugoslav government. There was no shortage of corrupt officials, but Midgley was the one to whom Hašek had an introduction.

During the short journey Hašek just had time to wrap his fingers around "I Found a New Baby."

Varnov drove at breakneck speed. He had expected Larry to take the lot off them, so was now in a hurry to find another approachable dealer before the end of the night. He wanted to be back inside the frontier before daybreak to minimize the risk of further attack.

It was so easy, laughably easy. The jeep screeched to a halt before a large fortified building and Varnov leapt out, saying this particular dealer might take the stuff, but then again, they'd never dealt with him before, so there was no guarantee. Hašek said he would try a dealer he knew of in the next street and report back. Varnov and Jensen, presumably having heard but not acknowledging his comment, disappeared into the building.

He walked east on the Bulevar Revolucije for two hundred meters, then turned up the Milana Rakica. Three blocks up he turned left and spoke into an intercom.

"So what do you need these visas for?" asked Midgley authoritatively, ushering Hašek through into a leatherbound-book-lined study at the rear of the apartment.

"Very civilized," Hašek said, looking around.

"I try," Midgley replied, looking pleased, "to maintain standards. Drink . . . ?" He looked at Hašek. "Oh no, of course not. Excuse me."

"I'll have a drink. Scotch and water. I developed a taste for it in Berlin."

"Oh really?" Midgley nervously poured Scotch from a decanter and iced water from a jug. "And when were you in Berlin?"

"Eight years ago. I knew an American woman there. We drank a lot of Scotch. She moved away. . . . Now, about the visas?"

"Of course." Midgley passed Hašek the tumbler of Scotch. He took the drink and waited for the other man to turn away, but he didn't, so Hašek tipped the contents of the glass down his throat in one go. Apparently slightly unnerved, Midgley turned and crossed to a desk. He opened a drawer, rummaged around inside, and found a pair of half-moon spectacles, which he put on, then continued his search.

Hašek hoped the Scotch and water had taken an undamaged route into his gut. Had it seeped out through a wound anywhere, he would be unable to feel the dampness and so would drip unawares on the Englishman's floor. It wasn't that he cared to avoid offending propriety; he just didn't want to telegraph his weaknesses to this man.

"A return transit visa, is it?" Midgley asked. A swathe of thick, black, greased hair had fallen down over his forehead. He tried to smooth it back into place.

"I only need to see her for two minutes."

"The trouble is," Midgley began, "they are in great demand and very short supply. It's mothers, you see, wanting for some morbid reason to come down and look for their dead children. Here in Belgrade, mainly. I don't know if you've noticed how few children there are in Tirana. They're mostly retained in Belgrade."

"I don't see the sense in that, when Belgrade is far more dangerous than Tirana."

"No, well, Mr. Hašek, that's really not your province, is it, rational thought and reasoning? So I really shouldn't worry about it, if I were you."

Midgley was clearly hiding something, but as he had so rightly pointed out, it didn't concern Hašek. The visas did.

"Look, Midgley, I want the visas and I want them now. I have the money you require." He took out a wad of bills. "I cannot wait any longer." He threw the money onto the desk. Midgley picked it up, flicked through the notes, and nodded.

"Yes, well, allow me just to make things look official." He took a rubber stamp, inked it, and pressed it on the small squares of paper on his blotter. In a hurry now to conclude the business, he handed the papers to Hašek. The Czech took them and turned to go. He paused with his hand on the door handle, as if something had occurred to him.

"I don't suppose," he began, facing Midgley again, "you possess such a thing as a saxophone?"

"That's it," she said. "That's for me. It's what I've been waiting for."

The clerk peered through large, round glasses like goggles, at the paper coming out of the machine.

"Hella Elizabeth Barton," he read out loud. "Do you have your ID?"

"I already showed it you," she said impatiently.

"Your ID," said the impassive clerk.

She searched in her pockets and finally produced the right card.

"Thank you," he said. "You may take these." He

handed her the replicated visas and a detailed note from
Hašek.

She left the replication unit and marched briskly down
Franklin Strasse to Ernst-Reuter-Platz, where she boarded
a U-bahn train to Hallesches Tor. She studied the visas.
They authorized her to cross over the Wall to East Berlin
and thence to travel through East Germany, Czechoslovakia, and Hungary to Yugoslavia. The return journey was
not to begin later than twenty-four hours after the outward trip.

Referring to her map, she saw that she would probably
pass through Cheb in Czechoslovakia, very close to the
borders with East and West Germany, where Hašek, then
a member of the Czech Jazz Section, had triggered the
start of the war by escaping to the West. Czech guards
fired after him, missed, and got two West German guards,
whose colleagues retaliated. The rest was history, with
Eastwood sanctioning the deployment and use of stock-
piled chemical weapons, and Britain, France, Austria, and
West Germany lining up behind him.

Barton's train crossed under the Wall and trundled
through the ghost stations on its way to Friedrichstrasse,
where she would make the official crossing.

As her train rattled across the bridge over the Danube,
in its final approach to the Beograd-Dunav Station, the
strange feeling that had hung over her all the way from
Germany sank down, becoming increasingly palpable. In
Belgrade, she was not going to find quite what she had
been expecting.

Apart from this, she had been suffering from asthma
since descending from the Moravian Heights, and it got
worse the farther south she came. She cursed her stupidity
in not having her insufflator with her at all times—she
hadn't thought of it as she rushed, without going home
first, from the replication unit to the Wall to start her
journey. As well as the presumed effect of the spores and
dust, which Trefzger had mentioned, her asthma was further aggravated by the anxiety she felt.

She got up and went to the bathroom to see if a drink of
water would improve her condition. It didn't. She looked
at herself in the broken mirror and searched for the beauty

she had been told was there. Yes, it was, but only to someone who saw her face and remembered what it had looked
like before. They could kid themselves that the ravages of
war and stress left only temporary scars. She could kid
herself, in her less pessimistic moments. She swept her
long hair back, tugging her fingers through the knots.

There was no soap. The water ran in rivulets away from
the oil in her skin. She was at least able to poke the little
bits of dirt out of the corners of her eyes.

She left the bathroom, her breathing more labored.

He waited in the room where he, Varnov, and Jensen
had surprised the Americans and Czechs.

He sat on a wooden chair in the middle of the room and
mimed "Just You Just Me" on the tenor saxophone he'd
bought after leaving the replication unit. He'd retained
enough money from the sale of the organs to cover the
cost of the instrument, possibly the only one on sale in
Belgrade.

He lacked only one thing now: that which Barton
would give him—breath to sound the notes.

He could almost hear "Now's the Time" as he worked
it out on the keys. What he didn't hear was the door
opening. She was suddenly there, on the threshold, panting and wheezing with obvious pain. Behind her a small
form lingered.

Hašek rose to his feet, placing his saxophone on the
chair.

"Hella . . ." he said flatly. "Is it asthma?" He was incapable of expressing concern he didn't feel.

"Yes," she wheezed. "But how can you talk?"

"Just using the air that gets into the body. It's enough
for speech but not enough for what I want to do. . . .
Your asthma is bad."

"Yes. It's all . . . the shit in the air and . . . and
finding him . . . here in Belgrade . . ." Whereupon, she
brought out from behind her a young boy, whose eyes
stared dully. His face looked tight and bluish gray, sug-
gesting death by asphyxiation. Hašek and the boy looked
at each other, neither face registering anything.

Hašek spoke: "Hella, come here. You know what I want."

"No, I can't," she said.

"Hella. You don't have to worry. I just want to breathe again. You will go freely and I will never seek you out. My oath."

"I believe you, Hašek . . . but it changes nothing. . . . I can't . . . The boy . . ."

"But I asked you to come. You came. Please. One minute. Then you can go."

"You don't understand."

"I want to breathe," he shouted. "I want to play music. Breathe into me. Kiss me!"

"No." She shook her head, as her chest continued to heave for gulps of air. "The boy, Hašek . . . Look at him. . . . He's ours."

Hašek looked, saw nothing. He needed the woman's breath. Music mattered. Nothing else was important, until he actually blew a note.

"I've spent the whole day . . . agonizing. . . . But if my asthma will allow me . . . to resurrect anyone . . . it must be Alex, our son."

A car drew up outside the building and doors slammed.

"I'm sorry, Hašek," she said, kneeling down to eye-level with the boy and taking his head in her hands. She placed her mouth over his passive lips, pinched his nostrils together, took a deep breath, and blew. Steps echoed hollowly on the stairs. She repeated the process and almost lost consciousness, so acute was her own breathing difficulty. She gave a final push and at the same time the doorway yielded two intruders, Varnov and Jensen.

Whether they'd come back for him or for fresh bodies to plunder, Hašek didn't know.

Barton looked up, startled then horrified. The boy fell from her grasp. Before she could reach him again, Varnov's club struck her jaw, smashing it and embedding her lower teeth into her upper gums, firmly scotching any hopes of further resuscitation.

Over by the wall, the boy twitched.

Jensen swung a spiked, macelike weapon and advanced on Hašek. The Czech searched his person for a weapon; he found a small knife, which he stuck out in front of him like a straw before a tornado. The mace crunched into the hand that held the knife and its swing severed the weakened wrist, carrying the hand away on its spikes like a trophy.

One instinct defeated the other, and Hašek grabbed the saxophone with his remaining hand. He mastered the awkward balance and brandished the instrument. Jensen made a pass and missed as Hašek ducked and swung low, scoring a hit and shattering the woman's tibia, but losing his improvised weapon in the process. The saxophone spun on the floor and Jensen kicked it away as she fell.

Hašek reached for the saxophone, but Jensen, no less formidable an opponent on the ground, had swung her mace and caught his elbow, snapping the joint and thrusting bone up through the skin.

Virtually defenseless now, Hašek glanced around, saw Barton desperately trying to fend off Varnov's killing blow. He saw also, in the instant before Jensen's spikes relieved him of that facility, the boy who was apparently his son, slipping otherwise unnoticed through the open doorway.

On the Far Side of the Cadillac Desert with Dead Folks

BY JOE R. LANSDALE

(For David Schow, a story of The Bad Guys and The Bad Guys)

[1]

After a month's chase, Wayne caught up with Calhoun one night at a little honky-tonk called Rosalita's. It wasn't that Calhoun had finally gotten careless, it was just that he wasn't worried. He'd killed four bounty hunters so far, and Wayne knew a fifth didn't concern him.

The last bounty hunter had been the famous Pink Lady McGuire—one mean, mama—three hundred pounds of rolling, ugly meat that carried a twelve-gauge Remington pump and a bad attitude. Story was, Calhoun jumped her from behind, cut her throat, and as a joke, fucked her before she bled to death. This not only proved to Wayne that Calhoun was a dangerous sonofabitch, it also proved he had bad taste.

Wayne stepped out of his '57 Chevy reproduction, pushed his hat back on his forehead, opened the trunk, and got the sawed-off double barrel and some shells out of there. He already had a .38 revolver in the holster at his side and a bowie knife in each boot, but when you went into a place like Rosalita's it was best to have plenty of backup.

Wayne put a handful of shotgun shells in his shirt pocket, snapped the flap over them, looked up at the red-and-blue neon sign that flashed ROSALITA'S: COLD BEER

AND DEAD DANCING, found his center, as they say in Zen, and went on in.

He held the shotgun against his leg, and as it was dark in there and folks were busy with talk or drinks or dancing, no one noticed him or his artillery right off.

He spotted Calhoun's stocky, black-hatted self immediately. He was inside the dance cage with a dead buck-naked Mexican girl of about twelve. He was holding her tight around the waist with one hand and massaging her rubbery ass with the other like it was a pillow he was trying to shape. The dead girl's handless arms flailed on either side of Calhoun, and her little tits pressed to his thick chest. Her wire-muzzled face knocked repeatedly at his shoulder and drool whipped out of her mouth in thick spermy ropes, stuck to his shirt, faded and left a patch of wetness.

For all Wayne knew, the girl was Calhoun's sister or daughter. It was that kind of place. The kind that had sprung up immediately after that stuff had gotten out of a lab upstate and filled the air with bacterium that brought dead humans back to life, made their basic motor functions work and made them hungry for human flesh; made it so if a man's wife, daughter, sister, or mother went belly up and he wanted to turn a few bucks, he might think: "Damn, that's tough about ole Betty Sue, but she's dead as hoot-owl shit and ain't gonna be needing nothing from here on out, and with them germs working around in her, she's just gonna pull herself out of the ground and cause me a problem. And the ground out back of the house is harder to dig than a calculus problem is to work, so I'll just toss her cold ass in the back of the pickup next to the chain saw and the barbed-wire roll haul her across the border and sell her to the Meat Boys to sell to the tonks for dancing.

"It's a sad thing to sell one of your own, but shit, them's the breaks. I'll just stay out of the tonks until all the meat rots off her bones and they have to throw her away. That way I won't go in some place for a drink and see her up there shaking her dead tits and end up going sentimental and dewey-eyed in front of one of my buddies or some ole two-dollar gal."

This kind of thinking supplied the dancers. In other parts of the country, the dancers might be men or children, but here it was mostly women. Men were used for hunting and target practice.

The Meat Boys took the bodies, cut off the hands so they couldn't grab, ran screws threw their jaws to fasten on wire muzzles so they couldn't bite, sold them to the honky-tonks about the time the germ started stirring.

Tonk owners put them inside wire enclosures up front of their joints, started music, and men paid five dollars to get in there and grab them and make like they were dancing when all the women wanted to do was grab and bite, which muzzled and handless, they could not do.

If a man liked his partner enough, he could pay more money and have her tied to a cot in the back and he could get on her and do some business. Didn't have to hear no arguments or buy presents or make promises or make them come. Just fuck and hike.

As long as the establishment sprayed the dead for maggots and kept them perfumed and didn't keep them so long hunks of meat came off on a fella's dick, the customers were happy as flies on shit.

Wayne looked to see who might give him trouble, and figured everyone was a potential customer. The six foot two, two-hundred fifty pound bouncer being the most immediate concern.

But, there wasn't anything to do but to get on with things and handle problems when they came up. He went into the cage where Calhoun was dancing, shouldered through the other dancers and went for him.

Calhoun had his back to Wayne, and as the music was loud, Wayne didn't worry about going quietly. But Calhoun sensed him and turned with his hand full of a little .38.

Wayne clubbed Calhoun's arm with the barrel of the shotgun. The little gun flew out of Calhoun's hand and went skidding across the floor and clanked against the metal cage.

Calhoun wasn't outdone. He spun the dead girl in front of him and pulled a big pigsticker out of his boot and held it under the girl's armpit in a threatening manner, which with a knife that big was no feat.

Wayne shot the dead girl's left kneecap out from under her and she went down. Her armpit trapped Calhoun's knife. The other men deserted their partners and went over the wire netting like squirrels.

Before Calhoun could shake the girl loose, Wayne stepped in and hit him over the head with the barrel of the shotgun. Calhoun crumpled and the girl began to crawl about on the floor as if looking for lost contacts.

The bouncer came in behind Wayne, grabbed him under the arms and tried to slip a full nelson on him.

Wayne kicked back on the bouncer's shin and raked his boot down the man's instep and stomped his foot. The bouncer let go. Wayne turned and kicked him in the balls and hit him across the face with the shotgun.

The bouncer went down and didn't even look like he wanted up.

Wayne couldn't help but note he liked the music that was playing. When he turned he had someone to dance with.

Calhoun.

Calhoun charged him, hit Wayne in the belly with his head, knocked him over the bouncer. They tumbled to the floor and the shotgun went out of Wayne's hands and scraped across the floor and hit the crawling girl in the head. She didn't even notice, just kept snaking in circles, dragging her blasted leg behind her like a skin she was trying to shed.

The other women, partnerless, wandered about the cage. The music changed. Wayne didn't like this tune as well. Too slow. He bit Calhoun's earlobe off.

Calhoun screamed and they grappled around on the floor. Calhoun got his arm around Wayne's throat and tried to choke him to death.

Wayne coughed out the earlobe, lifted his leg and took the knife out of his boot. He brought it around and back and hit Calhoun in the temple with the hilt.

Calhoun let go of Wayne and rocked on his knees, then collapsed on top of him.

Wayne got out from under him and got up and kicked

him in the head a few times. When he was finished, he put
the bowie in its place, got Calhoun's .38 and the shotgun.
To hell with pig sticker.

A dead woman tried to grab him, and he shoved her
away with a thrust of his palm. He got Calhoun by the
collar, started pulling him toward the gate.

Faces were pressed against the wire, watching. It had
been quite a show. A friendly cowboy type opened the
gate for Wayne and the crowd parted as he pulled Calhoun by. One man felt helpful and chased after them and
said, "Here's his hat, Mister," and dropped it on
Calhoun's face and it stayed there.

Outside, a professional drunk was standing between two
cars taking a leak on the ground. As Wayne pulled Calhoun past, the drunk said, "Your buddy don't look so
good."

"Look worse than that when I get him to Law Town,"
Wayne said.

Wayne stopped by the '57, emptied Calhoun's pistol and
tossed it as far as he could, then took a few minutes to
kick Calhoun in the ribs and ass. Calhoun grunted and
farted, but didn't come to.

When Wayne's leg got tired, he put Calhoun in the passenger seat and handcuffed him to the door.

He went over to Calhoun's '62 Impala replica with the
plastic bull horns mounted on the hood—which was how
he had located him in the first place, by his well known
car—and kicked the glass out of the window on the driver's side and used the shotgun to shoot the bull horns off.
He took out his pistol and shot all the tires flat, pissed on
the driver's door, and kicked a dent in it.

By then he was too tired to shit in the backseat, so he
took some deep breaths and went back to the '57 and
climbed in behind the wheel.

Reaching across Calhoun, he opened the glove box and
got out one of his thin, black cigars and put it in his
mouth. He pushed the lighter in, and while he waited for
it to heat up, he took the shotgun out of his lap and
reloaded it.

A couple of men poked their heads outside of the tonk's
door, and Wayne stuck the shotgun out the window and

fired above their heads. They disappeared inside so fast they might have been an optical illusion.

Wayne put the lighter to his cigar, picked up the wanted poster he had on the seat, and set fire to it. He thought about putting it in Calhoun's lap as a joke, but didn't. He tossed the flaming poster out the window.

He drove over close to the tonk and used the remaining shotgun load to shoot at the neon ROSALITA'S sign. Glass tinkled onto the tonk's roof and onto the gravel drive.

Now if he only had a dog to kick.

He drove away from there, bound for the Cadillac Desert, and finally Law Town on the other side.

[2]

The Cadillacs stretched for miles, providing the only shade in the desert. They were buried nose down at a slant, almost to the windshields, and Wayne could see skeletons of some of the drivers in the car, either lodged behind the steering wheels or lying on the dashboards against the glass. The roof and hood guns had long since been removed and all the windows on the cars were rolled up, except for those that had been knocked out and vandalized by travelers, or dead folks looking for goodies.

The thought of being in one of those cars with the windows rolled up in all this heat made Wayne feel even more uncomfortable than he already was. Hot as it was, he was certain even the skeletons were sweating.

He finished pissing on the tire of the Chevy, saw the piss had almost dried. He shook the drops off, watched them fall and evaporate against the burning sand. Zipping up, he thought about Calhoun, and how when he'd pulled over earlier to let the sonofabitch take a leak, he'd seen there was a little metal ring through the head of his dick and a Texas emblem dangling from that. He could understand the Texas emblem, being from there himself, but he couldn't for the life of him imagine why a fella would do that to his general. Any idiot who would put a ring through the head of his pecker deserved to die, innocent or not.

Wayne took off his cowboy hat and rubbed the back of his neck and ran his hand over the top of his head and back again. The sweat on his fingers was thick as lube oil, and the thinning part of his hairline was tender; the heat was cooking the hell out of his scalp, even through the brown felt of his hat.

Before he put his hat on, the sweat on his fingers was dry. He broke open the shotgun, put the shells in his pocket, opened the Chevy's back door and tossed the shotgun on the floorboard.

He got in the front behind the wheel and the seat was hot as a griddle on his back and ass. The sun shone through the slightly tinted windows like a polished chrome hubcap; it forced him to squint.

Glancing over at Calhoun, he studied him. The fucker was asleep with his head thrown back and his black wilted hat hung precarious on his head—it looked jaunty almost. Sweat oozed down Calhoun's red face, flowed over his eyelids and around his neck, running in riverlets down the white seat covers, drying quickly. He had his left hand between his legs, clutching his balls, and his right was on the arm rest, which was the only place it could be since he was handcuffed to the door.

Wayne thought he ought to blow the bastard's brains out and tell God he died. The shithead certainly needed shooting, but Wayne didn't want to lose a thousand dollars off his reward. He needed every penny if he was going to get that wrecking yard he wanted. The yard was the dream that went before him like a carrot before a donkey, and he didn't want anymore delays. If he never made another trip across this goddamn desert, that would suit him fine.

Pop would let him buy the place with the money he had now, and he could pay the rest out later. But that wasn't what he wanted to do. The bounty business had finally gone sour, and he wanted to do different. It wasn't any goddamn fun anymore. Just met the dick cheese of the earth. And when you ran the sonofabitches to ground and put the cuffs on them, you had to watch your ass till you got them turned in. Had to sleep with one eye open and a hand on your gun. It wasn't anyway to live.

And he wanted a chance to do right by Pop. Pop had been like a father to him. When he was a kid and his mama was screwing the Mexicans across the border for the rent money, Pop would let him hang out in the yard and climb on the rusted cars and watch him fix the better ones, tune those babies so fine they purred like dick-whipped women.

When he was older, Pop would haul him to Galveston for the whores and out to the beach to take potshots at all the ugly, fucked-up critters swimming around in the Gulf. Sometimes he'd take him to Oklahoma for the Dead Roundup. It sure seemed to do the old fart good to whack those dead fuckers with a tire iron, smash their diseased brains so they'd lay down for good. And it was a challenge. Cause if one of those dead buddies bit you, you could put your head between your legs and kiss your rosy ass goodbye.

Wayne pulled out of his thoughts of Pop and the wrecking yard and turned on the stereo system. One of his favorite country-and-western tunes whispered at him. It was Billy Conteegas singing, and Wayne hummed along with the music as he drove into the welcome, if mostly ineffectual, shadows provided by the Cadillacs.

> My baby left me,
> She left me for a cow,
> But I don't give a flying fuck,
> She's gone radioactive now,
> Yeah, my baby left me,
> Left me for a six-tittied cow.

Just when Conteegas was getting to the good part, doing the trilling sound in his throat he was famous for, Calhoun opened his eyes and spoke up.

"Ain't it bad enough I got to put up with the fucking heat and your fucking humming without having to listen to that shit? Ain't you got no Hank Williams stuff, or maybe some of that nigger music they used to make? You know, where the coons harmonize and one of them sings like his nuts are cut off."

"You just don't know good music when you hear it, Calhoun."

Calhoun moved his free hand to his hatband, found one of his few remaining cigarettes and a match there. He struck the match on his knee, lit the smoke and coughed a few rounds. Wayne couldn't imagine how Calhoun could smoke in all this heat.

"Well, I may not know good music when I hear it, capon, but I damn sure know bad music when I hear it. And that's some bad music."

"You ain't got any kind of culture, Calhoun. You been too busy raping kids."

"Reckon a man has to have a hobby," Calhoun said, blowing smoke at Wayne. "Young pussy is mine. Besides, she wasn't in diapers. Couldn't find one that young. She was thirteen. You know what they say. If they're old enough to bleed, they're old enough to breed."

"How old they have to be for you to kill them?"

"She got loud."

"Change channels, Calhoun."

"Just passing the time of day, capon. Better watch yourself bounty hunter, when you least expect it, I'll bash your head."

"You're gonna run your mouth one time too many, Calhoun, and when you do, you're gonna finish this ride in the trunk with ants crawling on you. You ain't so priceless I won't blow you away."

"You lucked out at the tonk, boy. But there's always tomorrow, and every day can't be like at Rosalita's."

Wayne smiled. "Trouble is, Calhoun, you're running out of tomorrows."

[3]

As they drove between the Cadillacs, the sky fading like a bad bulb, Wayne looked at the cars and tried to imagine what the Chevy-Cadillac Wars had been like, and why they had been fought in this miserable desert. He had heard it was a hell of a fight, and close, but the outcome had been Chevy's and now they were the only cars Detroit made. And as far as he was concerned, that was the only thing about Detroit that was worth a damn. Cars.

He felt that way about all cities. He'd just as soon lie down and let a diseased dog shit in his face than drive through one, let alone live in one.

Law Town being an exception. He'd go there. Not to live, but to give Calhoun to the authorities and pick up his reward. People in Law Town were always glad to see a criminal brought in. The public executions were popular and varied and brought in a steady income.

Last time he'd been to Law Town he'd bought a front-row ticket to one of the executions and watched a chronic shoplifter, a red-headed rat of a man, get pulled apart by being chained between two souped-up tractors. The execution itself was pretty brief, but there had been plenty of buildup with clowns and balloons and a big-tittied stripper who could swing her tits in either direction to boom-boom music.

Wayne had been put off by the whole thing. It wasn't organized enough and the drinks and food were expensive and the front-row seats were too close to the tractors. He had gotten to see that the red-head's insides were brighter than his hair, but some of the insides got sprinkled on his new shirt, and cold water or not, the spots hadn't come out. He had suggested to one of the management that they put up a big plastic shield so the front row wouldn't get splattered, but he doubted anything had come of it.

They drove until it was solid dark. Wayne stopped and fed Calhoun a stick of jerky and some water from his canteen. Then he handcuffed him to the front bumper of the Chevy.

"See any snakes, Gila monsters, scorpions, stuff like that," Wayne said, "yell out. Maybe I can get around here in time."

"I'd let the fuckers run up my asshole before I'd call you," Calhoun said.

Leaving Calhoun with his head resting on the bumper, Wayne climbed in the backseat of the Chevy and slept with one ear cocked and one eye open.

Before dawn Wayne got Calhoun loaded in the '57 and

they started out. After a few minutes of sluicing through
the early morning grayness, a wind started up. One of
those weird desert winds that come out of nowhere. It
carried grit through the air at the speed of bullets, hit the
'57 with a sound like rabid cats scratching.

The sand tires crunched on through, and Wayne turned
on the windshield blower, the sand wipers, and the
headbeams, and kept on keeping on.

When it was time for the sun to come up, they couldn't
see it. Too much sand. It was blowing harder than ever
and the blowers and wipers couldn't handle it. It was piling up. Wayne couldn't even make out the Cadillacs anymore.

He was about to stop when a shadowy, whalelike shape
crossed in front of him and he slammed on the brakes,
giving the sand tires a workout. But it wasn't enough.

The '57 spun around and rammed the shape on
Calhoun's side. Wayne heard Calhoun yell, then felt himself thrown against the door and his head smacked metal
and the outside darkness was nothing compared to the
darkness into which he descended.

[4]

Wayne rose out of it as quickly as he had gone down.
Blood was trickling into his eyes from a slight forehead
wound. He used his sleeve to wipe it away.

His first clear sight was of a face at the window on his
side; a sallow, moon-terrain face with bulging eyes and an
expression like an idiot contemplating sandscrit. On the
man's head was a strange, black hat with big round ears,
and in the center of the hat, like a silver tumor, was the
head of a large screw. Sand lashed at the face, embedded
in it, struck the unblinking eyes and made the round-eared
hat flap. The man paid no attention. Though still dazed,
Wayne knew why. The man was one of the dead folks.

Wayne looked in Calhoun's direction. Calhoun's door
had been mashed in and the bending metal had pinched
the handcuff attached to the arm rest in two. The blow
had knocked Calhoun to the center of the seat. He was
holding his hand in front of him, looking at the dangling

cuff and chain as if it were a silver bracelet and a line of pearls.

Leaning over the hood, cleaning the sand away from the windshield with his hands, was another of the dead folks. He too was wearing one of the round-eared hats. He pressed a wrecked face to the clean spot and looked in at Calhoun. A string of snot-green saliva ran out of his mouth and onto the glass.

More sand was wiped away by others. Soon all the car's glass showed the pallid and rotting faces of the dead folks. They stared at Wayne and Calhoun as if they were two rare fish in an aquarium.

Wayne cocked back the hammer of the .38.

"What about me," Calhoun said. "What am I supposed to use."

"Your charm," Wayne said, and at that moment, as if by signal, the dead folk faded away from the glass, leaving one man standing on the hood holding a baseball bat. He hit the glass and it went into a thousand little stars. The bat came again and the heavens fell and the stars rained down and the sand storm screamed in on Wayne and Calhoun.

The dead folks reappeared in full force. The one with the bat started through the hole in the windshield, unheeding of the jags of glass that ripped his ragged clothes and tore his flesh like damp cardboard.

Wayne shot the batter through the head, and the man, finished, fell through, pinning Wayne's arm with his body.

Before Wayne could pull his gun free, a woman's hand reached through the hole and got hold of Wayne's collar. Other dead folks took to the glass and hammered it out with their feet and fist. Hands were all over Wayne; they felt dry and cool like leather seat covers. They pulled him over the steering wheel and dash and outside. The sand worked at his flesh like a cheese grater. He could hear Calhoun yelling, "Eat me, motherfuckers, eat me and choke."

They tossed Wayne on the hood of the '57. Faces leaned over him. Yellow teeth and toothless gums were very near. A road kill odor washed through his nostrils. He thought: now the feeding frenzy begins. His only consolation was that there were so many dead folks there wouldn't be enough of him left to come back from the dead. They'd probably have his brain for dessert.

But no. They picked him up and carried him off. Next thing he knew was a clearer view of the whale-shape the '57 had hit. It was a yellow school bus.

The door to the bus hissed open. The dead folks dumped Wayne inside on his belly and tossed his hat after him. They stepped back and the door closed, just missing Wayne's foot.

Wayne looked up and saw a man in the driver's seat smiling at him. It wasn't a dead man. Just fat and ugly. He was probably five feet tall and bald except for a fringe of hair around his shiny bald head the color of a shit ring in a toilet bowl. He had a nose so long and dark and malignant looking it appeared as if it might fall off his face at any moment, like an overripe banana. He was wearing what Wayne first thought was a bathrobe, but proved to be a robe like that of a monk. It was old and tattered and moth-eaten and Wayne could see pale flesh through the holes. An odor wafted from the fat man that was somewhere between the smell of stale sweat, cheesy balls and an upwiped asshole.

"Good to see you," the fat man said.

"Charmed," Wayne said.

From the back of the bus came a strange, unidentifiable sound. Wayne poked his head around the seats for a look.

In the middle of the aisle, about halfway back, was a nun. Or sort of a nun. Her back was to him and she wore a black-and-white nun's habit. The part that covered her head was traditional, but from there down was quite a departure from the standard attire. The outfit was cut to the middle of her thighs and she wore black fishnet stockings and thick high heels. She was slim with good legs and a high little ass that, even under the circumstances, Wayne couldn't help but appreciate. She was moving one hand above her head as if sewing the air.

Sitting on the seats on either side of the aisle were dead folks. They all wore the round-eared hats, and they were responsible for the sound.

They were trying to sing.

He had never known dead folks to make any noise outside of grunts and groans, but here they were singing. A toneless sort of singing to be sure, some of the words garbled and some of the dead folks just opening and closing their mouths soundlessly, but, by golly, he recognized the tune. It was "Jesus Loves Me."

Wayne looked back at the fat man, let his hand ease down to the bowie in his right boot. The fat man produced a little .32 automatic from inside his robe and pointed at Wayne.

"It's small caliber," the fat man said, "but I'm a real fine shot, and it makes a nice, little hole."

Wayne quit reaching in his boot.

"Oh, that's all right," said the fat man. "Take the knife out and put it on the floor in front of you and slide it to me. And while you're at it, I think I see the hilt of one in your other boot."

Wayne looked back. The way he had been thrown inside the bus had caused his pants legs to hike up over his boots, and the hilts of both his bowie's were revealed. They might as well have had blinking lights on them.

It was shaping up to be a shitty day.

He slid the bowies to the fat man, who scooped them up nimbly and dumped them on the other side of his seat.

The bus door opened and Calhoun was tossed in on top of Wayne. Calhoun's hat followed after.

Wayne shrugged Calhoun off, recovered his hat, and put it on. Calhoun found his hat and did the same. They were still on their knees.

"Would you gentleman mind moving to the center of the bus?"

Wayne led the way. Calhoun took note of the nun now, said, "Man, look at that ass."

The fat man called back to them. "Right there will do fine."

Wayne slid into the seat the fat man was indicating with a wave of the .32, and Calhoun slid in beside him. The dead folks entered now, filled the seats up front, leaving only a few stray seats in the middle empty.

Calhoun said, "What are those fuckers back there making that noise for?"

"They're singing," Wayne said. "Ain't you got no churchin'?"

"Say they are." Calhoun turned to the nun and the dead folks and yelled, "Ya'll know any Hank Williams?"

The nun did not turn and the dead folks did not quit their toneless singing.

"Guess not," Calhoun said. "Seems like all the good music's been forgotten."

The noise in the back of the bus ceased and the nun came over to look at Wayne and Calhoun. She was nice in front too. The outfit was cut from throat to crotch, laced with a ribbon, and it showed a lot of tit and some tight, thin, black panties that couldn't quite hold in her escaping pubic hair, which grew as thick and wild as kudzu. When Wayne managed to work his eyes up from that and look at her face, he saw she was dark-complected with eyes the color of coffee and lips made to chew on.

Calhoun never made it to the face. He didn't care about faces. He sniffed, said into her crotch, "Nice snatch."

The nun's left hand came around and smacked Calhoun on the side of the head. He grabbed her wrist, said, "Nice arm, too."

The nun did a magic act with her right hand; it went behind her back and hiked up her outfit and came back with a double-barreled derringer. She pressed it against Calhoun's head.

Wayne bent forward, hoping she wouldn't shoot. At that range the bullet might go through Calhoun's head and hit him too.

"Can't miss," the nun said.

Calhoun smiled. "No you can't," he said, and let go of her arm.

She sat down across from them, smiled, and crossed her legs high. Wayne felt his Levis snake swell and crawl against the inside of his thigh.

"Honey," Calhoun said, "you're almost worth taking a bullet for."

The nun didn't quit smiling. The bus cranked up. The sand blowers and wipers went to work, and the windshield turned blue, and a white dot moved on it between a series of smaller white dots.

Radar. Wayne had seen that sort of thing on desert vehicles. If he lived through this and got his car back, maybe
he'd rig up something like that. And maybe not, he was
sick of the desert.

Whatever, at the moment, future plans seemed a little
out of place.

Then something else occurred to him. Radar. That
meant these bastards had known they were coming and
had pulled out in front of them on purpose.

He leaned over the seat and checked where he figured
the '57 hit the bus. He didn't see a single dent. Armored,
most likely. Most school buses were these days, and that's
what this had been. It probably had bullet-proof-glass and
puncture-proof sand tires too. School buses had gone that
way on account of the race riots and the sending of mutated calves to school just like they were humans. And
because of the Codgers—old farts who believed kids ought
to be fair game to adults for sexual purposes, or for knocking around when they wanted to let off some tension.

"How about unlocking this cuff?" Calhoun said. "It
ain't for shit now anyway."

Wayne looked at the nun. "I'm going for the cuff key in
my pants. Don't shoot."

Wayne fished it out, unlocked the cuff, and Calhoun let
it slide to the floor. Wayne saw the nun was curious and he
said, "I'm a bounty hunter. Help me get this man to Law
Town and I could see you earn a little something for your
troubles."

The woman shook her head.

"That's the spirit," Calhoun said. "I like a nun that
minds her own business . . . You a real nun?"

She nodded.

"Always talk so much?"

Another nod.

Wayne said, "I've never seen a nun like you. Not
dressed like that and with a gun."

"We are a small and special order," she said.

"You some kind of Sunday school teacher for these
dead folks?"

"Sort of."

"But with them dead, ain't it kind of pointless? They ain't got no souls now, do they?"

"No, but their work adds to the glory of God."

"Their work?" Wayne looked at the dead folks sitting stiffly in their seats. He noted that one of them was about to lose a rotten ear. He sniffed. "They may be adding to the glory of God, but they don't do much for the air."

The nun reached into a pocket on her habit and took out two round objects. She tossed one to Calhoun, and one to Wayne. "Menthol lozenges. They help you stand the smell."

Wayne unwrapped the lozenge and sucked on it. It did help overpower the smell, but the menthol wasn't all that great either. It reminded him of being sick.

"What order are you?" Wayne asked.

"Jesus Loved Mary," the nun said.

"His mama?" Wayne said.

"Mary Magdalene. We think he fucked her. They were lovers. There's evidence in the scriptures. She was a harlot and we have modeled ourselves on her. She gave up that life and became a harlot for Jesus."

"Hate to break it to you, sister," Calhoun said, "but that do-gooder Jesus is as dead as a post. If you're waiting for him to slap the meat to you, that sweet thing of yours is going to dry up and blow away."

"Thanks for the news," the nun said. "But we don't fuck him in person. We fuck him in spirit. We let the spirit enter into men so they may take us in the fashion Jesus took Mary."

"No shit?"

"No shit."

"You know, I think I feel the old boy moving around inside me now. Why don't you shuck them drawers, honey, throw back in that seat there and let ole Calhoun give you a big load of Jesus."

Calhoun shifted in the nun's direction.

She pointed the derringer at him, said, "Stay where you are. If it were so, if you were full of Jesus, I would let you have me in a moment. But you're full of the Devil, not Jesus."

"Shit, sister, give ole Devil a break. He's a fun kind of

guy. Let's you and me mount up . . . Well, be like that. But if you change your mind, I can get religion at a moment's notice. I dearly love to fuck. I've fucked everything I could get my hands on but a parakeet, and I'd have fucked that little bitch if I could have found the hole."

"I've never known any dead folks to be trained," Wayne said, trying to get the nun talking in a direction that might help, a direction that would let him know what was going on and what sort of trouble he had fallen into.

"As I said, we are a very special order. Brother Lazarus," she waved a hand at the bus driver, and without looking he lifted a hand in acknowledgement, "is the founder. I don't think he'll mind if I tell his story, explain about us, what we do and why. It's important that we spread the word to the heathens."

"Don't call me no fucking heathen," Calhoun said. "This is heathen, riding around in a fucking bus with a bunch of stinking dead folks with funny hats on. Hell, they can't even carry a tune."

The nun ignored him. "Brother Lazarus was once known by another name, but that name no longer matters. He was a research scientist, and he was one of those who worked in the laboratory where the germs escaped into the air and made it so the dead could not truly die as long as they had an undamaged brain in their heads.

"Brother Lazarus was carrying a dish of the experiment, the germs, and as a joke, one of the lab assistants pretended to trip him, and he, not knowing it was a joke, dodged the assistant's leg and dropped the dish. In a moment, the air conditioning system had blown the germs throughout the research center. Someone opened a door, and the germs were loose on the world.

"Brother Lazarus was consumed by guilt. Not only because he dropped the dish, but because he helped create it in the first place. He quit his job at the laboratory, took to wandering the country. He came out here with nothing more than basic food, water and books. Among these books was the Bible, and the lost books of the Bible: the Apocrypha and the many cast-out chapters of the New Testament. As he studied, it occurred to him that these cast out books actually belonged. He was able to interpret their higher meaning, and an angel came to him in a dream and told him of another book, and Brother Lazarus took up his pen and recorded the angel's words, direct from God, and in this book, all the mysteries were explained."

"Like screwing Jesus," Calhoun said.

"Like screwing Jesus, and not being afraid of words that mean sex. Not being afraid of seeing Jesus as both God and man. Seeing that sex, if meant for Christ and the opening of the mind, can be a thrilling and religious experience, not just the rutting of two savage animals.

"Brother Lazarus roamed the desert, the mountains, thinking of the things the Lord had revealed to him, and lo and behold, the Lord revealed yet another thing to him. Brother Lazarus found a great amusement park."

"Didn't know Jesus went in for rides and such," Calhoun said.

"It was long deserted. It had once been part of a place called Disneyland. Brother Lazarus knew of it. There had been several of these Disneylands built about the country, and this one had been in the midst of the Chevy-Cadillac Wars, and had been destroyed and sand had covered most of it."

The nun held out her arms. "And in this rubble, he saw a new beginning."

"Cool off, baby," Calhoun said, "before you have a stroke."

"He gathered to him men and women of a like mind and taught the gospel to them. The Old Testament. The New Testament. The Lost Books. And his own Book of Lazarus, for he had begun to call himself Lazarus. A symbolic name signifying a new beginning, a rising from the dead and coming to life and seeing things as they really are."

The nun moved her hands rapidly, expressively as she talked. Sweat beaded on her forehead and upper lip.

"So he returned to his skills as a scientist, but applied them to a higher purpose—God's purpose. And as Brother Lazarus, he realized the use of the dead. They could be taught to work and build a great monument to the glory of God. And this monument, this coed institution of monks and nuns, would be called Jesus Land."

At the word "Jesus," the nun gave her voice an extra trill, and the dead folks, cued, said together, "Eees num be prased."

"How the hell did you train them dead folks?" Calhoun said. "Dog treats?"

"Science put to the use of our Lord Jesus Christ, that's how. Brother Lazarus made a special device he could insert directly into the brains of dead folks, through the tops of their heads, and the device controls certain cravings. Makes them passive and responsive—at least to simple commands. With the regulator, as Brother Lazarus calls the device, we have been able to do much positive work with the dead."

"Where do you find these dead folks?" Wayne asked.

"We buy them from the Meat Boys. We save them from amoral purposes."

"They ought to be shot through the head and put in the goddamn ground," Wayne said.

"If our use of the regulator and the dead folks was merely to better ourselves, I would agree. But it is not. We do the Lord's work."

"Do the monks fuck the sisters?" Calhoun asked.

"When possessed by the Spirit of Christ. Yes."

"And I bet they get possessed a lot. Not a bad setup. Dead folks to do the work on the amusement park—"

"It isn't an amusement park now."

"—and plenty of free pussy. Sounds cozy. I like it. Old shithead up there's smarter than he looks."

"There is nothing selfish about our motives or those of Brother Lazarus. In fact, as penance for loosing the germ on the world in the first place, Brother Lazarus injected a virus into his nose. It is rotting slowly."

"Thought that was quite a snorkel he had on him," Wayne said.

"I take it back," Calhoun said. "He *is* as dumb as he looks."

"Why do the dead folks wear those silly hats?" Wayne asked.

"Brother Lazarus found a storeroom of them at the site

of the old amusement park. They are mouse ears. They
represent some cartoon animal that was popular once and
part of Disneyland. Mickey Mouse, he was called. This
way we know which dead folks are ours, and which ones
are not controlled by our regulators. From time to time,
stray dead folks wander into our area. Murder victims.
Children abandoned in the desert. People crossing the desert who died of heat or illness. We've had some of the
sisters and brothers attacked. The hats are a precaution."

"And what's the deal with us?" Wayne asked.

The nun smiled sweetly. "You, my children, are to add
to the glory of God."

"Children?" Calhoun said. "You call an alligator a lizard, bitch?"

The nun slid back in the seat and rested the derringer in
her lap. She pulled her legs into a cocked position, causing
her panties to crease in the valley of her vagina; it looked
like a nice place to visit, that valley.

Wayne turned from the beauty of it and put his head
back and closed his eyes, pulled his hat down over them.
There was nothing he could do at the moment, and since
the nun was watching Calhoun for him, he'd sleep, store
up and figure what to do next. If anything.

He drifted off to sleep wondering what the nun meant
by, "You, my children, are to add to the glory of God."

He had a feeling that when he found out, he wasn't
going to like it.

[5]

He awoke off and on and saw that the sunlight filtering
through the storm had given everything a greenish color.
Calhoun seeing he was awake, said, "Ain't that a pretty
color? I had a shirt that color once and liked it lots, but I
got in a fight with this Mexican whore with a wooden leg
over some money and she tore her. I punched that little
bean bandit good."

"Thanks for sharing that," Wayne said, and went back
to sleep.

Each time he awoke it was brighter, and finally he
awoke to the sun going down and the storm having died

out. But he didn't stay awake. He forced himself to close his eyes and store up more energy. To help him nod off he listened to the hum of the motor and thought about the wrecking yard and Pop and all the fun they could have, just drinking beer and playing cars and fucking the border women, and maybe some of those mutated cows they had over there for sell.

Nah. Nix the cows, or any of those genetically altered critters. A man had to draw the line somewhere, and he drew it at fucking critters, even if they had been bred so that they had human traits. You had to have some standards.

Course, those standards had a way of eroding. He remembered when he said he'd only fuck the pretty ones. His last whore had been downright scary looking. If he didn't watch himself he'd be as bad as Calhoun, trying to find the hole in a parakeet.

He awoke to Calhoun's elbow in his ribs and the nun was standing beside their seat with the derringer. Wayne knew she hadn't slept, but she looked bright-eyed and bushy-tailed. She nodded toward their window, said, "Jesus Land."

She had put that special touch in her voice again, and the dead folks responded with, "Fees num be prased."

It was good and dark now, a crisp night with a big moon the color of hammered brass. The bus sailed across the white sand like a mystical schooner with a full wind in its sails. It went up an impossible hill toward what looked like an aurora borealis, then dove into an atomic rainbow of colors that filled the bus with fairy lights.

When Wayne's eyes became accustomed to the lights, and the bus took a right turn along a precarious curve, he glanced down into the valley. An aerial view couldn't have been any better than the view from his window.

Down there was a universe of polished metal and twisted neon. In the center of the valley was a great statue of Jesus crucified that must have been twenty-five stories high. Most of the body was made of bright metals and multicolored neon, and much of the light was coming from that. There was a crown of barbed wire wound several times around a chromium plate of a forehead and

some rust-colored strands of neon hair. The savior's eyes
were huge, green strobes that swung left and right with
the precision of an oscillating fan. There was an ear to ear
smile on the savior's face and the teeth were slats of spar-
kling metal with wide cavity-black gaps between them.
The statue was equipped with a massive dick of polished,
interwoven cables and coils of neon; the dick was thicker
and more solid looking than the arthritic steel-tube legs on
either side of it; the head of it was made of an enormous
spotlight that pulsed the color of irritation.

The bus went around and around the valley, descending
like a dead roach going down a slow drain, and finally the
road rolled out straight and took them into Jesus Land.

They passed through the legs of Jesus, under the throbbing head of his cock, toward what looked like a small
castle of polished gold bricks with an upright drawbridge
interlayed with jewels.

The castle was only one of several tall structures that
appeared to be made of rare metals and precious stones:
gold, silver, emeralds, rubies and sapphires. But the closer
they got to the buildings, the less fine they looked and the
more they looked like what they were: stucco, cardboard,
phosphorescent paint, colored spotlights, and bands of
neon.

Off to the left Wayne could see a long, open shed full of
vehicles, most of them old school buses. And there were
unlighted hovels made of tin and tar paper; homes for the
dead, perhaps. Behind the shacks and the bus barn rose
skeletal shapes that stretched tall and bleak against the
sky and the candy-gem lights; shapes that looked like the
bony remains of beached whales.

On the right, Wayne glimpsed a building with an open
front that served as a stage. In front of the stage were
chairs filled with monks and nuns. On the stage, six
monks—one behind a drum set, one with a saxophone, the
others with guitars—were blasting out a loud, rocking
rhythm that made the bus shake. A nun with the front of
her habit thrown open, her headpiece discarded, sang into
a microphone with a voice like a suffering angel. The voice
screeched out of the amplifiers and came in through the
windows of the bus, crushing the sound of the engine. The

nun crowed "Jesus" so long and hard it sounded like a plea from hell. Then she lept up and came down doing the splits, the impact driving her back to her feet as if her ass had been loaded with springs.

"Bet that bitch can pick up a quarter with that thing," Calhoun said.

Brother Lazarus touched a button, the pseudo-jeweled drawbridge lowered over a narrow moat, and he drove them inside.

It wasn't as well lighted in there. The walls were bleak and gray. Brother Lazarus stopped the bus and got off, and another monk came on board. He was tall and thin and had crooked buck teeth that dented his bottom lip. He also had a twelve-gauge pump shotgun.

"This is Brother Fred," the nun said. "He will be your tour guide."

Brother Fred forced Wayne and Calhoun off the bus, away from the dead folks in their mouse-ear hats and the nun in her tight, black panties, jabbed them along a dark corridor, up a swirl of stairs and down a longer corridor with open doors on either side and rooms filled with dark and light and spoiled meat and guts on hooks and skulls and bones lying about like discarded walnut shells and broken sticks; rooms full of dead folks (truly dead) stacked neat as firewood, and rooms full of stone shelves stuffed with beakers of fiery-red and sewer green and sky blue and piss yellow liquids, as well as glass coils through which other colored fluids fled as if chased, smoked as if nervous, and ran into big flasks as if relieved; rooms with platforms and tables and boxes and stools and chairs covered with instruments or dead folks or dead-folk pieces or the asses of monks and nuns as they sat and held charts or tubes or body parts and frowned at them with concentration, lips pursed as if about to explode with some earth-shattering pronouncement; and finally they came to a little room with a tall, glassless window that looked out upon the bright, shiny mess that was Jesus Land

The room was simple. Table, two chairs, two beds—one on either side of the room. The walls were stone and unadorned. To the right was a little bathroom without a door.

Wayne walked to the window and looked out at Jesus Land pulsing and thumping like a desperate heart. He listened to the music a moment, leaned over and stuck his head outside.

They were high up and there was nothing but a straight drop. If you jumped, you'd wind up with the heels of your boots under your tonsils.

Wayne let out a whistle in appreciation of the drop. Brother Fred thought it was a compliment for Jesus Land. He said, "It's a miracle, isn't it?"

"Miracle?" Calhoun said. "This goony light show? This ain't no miracle. This is for shit. Get that nun on the bus back there to bend over and shit a perfectly round turd through a hoop at twenty paces, and I'll call that a miracle, Mr. Fucked-up Teeth. But this Jesus Land crap is the dumbest, fucking idea since dog sweaters.

"And look at this place. You could use some knick-knacks or something in here. A picture of some ole naked gal doing a donkey, couple of pigs fucking. Anything. And a door on the shitter would be nice. I hate to be straining out a big one and know someone can look in on me. It ain't decent. A man ought to have his fucking grunts in private. This place reminds me of a motel I stayed at in Waco one night, and I made the goddamn manager give me my money back. The roaches in that shit hole were big enough to use the shower."

Brother Fred listened to all this without blinking an eye, as if seeing Calhoun talk was as amazing as seeing a frog sing. He said, "Sleep tight, don't let the bed bugs bite. Tomorrow you start to work."

"I don't want no fucking job," Calhoun said.

"Goodnight, children," Brother Fred said, and with that he closed the door and they heard it lock, loud and final as the clicking of the drop board on a gallows.

[6]

At dawn, Wayne got up and took a leak, went to the window to look out. The stage where the monks had played and the nun had jumped was empty. The skeletal shapes he had seen last night were tracks and frames from rides long abandoned. He had a sudden vision of Jesus and his disciples riding a roller coaster, their long hair and robes flapping in the wind.

The large crucified Jesus looked unimpressive without its lights and night's mystery, like a whore in harsh sunlight with makeup gone and wig askew.

"Got any ideas how we're gonna get out of here?"

Wayne looked at Calhoun. He was sitting on the bed, pulling on his boots.

Wayne shook his head.

"I could use a smoke. You know, I think we ought to work together. Then we can try to kill each other."

Unconsciously, Calhoun touched his ear where Wayne had bitten off the lobe.

"Wouldn't trust you as far as I could kick you."

"I hear that. But I give my word. And my word's something you can count on. I won't twist it."

Wayne studied Calhoun, thought: Well, there wasn't anything to lose. He'd just watch his ass.

"All right," Wayne said. "Give me your word you'll work with me on getting us out of this mess, and when we're good and free, and you say your word has gone far enough, we can settle up."

"Deal," Calhoun said, and offered his hand.

Wayne looked at it.

"This seals it," Calhoun said.

Wayne took Calhoun's hand and they shook.

[7]

Moments later the door unlocked and a smiling monk with hair the color and texture of mold fuzz came in with Brother Fred, who still had his pump shotgun. There were two dead folks with them. A man and a woman. They wore torn clothes and the mouse-ear hats. Neither looked long dead or smelled particularly bad. Actually, the monks smelled worse.

Using the barrel of the shotgun, Brother Fred poked them down the hall to a room with metal tables and medical instruments.

Brother Lazarus was on the far side of one of the tables.

He was smiling. His nose looked especially cancerous this morning. A white pustle the size of a thumb tip had taken up residence on the left side of his snout, and it looked like a pearl onion in a turd.

Nearby stood a nun. She was short with good, if skinny, legs, and she wore the same outfit as the nun on the bus. It looked more girlish on her, perhaps because she was thin and small-breasted. She had a nice face and eyes that were all pupil. Wisps of blond hair crawled out around the edges of her headgear. She looked pale and weak, as if wearied to the bone. There was a birthmark on her right cheek that looked like a distant view of a small bird in flight.

"Good morning," Brother Lazarus said. "I hope you gentlemen slept well."

"What's this about work?" Wayne said.

"Work?" Brother Lazarus said.

"I described it to them that way," Brother Fred said. "Perhaps an impulsive description."

"I'll say," Brother Lazarus said. "No work here, gentlemen. You have my word on that. We do all the work. Lie on these tables and we'll take a sampling of your blood."

"Why?" Wayne said.

"Science," Brother Lazarus said. "I intend to find a cure for this germ that makes the dead come back to life, and to do that, I need living human beings to study. Sounds kind of mad scientist, doesn't it? But I assure you, you've nothing to lose but a few drops of blood. Well, maybe more than a few drops, but nothing serious."

"Use your own goddamn blood," Calhoun said.

"We do. But we're always looking for fresh specimens. Little here, little there. And if you don't do it, we'll kill you."

Calhoun spun and hit Brother Fred on the nose. It was a solid punch and Brother Fred hit the floor on his butt, but he hung on to the shotgun and pointed it up at Calhoun. "Go on," he said, his nose streaming blood. "Try that again."

Wayne flexed to help, but hesitated. He could kick Brother Fred in the head from where he was, but that might not keep him from shooting Calhoun, and there would go the extra reward money. And besides, he'd given his word to the bastard that they'd try and help each other survive until they got out of this.

The other monk clasped his hands and swung them into the side of Calhoun's head, knocking him down. Brother Fred got up, and while Calhoun was trying to rise, he hit him with the stock of the shotgun in the back of the head, hit him so hard it drove Calhoun's forehead into the floor. Calhoun rolled over on his side and lay there, his eyes fluttering like moth wings.

"Brother Fred, you must learn to turn the other cheek," Brother Lazarus said. "Now put this sack of shit on the table."

Brother Fred checked Wayne to see if he looked like trouble. Wayne put his hands in his pockets and smiled.

Brother Fred called the two dead folks over and had them put Calhoun on the table. Brother Lazarus strapped him down.

The nun brought a tray of needles, syringes, cotton and bottles over, put it down on the table next to Calhoun's head. Brother Lazarus rolled up Calhoun's sleeve and fixed up a needle and stuck it in Calhoun's arm, drew it full of blood. He stuck the needle through the rubber top of one of the bottles and shot the blood into that.

He looked at Wayne and said, "I hope you'll be less trouble."

"Do I get some orange juice and a little cracker afterwards?" Wayne said.

"You get to walk out without a knot on your head," Brother Lazarus said.

"Guess that'll have to do."

Wayne got on the table next to Calhoun and Brother Lazarus strapped him down. The nun brought the tray over and Brother Lazarus did to him what he had done to Calhoun. The nun stood over Wayne and looked down at his face. Wayne tried to read something in her features but couldn't find a clue.

When Brother Lazarus was finished he took hold of Wayne's chin and shook it. "My, but you two boys look healthy. But you can never be sure. We'll have to run the blood through some tests. Meantime, Sister Worth will

run a few additional tests on you, and," he nodded at the
unconscious Calhoun, "I'll see to your friend here."

"He's no friend of mine," Wayne said.

They took Wayne off the table, and Sister Worth and
Brother Fred and his shotgun, directed him down the hall
into another room.

The room was lined with shelves that were lined with
instruments and bottles. The lighting was poor, most of it
coming through a slatted window, though there was an
anemic yellow bulb overhead. Dust motes swam in the air.

In the center of the room on its rim was a great, spoked
wheel. It had two straps well spaced at the top, and two
more at the bottom. Beneath the bottom straps were
blocks of wood. The wheel was attached in back to an
upright metal bar that had switches and buttons all over
it.

Brother Fred made Wayne strip and get up on the wheel
with his back to the hub and his feet on the blocks. Sister
Worth strapped his ankles down tight, then he was made
to put his hands up, and she strapped his wrists to the
upper part of the wheel.

"I hope this hurts a lot," Brother Fred said.

"Wipe the blood off your face," Wayne said. "It makes
you look silly."

Brother Fred made a gesture with his middle finger that
wasn't religious and left the room.

[8]

Sister Worth touched a switch and the wheel began to
spin, slowly at first, and the bad light came through the
windows and poked through the rungs and the dust swam
before his eyes and the wheel and its spokes threw twisting
shadows on the wall.

As he went around, Wayne closed his eyes. It kept him
from feeling so dizzy, especially on the down swings.

On a turn up, he opened his eyes and caught sight of
Sister Worth standing in front of the wheel staring at him.
He said, "Why?" and closed his eyes as the wheel dipped.

"Because Brother Lazarus says so," came the answer
after such a long time Wayne had almost forgotten the

question. Actually, he hadn't expected a response. He was surprised that such a thing had come out of his mouth, and he felt a little diminished for having asked.

He opened his eyes on another swing up, and she was moving behind the wheel, out of his line of vision. He heard a snick like a switch being flipped and lightning jumped through him and he screamed in spite of himself. A little fork of electricity licked out of his mouth like a reptile tongue tasting air.

Faster spun the wheel and the jolts came more often and he screamed less loud, and finally not at all. He was too numb. He was adrift in space wearing only his cowboy hat and boots, moving away from earth very fast. Floating all around him were wrecked cars. He looked and saw that one of them was his '57, and behind the steering wheel was Pop. Sitting beside the old man was a Mexican whore. Two more were in the backseat. They looked a little drunk.

One of the whores in back pulled up her dress and pressed her naked ass against the window, cocked it high up so he could see her pussy. It looked like a taco that needed a shave.

He smiled and tried to go for it, but the '57 was moving away, swinging wide and turning its tail to him. He could see a face at the back window. Pop's face. He had crawled back there and was waving slowly and sadly. A whore pulled Pop from view.

The wrecked cars moved away too, as if caught in the vacuum of the '57's retreat. Wayne swam with his arms, kicked with his legs, trying to pursue the '57 and the wrecks. But he dangled where he was, like a moth pinned to a board. The cars moved out of sight and left him there with his arms and legs stretched out, spinning amidst an infinity of cold, uncaring stars.

". . . how the tests are run . . . marks everything about you . . . charts it . . . EKG, brain waves, liver . . . everything . . . it hurts because Brother Lazarus wants it to . . . thinks I don't know these things . . . that I'm slow . . . I'm slow, not stupid . . . smart really . . . used to be a scientist . . . before the accident . . . Brother Lazarus is not holy . . . he's mad . . .

328 OF THE DEAD

made the wheel because of the Holy Inquisition . . . knows a lot about the Inquisition . . . thinks we need it again . . . for the likes of men like you . . . the unholy, he says . . . But he just likes to hurt . . . I know."

Wayne opened his eyes. The wheel had stopped. Sister Worth was talking in her monotone, explaining the wheel. He remembered asking her "Why" about three thousand years ago.

Sister Worth was staring at him again. She went away and he expected the wheel to start up, but when she returned, she had a long, narrow mirror under her arm. She put it against the wall across from him. She got on the wheel with him, her little feet on the wooden platforms beside his. She hiked up the bottom of her habit and pulled down her black panties. She put her face close to his, as if searching for something.

"He plans to take your body . . . piece by piece . . . blood, cells, brain, your cock . . . all of it . . . He wants to live forever."

She had her panties in her hand, and she tossed them. Wayne watched them fly up and flutter to the floor like a dying bat.

She took hold of his dick and pulled on it. Her palms was cold and he didn't feel his best, but he began to get hard. She put him between her legs and rubbed his dick between her thighs. They were as cold as her hands, and dry.

"I know him now . . . know what he's doing . . . the dead germ virus . . . he was trying to make something that would make him live forever . . . it made the dead come back . . . didn't keep the living alive, free of old age. . . ."

His dick was throbbing now, in spite of the coolness of her body.

"He cuts up dead folks to learn . . . experiments on them . . . but the secret of eternal life is with the living . . . that's why he wants you . . . you're an outsider . . . those who live here he can test . . . but he must keep them alive to do his bidding . . . not let them know how he really is . . . needs your insides and the other man's . . . he wants to be a God . . . flies high above us in a little plane and looks down . . . Likes to think he is the creator, I bet . . ."

"Plane?"

"Ultra-light."

She pushed his cock inside her, and it was cold and dry in there, like liver left overnight on a drainboard. Still, he found himself ready. At this point, he would have gouged a hole in a turnip.

She kissed him on the ear and alongside the neck; cold little kisses, dry as toast.

". . . thinks I don't know . . . But I know he doesn't love Jesus. . . . He loves himself, and power. . . . He's sad about his nose . . ."

"I bet."

"Did it in a moment of religious fever . . . before he lost the belief. . . . Now he wants to be what he was. . . . A scientist. He wants to grow a new nose . . . knows how . . . saw him grow a finger in a dish once . . . grew it from the skin off a knuckle of one of the brothers . . . He can do all kinds of things."

She was moving her hips now. He could see over her shoulder into the mirror against the wall. Could see her white ass rolling, the black habit hiked up above it, threatening to drop like a curtain. He began to thrust back, slowly, firmly.

She looked over her shoulder into the mirror, watching herself fuck him. There was a look more of study than rapture on her face.

"Want to feel alive," she said. "Feel a good, hard dick. . . . Been too long."

"I'm doing the best I can," Wayne said. "This ain't the most romantic of spots."

"Push so I can feel it."

"Nice," Wayne said. He gave it everything he had. He was beginning to lose his erection. He felt as if he were auditioning for a job and not making the best of impressions. He felt like a knothole would be dissatisfied with him.

She got off of him and climbed down.

"Don't blame you," he said.

She went behind the wheel and touched some things on

the upright. She mounted him again, hooked her ankles behind his. The wheel began to turn. Short electrical shocks leaped through him. They weren't as powerful as before. They were invigorating. When he kissed her it was like touching his tongue to a battery. It felt as if electricity was racing through his veins and flying out the head of his dick; he felt as if he might fill her with lightning instead of come.

The wheel creaked to a stop; it must have had a timer on it. They were upside down and Wayne could see their reflection in the mirror; they looked like two lizards fucking on a window pane.

He couldn't tell if she had finished or not, so he went ahead and got it over with. Without the electricity he was losing his desire. It hadn't been an A-one piece of ass, but hell, as Pop always said, "Worse pussy I ever had was good."

"They'll be coming back," she said. "Soon. . . . Don't want them to find us like this. . . . Other test to do yet."

"Why did you do this?"

"I want out of the order. . . . Want out of this desert. . . . I want to live. . . . And I want you to help me."

"I'm game, but the blood is rushing to my head and I'm getting dizzy. Maybe you ought to get off me."

After an eon she said, "I have a plan."

She untwined from him and went behind the wheel and hit a switch that turned Wayne upright. She touched another switch and he began to spin slowly, and while he spun and while lightning played inside him, she told him her plan.

[9]

"I think ole Brother Fred wants to fuck me," Calhoun said. "He keeps trying to get his finger up my asshole."

They were back in their room. Brother Fred had brought them back, making them carry their clothes, and now they were alone again, dressing.

"We're getting out of here," Wayne said. "The nun, Sister Worth, she's going to help."

"What's her angle?"

"She hates this place and wants my dick. Mostly, she hates this place."

"What's the plan?"

Wayne told him first what Brother Lazarus had planned. On the morrow he would have them brought to the room with the steel tables, and they would go on the tables, and if the tests had turned out good, they would be pronounced fit as fiddles and Brother Lazarus would strip the skin from their bodies, slowly, because according to Sister Worth he liked to do it that way, and he would drain their blood and percolate it into his formulas like coffee, cut their brains out and put them in vats and store their veins and organs in freezers.

All of this would be done in the name of God and Jesus Christ (Eees num be prased) under the guise of finding a cure for the dead folks germ. But it would all instead be for Brother Lazarus who wanted to have a new nose, fly his ultra-light above Jesus Land and live forever.

Sister Worth's plan was this:

She would be in the dissecting room. She would have guns hidden. She would make the first move, a distraction, then it was up to them.

"This time," Wayne said, "one of us has to get on top of that shotgun."

"You had your finger up your ass in there today, or we'd have had them."

"We're going to have surprise on our side this time. Real surprise. They won't be expecting Sister Worth. We can get up there on the roof and take off in that ultra-light. When it runs out of gas we can walk, maybe get back to the '57 and hope it runs."

"We'll settle our score then. Who ever wins keeps the car and the split tail. As for tomorrow, I've got a little ace."

Calhoun pulled on his boots. He twisted the heel of one of them. It swung out and a little knife dropped into his hand. "It's sharp," Calhoun said. "I cut a Chinaman from gut to gill with it. It was easy as sliding a stick through fresh shit."

"Been nice if you'd had that ready today."

"I wanted to scout things out first. And to tell the truth,

I thought one pop to Brother Fred's mouth and he'd be out of the picture."

"You hit him in the nose."

"Yeah, goddammit, but I was aiming for his mouth."

[10]

Dawn and the room with the metal tables looked the same. No one had brought in a vase of flowers to brighten the place.

Brother Lazarus's nose had changed however; there were two pearl onions nestled in it now.

Sister Worth, looking only a little more animated than yesterday, stood nearby. She was holding the tray with the instruments. This time the tray was full of scalpels. The light caught their edges and made them wink.

Brother Fred was standing behind Calhoun, and Brother Mold Fuzz was behind Wayne. They must have felt pretty confident today. They had dispensed with the dead folks.

Wayne looked at Sister Worth and thought maybe things were not good. Maybe she had lied to him in her slow talking way. Only wanted a little dick and wanted to keep it quiet. To do that, she might have promised anything. She might not care what Brother Lazarus did to them.

If it looked like a double cross, Wayne was going to go for it. If he had to jump right into the mouth of Brother Fred's shotgun. That was a better way to go than having the hide peeled from your body. The idea of Brother Lazarus and his ugly nose leaning over him did not appeal at all.

"It's so nice to see you," Brother Lazarus said. "I hope we'll have none of the unpleasantness of yesterday. Now, on the tables."

Wayne looked at Sister Worth. Her expression showed nothing. The only thing about her that looked alive was the bent wings of the bird birthmark on her cheek.

All right, Wayne thought, I'll go as far as the table, then I'm going to do something. Even if it's wrong.

He took a step forward, and Sister Worth flipped the

contents of the tray into Brother Lazarus's face. A scalpel went into his nose and hung there. The tray and the rest of its contents hit the floor.

Before Brother Lazarus could yelp, Calhoun dropped and wheeled. He was under Brother Fred's shotgun and he used his forearm to drive the barrel upwards. The gun went off and peppered the ceiling. Plaster sprinkled down.

Calhoun had concealed the little knife in the palm of his hand and he brought it up and into Brother Fred's groin. The blade went through the robe and buried to the hilt.

The instant Calhoun made his move, Wayne brought his forearm back and around into Brother Mold Fuzz's throat, then turned and caught his head and jerked that down and kneed him a couple of times. He floored him by driving an elbow into the back of his neck.

Calhoun had the shotgun now, and Brother Fred was on the floor trying to pull the knife out of his balls. Calhoun blew Brother Fred's head off, then did the same for Brother Mold Fuzz.

Brother Lazarus, the scalpel still hanging from his nose, tried to run for it, but he stepped on the tray and that sent him flying. He landed on his stomach. Calhoun took two deep steps and kicked him in the throat. Brother Lazarus made a sound like he was gargling and tried to get up.

Wayne helped him. He grabbed Brother Lazarus by the back of his robe and pulled him up, slammed him back against a table. The scalpel still dangled from the monk's nose. Wayne grabbed it and jerked, taking away a chunk of nose as he did. Brother Lazarus screamed.

Calhoun put the shotgun in Brother Lazarus's mouth and that made him stop screaming. Calhoun pumped the shotgun. He said, "Eat it," and pulled the trigger. Brother Lazarus's brains went out the back of his head riding on a chunk of skull. The brains and skull hit the table and sailed onto the floor like a plate of scrambled eggs pushed the length of a cafe counter.

Sister Worth had not moved. Wayne figured she had used all of her concentration to hit Brother Lazarus with the tray.

"You said you'd have guns," Wayne said to her.

She turned her back to him and lifted her habit. In a

belt above her panties were two .38 revolvers. Wayne
pulled them out and held one in each hand. "Two-Gun
Wayne," he said.

"What about the ultra-light?" Calhoun said. "We've
made enough noise for a prison riot. We need to move."

Sister Worth turned to the door at the back of the room,
and before she could say anything or lead, Wayne and
Calhoun snapped to it and grabbed her and pushed her
toward it.

There were stairs on the other side of the door and they
took them two at a time. They went through a trap door
and onto the roof and there, tied down with bungie straps
to metal hoops, was the ultra-light. It was blue-and-white
canvas and metal rods, and strapped to either side of it
was a twelve-gauge pump and a bag of food and a canteen
of water.

They unsnapped the roof straps and got in the two
seater and used the straps to fasten Sister Worth between
them. It wasn't comfortable, but it was a ride.

They sat there. After a moment, Calhoun said, "Well?"

"Shit," Wayne said. "I can't fly this thing."

They looked at Sister Worth. She was staring at the
controls.

"Say something, dammit," Wayne said.

"That's the switch," she said. "That stick . . . forward
is up, back brings the nose down . . . side to side. . . ."

"Got it."

"Well shoot this bastard over the side," Calhoun said.

Wayne cranked it, gave it the throttle. The machine
rolled forward, wobbled.

"Too much weight," Wayne said.

"Throw the cunt over the side," Calhoun said.

"It's all or nothing," Wayne said.

The ultra-light continued to swing its tail left and right,
but leveled off as they went over the edge.

They sailed for a hundred yards, made a mean curve
Wayne couldn't fight, and fell straight away into the statue
of Jesus, striking it in the head, right in the midst of the
barbed wire crown. Spot lights shattered, metal groaned,
the wire tangled in the nylon wings of the craft and held it.
The head of Jesus nodded forward, popped off and shot

out on the electric cables inside like a Jack-in-the-Box. The cables popped tight a hundred feet from the ground and worked the head and the craft like a yo-yo. Then the barbed wire crown unraveled and dropped the craft the rest of the way. It hit the ground with a crunch and a rip and a cloud of dust.

The head of Jesus bobbed above the shattered craft like a bird preparing to peck a worm.

[11]

Wayne crawled out of the wreckage and tried his legs. They worked.

Calhoun was on his feet cussing, unstrapping the guns and supplies.

Sister Worth lay in the midst of the wreck, the nylon and aluminum supports folded around her like butterfly wings.

Wayne started pulling the mess off of her. He saw that her leg was broken. A bone punched out of her thigh like a sharpened stick. There was no blood.

"Here comes the church social," Calhoun said.

The word was out about Brother Lazarus and the others. A horde of monks, nuns and dead folks, were rushing over the drawbridge. Some of the nuns and monks had guns. All of the dead folks had clubs. The clergy was yelling.

Wayne nodded toward the bus barn, "Let's get a bus."

Wayne picked up Sister Worth, cradled her in his arms, and made a run for it. Calhoun, carrying only the guns and the supplies, passed them. He jumped through the open doorway of a bus and dropped out of sight. Wayne knew he was jerking wires loose and trying to hotwire them a ride. Wayne hoped he was good at it, and fast.

When Wayne got to the bus, he laid Sister Worth down beside it and pulled the .38 and stood in front of her. If he was going down he wanted to go like Wild Bill Hickok. A blazing gun in either fist and a woman to protect.

Actually, he'd prefer the bus to start.

It did.

Calhoun jerked it in gear, backed it out and around in

front of Wayne and Sister Worth. The monks and nuns had started firing and their rounds bounced off the side of the armored bus.

From inside Calhoun yelled, "Get the hell on."

Wayne stuck the guns in his belt, grabbed up Sister Worth and lept inside. Calhoun jerked the bus forward and Wayne and Sister Worth went flying over a seat and into another.

"I thought you were leaving," Wayne said.

"I wanted to. But I gave my word."

Wayne stretched Sister Worth out on the seat and looked at her leg. After that tossing Calhoun had given them, the break was sticking out even more.

Calhoun closed the bus door and checked his wing-mirror. Nuns and monks and dead folks had piled into a couple of buses, and now the buses were pursuing them. One of them moved very fast, as if souped up.

"I probably got the granny of the bunch," Calhoun said.

They climbed over a ridge of sand, then they were on the narrow road that wound itself upwards. Behind them, one of the buses had fallen back, maybe some kind of mechanical trouble. The other was gaining.

The road widened and Calhoun yelled, "I think this is what the fucker's been waiting for."

Even as Calhoun spoke, their pursuer put on a burst of speed and swung left and came up beside them, tried to swerve over and push them off the road, down into the deepening valley. But Calhoun fought the curves and didn't budge.

The other bus swung its door open and a nun, the very one who had been on the bus that brought them to Jesus Land, stood there with her legs spread wide, showing the black-pantied mound of her crotch. She had one arm bent around a seat post and was holding in both hands the ever-popular clergy tool, the twelve-gauge pump.

As they made a curve, the nun fired a round into the window next to Calhoun. The window made a cracking noise and thin crooked lines spread in all directions, but the glass held.

She pumped a round into the chamber and fired again.

Bullet proof or not, this time the front sheet of glass fell away. Another well-placed round and the rest of the glass would go and Calhoun could wave his head good-bye.

Wayne put his knees in a seat and got the window down. The nun saw him, whirled and fired. The shot was low and hit the bottom part of the window and starred it and pelleted the chassis.

Wayne stuck the .38 out the window and fired as the nun was jacking another load into position. His shot hit her in the head and her right eye went big and wet, and she swung around on the pole and lost the shotgun. It went out the door. She clung there by the bend of her elbow for a moment, then her arm straightened and she fell outside. The bus ran over her and she popped red and juicy at both ends like a stomped jelly roll.

"Waste of good pussy," Calhoun said. He edged into the other bus, and it pushed back. But Calhoun pushed harder and made it hit the wall with a screech like a panther.

The bus came back and shoved Calhoun to the side of the cliff and honked twice for Jesus.

Calhoun down-shifted, let off the gas, allowed the other bus to soar past by half a length. Then he jerked the wheel so that he caught the rear of it and knocked it across the road. He speared it in the side with the nose of his bus and the other started to spin. It clipped the front of Calhoun's bus and peeled the bumper back. Calhoun braked and the other bus kept spinning. It spun off the road and down into the valley amidst a chorus of cries.

Thirty minutes later they reached the top of the canyon and were in the desert. The bus began to throw up smoke from the front and make a noise like a dog strangling on a chicken bone. Calhoun pulled over.

[12]

"Goddamn bumper got twisted under there and it's shredded the tire some," Calhoun said. "I think if we can peel the bumper off, there's enough of that tire to run on."

Wayne and Calhoun got hold of the bumper and pulled but it wouldn't come off. Not completely. Part of it had been creased, and that part finally gave way and broke off from the rest of it.

"That ought to be enough to keep from rubbing the tire," Calhoun said.

Sister Worth called from inside the bus. Wayne went to check on her. "Take me off the bus," she said in her slow way. ". . . I want to feel free air and sun."

"There doesn't feel like there's any air out there," Wayne said. "And the sun feels just like it always does. Hot."

"Please."

He picked her up and carried her outside and found a ridge of sand and laid her down so her head was propped against it.

"I . . . I need batteries," she said.

"Say what?" Wayne said.

She lay looking straight into the sun. "Brother Lazarus's greatest work . . . a dead folk that can think . . . has memory of the past. . . . Was a scientist too . . ." Her hand came up in stages, finally got hold of her head gear and pushed it off.

Gleaming from the center of her tangled blond hair was a silver knob.

"He . . . was not a good man . . . I am a good woman . . . I want to feel alive . . . like before . . . batteries going . . . brought others."

Her hand fumbled at a snap pocket on her habit. Wayne opened it for her and got out what was inside. Four batteries.

"Uses two . . . simple."

Calhoun was standing over them now. "That explains some things," he said.

"Don't look at me like that . . ." Sister Worth said, and Wayne realized he had never told her his name and she had never asked. "Unscrew . . . put the batteries in. . . . Without them I'll be an eater. . . . Can't wait too long."

"All right," Wayne said. He went behind her and propped her up on the sand drift and unscrewed the metal shaft from her skull. He thought about when she had fucked him on the wheel and how desperate she had been to feel something, and how she had been cold as flint and lustless. He remembered how she had looked in the mirror hoping to see something that wasn't there.

He dropped the batteries in the sand and took out one of the revolvers and put it close to the back of her head and pulled the trigger. Her body jerked slightly and fell over, her face turning toward him.

The bullet had come out where the bird had been on her cheek and had taken it completely away, leaving a bloodless hole.

"Best thing," Calhoun said. "There's enough live pussy in the world without you pulling this broken-legged dead thing around after you on a board."

"Shut up," Wayne said.

"When a man gets sentimental over women and kids, he can count himself out."

Wayne stood up.

"Well boy," Calhoun said. "I reckon it's time."

"Reckon so," Wayne said.

"How about we do this with some class? Give me one of your pistols and we'll get back-to-back and I'll count to ten, and when I get there, we'll turn and shoot."

Wayne gave Calhoun one of the pistols. Calhoun checked the chambers, said, "I've got four loads."

Wayne took two out of his pistol and tossed them on the ground. "Even Steven," he said.

They got back-to-back and held the guns by their legs.

"Guess if you kill me you'll take me in," Calhoun said. "So that means you'll put a bullet through my head if I need it. I don't want to come back as one of the dead folks. Got your word on that?"

"Yep."

"I'll do the same for you. Give my word. You know that's worth something."

"We gonna shoot or talk?"

"You know, boy, under different circumstances, I could have liked you. We might have been friends."

"Not likely."

Calhoun started counting, and they started stepping. When he got to ten, they turned.

Calhoun's pistol barked first, and Wayne felt the bullet

punch him low in the right side of his chest, spinning him slightly. He lifted his revolver and took his time and shot just as Calhoun fired again.

Calhoun's second bullet whizzed by Wayne's head. Wayne's shot hit Calhoun in the stomach.

Calhoun went to his knees and had trouble drawing a breath. He tried to lift his revolver but couldn't; it was as if it had turned into an anvil.

Wayne shot him again. Hitting him in the middle of the chest this time and knocking him back so that his legs were curled beneath him.

Wayne walked over to Calhoun, dropped to one knee and took the revolver from him.

"Shit," Calhoun said. "I wouldn't have thought that for nothing. You hit?"

"Scratched."

"Shit."

Wayne put the revolver to Calhoun's forehead and Calhoun closed his eyes and Wayne pulled the trigger.

[13]

The wound wasn't a scratch. Wayne knew he should leave Sister Worth where she was and load Calhoun on the bus and haul him in for bounty. But he didn't care about the bounty anymore.

He used the ragged piece of bumper to dig them a shallow side-by-side grave. When he finished, he stuck the fender fragment up between them and used the sight of one of the revolvers to scratch into it: HERE LIES SISTER WORTH AND CALHOUN WHO KEPT HIS WORD.

You couldn't really read it good and he knew the first real wind would keel it over, but it made him feel better about something, even if he couldn't put his finger on it.

His wound had opened up and the sun was very hot now, and since he had lost his hat he could feel his brain cooking in his skull like meat boiling in a pot.

He got on the bus, started it and drove through the day and the night and it was near morning when he came to the Cadillacs and turned down between them and drove until he came to the '57.

When he stopped and tried to get off the bus, he found he could hardly move. The revolvers in his belt were stuck to his shirt and stomach because of the blood from his wound.

He pulled himself up with the steering wheel, got one of the shotguns and used it for a crutch. He got the food and water and went out to inspect the '57.

It was for shit. It had not only lost its windshield, the front end was mashed way back and one of the big sand tires was twisted at such an angle he knew the axle was shot.

He leaned against the Chevy and tried to think. The bus was okay and there was still some gas in it, and he could get the hose out of the trunk of the '57 and siphon gas out of its tanks and put it in the bus. That would give him a few miles.

Miles.

He didn't feel as if he could walk twenty feet, let alone concentrate on driving.

He let go of the shotgun, the food and water. He scooted onto the hood of the Chevy and managed himself to the roof. He lay there on his back and looked at the sky.

It was a clear night and the stars were sharp with no fuzz around them. He felt cold. In a couple of hours the stars would fade and the sun would come up and the cool would give way to heat.

He turned his head and looked at one of the Cadillacs and a skeleton face pressed to its windshield, forever looking down at the sand.

That was no way to end, looking down.

He crossed his legs and stretched out his arms and studied the sky. It didn't feel so cold now, and the pain had almost stopped. He was more numb than anything else.

He pulled one of the revolvers and cocked it and put it to his temple and continued to look at the stars. Then he closed his eyes and found that he could still see them. He was once again hanging in the void between the stars wearing only his hat and cowboy boots, and floating about him were the junk cars and the '57, undamaged.

The cars were moving toward him this time, not away. The '57 was in the lead, and as it grew closer he saw Pop behind the wheel and beside him was a Mexican puta, and in the back, two more. They were all smiling and Pop honked the horn and waved.

The '57 came alongside him and the back door opened. Sitting between the whores was Sister Worth. She had not been there a moment ago, but now she was. And he had never noticed how big the backseat of the '57 was.

Sister Worth smiled at him and the bird on her cheek lifted higher. Her hair was combed out long and straight and she looked pink-skinned and happy. On the floor-board at her feet was a chest of iced beer. Lone Star, by God.

Pop was leaning over the front seat, holding out his hand, and Sister Worth and the whores were beckoning him inside.

Wayne worked his hands and feet, found this time that he could move. He swam through the open door, touched Pop's hand, and Pop said, "It's good to see you, son," and at the moment Wayne pulled the trigger, Pop pulled him inside.

Dead Giveaway

BY BRIAN HODGE

Every night, without fail, it began like this:

MUSIC: opening of Gustav Holst's "Mars, Bringer of War"

. . . A dark and brooding piece of music if ever there was one. Next came the announcer, cheerful, bouncy as a beachball. Monty didn't know where they'd found the guy, but he was the best Don Pardo soundalike he'd ever heard.

ANNCR, VO: Drop what you're doing . . . it'll still be there! Come on! Join us now for the most unpredictable hour on television . . . *Deaaaad Giveawaaaaay!*

Every night, without fail. Seven nights a week, live on the air, and no reruns.

When Monty first checked his watch, it was a half hour to show time. He slumped a little deeper into the chair in his dressing room. Time on his hands. Time to kill. Would that lead to blood on his hands?

Too late, Monty! It's already there!

So he reached out onto the counter before him and plucked his bottle of Chivas Regal from the carpet of dust beneath it. And drank until it burned. Penance. A little later he was comfortably numb. And could live with himself again.

Time was that Monty Olson lived with just about everybody. In spirit, if not body. He traveled the airwaves, waltzing into bright, sunlit living rooms and bedrooms, borne on the wings of daytime TV. Always a guest, never an intruder, forever welcome. Shows such as *Deal of the Century* and *Bet You a Million* had made him a star. And was he loved? Oh was he ever . . . because he was the

man with the cash, the man with the prizes, the man with
the motherlode.

The man with the million-dollar smile.

It was a little tougher to conjure up that smile these
days, the big one that wrapped the corners of his mouth
almost back to his wisdom teeth. But he managed. Once a
pro, always a pro.

Who would have ever guessed it? he wondered for maybe
the billionth time since waking up to find that he and
everyone else unfamiliar with the rigors of rigor mortis
were in a declining minority. *Who'd've guessed that they'd
still want to be entertained?*

Monty fortified himself with another character-building
gulp of scotch and reached for his makeup case. He did his
own makeup these days, wondering why he bothered. His
face was a little flabbier, a little looser, with a few more
broken veins mapping his nose. But he was still a regular
Clark Gable by comparison with the rest of the folks on
the show. Monty peered at the lines webbing from the
corners of his eyes and mouth and did his best to erase
them with a little pancake makeup.

They still want to be entertained.

It wasn't *that* crazy a notion, not when you gave it time
to sink into your already shell-shocked head. Because
back in the days when the dead suddenly weren't obliged
to stay in their holes and their morgue drawers anymore,
Monty had found himself wandering the streets. He didn't
want much, only to avoid becoming lunch for some newly
awakened cadaver, and maybe to link up with someone
else whose blood still ran warm. And he'd seen the zombies in their homes. There they were—by themselves, in
pairs, as entire families—parked in front of their televisions just as before, as if nothing whatsoever had changed.
Even when all the networks and independent stations had
dropped from the airwaves like fruit from a dying tree,
they watched the blank screens anyway. Mesmerized by
the static.

The watching dead, waiting to be entertained.

Most of the zombies weren't that bright. Most of them
weren't much more than two-legged dinosaurs in search of
the nearest tar pit to blunder into. But some of them—

perhaps those who'd been the sharpest and shrewdest to begin with—had managed to retain enough intelligence that it was downright scary in itself. You looked into those glassy eyes and found that they weren't quite as dull as you'd thought. Or hoped. Yep, the lights were still on and somebody was still at home up there . . . only now the resident's priorities had been turned on their heads.

Such a creature was Brad Bernerd. Here in New York, he'd been a fast-track network executive with a string of hit shows as long as your arm. Some people, before the demise of what Monty was beginning to regard nostalgically as The Old World, had said that Brad Bernerd was going to launch his own network.

It came about a lot differently than expected, but he got his chance after all.

Monty had wandered up to the studio soundstage of *Deal of the Century* one day, a huge and silenced amphitheater where even the echoes of past applause had died. He stood at center stage, where he'd spent nearly half of his forty-three years, feeling the glorious pressure of the lights burning through him . . . and he was ready to blow his brains out and die where he'd lived his finest hours.

Except that Brad Bernerd had picked that moment to make an entrance.

He didn't look much different than Monty remembered, except for a fist-sized dent in the right side of his head. He moved more slowly, more deliberately, but he still managed to carry himself with a little pride. A little arrogance, even after death.

Monty just about piddled his pants like a three-year-old when he looked into those unblinking eyes and saw that they recognized him.

They stared forever.

"I have a job for you," Bernerd said at last. The voice held little of its old animated enthusiasm . . . but that didn't mean it had lost its power to persuade.

Hey guy, no reason to cash in your chips now, was what it boiled down to. Not when the show must go on. Not when I can put you back on the air. Not when you can reclaim your place in the limelight.

And thus was born the first television program conceived entirely for zombies. I want my ZTV.

Monty checked his watch one last time, found that the zero hour had just about drawn nigh once again. He suckled a final pull from the Chivas and left it behind when the knock came at the door, right on schedule.

"Time for the show," said Brad Bernerd when Monty opened the door. "It's show time, my man."

Yeah, like I really need a reminder NIGHT AFTER NIGHT!

Monty wound his way backstage among the skeleton crew that kept the cameras rolling and the lights burning. The boys in the band who kept the show on the road. They needed to do something about the ventilation, but Monty had gotten used to the week-old roadkill smell months ago. Once a pro, always a pro.

How do you do it? they used to ask him, the admirers, the hangers-on. *How do you manage to seem so on top of the world every single show?*

No sweat, he'd tell them. It was simply a matter of knowing the right buttons and what to do with them. Turn on the adrenaline. Turn on the smile. The charm. The juice. But just as important, turn off the mind. And the conscience. After all, how long can you live with yourself if you acknowledge that your mission in life is encouraging people to debase themselves for cash?

The switches were just about all in the proper on/off positions by the time he strolled over to stage left, behind the three huge doors. The crew was putting the final touches on the displays. Now and again, a foreman would have to restrain an overzealous stagehand from helping himself to one of the prizes.

"I rec . . . recog . . . hey I know you." A weak voice from the cage behind Door Number Three. The lights were dimming, and it was tough to tell who the voice belonged to. Still warm and breathing, of course, if she was in the cage. Monty was the only live one that walked *these* hallowed halls.

"I *know* you." The voice was thick, but clear.

He was drawn to her voice as a moth to the flame, briefly wondering why she was able to speak coherently.

Everyone else in the cage had surrendered to the doses of Thorazine administered earlier. Good old Thorazine. It made the live ones so much more docile. Kept them from agitating the audience. *And* the master of ceremonies.

"Please let me out . . . please . . . ?" She knelt on the cage floor, her face framed by long dark hair. She wore a red-and-white skirt and a dirty white V-neck sweater with a large red M on the front. Her hands clutched the bars so tightly they looked albino. "Please?"

All switches in place, all systems go.

"Can't do that, babe," he said, and just to charm the fear out of her, he gave her a great big Monty Olson smile. A fine one it was, too, one to rival any from The Old World. When you got it, flaunt it.

"How can you . . . sell us out like this? You're still one of us." She gestured toward the identically dressed girls sharing the cage with her. "You're not one of *them.*" She was beginning to cry, her eyes glassy but not blank, as she fought an uphill battle against the Thorazine. "How can you sell us out?"

"They'll get you one way or another, and they're the ones calling the shots these days. They're the ones signing my paycheck, as it were. They let me live." Monty knelt down close to her, his voice almost fatherly, "Remember Andy Warhol? Hmmm? A long time ago he said that everyone was going to be famous for fifteen minutes. Remember that? Well, this is your night, babe. You're gonna be seen from coast to coast tonight."

She stared at him, clawing for a little more comprehension, and her fingers opened and trailed down the bars. She stared at the spot they'd been holding.

"Try to make the best of it," he said, and left her. He had a lapel mike to clip on.

"Show time," called Bernerd from the shadows. "Look alive, folks."

Bernerd cued the guy in the sound booth, a forever-young fellow called Deadhead, since he'd died and was then reborn in a Grateful Dead T-shirt. Deadhead's job was to play the proper music at the proper times. He juggled several cassette tapes and managed to do a remarkable job of keeping them sorted.

The music: "Mars, Bringer of War," throbbing with menace.

The lights: coming up from dim.

The cameras: red tally lights winking on, lenses focusing, slack gray faces staring into the viewfinders.

The pseudo–Don Pardo: "Drop what you're doing . . . it'll still be there! Come on! Join us now for the most unpredictable hour on television . . . *Deaaaad Giveawaaaaay!*"

Monty cemented that huge smile across his face and came striding onstage, sharp and natty in his slacks and sports jacket. The bulge under the left sleeve was barely noticeable. Doors One, Two, and Three were at his left, and the enormous wheel of opportunity at his right. Down he went, down to the very lip of the stage as the curtain rose, the final barrier removed. . . .

And there they were. His audience.

They sat politely, somewhere around a thousand of them, somewhere around two thousand unblinking eyes staring back at him. Some of them clapped, or tried their best, clumsy hands slapping together like pairs of gutted fish. Others cheered, sounding like contented cattle lowing gently into the night. A sea of gray faces, agate eyes.

Let me entertain you, let me make you smile.

"Right you are, this is *Dead Giveaway,* and my name's Monty Olson. Good-looking crowd tonight, wow. Well hey! I know you hate waiting for the fun to start about as much as I hate long monologues, so let's just get right down to it, what do you say?"

The studio audience murmured its agreement, mottled gray heads bobbing here and there. Monty went striding back toward the wheel, feeling more vital than he had all day. The lights, the cameras, the smell of makeup . . . he knew no better nourishment.

"One thing before we get started, let's run through the rules, shall we? They're simple enough, in keeping with most of your minds out there. Each contestant gets one spin at the wheel, where they can be an instant winner or loser. If the wheel stops on a number, they'll win one of our big prizes behind the three doors. And trust your old Uncle Monty, we've got some real goodies behind there tonight. Only one word of warning . . . just don't commit the Big No-No. We all know what that is and what that means, don't we, ha ha haaaa!"

As Monty patted the bulge beneath his sleeve, there came from the audience a thick rumbling that was probably laughter.

"So! Who's our first contestant tonight?"

Deadhead began playing Roy Orbison's "Oh Pretty Woman" as the announcer introduced the shape beginning to move onstage.

"She's a hometown career girl from mid-Manhattan, a former director of sales and training at a downtown bank. First up tonight on *Dead Giveaway* . . . please welcome Cynthia!"

Again, that dead-fish splatter of applause. There were several agitated moans that in The Old World might've been wolf whistles. Cynthia shuffled toward the wheel, tall and angular in the moldering remnants of a pin-striped business dress and jacket. Her mouth was a cruel red splash of lipstick against a white face the texture of dried-out Play Doh.

"Welcome, Cynthia, welcome," Monty said. "Gosh, you sound like a lady who has it all together. So tell me, what do you owe your success to?"

"Brains," she said with a lopsided grin.

Monty dug deep and chortled out a big belly laugh. He had her step up to the wheel, and she gripped one of the many handles circling its edge and gave it a good shove. An overhead camera flashed the spinning image onto the studio monitors. Numbers and prizes alike flicked past the marker, a blur at first, then gradually coming into focus as the wheel lost momentum. At last the marker settled on a huge numeral 2.

"How 'bout that, a big winner first time out tonight!" Monty boomed. On went the wraparound smile. "Tell her what she's won!"

Door Number Two eased upward to reveal a display that resembled the back room of a well-stocked butcher shop. Stainless-steel tables and white-cloaked gurneys were loaded nearly to the point of collapse. A groan of envy rippled through the audience.

The studio monitors and home viewers were then treated to stock newsreel footage of a suburban neighborhood reduced to the apparent aftermath of a war zone. Weeping rescue workers crawled past mounds of burning rubble, extracting victims whole and in part from wreckage twisted beyond recognition.

"Who'll ever forget last May twenty-third?" said the announcer, as cheerful and bouncy as ever. "Flight nine-oh-one out of O'Hare Airport? It crashed a minute after takeoff, but the nation's third-worst airline disaster is *your* gain, Cynthia. Direct to you from cold storage in the Cook County Morgue, it's the last of flight nine-oh-one! Courtesy of *Dead Giveaway.*"

Whatever remained of Cynthia's professional composure was abandoned where she stood. She went lurching toward Door Two in a stiff-legged hobble, falling toward the nearest table and overturning it in an avalanche of assorted parts. Two cameras zoomed in and caught her delight . . . the sweet taste of victory.

The next contestant was a trim lady wearing a tattered dress belted around the waist and a string of pearls. Earrings showed through the matted filth of once-carefully coiffed hair. Her name was June, a housewife from Mayfield, Ohio, and she lumbered away an instant winner, the proud owner of the thigh and lower leg of what the announcer said had been a marathon runner.

A Brooklyn construction laborer named Carl was up next, entering to the strains of "Born in the U.S.A." His blue workshirt was stained in numerous places where it puckered into the flesh of his belly and chest, and his shoulders looked as broad as a freezer door.

"Whoa, Carl, let's be careful, okay?" Monty said, laughing. "That wheel's gotta last us the rest of the night, you know."

Carl grunted, and a low moan escaped the crowd as he clutched the handle, lurching when he spun the wheel. Then, with the sound of a large, half-rotten carrot snapping in two, the zombie's arm parted company with his shoulder. The arm slithered out of its sleeve like a great gray worm, the hand still holding fast to the wheel. Carl watched in dumbfounded surprise as his arm spun in broad circles, like the last remnant of a child desperate to remain aboard a merry-go-round. Carl looked up, mouth agape, eyes bovine in their stupidity.

Silence, save for the clattering of the marker.

Then a red beacon, and the sound of a buzzer ripsawing through the studio.

"Uh-oh, that's it! The Big No-No!" cried Monty. "Self-dismemberment *is* grounds for automatic disqualification!" He reached inside his jacket and pulled out a long-barreled .38, leveling it at the zombie's head. "Too bad, Carl. That was a good spin, too."

The audience uttered a mournful groan at the gunshot, at the mushrooming of the back of Carl's head into gray and maroon, at the thud of his body on the soundstage floor. A pair of stagehands shuffled out to drag the remains away; one licked his fingers when the job was done. Monty reholstered the .38 and grinned broadly and hunched his shoulders. Always a laff-a-minute here on *Dead Giveaway*.

And on and on it went, a constant, plodding parade of the undead coming to claim their prizes. Shawn, the California beach bum who still had shards of a surfboard sticking from his chest, walked away with a four-pack of heads of various network executives Bernerd hadn't liked. Millicent, who'd been killed shortly after her debutante coming-out party, won the massive arm of a weightlifter and wore it around her neck like a fine fur. And on and on . . .

Until, at last, the final contestant.

"Looks like the old clock on the wall says we're just about out of time," Monty said. "But hey, let's squeeze in one more, what do you say? Who's up next?"

"Well, Monty, he comes to us from the lower east side, and his interests are slam-dancing and graffiti. Six-foot-two, hair of blue, just call him Fang!"

An imposingly tall figure emerged from offstage, made even taller by the blue spikes of hair exploding from his head at all angles. Beneath a loose black-mesh shirt, his sunken chest was crisscrossed with chains. His upper lip was eaten away entirely up to his nose, giving him a perpetual snarl. Fang took his place at the wheel.

"Last spin of the night, Fang," Monty said. "Let's give
'em a good one."

And good it was. The wheel spun forever, slowing at
last with a clattering of the marker blade. Finally it came
to rest on a large 3, and the crowd broke into a smattering
of applause.

"Whoa ho ho ho, what luck!" Monty roared; the best he
could tell, Fang was grinning. "Another big winner! What
have we got for him?"

"They're young! They're nubile! They're fresh from
Hollywood! And they're all yours, Fang! The entire female
cast of last spring's drive-in theater epic, *Cheerleader
Party Massacre*!"

Door Number Three was up by now, and behind it sat a
cage filled with aspiring starlets in identical red-and-white
suits. What a shame, to have spent years hoping and
dreaming for the big break, that shot on prime-time TV
. . . and to miss it due to Thorazine. It had kicked in
hard and heavy, leaving them about as excited as a basket
of vegetables. Except for . . .

The audience was in, for them, a frenzy of excitement.
Some were standing, arms waving like stalks of wheat in a
summer breeze. Others stomped their feet to no apparent
rhythm. Deadhead started some new music, angry guitars
and shrieking vocals. Old Blue Eyes it wasn't. The Dead
Kennedys, maybe?

Except for . . .

Fang was in a frenzy of his own, twitching in time with
the music like a spastic during a seizure. His head bristled
like a mace. Several of the earlier contestants wandered
back onstage for the party atmosphere of the closing credits. Cynthia, with a good deal of Flight 901 smeared across
her face. Shawn and his cooler of heads. Millicent, model-
ing her new arm. Fang twitched and slammed himself into
Cynthia; an ear went sailing across the soundstage like a
crinkled little Frisbee.

And yet Monty found himself unable to tear his eyes
away from the girl he'd spoken to before the show. She
clung to the front of the cage, swimming upstream against
the current of a Thorazine haze while the rest of the star-

lets slumped in catatonic heaps. Her knuckles showed white against the steel bars.

She's not supposed to do that! She's supposed to be out of it!

She looked thin, painfully so, and no doubt it had been a good long while since her hair had been washed. Her lips trembled, and her eyes loomed huge against the pale of her face. Eyes that fixed, eyes that accused.

Eyes that started rearranging those internal switches. Off went the smile, off went the juice.

"Help me, please," she said, though over the racket on the stage he couldn't hear her, could only read her lips. "Everybody's got a price, what's yours? Is it this?"

And then, in a pathetic attempt at seduction, the girl fumbled with one side of her sweater and tugged it down. Ragged fingernails left red streaks on her skin. And there she stayed, holding the bar in one hand and her sweater in the other. Gauging his price.

Monty suddenly wanted to be sick. Not entirely from the prospect of her inevitable fate . . . but from the quick glimpse at just what it was that he was made of.

Everybody's got a price, what's yours . . .

In the absurd simplicity of her offer, she'd somehow managed to show him a truth that had always eluded him before: Greed is the one thing death can't conquer. Love can succumb before it, and loyalty. Friendship and honor. Morality and dignity and even humanity. But not greed, oh no. Greed has an indefinite lifespan all its own, and thrives in the stony soil that can kill the rest.

He gave her the first genuine smile he'd given in years.

Monty reached beneath his jacket to finger the grip of the .38. *At least it'd be the merciful way out. And then a bullet for me, maybe?*

He pulled the gun out, letting his arm hang by his side. The girl saw, and understood. And in pulling her sweater back up, accepted. Her glazed eyes shut and her face tilted slightly toward an unseen sky. *Make it quick,* she seemed to be saying.

And then a bullet for me? No, I can't do that, can't do that at all. Because Heaven help me, I need this stage more.

Make it quick? Okay, that much he could do.

Except that by the time he got the gun halfway up, it was plucked cleanly from his hand.

Monty hadn't noticed that Brad Bernerd had sidled over beside him. But now they stood face to rotten face. Bernerd was smarter than he looked, Monty knew that. Apparently he was stronger and quicker, as well.

Before Monty could move, Bernerd pointed the revolver's muzzle at his lower thigh and pulled the trigger.

The thunderclap of gunpowder aside, the effect was much like getting clubbed with a concrete block. Monty felt his leg suddenly swatted out from beneath him, and the next thing he knew he was on his side on the floor, tasting dust.

The gunshot brought everything to a halt . . . the announcer's closing voice-over, Fang's slam-dancing, Millicent's preening. Even Deadhead killed the music. Everything stopped except the silent scrolling of the credits on the monitors. Once again, Monty was the center of undivided attention. At the bottom of a sea of staring eyes.

He propped himself up on one elbow, grunting, chilly sweat trickling from his scalp. The lights didn't feel quite so warm anymore. He gazed up into Bernerd's runny eyes.

"It would've happened anyway," Bernerd said. He slowly cocked his dented head toward Door Number Three. "She didn't matter."

Monty's mouth gaped. He figured that his eyes were as blank and his brain as empty as everyone else's around him. "Then why?" was all he could say.

"The ratings," Bernerd said. "Time for a change. Your ratings are slipping."

And as Monty pondered this great imponderable, Bernerd simply turned and walked away. The credits rolled on, and the rest of them began to move again, closing in as surely as the cameras. They mounted the stage from the amphitheater . . . by themselves, in pairs, as entire families. Converging on him with unblinking, hungry eyes.

My ratings? Slipping? SLIPPING? The thought was too great, and it snapped his already fragile mind in two with pencil-thin ease.

He felt the first insistent tug at the bullet wound in his thigh, saw the cameras leering in.

But the eyes of the world are on me now! he thought. *And its hands . . . and quite a few teeth . . .*

Audience participation at its finest.

Jerry's Kids Meet Wormboy

BY DAVID J. SCHOW

Eating 'em was more fun than blowing their gnarly green heads off. But why dicker when you could do both?

The fresher ones were blue. That was important if you wanted to avoid cramps, salmonella. Eat a green one and you'd be yodeling down the big porcelain megaphone in no time.

Wormboy used wire cutters to snip the nose off the last bullet in the foam block. He snugged the truncated cartridge into the cylinder of his short-barrel .44. When fired, the flattened slugs pancaked on impact and would disintegrate any geek's head into hash. The green guys weren't really zombies, because no voodoo had played a part. They were all geeks, all slow as syrup and stupid as hell, and Wormboy loved it that way. It meant he would not starve in this cowardly new world. He was eating; millions weren't.

Wormboy's burden was great.

It hung from his Butthole Surfers T-shirt. He had scavenged dozens of such shirts from a burned-out rock shop, all Extra Extra Large, all screaming about bands he had never heard of—Dayglo Abortions, Rudimentary Penii, Shower of Smegma, Fat & Fucked Up. Wormboy's big personal in-joke was one that championed a long-gone album titled *Giving Head to the Living Dead*.

The gravid flab of his teats distorted the logo, and his surplus flesh quivered and swam, shoving around his clothing as though some subcutaneous revolution was aboil. Pasty and pocked, his belly depended earthward, a vast sandbag held at bay by a wide weight lifter's belt, notched low. The faintest motion caused his hectares of skin to bobble like mercury.

Wormboy was more than fat. He was a crowd of fat people. A single mirror was insufficient to the task of containing his image.

The explosion buzzed the floor beneath his hitops. Vibrations slithered from one thick stratum of dermis to the next, bringing him the news.

The sound of a Bouncing Betty's boom-boom always worked like a Pavlovian dinner gong. It could smear a smile across his jowls and start his tummy to percolating. He snatched up binoculars and stampeded out into the graveyard.

Valley View Memorial Park was a classic cemetery, of a venerable lineage far preceding the ordinances that required flat monument stones to note the dearly departed. The granite and marble jutting from its acreage was the most ostentatious and artfully hewn this side of a Universal Studios monster movie boneyard. Stone-cold angels reached toward heaven. Stilted verse, deathlessly chiseled, eulogized the departees—vanity plates in a suburbia for the lifeless. It cloyed.

Most of the graves were unoccupied. They had prevailed without the fertilization of human decay and were now choked with loam and healthy green grass. The tenants had clawed out and waltzed off several seasons back.

A modest road formed a spiral ascent path up the hill and terminated in a cul-de-sac fronting Wormboy's current living quarters. Midway up, it was interrupted by a trench ten feet across. Wormboy had excavated this "moat" using the cemetery's scoop-loader, and seeded it with lengths of two-inch pipe sawn at angles to form funnel-knife style pungi sticks. Tripwires knotted gate struts to tombstones to booby traps, and three hundred antipersonnel mines lived in the earth. Every longitude and latitude of Valley View had been lovingly nurtured into a Gordian knot of killpower that Wormboy had christened his spiderweb.

The Bouncing Bettys had been a godsend. Anything that wandered in unbidden would get its legs blown off or become immovably gaffed in the moat.

Not long after the geeks woke up, shucked dirt, and ambled off with their yaps drooping open, Wormboy had claimed Valley View for his very own. He knew the dead tended to "home" toward places that had been important to them back when they weren't green. Ergo, never would they come trotting home to a graveyard.

Wormboy's previous hideout had been a National Guard armory. Too much traffic in walking dead weekend warriors, there. Blowing them into unwalking lasagna cost too much time and powder. After seven Land-Rover-loads of military rock and roll, Wormy's redecoration of Valley View was complete. The graveyard was one big mechanized ambush. The reception building and nondenominational chapel were ideally suited to his needs . . . and breadth. Outfitting the prep room was more stainless steel than a French kitchen in Beverly Hills; where stiffs were once dressed for interment, Wormboy now dressed them out for din-din. There was even a refrigerated morgue locker. Independent generators chugged out wattage. His only real lament was that there never seemed to be enough videotapes to keep him jolly. On the nonfiction front he favored Julia Child.

The binocs were overpriced army jobs with an illuminated reticle. Wormboy thumbed up his bottle-bottom fish-eye specs, focused, and swept the base of the hill. Smoke was still rising from the breach point. Fewer geeks blundered in these days, but now and again he could still snag one.

That was peculiar. As far as Wormboy could reckon, geeks functioned on the level of pure motor response with a single directive—seek food—and legs that made their appetites mobile. Past year one the locals began to shun Valley View altogether, almost as though the geek grapevine had warned them the place was poison. Could be that Valley View's primo kill rate had made it the crucible of the first bona fide zombie superstition.

God only knew what they were munching in the cities by now. As the legions of ambulatory expirees had swelled, their preferred food—live citizens—had gone underground. Survivors of what Wormboy called Zombie Apocalypse had gotten canny or gotten eaten. Geek soci-

ety itself was like a gator pit; he'd seen them get pissed off
and chomp hunks out of one another. Though their irradi-
ated brains kept their limbs supple and greased with oxy-
genated blood, they were still dead . . . and dead people
still rotted. Their structural integrity (not to mention their
freshness) was less than a sure bet past the second or third
Halloween. Most geeks Wormy spotted nowadays were
minus a major limb. They digested, but did not seem to
eliminate. Sometimes the older ones simply exploded.
They clogged up with gas and decaying food until they hit
critical mass, then *kerblooey*—steaming gobbets of brown
crap all over the perimeter. It was enough to put you off
your dinner.

Life was so weird. Wormboy felt like the only normal
person left.

This movable feast, this walking smorgasbord, could
last another year or two at max, and Wormboy knew it.
His fortifications insured that he would be ready for whatever followed, when the world changed again. For now, it
was a matchless chow-down, and grand sport.

The ATV groaned and squeaked its usual protests when
he settled into its saddle. A rack welded to the chassis
secured geek tools—pinch bar, fire ax, scattergun sheaths,
and a Louisville Slugger with a lot of chips, nicks, and
dried blood. The all-terrain bike's balloon tires did not
burst. Wormboy kick-started and puttered down to meet
his catch of the day.

Geeks could sniff human meat from a fair distance.
Some had actually gotten around to elementary tool use.
But their maze sense was zero-zero. They always tried to
proceed in straight lines. Even for a nongeek it took a load
of deductive logic just to pick a path toward Valley View's
chapel without getting divorced from your vitals, and
much more time than generally elapsed between
Wormboy's feedings. Up on this hilltop, his security was
assured.

He piloted the ATV down his special escape path, twisting and turning, pausing at several junctures to gingerly
reconnect tripwires behind him. He dropped his folding
metal army fording bridge over the moat and tootled
across.

Some of the meat hung up in the heat flash of the explosion was still sizzling on the ground in charred clumps. Dragging itself doggedly up the slope was half a geek, still aimed at the chapel and the repast that was Wormboy. Everything from its navel down had been blown off.

Wormboy unracked the pinch bar. One end had been modified to take a ten-pound harpoon head of machined steel. A swath of newly muddied earth quickly became a trail of strewn organs resembling smashed fruit. The geek's brand-new prone carriage had permitted it to evade some of the Bouncing Betty trips. Wormboy frowned. His announcement was pointed—and piqued—enough to arrest the geek's uphill crawl.

"Welcome to hell, dork breath."

It humped around on its palms with all the grace of a beached haddock. Broken rib struts punched through at jigsaw angles and mangled innards swung from the mostly empty chest cavity like pendant jewels. One ear had been sheared off; the side of its head was caked in thick blood, dirt, and pulverized tissue that reminded Wormboy of a scoop of dog food. It sought Wormboy with bleary drunkard's eyes, virulently jaundiced and discharging gluey fluid like those of a sick animal.

It was wearing a besmirched Red Cross arm band.

A long, gray-green rope of intestine had paid out behind the geek. It gawped with dull hunger, then did an absurd little push-up in order to bite it. Teeth crunched through geek-gut and gelid black paste evacuated with a blatting fart noise. *Sploot!*

Disinclined toward autocannibalism, it tacked again on Wormboy. A kidney peeled loose from a last shred of muscle and rolled out to burst apart in the weeds. The stench was unique.

Impatient, Wormy shook his head. Stupid geeks. "C'mon, fuckface, come and get it." He waggled his mighty belly, then held out the rib roast of his forearm. "You want Cheez Whiz on it or what? C'mon. Chow time."

It seemed to catch the drift. Mouth champing and slavering, eyes straying off in two directions, it resumed its quest, leaving hanks and clots of itself behind all the way down.

It was too goddamned slow . . . and wasting too many choice bits.

Hefting the pinch bar, Wormboy hustled up the slope. He slammed one of his size thirteens thunderously down within biting range and let the geek fantasize for an instant about what a crawfull of Wormboy Platter would taste like. Greedy. Then he threw all his magnificent tonnage behind a downward thrust, spiking his prey between the shoulder blades and staking it to the ground with a moist crunch.

It thrashed and chewed air. Wormy waved bye-bye in its face. "Don't go 'way, now." He let the geek watch him pick his way back down to the ATV. He wanted it to see him returning with the ax. Sweat had broken freely; the exertion already had Wormboy huffing and aromatic, but he loved this part almost as much as swallowing that old-time home cookin'.

The ax hissed down overhand. A bilious rainbow of decomposing crap hocked from the neck stump while the blue head pinballed from one tombstone to the next. It thonked to rest against the left rear wheel of the ATV.

Wormboy lent the half torso a disappointed inspection. Pickings were lean; this geek had been on the hoof too long. Burger night again.

He looked behind him and sure enough, the lone head was fighting like hell to redirect itself. Hair hung in its eyes, the face was caved in around the flattened nose, the whole of it now oozing and studded with cockleburs . . . but by God it tipped over, embedded broken teeth into packed dirt, and tried to pull itself toward Wormy. It was that hungry.

Wormboy went down to meet it, humming. He secured the ax in its metal clip and drew the ball bat.

Busting a coconut was tougher. The geek's eyes stayed open. They never flinched when you hit them. On the second bash, curds of blood-dappled brain jumped out to meet the air.

It ceased moving then, except to crackle and collapse. The cheesy brain-stuff was the color of fishbellies.

Wormboy pulled free a mucilaginous fistfull and brandished it before the open, unseeing eyes. He squeezed hard. Glistening spirals unfurled between his fingers with a greasy macaroni noise.

"I win again."

He licked the gelid residue off his trigger finger and smacked his lips. By the time he got back to the torso with a garbage bag, the Red Cross arm band was smoldering. He batted it away. It caught in midair and flared, newborn fire gobbling up the swatch of cloth and the symbol emblazoned thereon, leaving Wormboy alone to scratch his head about what it might have meant.

Little Luke shot twin streamers of turbid venom into the urine specimen cup like a good Christian, providing. He did not mind being milked (not that he'd been asked); it was a necessary preamble to the ritual. He played his part and was provided for—a sterling exemplar of God's big blueprint. His needle fangs were translucent and fragile looking. Cloudy venom pooled in the cup.

Maintaining his grip just behind Little Luke's jaws, the Right Reverend Jerry thanked his Lord for this bounty, that the faithful might take communion and know His peace. He kissed Little Luke on the head and dropped all four feet of him back into the pet caddy. Little Luke's Love Gift had been generous today. Perhaps even serpents knew charity.

Jerry pondered charity, and so charitably ignored the fact that his eldest deacon was leaking. Deacon Moe stood in the vestibule, his pants soaked and dripping, weaving back and forth. He was not breathing, and his eyes saw only the specimen cup. The odor that had accompanied him into the tiny room was that of maggoty sausage. He was a creature of wretchedness, without a doubt . . . but was also proof to the Right Reverend Jerry that the myth had delivered at last, and skeptics be damned.

The dead had risen from their graves to be judged. If that was not a miraculous proof, what was? The regular viewers of Jerry's tricounty video ministry had been long satisfied by more pallid miracles—eased sprains, restored control of the lower tract, that sort of thing. Since this ukase had flown down from heaven, it would be foolish to shun its opportunities.

Jerry savored the moment the dead ones had walked. It had vindicated his lagging faith, dispelling in an instant the doubts that had haunted his soul for a lifetime. There *was* a One True God, and there *was* a Judgment Day, and there *was* an Armageddon, and there was *bound* to be a Second Coming, and as long as the correct events came to pass, who cared if their order had been juggled a bit? The Lord had been known to work in mysterious ways before.

Once his suit had been blazing white, and pure. With faith, it would shine spotlessly again. Right now he did not mind the skunky miasma exuding from the pits of what had once been a fifteen-hundred-dollar jacket. It helped blanket the riper and more provocative stench of Deacon Moe's presence. The congregation was on the move, and there was little time for dapper grooming in midhegira.

Jerry beckoned Deacon Moe forward to receive communion. From the way poor Moe shambled, this might be his last chance to drink of the Blood . . . since none of the faithful had meshed teeth lately on the Body, or any facsimile thereof.

He had visited an abandoned library, and books had told him what rattlesnake venom could do.

In human beings, it acts as a neurotoxin and nerve-impulse blocker, jamming the signals of the brain by preventing acetylcholine from jumping across nerve endings. The brain's instructions are never delivered. First comes facial paralysis, then loss of motor control. Heart and lungs shut down, and the victim drowns in his own backed up fluids. Hemolytic, or blood-destroying, factors cause intense local pain. Jerry had tasted the venom he routinely fed his quartet of deacons. Nothing to worry about, as long as your stomach lining had no tiny holes in it. The bright yellow liquid was odorless, with a taste at first astringent, then sweetish. It numbed the lips. There was so much books could not know.

In walking dead human beings, Jerry discovered that the venom, administered orally, easily penetrated the cheesecloth of their internal pipework and headed straight for the motor centers of the brain, unblocking them, allowing Jerry to reach inside with light hypnosis to tinker. He could program his deacons not to eat him. More important, this imperative could then be passed among the faithful in the unspoken and mystical way that seemed reserved to only these special children of God.

A talent for mesmerization came effortlessly to a man who had devoted years to charming the camera's unblinking and all-seeing eye. Jerry preferred to consider his ability innate, a divine, God-granted sanction approved for the use he made of it. *Don't eat the Reverend.*

Deacon Moe's coated tongue moistened cracked and greenish lips, not in anticipation, but as a wholly preconditioned response. The demarcations of the urine specimen cup showed a level two ounces. Little Luke could be fully milked slightly more often than once per month, if Jerry's touch was gentle and coaxing. The cup was tilted to Deacon Moe's lips and the poison was glugged down *in nomine Patris, et Filii . . .*

"And God waved His hand," Jerry belted out.

"And when God did wave His hand, He cleansed the hearts of the wicked of evil. He scoured out the souls of the wolves, and set His born-agains to the task of reclaiming the earth in His name. The Scriptures were right all along—the meek inherited. Now the world grows green and fecund again. Now the faithful must seek strength from their most holy Maker. The damned Sodom and Gomorrah of New York and Los Angeles have fallen to ruin, their false temples pulled down to form the dust that makes the clay from which God molds the God-fearing Christian. Our God is a loving God, yet a wrathful God, and so he struck down those beyond redemption. He closed the book on secular humanism. His mighty Heel stamped out radical feminism. His good right Fist meted out rough justice to the homosexuals; his good left Fist likewise silenced the pagans of devilspawn rock and roll. And He did spread His arms wide to gather up the sins of this evil world, from sexual perversion to drug addiction to Satan worship. And you might say a *memo* came down from the desk of the Lord, and major infidel butt got kicked doubleplusgood!"

Now he was cranking, impassioned, his pate agleam with righteous perspiration. His hands clasped Deacon Moe's shoulders. His breath misted the zombie's dead-ahead eyes. His conviction was utter. Moe salivated.

"And now the faithful walk the land, brother, as a mighty army. God's legions grow by the day, by the hour, the minute, as we stand here and reaffirm our faith in His name. We are all children of God, and God is a loving Father who provides for His children, yes. Yes, we must make sacrifices. But though our bellies be empty today, our hearts are full up with God's goodness!" His voice was cracking now; it was always good to make it appear as though some passion was venting accidentally. "From that goodness you and I must draw the strength to persevere until tomorrow, when the Millenium shall come and no child of the Lord shall want. Peace is coming! Food is coming! Go forth unto the congregation, Deacon Moe, and spread this good news! Amen! Amen! Amen!"

Deacon Moe wheezed, his arid throat rasping out an acknowledgment that sounded like an asthmatic trying to say *rruuaah* through a jugfull of snot. Jerry spun him aboutface and impelled him through the curtain to disseminate the Word. He heard Moe's stomachload of accumulated venom slosh. Corrosion was running amok in there. Any second now, gravity might fill Deacon Moe's pants with his own zombified tripe.

Tonight they were billeted in an actual church. Most of the faithful loitered about the sanctuary. The deacons led them through Jerry's motions; the response quotient of the total group, twoscore and ten, was about as dependable as a trained but retarded lab rat. Less control, and Jerry would have starred at his own Last Supper months ago. Right now he saw his congregation only as vessels itching to be filled with the prose of the Lord. He tried to keep them fed as best he could manage.

He was most proud of the glorious day he had commenced his cross-country revival. He strode boldly into the murk of a Baton Rouge honky-tonk and let God say howdy-do to a nest of musicians calling themselves Slim Slick and His Slick Dicks. Marching right behind him were twenty hungry born-agains. That holy purge, that first big feed with which he had blessed his new congregation, would forever burn brightly in a special corner of his heart. Slim Slick, et al., had seen the light. Some of them had joined the marching ministry, those that had not been too chewed up to locomote.

Like Jesus to the temple, the Right Reverend Jerry came not to destroy, but to fulfill. To fill full.

He poked his snakestick into the hatch of the pet caddy. Nobody buzzed. Nobody could. Rattling tended to upset the faithful, so he had soaked the rattle of each of his four Little wine-makers until it rotted into silence. Little Matthew was disengaged from the tangle of his brothers. Eastern diamondbacks were rightly feared for their size and high venom delivery; full-contact bites were almost always fatal. Little Matt was five feet long, with large glands that would effortlessly yield a Love Gift that could convert six hundred sixty-six adults to the cause, and wasn't *that* a significant coincidence of mathematics? Jerry had to push the figures a smidgen, converting milligrams to grains to ounces. How a lethal dosage was administered was a big variable. But the final number summoned by his calculator was 666, repeating to infinity. That was how many sinners could swing low on three ounces of Little Matt's finest kind. To Jerry, that number was a perfect sign . . . and wasn't that what really counted in the Big Book? Perfection just tickled God green.

Deacon Curly had not come forth to receive communion. Perhaps he had wandered astray?

Back in the days before it had become synonymous with smut, the Right Reverend Jerry had enjoyed comedy. Upon his nameless deacons he had bestowed the names of famous funnymen. As the ramrods wore out or were retired, Jerry's list of names dwindled. Just now, the deacons in charge were Moe, Curly, W.C., and Fatty. Curly was running late. Tardiness was a sin.

Jerry felt secure that his flock would follow him even without the able assistance of his deacons. He represented the Big Guy, but his course work with Graham and Hummell pealed just as righteously. His tent-revival roots ran deep and wide, he had always trodden the upward path.

and his congregation now burgeoned beneath his loving ministrations.

When he sermonized, the born-agains seemed to forget their earthly hungers. He could not pinpoint why, past his own Rock-solid certainty that the Word held the power to still the restless, and quiet gnawing bellies. There were other kinds of nourishment; these lost ones were spiritually starved as well. Jerry held dear a reverence for awareness and sheer faith, and fancied he saw both in the eyes of his congregation when he vociferated. He Witnessed this miracle in a most hallowed and traditional fashion, during a sermon, when he looked out upon the milling throng and just *knew*. The born-agains depended on him for the Word just as much as the deacons counted on him to deliver the holy imbibitions. Venom governed the deacons, but it had to be a new kind of faith that oversaw the members of the marching ministry. Had to be.

They needed saving. Jerry needed to save. Symbiosis, plain, ungarnished, and God-sanctioned as all get-out.

In a most everlasting way, they fed each other. Maybe it was not such a big whodunit, after all.

Still no sign of Deacon Curly in the sanctuary. Jerry motioned Deacon Fatty inside. Fatty's eye had popped out to hang from the stalk again. Jerry tucked it in and brushed the bugs from this deacon's shoulders, then reknotted the arm band which had drooped to the zombie's elbow. Each member of the new congregation wore a Red Cross—it seemed an appropriate symbol for the New Dawn, and Jerry needed a handy way to take quick head counts while on the march.

The sudden, flat *boom* of an explosion not far away made Jerry's heart slam on brakes. Deacon Fatty stood unimpressed, awaiting his communion, insects swimming in his free-flowing drool.

Orthodoxies had spent too long fucking up the world, so Wormboy had obliterated all of them with a snap of his knockwurst fingers. Enough was enough. Idiots fumbled about, living their lives by accident, begging nonexistent gods for unavailable mercies, trusting in supernatural beings and nebulous powers of good and evil that predetermined what breakfast cereal they ate. If there was any evil now, its name was either Starvation or Stupidity—two big items that could make you instant history. True Believers spent their lives preparing to die. Wormboy preferred fighting to live.

His survival ethics might become the first writ of a new doctrine. Another system would rise in time. Nobody ever really learned a goddamned thing.

He preferred heavy-caliber projectile peace of mind. Cordite calm. He had named his M60 Zombo and it was swell. One round made raspberry slush. Vaporize the head and the leftovers could not eat you or infect you with the geek germ.

And spraying on Pam kept them from sticking to the cookery.

Wormboy dumped his dishes in the steel tub sink and relaxed on his Valley View sofa. A basso toilet belch eased him into sleep, and he dreamed about the first person he had ever eaten.

Duke Mallett had dubbed him Wormboy because of his obesity and spotty complexion. Which, quoth Duke, indicated that 15th Street Junior High's resident wimp, blimp, pussywhip, and pariah sucked up three squares chock full 'o night crawlers each day, with squiggly snacks between. "Yo, Wormy—wotcha got in your locker? More WORMS, huh?" That was always good for a chorus of guffaws from Duke and 15th Street's other future convicts.

Duke smoked Camels. His squeeze, Stacy, had awesome boobs and a lot of pimples around her mouth. She used bubble-gum-flavored lipstick. Two weeks prior to becoming a high school freshman, Dukey wrapped a boosted Gran Torino around a utility pole at ninety. He, Stacy, and a pair of their joyriding accomplices were barbecued by sputtering wires and burning Hi-Test. Paramedics piled what parts they could salvage onto a single stretcher, holding their noses.

Tompkins Mortuary also provided local ambulance service, and when Wormboy caught wind he raced there, to grieve. Old Man Tompkins admired the fat kid's backbone in requesting to view the remains of his classmates. "I have to be sure!" Wormy blurted melodramatically, having re-

hearsed. Tompkins was of the mind that youngsters could never be exposed to death too soon, and so consented to give Wormboy a peek at the carbonized component mess filling Drawer Eight.

Wormboy thought Tompkins smelled like the biology lab at shark-dissecting time. While the old man averted his gaze with a sharp draw of untainted air, Wormboy sucked wind, fascinated. The flash-fried garbage staining the tray and blocking the drains was Duke. Harmless now. The sheer joy of this moment could not hold, so Wormboy quickly swiped a small sample. When Tompkins turned to look, he sheepishly claimed to have seen enough. He lied.

Later, alone, he wallowed.

The piece he had purloined turned out to be one of Duke's fricasseed eyeballs. It had heat-shrunken, wrinkled in a raisin pattern, deflated on one side, and petrified on the other . . . but without a doubt it was one of Duke's baby blues. The eye that had directed so much hatred at Wormboy was now in his very hand, subtracted of blaze and swagger and no more threatening than a squashed seed grape.

It gave under the pressure of his fingers, like stale cheese. He sniffed. It was sour, rather akin to the smell of an egg-shell in the trash, with no insides.

Wormboy popped it between his lips and bit down before his brain could say no. He got a crisp bacon crunch. His mental RPMs redlined as flavor billowed across his tongue and filled his meaty squirrel cheeks.

His mom would not have approved. This was . . . well, this was the sort of thing that was . . . just not done.

It was . . . a rush of liberation. It was the ultimate expression of revenge, of power wielded over Duke the dick-nosed shitheel. It was the nearest thing to sex Wormboy would ever experience. It was damned close to religious.

Once Wormboy was old enough, he began to work part-time for Old Man Tompkins after school. By then his future was cast, and his extra weight gain attracted no new notice.

At the National Guard armory he had tucked in quite a few Type-A boxed combat meals. The gel-packed mystery meat he pried from olive-drab tins was more disgusting than anything he had ever sliced off down at the morgue.

BONE appetit!

Wormboy's wet dream was just sneaking up on the gooshy part when another explosion jerked him back to reality and put his trusty .44 in his grasp quicker than a samurai's *katana.* It was getting to be a busy Monday.

His mountainous gut fluttered. *Brritt.* Lunch was still in there fighting. But what the binoculars revealed nudged his need for a bromo right out of his mind.

Two dozen geeks, maybe more, were lurching toward the front gates of Valley View. Wormboy's jaw unhinged. That did not stop his mouth from watering at the sight.

The Right Reverend Jerry unshielded his eyes and stared at the sinner on the hilltop as smoking wads of Deacon Fatty rained down on the faithful. He'd been in front. Something fist-sized and mulchy smacked Jerry's shoulder and blessed it with a smear of yellow. He shook detritus from his shoe and thought of Ezekiel 18:4. Boy, he was getting mad.

The soul that sinneth—it shall die!

Deacon Moe and Deacon Fatty had bitten the big one and bounced up to meet Jesus. The closer the congregation staggered to the churchyard, the better they could smell the sinner . . . and his fatted calves. The hour of deliverance—and dinner—so long promised by Jerry seemed at hand.

Jerry felt something skin past his ear at two hundred per. Behind him, another of the born-agains came unglued, skull and eyes and brains all cartwheeling off on different trajectories. Jerry stepped blind and his heel skidded through something moist and slick; his feet took to the air and his rump introduced itself to the pavement and much, much more of Deacon Fatty. More colors soaked into his coat of many.

The Right Reverend Jerry involuntarily took his Lord's name in vain.

At the next flat crack of gunshot one more of the faithful burst into a pirouette of flying parts. Chunks and stringers splattered the others, who had the Christian grace not to take offense.

Jerry scrambled in the puddle of muck, his trousers

slimed and adherent, his undies coldly bunched. Just as wetly, another born-again ate a bullet and changed tense from present to past. Jerry caught most in the bazoo.

It was high time for him to bull in and start doing God's work.

Wormboy cut loose a throat-rawing war whoop—no melodrama, just joy at what was heading his way. The guy bringing up the rear did not twitch and lumber the way geeks usually did, so Wormy checked him out through the scope of the high-power Remington. He saw a dude in a stained suit smearing macerated suet out of his eyes and hopping around in place with Donald Duck fury.

He wore a Red Cross arm band, as did the others. End of story. Next case.

Wormy zeroed a fresh geek in his crosshairs, squeezed off, and watched the head screw inside out in a pizza-colored blast of flavor. With a balletic economy of motion for someone his size, he ejected the last of the spent brass and left the Remington open-bolted while he unracked his M60. Zombo was hot for mayhem. Zombo was itching to pop off and hose the stragglers. Wormy draped a stretch belt of high-velocity armor piercers over one sloping hillock of shoulder. The sleek row of shell casings obscured the Dirty Rotten Imbeciles logo on his T-shirt.

Dusting was done. Now it was casserole time. Zombo lived. Zombo ruled.

The next skirmish line of Bouncing Bettys erupted. They were halfway to the moat. The stuff pattering down from the sky sure looked like manna.

Jerry let 'em have it in his stump-thumper's bray, full bore: "Onward, onward! Look unto me, and be ye saved, all the ends of the earth!" Isaiah 45:22 was always a corker for rousing the rabble.

By now each and every born-again had scented the plump demon on the hilltop. He was bulk and girth and mass and calories and salvation. Valley View's iron portals were smashed down and within seconds, a holy wave of living-dead arms, legs and innards were airborne and graying out the sunlight.

"Onward!" Jerry frothed his passion to scalding and

dealt his nearest disciple a fatherly shove in the direction of the enemy. The sinner. The monster. *"Onward!"*

The flat of Jerry's palm met all the resistance of stale oatmeal. A fresh cow patty had more tensile strength and left less mess. He ripped his hand free with a yelp and gooey webs followed it backward.

The born-again gawped hollowly at the tunnel where its left tit used to be, then stumped off, sniffing fresh Wormboy meat.

The explosions became deafening, slamming one into the next, thunderclaps that mocked God. In the interstices, Jerry heard a low, vicious chuddering—not a heavenly sound, but an evil noise unto the Lord that was making the faithful go to pieces faster than frogs with cherry bombs inside.

He tried to snap off the maggot-ridden brown jelly caking his hand and accidentally boffed Deacon Moe in the face. The zombie's nose tore halfway off and dangled. Moe felt no pain. He had obediently brought the pet caddy, whose occupants writhed and waxed wroth.

Zombo hammered out another gunpowder benediction, and Jerry flung himself down to kiss God's good earth. Hot tracers ate pavement and jump-stitched through Deacon Moe in a jagged line. The pet carryall took two big hits and fell apart. Moe did likewise. His ventilated carcass did a juice dump, and the Right Reverend Jerry found himself awash in gallons of zombie puree plus four extremely aggravated rattlesnakes.

He never found out who was the first to betray him. The first bite pegged him right on the balls, and he howled.

Deacon Moe, his work on this world finished, keeled over with a splat. It was like watching a hot cherry pie hit a concrete sidewalk.

Wormboy rubbed his eyes. Zombo had *missed.* It wasn't just the salt sting of sweat that had spoiled his aim. His vision was bollixed. The oily drops standing out on his pate were ice cold.

It was probably someone's something he ate.

Zombo grew too heavy, too frying-pan hot to hold. Zombo's beak kept dipping, pissing away good ammo to spang off the metal spikes crowding the moat. Wormboy

gritted his teeth, clamped his clammy trigger finger down
hard, and seesawed the muzzle upward with a bowel-
clenching grunt. He felt himself herniate below his weight
lifter's belt. Zombo spoke. Geeks blocked tracers, caught
fire, and sprang apart at the seams. Those in front were
buffaloed into the moat by those behind. They seated
permanently onto the pungi pipes with spongy noises of
penetration, to wriggle and gush bloodpus and reach im-
potently toward Wormboy.

Zombo demanded a virgin belt of slugs.

Wormboy's appetite had churned into a world-class acid
bath of indigestion. This night would belong to Maalox.

It took no time for the air to clog with the tang of
blackened geek beef. One whiff was all it took to make
Wormboy ralph long and strenuously into the moat.
Steaming puke pasted a geek who lay skewered through
the back, facing the sky, mouth agape. It spasmed and
twisted on the barbs, trying to lap up as much fresh hot
barf as it could collect.

Zombo tagged out. Wormboy unholstered his .44 and
sent a pancaking round into Barf-eater's brain pan. Its
limbs stiffened straight as the hydrostatic pressure blew its
head apart into watermelon glop. Then it came undone
altogether, collapsing into a pool of diarrhetic putresence
that bubbled and flowed amidst the pipework.

Now everything looked like vomit. Wormy's ravaged
stomach said heave-ho to that, too, and constricted to ex-
pel what was no longer vomitable. This time he got blood,
shooting up like soda pop to fizz from both nostrils. He
spat and gagged, crashing to his knees. His free hand vanished into the fat cushion of his stomach, totally inade-
quate to the task of clutching it.

The Right Reverend Jerry saw the sinner genuflect.
God was still in Jerry's corner, whacking away, world
without end, hallelujah, amen.

Jerry's left eye was smeared down his cheek like a
lanced condom. Little Paul's fang had put it out. Must
have offended him. Jerry seized Little Paul and dashed his
snaky brains out against the nearest headstone. Then he
began his trek up the hill, through the valley of death,
toting the limp, dead snake as a scourge. Consorting with

serpents had won him a double share of bites, and he knew the value of immunization. He stung all over and was wobbly on his feet . . . but so far, he was still chugging.

This must be hell, he thought dazedly when he saw most of his congregation sliced, diced, and garnishing Valley View's real estate. Tendrils of smoke curled heavenward from the craters gouged rudely in the soil. Dismembered limbs hung, spasming. A few born-agains had stampeded over the fallen and made it all the way to the moat.

Jerry could feel his heart thudding, pushing God knew how much snakebite nectar through his veins. He could feel the power working inside him. Blood began to drip freely from his gums, slathering his lips. His left hand snapped shut into a spastic claw and stayed that way. His good eye tried to blink and could not; it was frozen open. The horizon tilted wildly. Down below, his muscles surrendered and shit and piss came express delivery.

As he neared his children, he wanted to raise his voice in the name of the Lord and tell them the famine was ended, to hoot and holler about the feast at last. He lost all sensation in his legs instead. He tumbled into the violence-rent earth of the graveyard and began to drag himself forward with his functioning hand, the one still vised around the remains of Little Paul.

He wanted to shout, but his body had gotten real stupid real fast. What came out, in glurts of blood-flecked foam, was *He ham niss ed begud!*

Just the sound of that voice made Wormboy want to blow his ballast all over again.

Jerry clawed onward until he reached the lip of the pit. The born-agains congregated around him. His eye globbed on his face, his body jittering as the megadose of poison grabbed hold, he nevertheless raised his snake and prepared to declaim.

Wormboy dragged his magnum into the firing line and blew the evangelist's mushmouthed head clean off before the mouth could pollute the air with anything further.

"That's better," he ulped, gorge pistoning.

Then he vomited again anyway and blacked out.

* * *

Weirder things have happened, his brain insisted right before he came to. None of it had been a dream.

One eye was shut against the dark of dirt and his nose was squashed sideways. Over the topography of regurgitated lunch in front of his face, he watched.

He imagined the Keystone Kops chowing down on a headless corpse. Meat strips were ripped and gulped without the benefit of mastication, each glistening shred sliding down gullets like a snake crawling into a wet, red hole. One geek was busily chomping a russet ditch into a Jerry drumstick with the foot still attached. Others played tug-o-war with slick spaghetti tubes of intestine or wolfed double facefuls of the thinner, linguini strands of tendon and ligaments—all marinated in that special, extra-chunky maroon secret sauce.

Wormboy's own tummy grumbled jealously. It was way past dinnertime. The remaining geeks would not leave, not with Wormboy uneaten. He'd have to crop 'em right now, unless he wanted to try mopping up in total darkness and maybe waiting until sunup to dine.

He saw one of the geeks in the moat squirm free of a pungi pipe. Its flesh no longer meshed strongly enough for the barbs to hold it. It spent two seconds wobbling on its feet, then did a header onto three more spikes. Ripe plugs of rotten tissue bounced upward and acid bile burbled forth.

Wormboy rolled toward Zombo, rising like a wrecked semi righting itself. His brain rollercoastered; his vision strained to focus; what the fuck had been wrong with lunch? He was no more graceful than a geek, himself, now. He put out one catcher's-mitt hand to steady his balance against a massive headstone memorializing somebody named Eugene Roach, *Loving Father.* Mr. Roach had himself lurched off to consume other folks' children a long time ago.

What happened, happened fast.

Wormboy had to pitch his full weight against the tombstone just to keep from keeling over. When he leaned, there came a sound like hair being levered out by the roots. His eyes bugged and before he could arrest his own momentum, the headstone hinged back, disengaging from Valley View's overnourished turf. Arms windmilling, Wormy fell on top of it. His mind registered a flashbulb image of the tripwire, twanging taut to do its job.

The mine went off with an eardrum-compressing clap of bogus thunder. Two hundred pounds of granite and marble took to the air right behind nearly four hundred pounds of Wormboy, who was catapulted over the moat and right into the middle of the feeding frenzy on the far side.

It was the first time in his life he had ever done a complete somersault.

With movie slo-mo surreality, he watched his hunky magnum pal drop away from him like a bomb from a zeppelin. It landed with the trigger guard snugged around one of the moat's deadly metal speartips. The firmly impaled Deacon W.C. was leering down the bore when it went bang. Everything above the Adam's apple rained down to the west as goulash and flip chips.

Wormboy heard the shot but did not witness it. Right now his overriding concern was impact.

A geek turned and saw him, raising its arms as if in supplication, or a pathetic attempt to catch the UFO that isolated it in the center of a house-sized, ever-growing shadow.

Eugene Roach's overpriced monument stone veered into the moat. The mushy zombie watched it right up until the second it hit. The fallout was so thick you could eat it with a fondue fork.

Wormboy clamped shut his eyes, screamed, and bellied in headfirst. Bones snapped when he landed. Only the yellows of the geek's eyes were visible at the end. It liquefied with a *poosh* and became a wet stain at the bottom of the furrow dug by Wormboy's touchdown.

All heads turned.

His brain was like a board room choked with yelling stockbrokers. The first report informed him that aerial acrobatics did not agree with his physique. The second enumerated fractures, shutdown, concussion, an eardrum that had popped with the explosive decompression of a pi-

mento being vacuumed from an olive, the equitable distri-
bution of slag-hot agony to every outback and tributary of
his vast body . . . and the dead taste of moist dirt.

The third was a surprise news flash: He had not been
gourmandized down to nerve peels and half a dozen red
corpuscles. Yet.

He filed a formal request to roll back his eyelids and it
took about an hour to go through channels.

He saw stars, but they were in the postmidnight sky
above him. He lay on his back, legs straight, arms out in a
plane shape. What a funny.

Eight pairs of reanimated dead eyes appraised him.

They've got me, dead bang, he thought. For more than
a year they've whiffed me and gotten smithereened . . .
and now I've jolly well been served up to them airfreight,
gunless, laid out flat on my flab. Maybe they waited just so
I could savor the sensual cornucopia of being devoured
alive firsthand. Dr. Moreau time, kids. Time for Uncle
Wormy to check out for keeps.

He tried to wiggle numb fingers at them. "Yo, dudes."
It was all he could think of to do.

The zombies surrounding him—three up, three down,
one at his feet, and one at his head—rustled as though
stirred by a soft breeze. They communed.

The skull of the Right Reverend Jerry had been perched
on his chest. He could barely see it up there. The blood-
dyed and tooth-scored fragments had been leaned together
into a fragile sort of card ossuary. He could see that his
bullet had gone in through Jerry's left eyebrow. Good
shot.

His insides convulsed and he issued a weak cough. The
skull clattered apart like an inadequately glued clay pot.

More commotion, among the zombies.

The Right Reverend Jerry had been gnawed down to a
jackstraw clutter of bones; the bones had been cracked,
their marrow greedily drained. All through the feast, there
he had been, mere feet distant, representing bigger por-
tions for everybody. He had gone unmolested for hours.
Instead of tucking in, they had gathered round and waited
for him to wake up. They had flipped him over, touched
him without biting. They had pieced together Jerry's

headbone and seen it blown apart by a cough. They had Witnessed, all right.

He considered the soda-cracker fragments of skull and felt the same rush of revelation he had experienced with Duke Mallett's eyeball. So fitting, now, to savor that crunchy stone-ground goodness.

The eyes that sought him did not judge. They did not see a grotesquely obese man who snarfed up worms and eyeballs and never bathed. The watchers did not snicker in a Duke Mallett drawl, or reject him, or find him lacking in any social particular. They had waited for him to revive. Patiently, on purpose, they had waited. For him.

They had never sought to eat of his lard or drink of his cholesterol. The Right Reverend Jerry had taught them that there were hungers other than physical.

One of his legs felt busted, but with effort he found himself capable of hiking up onto both elbows. The zombies shuffled dutifully back to make room for him to rise, and when he did not, they helped him, wrestling him erect like dogfaces hoisting the Stars and Stripes on Iwo Jima. He realized that if he cared to order them to march into one of Valley View's crematory ovens according to height, they'd gladly comply.

He had, at last, gained the devoted approval of a peer group.

And any second now, some asshole would try to whore up this resurrection for posterity in a big, bad, black book . . . and get it all wrong. He decided that anybody who tried would have a quick but meaningful confab with Zombo.

I win again. He had thought this many times before, in reference to those he once dubbed geeks. Warmth flooded him. *He* was not a geek . . . therefore *they* were not.

What he finally spake unto them was something like: "Aww . . . shit, you guys, I guess we oughta go hustle up some potluck, huh?"

He began by passing out the puzzle pieces of the Right Reverend Jerry's skull. As one, they all took and ate without breathing.

And they saw that it was good.

Eat Me

BY ROBERT R. McCAMMON

A question gnawed, day and night, at Jim Crisp. He pondered it as he walked the streets, while a dark rain fell and rats chattered at his feet; he mulled over it as he sat in his apartment, staring at the static on the television screen hour after hour. The question haunted him as he sat in the cemetery on Fourteenth Street, surrounded by empty graves. And this burning question was: when did love die?

Thinking took effort. It made his brain hurt, but it seemed to Jim that thinking was his last link with life. He used to be an accountant, a long time ago. He'd worked with a firm downtown for over twenty years, had never been married, hadn't dated much either. Numbers, logic, the rituals of mathematics had been the center of his life; now logic itself had gone insane, and no one kept records anymore. He had a terrible sensation of not belonging in this world, of being suspended in a nightmare that would stretch to the boundaries of eternity. He had no need for sleep any longer; something inside him had burst a while back, and he'd lost the ten or twelve pounds of fat that had gathered around his middle over the years. His body was lean now, so light sometimes a strong wind knocked him off his feet. The smell came and went, but Jim had a caseload of English Leather in his apartment and he took baths in the stuff.

The open maw of time frightened him. Days without number lay ahead. What was there to do, when there was nothing to be done? No one called the roll, no one punched the time-clock, no one set the deadlines. This warped freedom gave a sense of power to others; to Jim it was the most confining of prisons, because all the symbols of order—stoplights, calendars, clocks—were still there, still working, yet they had no purpose or sense, and they reminded him too much of what had been before.

As he walked, aimlessly, through the city's streets he saw others moving past, some as peaceful as sleepwalkers, some raging in the grip of private tortures. Jim came to a corner and stopped, instinctively obeying the DON'T WALK sign; a high squealing noise caught his attention, and he looked to his left.

Rats were scurrying wildly over one of the lowest forms of humanity, a half-decayed corpse that had recently awakened and pulled itself from the grave. The thing crawled on the wet pavement, struggling on one thin arm and two sticklike legs. The rats were chewing it to pieces, and as the thing reached Jim, its skeletal face lifted and the single dim coal of an eye found him. From its mouth came a rattling noise, stifled when several rats squeezed themselves between the gray lips in search of softer flesh. Jim hurried on, not waiting for the light to change. He thought the thing had said *Whhhyyy?* and for that question he had no answer.

He felt shame in the coil of his entrails. When did love die? Had it perished at the same time as this living death of human flesh had begun, or had it already died and decayed long before? He went on, through the somber streets where the buildings brooded like tombstones, and he felt crushed beneath the weight of loneliness.

Jim remembered beauty: a yellow flower, the scent of a woman's perfume, the warm sheen of a woman's hair. Remembering was another bar in the prison of bones; the power of memory taunted him unmercifully. He remembered walking on his lunch hour, sighting a pretty girl and following her for a block or two, enraptured by fantasies. He had always been searching for love, for someone to be joined with, and had never realized it so vitally before now, when the gray city was full of rats and the restless dead.

Someone with a cavity where its face had been stumbled past, arms waving blindly. What once had been a child ran by him, and left the scent of rot in its wake. Jim lowered his head, and when a gust of hot wind hit him he lost his balance and would have slammed into a concrete wall if he hadn't grabbed hold of a bolted-down mailbox. He kept going, deeper into the city, on pavement he'd never walked when he was alive.

At the intersection of two unfamiliar streets he thought he heard music: the crackle of a guitar, the low grunting of a drumbeat. He turned against the wind, fighting the gusts that threatened to hurl him into the air, and followed the sound. Two blocks ahead a strobe light flashed in a cavernous entrance. A sign that read THE COURT-YARD had been broken out, and across the front of the building was scrawled BONEYARD in black spray paint. Figures moved within the entrance: dancers, gyrating in the flash of the strobes.

The thunder of the music repulsed him—the soft grace of Drahms remained his lullaby, not the raucous crudity of Grave Rock—but the activity, the movement, the heat of energy drew him closer. He scratched a maddening itch on the dry flesh at the back of his neck and stood on the threshold while the music and the glare blew around him. The Courtyard, he thought, glancing at the old sign. It was the name of a place that might once have served white wine and polite jazz music—a singles bar, maybe, where the lonely went to meet the lonely The Boneyard it was now, all right: a realm of dancing skeletons. This was not his kind of place, but still . . . the noise, lights, and gyrations spoke of another kind of loneliness. It was a singles bar for the living dead, and it beckoned him in.

Jim crossed the threshold, and with one desiccated hand he smoothed down his remaining bits of black hair.

And now he knew what hell must be like: a smoky, rot-smelling pandemonium. Some of the things writhing on the dance floor were missing arms and legs, and one thin figure in the midst of a whirl lost its hand; the withered flesh skidded across the linoleum, was crushed underfoot as its owner scrabbled after it, and then its owner was likewise pummeled down into a twitching mass. On the bandstand were two guitar players, a drummer, and a legless thing hammering at an electric organ. Jim avoided the dance floor, moving through the crowd toward the blue-neon bar. The drum's pounding offended him, in an obscene way; it reminded him too much of how his heartbeat used to feel before it clenched and ceased.

This was a place his mother—God rest her soul—would have warned him to avoid. He had never been one for nightlife, and looking into the decayed faces of some of these people was a preview of torments that lay ahead— but he didn't want to leave. The drumbeat was so loud it destroyed all thinking, and for a while he could pretend it was indeed his own heart returned to scarlet life; and that, he realized, was why the Boneyard was full from wall to wall. This was a mockery of life, yes, but it was the best to be had.

The bar's neon lit up the rotting faces like blue-shadowed Halloween masks. One of them, down to shreds of flesh clinging to yellow bone, shouted something unintelligible and drank from a bottle of beer; the liquid streamed through the fissure in his throat and down over his violet shirt and gold chains. Flies swarmed around the bar, drawn to the reek, and Jim watched as the customers pressed forward. They reached into their pockets and changepurses and offered freshly-killed rats, roaches, spiders, and centipedes to the bartender, who placed the objects in a large glass jar that had replaced the cash register. Such was the currency of the Dead World, and a particularly juicy rat bought two bottles of Miller Lite. Other people were laughing and hollering—gasping, brittle sounds that held no semblance of humanity. A fight broke out near the dance floor, and a twisted arm thunked to the linoleum to the delighted roar of the onlookers.

"I know you!" A woman's face thrust forward into Jim's. She had tatters of gray hair, and she wore heavy makeup over sunken cheeks, her forehead swollen and cracked by some horrible inner pressure. Her glittery dress danced with light, but smelled of gravedirt. "Buy me a drink!" she said, grasping his arm. A flap of flesh at her throat fluttered, and Jim realized her throat had been slashed. "Buy me a drink!" she insisted.

"No," Jim said, trying to break free. "No, I'm sorry."

"You're the one who killed me!" she screamed. Her grip tightened, about to snap Jim's forearm. "Yes you are! You killed me, didn't you?" And she picked up an empty beer bottle off the bar, her face contorted with rage, and started to smash it against his skull.

But before the blow could fall a man lifted her off her feet and pulled her away from Jim; her fingernails flayed to the bones of Jim's arm. She was still screaming, fighting to pull away, and the man, who wore a T-shirt with *Boneyard* painted across it, said, "She's a fresh one. Sorry, mac," before he hauled her toward the entrance. The woman's scream got shriller, and Jim saw her forehead burst open and ooze like a stomped snail. He shuddered, backing into a dark corner—and there he bumped into another body.

"Excuse me," he said. Started to move away. Glanced at whom he'd collided with.

And saw her.

She was trembling, her skinny arms wrapped around her chest. She still had most of her long brown hair, but in places it had diminished to the texture of spiderwebs and her scalp showed. Still, it was lovely hair. It looked almost healthy. Her pale blue eyes were liquid and terrified, and her face might have been pretty once. She had lost most of her nose, and gray-rimmed craters pitted her right cheek. She was wearing sensible clothes: a skirt and blouse and a sweater buttoned to the throat. Her clothes were dirty, but they matched. She looked like a librarian, he decided. She didn't belong in the Boneyard—but, then, where did anyone belong anymore?

He was about to move away when he noticed something else that caught a glint of frenzied light.

Around her neck, just peeking over the collar of her sweater, was a silver chain, and on that chain hung a tiny cloisonné heart.

It was a fragile thing, like a bit of bone china, but it held the power to freeze Jim before he took another step.

"That's . . . that's very pretty," he said. He nodded at the heart.

Instantly her hand covered it. Parts of her fingers had rotted off, like his own.

He looked into her eyes; she stared—or at least pretended to—right past him. She shook like a frightened deer. Jim paused, waiting for a break in the thunder, nervously casting his gaze to the floor. He caught a whiff of decay, and whether it was from himself or her he didn't know; what did it matter? He shivered too, not knowing what else to say but wanting to say something, anything, to make a connection. He sensed that at any moment the girl—whose age might be anywhere from twenty to forty, since Death both tightened and wrinkled at the same time —might bolt past him and be lost in the crowd. He thrust his hands into his pockets, not wanting her to see the exposed fingerbones. "This is the first time I've been here," he said. "I don't go out much."

She didn't answer. Maybe her tongue is gone, he thought. Or her throat. Maybe she was insane, which could be a real possibility. She pressed back against the wall, and Jim saw how very thin she was, skin stretched over frail bones. Dried up on the inside, he thought. Just like me.

"My name is Jim," he told her. "What's yours?"

Again, no reply. I'm no good at this! he agonized. Singles bars had never been his "scene", as the saying went. No, his world had always been his books, his job, his classical records, his cramped little apartment that now seemed like a four-walled crypt. There was no use in standing here, trying to make conversation with a dead girl. He had dared to eat the peach, as Eliot's Prufrock lamented, and found it rotten.

"Brenda," she said, so suddenly it almost startled him. She kept her hand over the heart, her other arm across her sagging breasts. Her head was lowered, her hair hanging over the cratered cheek.

"Brenda," Jim repeated; he heard his voice tremble. "That's a nice name."

She shrugged, still pressed into the corner as if trying to squeeze through a chink in the bricks.

Another moment of decision presented itself. It was a moment in which Jim could turn and walk three paces away, into the howling mass at the bar, and release Brenda from her corner; or a moment in which Brenda could tell him to go away, or curse him to his face, or scream with haunted dementia and that would be the end of it. The moment passed, and none of those things happened. There was just the drumbeat, pounding across the club, pounding like a counterfeit heart, and the roaches ran their race on the bar and the dancers continued to fling bits of flesh off their bodies like autumn leaves.

He felt he had to say something. "I was just walking. I didn't mean to come here." Maybe she nodded. Maybe; he couldn't tell for sure, and the light played tricks. "I didn't have anywhere else to go," he added.

She spoke, in a whispery voice that he had to strain to hear: "Me neither."

Jim shifted his weight—what weight he had left. "Would you . . . like to dance?" he asked, for want of anything better.

"Oh, no!" She looked up quickly. "No, I can't dance! I mean . . . I used to dance, sometimes, but . . . I can't dance anymore."

Jim understood what she meant; her bones were brittle, just as his own were. They were both as fragile as husks, and to get out on that dance floor would tear them both to pieces. "Good," he said. "I can't dance either."

She nodded, with an expression of relief. There was an instant in which Jim saw how pretty she must have been before all this happened—not pretty in a flashy way, but pretty as homespun lace—and it made his brain ache. "This is a loud place," he said. "Too loud."

"I've . . . never been here before." Brenda removed her hand from the necklace, and again both arms protected her chest. "I knew this place was here, but . . ." She shrugged her thin shoulders. "I don't know."

"You're . . ." *lonely,* he almost said. *As lonely as I am.* ". . . alone?" he asked.

"I have friends," she answered, too fast.

"I don't," he said, and her gaze lingered on his face for a few seconds before she looked away. "I mean, not in this place," he amended. "I don't know anybody here, except you." He paused, and then he had to ask the question: "Why did you come here tonight?"

She almost spoke, but she closed her mouth before the words got out. I know why, Jim thought. Because you're searching, just like I am. You went out walking, and maybe you came in here because you couldn't stand to be alone another second. I can look at you, and hear you screaming. "Would you like to go out?" he asked. "Walking, I mean. Right now, so we can talk?"

"I don't know you," she said, uneasily.

"I don't know you, either. But I'd like to."

"I'm . . ." Her hand fluttered up to the cavity where her nose had been. *"Ugly,"* she finished.

"You're not ugly. Anyway, I'm no handsome prince." He smiled, which stretched the flesh on his face. Brenda might have smiled, a little bit; again, it was hard to tell. "I'm not a crazy," Jim reassured her. "I'm not on drugs, and I'm not looking for somebody to hurt. I just thought . . . you might like to have some company."

Brenda didn't answer for a moment. Her fingers played with the cloisonné heart. "All right," she said finally. "But not too far. Just around the block."

"Just around the block," he agreed, trying to keep his excitement from showing too much. He took her arm—she didn't seem to mind his fleshless fingers—and carefully guided her through the crowd. She felt light, like a dry-rotted stick, and he thought that even he, with his shrunken muscles, might be able to lift her over his head.

Outside, they walked away from the blast of the Boneyard. The wind was getting stronger, and they soon were holding to each other to keep from being swept away. "A storm's coming," Brenda said, and Jim nodded. The storms were fast and ferocious, and their winds made the buildings shake. But Jim and Brenda kept walking, first around the block and then, at Brenda's direction, southward. Their bodies were bent like question marks; overhead, clouds masked the moon and blue streaks of electricity began to lance across the sky.

Brenda was not a talker, but she was a good listener. Jim told her about himself, about the job he used to have, about how he'd always dreamed that someday he'd have his own firm. He told her about a trip he once took, as a young man, to Lake Michigan, and how cold he recalled the water to be. He told her about a park he visited once, and how he remembered the sound of happy laughter and the smell of flowers. "I miss how it used to be," he said, before he could stop himself, because in the Dead World voicing such regrets was a punishable crime. "I miss beauty," he went on. "I miss . . . love."

She took his hand, bone against bone, and said, "This is where I live."

It was a plain brownstone building, many of the windows broken out by the windstorms. Jim didn't ask to go to Brenda's apartment; he expected to be turned away on the front steps. But Brenda still had hold of his hand, and now she was leading him up those steps and through the glassless door.

Her apartment, on the fourth floor, was even smaller than Jim's. The walls were a somber gray, but the lights revealed a treasure—pots of flowers set around the room and out on the fire escape. "They're silk," Brenda explained, before he could ask. "But they look real, don't they?"

"They look . . . wonderful." He saw a stereo and speakers on a table, and near the equipment was a collection of records. He bent down, his knees creaking, and began to examine her taste in music. Another shock greeted him: Beethoven . . . Chopin . . . Mozart . . . Vivaldi . . . Strauss. And, yes, even Brahms. "Oh!" he said, and that was all he could say.

"I found most of those," she said "Would you like to listen to them?"

"Yes. Please."

She put on the Chopin, and as the piano chords swelled, so did the wind, whistling in the hall and making the windows tremble.

And then she began to talk about herself: She had been a secretary, in a refrigeration plant across the river. Had never married, though she'd been engaged once. Her hobby was making silk flowers, when she could find the material. She missed ice cream most of all, she said. And summer—what had happened to summer, like it used to be? All the days and nights seemed to bleed together now, and nothing made any of them different. Except the storms, of course, and those could be dangerous.

By the end of the third record, they were sitting side by side on her sofa. The wind had gotten very strong outside;

the rain came and went, but the wind and lightning remained.

"I like talking to you," she told him. "I feel like . . . I've known you for a long, long time."

"I do too. I'm glad I came into that place tonight." He watched the storm and heard the wind shriek. "I don't know how I'm going to get home."

"You . . . don't have to go," Brenda said, very quietly. "I'd like for you to stay."

He stared at her, unbelieving. The back of his neck itched fiercely, and the itch was spreading to his shoulders and arms, but he couldn't move.

"I don't want to be alone," she continued. "I'm always alone. It's just that . . . I miss touching. Is that wrong, to miss touching?"

"No. I don't think so."

She leaned forward, her lips almost brushing his, her eyes almost pleading. "Eat me," she whispered.

Jim sat very still. Eat me: the only way left to feel pleasure in the Dead World. He wanted it, too; he needed it, so badly. "Eat me," he whispered back to her, and he began to unbutton her sweater.

Her nude body was riddled with craters, her breasts sunken into her chest. His own was sallow and emaciated, and between his thighs his penis was a gray, useless piece of flesh. She reached for him, he knelt beside her body, and as she urged "Eat me, eat me," his tongue played circles on her cold skin; then his teeth went to work, and he bit away the first chunk. She moaned and shivered, lifted her head and tongued his arm. Her teeth took a piece of flesh from him, and the ecstasy arrowed along his spinal cord like an electric shock.

They clung to each other, shuddering, their teeth working on arms and legs, throat, chest, face. Faster and faster still, as the wind crashed and Beethoven thundered; gobbets of flesh fell to the carpet, and those gobbets were quickly snatched up and consumed. Jim felt himself shrinking, being transformed from one into two; the incandescent moment had enfolded him, and if there had been tears to cry, he might have wept with joy. Here was love, and here was a lover who both claimed him and gave her all.

Brenda's teeth closed on the back of Jim's neck, crunching through the dry flesh. Her eyes closed in rapture as Jim ate the rest of the fingers on her left hand—and suddenly there was a new sensation, a scurrying around her lips. The love wound on Jim's neck was erupting small yellow roaches, like gold coins spilling from a bag, and Jim's itching subsided. He cried out, his face burrowing into Brenda's abdominal cavity.

Their bodies entwined, the flesh being gnawed away, their shrunken stomachs bulging. Brenda bit off his ear, chewed, and swallowed it; fresh passion coursed through Jim, and he nibbled away her lips—they *did* taste like slightly overripe peaches—and ran his tongue across her teeth. They kissed deeply, biting pieces of their tongues off. Jim drew back and lowered his face to her thighs. He began to eat her, while she gripped his shoulders and screamed.

Brenda arched her body. Jim's sexual organs were there, the testicles like dark, dried fruit. She opened her mouth wide, extended her chewed tongue and bared her teeth; her cheekless, chinless face strained upward—and Jim cried out over even the wail of the wind, his body convulsing.

They continued to feast on each other, like knowing lovers. Jim's body was hollowed out, most of the flesh gone from his face and chest. Brenda's lungs and heart were gone, consumed, and the bones of her arms and legs were fully revealed. Their stomachs swelled. And when they were near explosion, Jim and Brenda lay on the carpet, cradling each other with skeletal arms, lying on bits of flesh like the petals of strange flowers. They were one now, each into the other—and what more could love be than this?

"I love you," Jim said, with his mangled tongue. Brenda made a noise of assent, unable to speak, and took a last love bite from beneath his arm before she snuggled close.

The Beethoven record ended; the next one dropped onto the turntable, and a lilting Strauss waltz began.

Jim felt the building shake. He lifted his head, one eye remaining and that one sated with pleasure, and saw the fire escape trembling. One of the potted plants was suddenly picked up by the wind. "Brenda," he said—and then the plant crashed through the glass and the stormwind came in, whipping around the walls. Another window blew in, and as the next hot wave of wind came, it got into the hollows of the two dried bodies and raised them off the floor like reed-ribbed kites. Brenda made a gasping noise, her arms locked around Jim's spinal cord and his handless arms thrust into her ribcage. The wind hurled them against the wall, snapping bones like matchsticks as the waltz continued to play on for a few seconds before the stereo and table went over. There was no pain, though, and no reason to fear. They were together, in this Dead World where love was a curseword, and together they would face the storm.

The wind churned, threw them one way and then the other—and as it withdrew from Brenda's apartment it took the two bodies with it, into the charged air over the city's roofs.

They flew, buffeted higher and higher, bone locked to bone. The city disappeared beneath them, and they went up into the clouds where the blue lightning danced.

They knew great joy, and at the upper limits of the clouds where the lightning was hottest, they thought they could see the stars.

When the storm passed, a boy on the north side of the city found a strange object on the roof of his apartment building, near the pigeon roost. It looked like a charred-black construction of bones, melded together so you couldn't tell where one bone ended and the other began. And in that mass of bones was a silver chain, with a small ornament. A heart, he saw it was. A white heart, hanging there in the tangle of someone's bones.

He was old enough to realize that someone—two people, maybe—had escaped the Dead World last night. Lucky stiffs, he thought.

He reached in for the dangling heart, and it fell to ashes at his touch.